MW00946745

HALLELUJAH

THE STORY OF THE COMING FORTH OF HANDEL'S MESSIAH

A N O V E L

J. SCOTT FEATHERSTONE

Warmest Wishes

ACW Press
Phoenix, Arizona 85013

Hallelujah: The story of the coming forth of Handel's *Messiah*
A Novel
Copyright ©2001 J. Scott Featherstone
All rights reserved

Cover design by Jeff Duncan and Alpha Advertising
Interior design by Pine Hill Graphics
Cover photo by Grant Heaton

Packaged by ACW Press
5501 N. 7th Ave., #502
Phoenix, Arizona 85013
www.acwpress.com
The views expressed or implied in this work do not necessarily reflect those of ACW Press.
Ultimate design, content, and editorial accuracy of this work is the responsibility of the author(s).

Library of Congress Cataloging-in-Publication Data

Featherstone, J. Scott.
   Hallelujah : the story of the coming forth of
  Handel's Messiah : a novel / J. Scott Featherstone. --
  1st ed.
    p. cm.
    ISBN 1-892525-64-X

   1. Handel, George Frideric, 1685-1759. Messiah--
Fiction. I. Title.

PS3606.E3844H35 2001   813'.6
                QBI01-701291

Printed in the United States of America.

*And the glory of the Lord shall be
revealed, and all flesh shall see it
together, for the mouth of the Lord
hath spoken it.*

Isaiah 11:7

For my wife, Lori, and my sons, Jacob, Joseph, Zachary, Samuel, Nathanael, and Benjamin. "If I could choose...they would all be you."

Acknowledgments

A VERY PERSONAL AND HEARTFELT THANKS TO ALL OF THE people who have touched this story since its inception. The road has been long, at times difficult; still, regrets are few and Good Samaritans have been many.

Humble thanks to my dear wife, my mother and father, and my wonderful family and friends for their unconditional support. They bless my life each and every day.

Special thanks to my dad for his many hours of editing and his innate goodness and integrity. He is the true Packrat.

Appreciation to Joe Featherstone and Kent Derricott. I am grateful for their early and earnest support and thank them for their vision.

Warm thanks to Lisa Motzkus, Mary Lynne Hansen, and Suzanne Pike for their many hours of editing and always improving the work; to Jeff Duncan and Fred Renich for their distinctive art and design efforts; to Grant and Linda Heaton for their elegant photography; to Bonnie Christensen, Brian and Sue Anderson, and Ron and Colette Waters, for reading, suggesting, and ever encouraging; to Hal, Cynthia, Dave and Susan for their confidence; to Ron Stone for helping me find the words; to Ryan Tibbetts, Roger Dibb, and Dave Ricks for all their great work and support; to Dave for being there in the night.

Contents

Preface

THE FIRST DAY OF MY SOPHOMORE YEAR IN HIGH SCHOOL, Mr. Zabriski, our choir director, stood at the front of class and announced that the combined choirs of the high school would be singing *Messiah* for our annual Christmas concert. I'm sure he could tell from our blank stares that we didn't understand, so he followed the statement up with, "Hallelujah chorus?" We all nodded.

Through the following months, we labored (that is a major understatement) through the many choruses of *Messiah*, doing our best to stay within a few measures of our director. The going was slow and difficult. We struggled with bars and measures—getting through an entire page was rare. Our day-to-day view of *Messiah* was so myopic that it was impossible for us to get a clear sense of what the end result would be. When it came time for the autumn concert, we were so preoccupied with *Messiah* that we hadn't practiced anything else. The concert was canceled.

On we went. During those brutal rehearsals, Mr. Z must have been tempted daily to fall back on "Sleigh Ride" or "Winter Wonderland," but somehow he stayed the course in spite of the obvious opposition of trying to guide an unwieldy number of teenagers on such a quest. I remember the cheers that went up from our bass section the first time that we finished the sixteenth note bars of "For unto us" at approximately the same time.

Then one day near the first week of November, something remarkable happened. The combined choirs of the school were asked to stay after school to rehearse. We, of course, complained about the imposition on our precious time, but, when the appointed hour came, the room was packed. It took several minutes to scare up anything that resembled order, but in time,

Mr. Z had us separated into sections and the accompanist began playing the introduction of the first chorus. To our amazement, the alto section came in on cue—"And the glory, the glory of the Lord."

The rest of us were so surprised by how strong they sounded that we all stood up straight and joined in on our entrance. At that moment, we all suddenly understood what had kept Mr. Z going through those long, arduous practices. The room filled with sound unlike any we would have ever supposed. It was miraculous. The hair on the back of my neck stood on end. As we sang, it seemed as if we were transported to a different place—a better place. We felt suddenly elevated, as if our song had somehow reached the heavens.

When the chorus finished, there was not a roar of cheers. Instead, there was silence—then we cheered. After that day, practice was no longer drudgery. We never again questioned the wonderful determination of our director who had beckoned us to betterment. We worked with new resolve and enthusiasm and managed to learn ten choruses before Christmas.

The concert was far from perfect, but it didn't matter. Our choir teacher had instilled in us a love and reverence for the music that we would never forget. I am eternally grateful for his decision to challenge us to walk a higher road. That experience changed my life.

Almost twenty years later, on a Sunday evening—the Sunday before Thanksgiving—I was standing alone in the kitchen doing dishes while my wife was putting little boys to bed. As is often the case on Sunday, I had *Messiah* playing on the stereo. Usually I sing along, but for some reason, that night I just listened. One of my favorite choruses from high school began to play.

"'And He shall purify the sons of Levi, that they may offer unto the Lord an offering in righteousness.'"

Suddenly, in my mind's eye, I could see a man sitting alone in the night, his head bent forward—writing. I could see the flickering candle on the desk next to him, papers strewn before him. His fingers were black with ink; a Bible lay opened on his desk.

The scene was one of despair—of loneliness. I somehow sensed that the man had lost everything. There was a heaviness all about him. It felt to me that the work he was doing was birthed in the darkest and most desperate hours of his life. That image stayed with me through a long, sleepless night. Finally, I got up and went in to the kitchen table, turned on *Messiah*, and wrote what I saw.

The following morning I went to the library and began researching how *Messiah* had come to be. I was humbled to find that what I had written the night before was in fact, true.

Since that night, the project has been in near constant evolution. There have been several edits and rewrites, but the story—including that original page—has remained intact.

I believe it's natural and right, at the conclusion of any truly meaningful experience, to ask if it was worth it. To that I say a heartfelt "yes." Our lives have been blessed and enriched by both the process and the words; we sincerely hope that yours will also.

Foreword

IN TWENTY-FOUR DAYS, GEORGE FREDERIC HANDEL WROTE
the entire score of his oratorio *Messiah*—an amazing feat by any standard. We have little information about what happened in that study during those three-plus weeks of creative catharsis. Handel did not keep a
journal of his thoughts and feelings. Like many great undertakings, the
vast majority of it took place in solitude.

Some scholars and writers contend that Handel's experience was not
of a spiritual nature, but the offspring of a creative burst, similar to others he'd had in the past. Indeed, Handel was notorious for prolific writing spells wherein he could write entire operas in a matter of a few weeks.

Others espouse the notion that Handel's motivation was purely
financial since he was burdened by debt when it was written.

In contrast, there are unconfirmed stories—based on word of
mouth from his manservant, Peter LeBlonde—that tell of Peter entering
Handel's study to find his master in tears and speaking of seeing the great
God in heaven surrounded by angels—of leaving food and returning
hours later to find it untouched.

Unfortunately, we have little substantive evidence to unequivocally
validate any presumption of Handel's intent or state of mind during those
twenty-four days. It is true that the remarkable feat of writing the entire
score in such a short time was not unique to *Messiah*, or without prece-
dent, but I believe that the most accurate barometer in ascertaining
Handel's personal experience may be his subsequent actions regarding
Messiah. If he would have treated his "sacred oratorio" in ways consistent
with other works, it would be easy to justify that his experience was purely
secular and that his motivation was principally financial, but I believe there
are overarching indications that his experience was also spiritual.

When Handel began writing *Messiah* he was a broken man. His last several attempts at opera had failed. The once hailed "Music Maker of the World" was at the lowest ebb of his career. His health was failing. He had an arthritic tic that pained every step he took. Critics publicly punished him. Creditors hounded him. Pride had nearly destroyed him. He was alone in every worldly way—yet perhaps he was not so alone.

During those twenty-four days, Handel lived with, pondered, and poured over some of the most poignant and prophetic canon of Christendom. The entire libretto was scriptural. Every verse put to song proclaims Jesus as divine, the King of kings and Lord of lords, the Redeemer and Savior of the human race, the Prince of Peace, the Lamb of God.

If Handel had any predisposition toward developing or increasing his faith in Christ's divinity, he certainly had the time and the circumstances necessary to facilitate having a spiritual experience. A principle that has been validated countless times, through all generations, is that adversity and humility are the crucible wherein the gold of discipleship is refined. If there is truth in the principle that one comes to know Christ in extremity, never was Handel more prepared for an encounter with deity.

Handel's actions subsequent to finishing the oratorio also shed light on his disposition concerning *Messiah*. He was reluctant to perform it. He made statements regarding *Messiah* that set it apart from the rest of his body of work. The fact that he only performed it during Lent could indicate that he felt it appropriate to attach the piece to a solemn religious season. Also, at no point in his life was he more in need of money, yet he gave the proceeds to charity. What he did with *Messiah* was singular and extraordinary.

If we judge Handel's experience writing the oratorio by his subsequent actions, we can reasonably justify that *Messiah* had special meaning to him. He treated it differently; he spoke of it differently; he altered his codicil to mention it specifically. Indeed, he was a changed man.

Lastly, beyond the purely musical aspects of *Messiah*, it would seem that any discussion as to the spiritual nature of the work must include comment as to whether its performance elicits a spiritual response. Obviously, any such assessment would be objective, but there may be value in attempting to discern if the music itself is inspiring only, or if there is an added spiritual dimension. Since the title and theme are centered on Christ, the Messiah—one might ask the question if *Messiah* is a conduit through which the Holy Spirit can witness to the divinity of Christ and His mission. If so, can we reasonably assume that creation of it could have been equally spiritual?

The Rough Places Plain

THERE ARE CERTAIN CHILDREN WHO SEE ONLY STARS IN THE darkest night sky—such was Peter, the one they called Packrat. Peter the Packrat was well known among the paupers, but it was not his thieving that gave him notoriety: it was his laugh, his smile, and his gait, none of which fit his circumstance. The Packrat's home was the street—his profession, the people in the street. He was an opportunist, taking advantage of everyone and everything that was availed to him. He earned the name Packrat because, even though he was a thief, he usually left something in place of what he took. It didn't matter that the actual value of what he stole was different from what he left behind. What did matter was that he was fair—unless the "dupe" was rich, then he did not care. He stole from the wealthy without conscience, since fairness was a principle that didn't apply to them anyway.

The Packrat never knew his mother and father; yet by his eighth year, he had developed the instincts of both. He could win bread like a father, and, like the mother he wished for, he could influence—usually for good, but ultimately for whatever conditions dictated. Although he had no parents, he did have family: brothers and sisters by circumstance, not by blood. He took particular care of the younger rodents, both those born in the street and those abandoned and left in the street, a distinction to which he placed particular significance.

In a place where everyone looked down, young Peter looked up. He somehow knew that he had nothing to do with how God had placed him in the world, but he did hold the Creator responsible for what happened beyond his inauspicious start and was liberal about letting Him know it.

"Show me what is rightfully yours,
And I'll show ya' what is wrongfully mine.
For God chose me to be poor,
So I can steal what is thine."

Thus, was the song of the Packrat. His lightness took away the heaviness of many. He skipped where others walked. He smiled when others despaired. He was rude, uncouth, and stained with dirt, but underneath it all was a simple little boy, full of life, full of wonder. He shined in a dull world.

There was nothing singular in the physicality of the Packrat. He was neither tall nor short. His hair was parchment colored; his skin—well, skin-colored. His face was somewhat freckled, barely visible through the dirt. He was, by all appearances, ordinary. And yet this ordinary boy was anything but ordinary.

His eye was bright and alert from spotting numerous ill-guarded coin purses. He could detect a shiny object in a gutter through the passing legs of a thousand pedestrians.

He trained his ears to hear the walls of London, which echoed the news of the street, including every vacant shop and sleeping vendor.

His nose was ever open. He loved the pungent odors of the street: fish, smoke, filth, tobacco, oil, and coal. These were the smells of his world. But there was one smell that he relished above all others: the smell of bread. He often walked Baker's Row just to fill his nose with the warm aroma of baking bread. He knew why the Bible called it the "staff of life," because he leaned on it every day.

"I can't think of a better crutch," he would laugh, with his mouth full of dough. Whenever he could procure a loaf, he would throw back his head and shout to the sky: "I've come under Your eye today, Lord, and I thank Ya' for it. I'm glad Ya' didn't blink during my brief crossin' t'day."

There was one smell, however, which the Packrat detested: the stench of wealth. To him, money was evil—not for inherent reasons, but because of what it apparently did to the possessor of it.

"It must stink," he mused. "The more a man has in his pocket, the higher he reaches his nose away from it."

If the Packrat caught a passing waft of violet or rose, he knew precisely the origin: a perfume-tainted handkerchief held to the lifted nose of a snobby aristocrat. He had no use for these people, for they seemed neither natural nor good-natured. He regarded those with wealth as The Given, since he could see no reasonable means by which the rich could have obtained that stature on their own merit.

"I know God is good, but not that good, for He errs every time a rich man is born."

Peter the Packrat had no stomach for the noble, and he was unabashedly vocal about it. This made him all the more popular among his kind. He could spot a man full of himself a half a block away. He could easily recognize the walk, the lilting head, and the raised nose. If the situation were such that he could not rob them of something, he made them pay in ridicule.

"Look down on us kindly, Lord, but save Your sore eyes for the rich."

The Packrat's days were spent touring. Sometimes he would pass the hours stepping from wall to fence to street lamp pedestal, trying his best to get a good view of what grown-ups see. Other days he would stay low, his eye to the ground, in order to get a good view of what rodents see. Generally, he used the atmosphere of the street as a reverse barometer. When a commotion would erupt, he typically went the opposite direction of the action to gain the advantage. If people were straining up on their tiptoes to see the milieu, he would look low. If something fell, and the eyes of the crowd searched downward, he would jump to a perch above the flap where he could clearly see over the sea of backs and behinds. He learned from experience that there was much to be gained by not following the crowd.

It was late in the day when he observed something extraordinary happening in the world above. The Packrat stayed low. Going was difficult, as there were more legs—rich legs—than usual to work through. It was a fertile field for a small thief, so he kept his eyes sharp. Above him he heard shouting—not the crass banter of street vendors vying for the best space, but eloquent voices using articulate words.

"Rantin's of the rich," Peter sighed under his breath.

Two distinct voices could be heard above the rest. It was the beginning of a series of events that the Packrat knew well. As he wandered about the bystander's legs, the crowd pressed into a ring. The Packrat couldn't help snickering as bodies began pushing against bodies.

"Easy pickin's," he chortled, knowing full well that there was absolutely no way anyone would notice the slight pressure of a small hand slipped into a coat pocket. What was even more pleasing was that he knew escape from the tightening crowd would be simple, since he would be moving against the flow of any pursuit. This was a principle of survival, learned early, which he employed whenever the opportunity presented itself. Even at a young age, the boy somehow knew there was a practical application for every natural phenomenon. He observed in order to learn.

When he and the other boys on the street tried to catch floaters in the gutter after a downpour, he discovered it was far more difficult to catch an object working against the swift current than with it.

The Packrat tested the lesson of the floaters on numerous occasions and found it to be an effective means of escape. The maneuver had two essential elements: speed and timing. It was a simple move. If a would-be assailant tried to head him off, he would cut back hard against the pursuer's angle of attack. The pursuer's momentum would carry him helplessly past the boy.

Cobbles made the maneuver even more effective. The Packrat's small feet could easily change direction in the cracks between cobbles. The large surface area of an adult's foot made turning difficult. The Packrat watched many a chaser attempt to change direction, lose footing on the slick stones, and tumble to the ground in a splay of cursing. By the time the fallen could react, the boy would have already disappeared into the crowded street. Dodging oncoming traffic became a game to him. As yet, the Packrat's record was perfect; no one had ever caught him head-on.

What the boy did fear, however, was pursuit from behind. His two best and most reliable advantages would be lost: sight and surprise. If pursued from the rear, escape was reduced to a simple contest of speed and endurance. Advantage adults. He avoided races of that nature except as a last resort.

The Packrat angled himself against the moving crowd. Several feet in front of him, he spied the perfect pocket. It was a finely tailored pocket, hand sewn on the outside of a gentleman's satin coat. Work of this quality did not come cheaply; the owner had money. Creases formed across the upper edge of the sagging pocket. Peter recognized that it was weighted down with heavy contents. He determined to focus all of his attention on that one pocket. One good take was far better than getting greedy and increasing the odds for capture by being careless.

He closed in.

"Don't be gettin' stupid," the Packrat whispered through his teeth.

The pitch and number of voices speaking in the group were decreasing. The Packrat knew precisely what this meant in the sequence of events leading up to the final confrontation. The fewer the voices, the closer the climax. His wait was paying off. He knew there would be some last words, followed by a brief moment when all would be still. The circle would then tighten one last time at the crucial moment of surrender or attack, depending upon the disposition of the opposing parties. That final moment of crowd shifting would be his chance to rise.

He waited.

One voice challenged, the other withstood.

Peter sat on his haunches, waiting to strike. He wondered what small indiscretion had resulted in this confrontation. He loved the facing-off of stuck-up rich men. There was only one thing he enjoyed more than two spoiled noblemen measuring their honor against one another: a good catfight. Women fighting was a rare treat. It usually only happened at a busy corner or intersection when several carriages became entangled. The women of the wheeled cages would only take the inconvenience so long before they would protrude from the small windows and begin shouting at drivers and each other. If one were very fortunate, carriage doors would open, and the contents would spill out onto the street for hair pulling, clawing, and dress tearing. The Packrat could fly through a crowded street like a lead ball from a gun at the sound of high-pitched screaming. But for now, this male altercation was good enough and most likely profitable.

The two principal voices began to crescendo. This would initiate the silence just prior to the final close of the ring. Peter's hands began to itch.

Peter crawled forward. The toes of polished leather shoes began to creak and tighten all around him as bodies leaned forward for a better view. He heard the shrill hiss of metal sliding against metal—the unmistakable sound of a sword sliding out of a scabbard. Whatever was happening up there was much more serious than usual. He sensed a unique tenseness in the crowd that he had only felt a few times before. He stretched his neck to catch a glimpse of those at the center of the ring, but he was not quite tall enough. He was halfway up the wooden spokes of the closest carriage wheel before he slapped himself for nearly forgetting why he was there. He dropped to the ground and moved back into place. Forward he reached, his hand nearly touching the goal.

Silence.

Like a wave, the crowd swelled forward. The boy gently slid his fingers down the inner lining of the pocket and touched leather. As his hand began to wrap around the prize, there was a blood-chilling scream. He heard the sharp whip of a blade cutting air, then a loud clang.

In one great surge, the crowd fell back, knocking him to the ground, his hand empty. The sound of steel falling on cobbles rang in his ears. Through cracks in the broken wall of legs, the Packrat saw a great body plummet to the ground. He heard the dull slap of flesh hitting against flat pavement. He didn't move for fear of being discovered. Something was very wrong.

He held his breath.

That's when he heard it.

The Packrat's ear caught hold of a tiny sound—a clinking, several feet in front of him. He scanned the ground for a coin. There it was, a flash of gold tumbling around and between the many shoes and legs, coming toward him. The shiny object danced in and out of sight until it finally came to rest inches in front of him. He quickly covered over the gold, scallop-shaped piece with a dirty hand. It instantly disappeared to everyone but him.

Only then did he venture a look upward to see if he had been discovered. Nothing! All eyes were focused on the fallen man. The Packrat scooped up the piece and lifted his hand to his eye. His fingers slowly opened. What he saw was golden but not what he expected. His eyes widened in wonderment.

Every Valley Exalted,
Every Mountain Made Low

THE KING'S THEATRE WAS FULL TO BURSTING. CARRIAGES of all sizes and class lined the alleys in every direction. Coachmen babbled; horses waited. There was titillating talk in the street of something extraordinary happening at tonight's opera performance. Quiet whispers quickly turned into excited "Ahhhs."

Many stopped during their traverse up the theatre steps to make sure their ears had heard correctly.

"Here? Tonight?" was a question asked repeatedly by anxious patrons.

Truly, there was something about the upcoming performance that had London's influential talking. The unexpected surprise was just the kind of thing that could provide gossip for days to come. Those lucky ones who had spent the day preparing to attend the opera would surely have the upper hand in all the upcoming conversations. Eyewitness testimony was a far more valuable commodity than hearsay. The right information, if exploited correctly, could be quite a coup in any social circle.

One thing was sure: tonight's performance of Johann Matheson's *Cleopatra* would provide fodder enough to consume or elevate many gossip players.

The run of *Cleopatra* was long by any standard—nearly five weeks—and yet receipts had not even begun to diminish. The wealthy of London had been most supportive of the effort.

"Glorious," was the word most used by the critics. *Cleopatra* was a resounding success, Matheson had made sure of it. In addition to a wonderful libretto and score, he had ingeniously created another draw that kept people coming long after the opera alone might have run its course. People were enamored with the idea that Matheson, the composer, was playing the lead role of Antonius. London responded by buying out nearly every available seat well in advance. That strategic ploy, along with Matheson's propensity to invite guest artists, was ample munition to acclaim the effort as a solid victory.

But the crackle of energy in the hall this night went far beyond being just another fine performance of a now aging opera run. To be certain, something special was about to take place. Expectations were palpable. In the last hour prior to the curtain rising, it was rumored that Matheson's guest musician for the evening was not just any artist, but the celebrated Saxon of whom they had heard so much talk.

Georg Friedrich Handel, the acclaimed artist and composer from Saxony, was invited by Matheson to accompany the orchestra on the harpsichord. The two musicians became friends when they worked and composed together years before in Hamburg. Consequently, to celebrate the reunion of their friendship, Matheson invited the German-born Handel to stand in at the harpsichord, much to the consummate delight of the audience.

As it happened, Handel was in London for a second time on leave from his duties as Kapellmeister to George, the Elector of Hanover. When Handel visited London during the year previous, he could not speak a stitch of English. Within a short time after arriving, he deduced that London was about to explode musically and he wanted to be at the center of it. He had dedicated his life to becoming the most renowned musician the world had ever known and London could be the springboard he needed to prove it. Here was a metropolitan pool large enough to make a big splash, and yet it was lagging behind other European cities in its output of artists. The opportunity was so well timed and tailored to him that Handel assumed that God had ordained it. It was the chance of a lifetime, and it was his to take.

He returned to his duties at Hanover, already studying the English language in preparation for the next opportunity he would have to travel to London. For months, he begged his employer, the Elector, to grant him a second leave of absence that he might go back again to England. Reluctantly, George of Hanover finally did allow his Kapellmeister to leave, but only upon the condition that he would return within a reasonable amount of time. Handel stretched the word "reasonable" far beyond what was initially intended. When the invitation came to make a guest appearance in *Cleopatra*, Handel was already long overdue. He didn't care. In the relatively short time he had been in London, his reputation had grown robustly. Those who heard him, hailed him simply as "The Saxon."

As Handel's popularity grew, his desire to return to Hanover diminished. The chamber music required by his employer in Germany was no match for the vast opportunities availed him in London. He stayed months beyond what could be rationalized, immersing himself in the music pool of London. He even took on the English spelling of his name: George Frederic Handel. He knew there would come a time of reckoning with his employer; for now, his mind was on London.

Though he had been in the city for some time, relatively few Londoners were fortunate enough to have heard him play. Those who had heard him heralded his unparalleled mastery of the harpsichord and organ.

There were some who found occasion to hear Handel in Rome, Venice, or Naples. They told stories of entire audiences rising to their feet with shouts of *"Viva il caro Sassone!"* The tales of his conquests in Italy spread through London's nobility like a firestorm, wholly consuming every conversation on the topic of music. English audiences had anxiously awaited his arrival.

Handel was ponderously large in stature, with a mighty temper to match. He was a curiosity, both for his eccentricities as well as his ability. It was rumored that he had a voracious appetite that could easily justify his hugeness. He would write his way through creative spells and eat through droughts. For different reasons he learned to appreciate both.

Handel's eyes often showed a lack of sleep—no sign of lacking could be seen anywhere else. But what was most astonishing to those who had witnessed his craft was that a man of such enormity could be so deft and nimble on the keys. It was said that his hand was indeed faster than the eye. Rumor had it that he often engaged in musical duels—matching bars with the finest players in Europe—in which he always triumphed. "A good thing," it was said, for he was also known to have a German temper. With the addition of English, it was purported that he could ably and skillfully explode into a tirade of cursing in four languages. It was oft said that he did not appear the artist he was. That was part of the allure of the man.

Handel was a Saxon; one word from his mouth betrayed his heritage. Although he learned to speak the Queen's English, his speech was heavily laced with a thick, German accent. This he exploited generously, as it proved to be extremely entertaining to the English aristocracy. He espoused the notion that entertainment was the key to success in this or any town. Unlike his German contemporary, Johann Sebastian Bach, who chose to enlighten audiences within the confines of his ecclesiastically appointed position, Handel chose to entertain first. Whether in conversation or music, he lived to please. He held firmly to the concept that people desired entertainment even above enlightenment; this he learned from the Italians. Receipts and subscriptions were secured by amusing and impressing. Indeed, Handel's gifts seemed to steer him toward that end, for he was blessed equally with unprecedented ability and peculiar idiosyncrasies. Handel was truly a novelty, and now he was in London.

From the onset of the opera, music echoed from the grand hall to the street outside the theatre. With each crescendo, doormen would stop their idle whispers to listen. When the music diminished, they would speculate on the transpirings within. Inside the theatre, every eye was open, every ear, forward.

Typically, a musician from one of the local chamber orchestras played the harpsichord through the first two acts and part way through the third. Following the tragic death of Antonius in Act III, when his role was finished on stage, Matheson would take over at the harpsichord, where he would accompany and lead the orchestra through the finale. That arrangement served the opera well throughout the run. It also provided the author a chance to perform in both the cast and orchestra, which he rightly relished.

The harpsichord lines were difficult. One of the most critically praised features of the opera was the command that Matheson took of both the instrument and orchestra during the final scenes of Act III and through the finale. He was no less compelling in the pit than he was on stage. On this night, however, it was not to be.

From the first stanza, the Saxon made easy work of the difficult harpsichord lines—which was astounding, considering he had never laid eyes on the *Cleopatra* score before. The arrangement to guest perform in the production happened so quickly, there was no time to schedule a rehearsal. It didn't matter; there was no doubt that Handel could hold his own and then some. Each time he had an entrance, people would rise up in their seats for a better look. During the more active harpsichord sections, Handel would bounce on his stool, causing his wig to dance on his head. By the time the first act was over, the audience could judge his interest and enthusiasm for the piece by the shake of his wig.

As the performance advanced through the first two acts and into the climactic death scenes of Act III, the anticipation was tangible. On stage, Antonius had just discovered the corpse of his beloved Cleopatra. He rose like a huge monolith over his fallen love in the center of the stage—his presence, dominating. He stood like a great monarch before the crowd, the orchestra swelling beneath him. Never had Matheson played the role with such majesty and power. He looked down upon his love, Cleopatra, her lifeless body crumpled and still.

His was a song of anguish, of unequivocal despair. Antonius thrust his grief upon the empathetic listener with each note of heart-wrenching melody. His whole soul was bared to all in sung agony. This was his moment; every eye was on him, every heart felt his pain.

Antonius slowly drew the sword from his scabbard and held it aloft, high over his head. Words of unrequited love flowed from his lips in perfect pitch and resolve. Antonius lowered the sword to the ground, hilt down.

The music rose feverishly.

With one final despairing groan, Antonius thrust himself down upon the cold steel blade.

He staggered, then fell to the ground, dead. His eternal love and devotion were sealed by his death. The last cry of song exhaled from his pierced lung.

No one dared breathe.

No one dared speak.

The dying notes of Antonius echoed through the theatre and antechambers below.

All was silent.

Then suddenly—sound.

The voice of one single instrument filled the immense void created by the fallen hero. Who dared break the spell of the tragic moment? The insensitive invasion of the poignant space left by Antonius's death was utterly appalling. The mere suggestion that anyone would be so brazen as to diminish the dramatic pinnacle they had just witnessed was unthinkable. In mortified unison, every eye in the theatre shifted from the fallen to the harpsichord.

At first, they looked on, aghast; seconds later, they were enthralled.

The conductor's guest was playing with a virtuosity that was stunning in every respect. His hands moved up and down the keyboard at a speed and agility never before witnessed in London. His finger dexterity was incomprehensible. The ostentatious spectacle of the opera seemed suddenly overdone and unwieldy as compared to the singular stirring sound that now filled their ears. The haunting strains of death gave way to the buoyant, invigorating music of life.

Mr. Handel sat tall and self-importantly, his wig slightly cock-eyed, the curls bobbing in time with his hands. So remarkable was his skill that even the corpse of Antonius raised his head to watch the amazing improvisation. While the audience watched, the orchestra waited.

Matheson waited.

For the moment, it was a cast of one. None dared invade the realm of genius, knowing their ordinariness would become thoroughly apparent.

From his prostrate place on stage, Matheson burned. This was his opera, his moment of triumph. And it was all eclipsed by his invited friend, who unwittingly unraveled the rightful place of the author. Matheson rose to his feet unnoticed and slunk offstage.

Meanwhile, Handel expertly transposed his way into the next orchestra entrance. With a wave of his hand, the cast and orchestra picked up the count, the opera continued without a missed measure. It was entirely remarkable.

The audience exploded in spontaneous applause, hardly believing what they had just heard.

Seconds later, Matheson was in the orchestra pit, still in costume, ready to take his place at the harpsichord. With a flick of his hand, he hailed Handel to move aside and allow him to take his place for the finale.

"Thank you. I will take it now." His presence was barely acknowledged.

"Give way, sir!" Matheson demanded. "Move aside."

"You're dead!" said Handel, without giving him a second look.

"I always accompany the finale myself. Give way!"

"Neither they, nor I, have ever seen the dead return to take over an orchestra." Handel did not budge.

Matheson grew more vexed with each passing moment. So conspicuous was the spectacle being played out in the orchestra, that even the audience forgot what was happening on stage. Opposing factions began to take personal interest in the controversy. A small number of patrons were incensed at Handel's impropriety. A far greater number sided with sheer prowess: Handel was their choice. Matheson's demands were followed by a few random shouts of affirmation. Handel's refusals were followed by enthusiastic applause. Upon hearing this, Handel sat heavier on the seat, but Matheson was still not willing to let go of his opera.

"It's my opera. You are a guest here."

"And making it a success—look at them." Handel glanced over the charmed audience. "You should thank me!"

Clearly, Handel was getting the upper hand. Matheson knew it. He was desperate.

"Unquestionably, the author can do better than anyone else—even you."

Handel's head whipped around toward Matheson. He had had enough. He anchored himself in place and began to exert himself on the instrument tenaciously. What the audience had heard before was a trifling compared to what Handel now offered them. He not only improvised, he improvised upon the score as he played it. He did not miss a note of what was on paper; he added to it. Far beyond what Matheson had written, Handel added a dimension of music that caused even Matheson to fall back, his eyes riveted on Handel's flying hands. The audience was stunned. No one had ever considered it possible to play with the speed and agility that Handel now exhibited. At that very moment, the same exact thought rested upon everyone in the room. Any prior controversy was over; Handel was the victor.

All at once, Matheson felt that every eye in the theatre was upon him. He cowered beneath the weight of it. He was the author, the lead, the director, and yet he was unwelcome. Matheson had but one thought: to flee.

Shame fell upon him like a pall of darkness. Slowly he backed away, wanting desperately not to be seen. Taunting cheers rang out from hoodlums in the crowd, trying to provoke even more mischief. Matheson turned toward the door at the side of the pit. It was but nine steps; to him it seemed a hundred.

He ran.

Seconds seemed hours. In his mind's eye he could see the distorted face of every jeering person in the theatre. Just when he was certain he would implode with embarrassment, he fell through the open portal into darkness. Behind him, he could hear a rise of applause as he disappeared through the door. His head was dizzy with anger and humiliation. He grasped for anything to steady himself. His groping hand caught hold of a side stage curtain. Shrouds of heavy velvet wrapped around him in layers of crimson. He twirled around and around until he was completely hidden in a protective cocoon. At last, he was safe, out from under the scrutinizing eye of the audience. As his hot breath heated his own temple, he could think of but one thing: revenge.

The opera continued under Handel's direction to the finish. All went magnificently as the chorus and orchestra played through the final bars. At the conclusion of the finale, the entire audience rose to its feet in appreciative ovation.

As was customary, the cast ceremoniously walked to the front of the stage one by one for their curtain call. Matheson knew he must take his place at the end of the line. As he waited in the dark aft of the stage for the understudies and supporting roles to finish, he determined to deafen his ears against what he was certain would meet him on stage. He closed his heart to the crowd, shielding himself from them with the armor of apathy.

When his turn finally came, he walked to center stage and bowed low. Nobly, he awaited their derision.

At first, he forced himself to hear nothing, but the noise grew. Try as he might, the sheer volume of it was irrepressible. Louder and louder in his head it rang, penetrating his deepest resolve to shut it out. Slowly his ears opened, but it was not ridicule that he heard, it was approbation.

Applause reverberated throughout the hall and his empty heart. He braved a look up—the audience was on its feet. All eyes were on him; open mouths cheered him. Strength came to his bent and arched back. He rose to full stature, standing tall as Antonius in all his might and glory.

He raised his outstretched arms to the crowd, drinking in their unrestrained admiration. He was more healed with each enduring moment of praise.

In turn, he bowed low to each section of the audience; the courtesy was reciprocated by a crescendo of applause and cheering from that section.

He then stepped forward to the front of the stage and bowed low one last time; thunderous applause erupted, far beyond what had been before. Matheson's soul swelled wide enough to accept it all. As he raised his head, fully expecting to behold a sea of adoring faces, he could not find one eye upon him. Instead, they were on Handel, who stood at the harpsichord shamelessly hailing the exuberant crowd. A second time he had upstaged Matheson in his very moment of triumph.

Matheson seethed.

He left in haste; few saw him go.

Matheson retreated to his dressing room, firmly resolved to do that which he had only contemplated minutes before. He stood in the half-light of the small square room.

Slowly, deliberately, he pulled a white cloth glove onto his trembling hand. The fabric tightened as the finger slots were filled and stretched. His other hand was then likewise robed. Matheson's two white hands disappeared into the shadows below the vanity before him, then rose again, revealing into the light a long, lavishly detailed case. He held the case horizontally as if holding a shallow pan full of water. He laid the case on a small table covered with loose sheets of music. The low burning candle on the corner of the table cast yellow highlights on the detailed etchings on the surface of the lid.

The case was expertly crafted from deep red mahogany. The lid was carved in the pattern of a long serpentine dragon; fire spewed from its jaws. The eye of the lizard was deeply set, a black hole in the dim candlelight.

Matheson's white hands rested, palms down, on the dragon; they stopped trembling. Now steady, his fingers clicked open the brass fasteners along the side of the case. He opened the lid, letting light penetrate to the inside. Firelight sparked off the honed blade of a blue-edged sword, shining sickly in the shadows of the case.

With one gloved hand, he gripped the sword by the hilt; with his other hand, he ran white fingers along the razor sharp edge of the blade. A small fleck of red began to soak through the fold of his gloved index finger.

Matheson stood to attention, his black shadow reaching ominously up the wall behind him. With a screeching metal hiss, he slid the sword into its scabbard. Matheson turned around. His face moved into the light spilling through the open door from the hallway. His gaze was distant, severe.

He walked to the door of his dressing room, pausing only to pick up his leather overgloves, then strode out the door of his cubicle and into the backstage hall. He walked past several cast and orchestra members mingling in the crowded corridor. He heard nothing; he spoke to no one. Without slowing, he pushed open the outer door of the theatre, his face grim. He squinted as the last rays of sunset raked across his face. He searched the crowd for one man.

Matheson found Handel near the backstage door, greeting and mixing with the theatre patrons. Matheson walked straight to Handel. Innocent attendees reached out congratulating hands to him, but he walked through them like bars on a turnstile.

Handel was so preoccupied with those closest to him that he had no warning of Matheson's coming. Matheson suddenly appeared from out of the throng, his face pallid. He stopped two paces short of Handel, who stood with his back to him.

Voices hushed.

"I invite a friend to be my guest. In return, you disgrace my honor. Did the applause mean that much to you?"

Bewildered, Handel turned to face him. Those standing closest stepped back apprehensively. Matheson pulled off his leather overgloves, then hurled them at Handel's feet. He drew his sword. People winced at the shrill scraping of the blade leaving the scabbard.

Handel grinned, not fully comprehending the gravity of Matheson's staunch determination.

"You wish to die again?" Handel laughed as he surveyed the group of onlookers pressing into a circle around them. "How many times must one man die before he is truly dead?"

A few in the crowd responded with nervous laughter, but Matheson was earnest. He was not amused, nor did he retreat. The only indication that he had heard at all was the slightest raise of the point of his sword. Handel looked into Matheson's eye—it was unyielding.

The Saxon sighed deeply, his gaze never leaving his challenger. The muscles in his face tightened. He stretched out his open hand to bystanders in the circle behind him. A gentleman pulled his sword and put the hilt into Handel's outstretched palm. Handel planted his feet firmly. He squared his shoulders to Matheson while holding the sword in front of him, blade down, pointed at his accuser's feet.

"You were mistaken, Johann. It was never a question of honor—and would not have been except that you made it so this very moment. I would not give way then, nor will I now."

The crowd pressed inward. Long the two stood, their eyes firmly locked on one another.

Suddenly, without warning, Matheson lunged at Handel, driving his sword squarely into his chest. There was a scream from within the crowd, followed by a deafening clang. Matheson's long, thin blade shattered into pieces as the two men plunged to the ground amid shards of silver. Handel's body crumpled and fell in a motionless pile.

All was still.

Onlookers looked on in helpless disbelief. Matheson rose to his feet, unharmed. He gazed at Handel who lay motionless on the ground. Guilt and regret stung at Matheson's conscience. He searched the crowd for an empathetic face, but there was not one to be found. He wished he could run and hide himself in a shroud of crimson velvet, but there was no portal through which to escape. His eyes came back to the fallen man lying before him.

"What have I done?" he cried. "What honor is there here? This is not what was meant to happen, surely you believe me." He clutched hold of a man in the crowd, then another. He randomly moved from person to person, begging for understanding.

"One of you must believe me. It was my opera—my opera. I had to do something. He made a mockery of me. Will you believe me? I did not mean for this to happen! You do believe that, don't you?"

All eyes stared at the lifeless body. The terrible burden of guilt that rested solely upon Matheson was more than his legs could hold. He fell to his knees with his face in his hands at the side of his victim.

Suddenly, Handel sat up. His eyes opened. He looked around the company, completely disoriented. One woman, who stood closest to Handel, fainted. Spectators looked on in horror as if they were seeing a ghost. In utter amazement and relief, Matheson breathed aloud.

"You're not dead."

"No one dies in this opera," Handel said in a daze.

His hand went to his chest, feeling for a wound. His coat was lacerated, but no blood. He looked up, his head cocked to the side; something was very peculiar. Handel searched through the broken pieces of sword on the ground around him. Others in the group followed suit and began to survey the ground for the missing clue to his being alive, anything that would solve the mystery. As the eyes of the all the crowd turned down, one pair of eyes turned upward.

From out of the crowd, a small dirty hand rose high. Slowly, the closed fist began to open. As the small fingers unraveled, the sun caught the edge of something metallic. There, in the middle of the dirt-stained palm was a brightly shining object: a large, gold-plated button. It was bent in half and partially severed from the blow of the sword. People gasped. They marveled as the young urchin who held the button approached Handel at the center of the ring, his prize held high. The stupefied crowd opened like the red sea for Israel—the boy passed through untouched. He stopped just short of Handel and looked up at the large man, then at his coat.

Handel pulled tight the folds of his coat. One large button, chest high, was missing. The boy held the button to the place where it had once hung on Handel's coat. It matched the other buttons perfectly. In one great breath, the crowd sighed in astonishment.

The ineffability of the entire circumstance was overwhelming. Matheson's sword had struck the button squarely, shattering the sword, but sparing Handel. A soiled street urchin stood in the middle of the noblest of London, holding the proof of the miracle in his soiled hand.

The boy stepped back from the gigantic oldster looming above him. He tipped back his head and laughed aloud to the sky.

"Ya' must think somethin' of this 'un, Lord." His eyes came back to Handel. "You're a lucky one, mate."

As quick as that, he was back through the open causeway in the crowd and gone from sight.

"Little thief! Someone stop him; Don't let him get away!" boomed Handel, but the boy outpaced his words and was gone before anyone could so much as get turned around.

Handel stood perplexed, his attire in complete disarray. When he noticed his dishevelment he began straightening his clothes and wiping the dirt off his pants and coat. When he spun around to face Matheson, his loose fitting wig slid completely catawampous on his head. Snickers were heard from the audience. Handel shook his head back and forth to try to shift the wig back to its proper place.

"No—leave it! It's straighter than usual," laughed Matheson. "God must have a purpose for you, else why so graciously guide my sword into your button?"

"He must enjoy a good tune now and then," replied Handel.

Matheson extended his open hand to the fallen. Handel looked first at the hand, then at the face of the owner. Like the sun coming out of gray clouds, a smile beamed on Handel's smudged face. He took hold of his friend's hand in a powerful grip and shook it vigorously. Matheson's voice rose above the throng: "Though thou drawest a sword at thy friend, yet despair not, for there may be a returning to favour, if thou openest thy mouth against thy friend, fear not, for there may be a reconciliation."

Handel enthusiastically nodded his agreement. His grip on Matheson's hand tightened as the two friends warmly embraced each other. Forgiveness and restitution were so fully felt that neither of the men heard the voice of the town crier the first time he called out the news.

The crier's voice rang out again from the nearby street corner. As people understood, their voices fell silent. The crowd began to disperse. Not until it was completely quiet did either Matheson or Handel hear the message being called through the streets:

"Her Majesty, Queen Anne, is dead."

The blood drained from Handel's face. The crier's voice continued.

"On this day, our beloved Queen has gone back to the God that made her. God save the Queen. Her Majesty, Queen Anne, is dead."

While most simply stared in disbelief at the news, Handel ran toward the crier, carelessly pushing through anyone or anything in his path. As he ran, he nervously muttered, "Queen Anne gone, it can't be. Who will succeed her? Who will follow?"

He moved with all the haste he could muster. He no longer cared about wigs or straightened clothes. He ran frantically to the bearer of the news.

"Please don't let it be him. No, it can't be."

Out of breath, he finally reached the town crier. Handel grabbed him by the arm and spun him around.

"Tell me, man, has the successor been named? Who will be crowned?"

"What? Let go of me." The messenger jerked his arm, but it did not come free.

Handel's grip tightened.

"Who will be the successor?"

"The settlement act of 1701 names him," the crier stammered.

Handel was out of patience. He seized the town crier with both hands and pulled him to his face; the man's toes barely touched the ground.

"Names whom? Whom does it name?"

"The son of the most excellent Princess Sophia: George, the Elector of Hanover," shouted the frightened man.

Handel's countenance fell.

The blood which in rashness had drained from his face now rushed back in. He became dizzy. Handel's firm grip on the town crier released; he dropped him flat on his feet. The man ran while he could.

Handel stood in utter disbelief, completely oblivious to the beggars who now thronged him on every side. Glass-eyed, he walked away to nowhere in particular; not even the beggars followed him. It was clear there was no point in continuing their pleas. He was numb to everyone and everything. He saw nothing but the ground one step ahead of him. He forgot about *Cleopatra*, forgot about Matheson. He had forsaken his employer to go to London. Now his employer was coming to him.

He stopped mid-step and pulled back the folds in his coat. He looked where the gold button had been; he wondered if it was providence or some demented irony that guided Matheson's sword into his button. He walked on, unaware of the passage of time or distance he had traveled. The new day was just starting to glow on the eastern horizon when he turned the corner onto Brook Street and arrived home.

Prepare Ye the Way of the Lord

THE STREET WAS PART DIRT AND PART PEBBLE. THE ORDER of the day was for occupants to pave and clean the specific and immediate area in front of their houses or shops. Good pebbles—raggstones or flints—were recommended. The rounded, fist-sized pebbles, or cobbles, were planted in the street in a staggered fashion, with approximately half of the stone exposed. The paving was difficult. Most people routinely complied, although in varying degrees. The patchwork result was better than nothing but far less than ideal.

The maintenance and cleanliness of the street were directly commensurate with the immediate occupant's sense of duty. Pot holes and puddles were often neglected as long as possible. Only if there were sections of the street in such poor repair as to warrant numerous complaints would a constable show up to demand that improvements be made. Generally, the level of tolerance was high while expectation was low.

As all traffic—whether foot or wheeled—came in contact with only the exposed surface of the cobbles, the stones were first honed smooth then polished by countless leather soles and iron-rimmed wheels. When wet, they became treacherously slick. It was not unusual to see people picking themselves up from a wet street. In winter, when freezing rain would fall in icy sheets, the streets were virtually impassable.

Usually, through the center of the street, there extended a long, narrow gutter. In spite of the fact that it was specifically intended for drainage, it was more often used to delineate the perimeter of one's responsibility. Occasionally, fights would break out between neighboring tenants in areas where the borders were not definitively clear. A good center gutter did much to promote community cooperation and general good will. Deep gutters were also dug along the outside edges of the street. When the rains came, water would drain to both the inside and outside gutters, forming silty streams and huge muddy puddles. In summer when the days were muggy, children would play in the muddy mess, much to the dismay of protective parents.

The busier the street, the noisier. The window-rattling ruckus of iron carriage wheels on cobbles could be maddening. Several carriages on the same block, echoing their plangent clamor back and forth between parallel granite walls, were more than most people could endure. Pedestrians walked with their hands over their ears. Small children would cry.

Late at night when the streets were deserted, the noise of a carriage on cobbles could be hauntingly disconcerting to a skittish walker. The crescendoing pulse of an on-coming horse and carriage hidden under a shroud of darkness could erode both courage and common sense. The indomitable approaching patter provided ample time for a nervous pedestrian's imagination to conjure up the most horrific of possible nightmares before the carriage would finally— and usually innocently—pass.

During daylight hours and the neighboring hour on either side, the street was in constant motion with a seemingly endless flow of humanity. Pedestrians and wheeled machines together filled the Strand from end to end. Like a long snake with numerous appendages reaching out from the main body, the long street would ebb and surge like the tide—not steady, but not still.

From above the street, the rhythmic throb had the hypnotic effect of numbing the unwary observer into believing that the snake had no bite. But a closer look revealed bulges within the serpent—aberrations in the belly. These boils were most deceptive, for it was within these social swellings that precious life was torturously sucked from those swallowed up by injustice: the helpless, the poor, the orphan. Nowhere was social disparity more apparent than in the street. Such were the cobbled streets of London in 1737.

There existed a communally understood hierarchy in the street. As with most social structures, it was both vertical and triangular by nature, with those of substance nearest the apex. In like fashion, the farther one could stay above the cobbled stones, the higher one's station in life. Simply stated: those who had, rode. They were the carriage people—individuals of influence who could afford to be on the street, but not in it.

The way of the carriage was the way of horses, wheels, and privilege. Wealth seldom walked. It was not unusual for the most lavish carriage wheel to hurl mud on the most miserable of men. Carriages were the giants of the street. Size and speed made them formidable, reprehensible, untouchable—until they stopped. Stillness rendered them reachable. Like flies caught in a jar, the carriage people were suddenly captive to be looked upon and loathed. Filthy hands were flung up at them to be filled, perhaps, with sympathy. For those below to make a pawn of one of the privileged was not an impropriety, but a leavening.

The masses endured below the carriage. For the common man, the street was life's arena. Where the street was swollen with people, there was commerce—merchants and customers, buying and selling. Money changing bred misery. The one followed the other like a dog waiting for scraps to fall from the master's table. When the tide of the street surged, it simply reflected the good fortune or fall of one in the nameless crowd.

Nearest the street existed the lowest class of Georgian London, in what was known as "the realm of the rodent." To live low was to know the damp, slimy underbelly of the snake. It was the way of gutters, ooze, puddles, holes, mud, and usually, misery. Here were children without homes, children without parents.

Most street urchins knew nothing of higher views or the innards of carriages. The only companion with which they were well acquainted was hunger. These unfortunate children could imagine no life other than the street. Their wretched days were dismally wrung out below the eyes of all. Many begged. Some tried to steal. Occasionally, one might catch a glimpse of a darting child, always followed by shouts of "Thief!" or "Robber!"

Their very existence relied on learning to fend for themselves in a thorny world. And yet, possibly because they were not far enough from God to know better, among the rodents were some of the best of humans. Like the northern goose, whose tiny, most precious plumes of down lay closest to the fowl, here also were some of the smallest and most precious of people dwelling closest to the foul. Here lived Peter the Packrat.

The Packrat was right; escape had been easy. By the time the crowd behind the opera house turned around, he was past them. None had so much as laid a finger on him. He knew it was stupid to walk right up to the big man who had been saved by the button, but it felt like a fitting end to such a bizarre event.

"Besides," he muttered, "they made a path 'tween 'em wide enough for the fattest a' noblemen to waddle through."

He smiled as he thrust his hand deep into his pocket. His fingers touched the button. From that moment on, each time he put his hand in his pocket, he breathed a little sigh of relief when his fingers touched the metal piece. Things in his pocket had an uncanny way of working their way out. He was almost certain that one day he would reach for it and it would be gone. He knew it was silly to become attached to anything that could be lost or stolen as easily as it had come to him, but the Packrat couldn't help himself. Never had anything at the bottom of his pocket piqued his curiosity so much as the thing that he now possessed. He thought about it constantly. Even his profession suffered because of it; open pockets passed by him unnoticed. He repeatedly caught himself absentmindedly turning it over and over in his hand in the bottom of his pocket.

Peter thought about trying to flatten it out with a rock, but he could not bring himself to do it. The bend in the middle was the one feature of his trophy that was most appealing to him. It caused him to wonder about the big man who was saved by the button.

"Who is the man God protects with a button?" he would wonder out loud. "I know Your ways are mysterious, Lord, but this time Ya' were a bit careless. Left a clue to Your riddle, didn't Ya'." He raised the button high in his open hand.

"And I've got it. Hah!"

Peter believed he had found a little miracle that would bring him luck because God himself had touched it with his finger. The sharp crease in the button where the sword had struck it was evidence of God's protecting hand. Peter memorized the divine bend. The button was slightly severed on one edge. He found the cut when he pricked his finger on it and tore away a piece of skin. The length of the crease had a shorn silver stripe where the sword shaved off the gold plating.

Peter had no thought of trading the button away or leaving it behind in place of some other stolen item. This was a prize he had every intention of keeping. He had come by it by pure providence; surely God wanted him to have it. He somehow knew that there was a reason that he was meant to have it. Perhaps someday it would save him, too. He took it from his pocket and stared at it.

"Thank Ya', Lord, for rollin' it my way—any closer and it would have landed right in my hand. But Ya' don't like makin' things that easy— always like me to do my part, don't Ya'?"

He flipped the button in his hand; other than the bend, it was fairly ordinary. There were some engravings of sorts, nothing royal or eminent. It was heavy for a button. It easily weighed more than all the buttons on the Packrat's shirt and pants combined. He stopped in front of a small shop window and held it up to his shirt. In the window reflection the button appeared almost as big as his head. It scared him. He felt as though he were issuing a challenge to all of London: "Jus' try to take this from me!"

He quickly shoved it back in his pocket and glanced around nervously. He hated how it made him feel to have gold dangling on the front of him. He never thought of it as an ornament again. It was simply a luck-button for the bottom of pockets, not for the dressing of coats.

As he skipped off down the street, he remembered that he still had work to do and must be about it. He had promised bread to the two abandoned rodents he had found the week before. He stumbled upon them in the empty coal pit behind the stairwell to the Boar's Head Pub.

They hadn't eaten in days and the little girl looked especially gaunt. Had it been winter, the two would have been dead before he found them, but the cool spring nights were more forgiving.

When the Packrat saw them hiding between the stairs he knew immediately that their parents had abandoned them. He didn't know the parents, but he hated them, nonetheless. A child born in the street was a travesty of life; a child deserted in the street was one of life's most pitiful tragedies. Peter considered it a premeditated act of selfishness. He couldn't imagine any reason for leaving a kid in the street. He, himself, had been abandoned; and by experience he had learned to recognize new orphans. Any kid who had spent any time in the street would know that the stairwell was temporary at best. Certainly there were scraps to be had, but inevitably someone would discover them and they would be put out and moved on. At the wrong time of year, that would be the worst of circumstances.

Transient children were the most unfortunate of vermin. There was nothing more pathetic than the homeless among the homeless. These were the children who lived or died by pure chance. Because they were nomads, they had no way of learning the territory and the opportunistic events of the day, the habits of the vendors and shopkeepers, the times when the inns throw out garbage to the dogs. What was worse, they had no family of rodents like themselves to rely on.

Peter spotted the two little ones and recognized at once that they were lost in the underprivileged world. He took them into his place and looked after them. He realized that helping them learn to help themselves would take time and effort. For now, he determined to help keep them alive, but not give them so much as to make them dependent. Self-reliance was what kept him alive, and he dared not take that power from them. Usually, he tried to be firm and unsympathetic to help them become independent, but tonight he had promised them bread, and he had yet to win it.

He went to the bakers who occasionally threw their ugly loaves his way but he was too late. He shopped the garbage of the pubs; there was nothing. Every time he thought about going home without bread, he could see the little girl's eyes and the boy's hands. Both would be disappointed.

Peter reached in his pocket and rubbed the button for luck. He pricked the same scabbed finger again and cursed.

He turned down an alley he usually avoided. He walked with his head down. As he sucked the blood from his wounded finger he suddenly heard footsteps in front of him. He glanced up to find that he was not alone. There was another shadow in the narrow passage ahead—a man.

Peter slowed to a stop.

He looked back in the direction from which he had come, then at the approaching man. His first thought was to turn around and run, but then he eyed the brown bag under the man's arm; it was full. He wondered how to distract the man and take the bag, but the alley was long and empty. There was little chance of escape short of simply being the faster runner. It was precisely the kind of pursuit he hated, an adult chasing him from behind. Even if he did get away, he was sure the deed would come back around when he didn't need it. Desperate deeds done within sight always did.

While Peter was strategizing, the man suddenly stopped. He stood a few paces in front of the Packrat. Peter seldom looked adults in the eye, especially adults in shoes he didn't recognize. He didn't want people to know his face too well or they might wrongly accuse him of a trespass done by a less-skilled thief.

He studied the man's shoes; they were weathered and well worn. Peter didn't recognize the shoes, but he could tell the man wasn't far from where he was in the world.

The Packrat's eyes ventured higher to the bag. He could see the heels of two loaves pointing straight at him from the open end. The man's hand went in the bag. Before Peter knew what he was doing, the hand was holding a loaf out to him.

Peter stepped back.

The hand didn't move, nor did the loaf.

"What the 'ell?" Peter wondered. He wasn't sure of the stranger's motive, but he was sure that what he saw was bread—and it was being held out to him.

Cautiously, he slid forward until the bread was within reach. The hand did not move. All at once, the Packrat caught hold of the loaf and jumped free of the man's reach. Nothing happened. The Packrat turned to flee but couldn't. He instinctively knew there would be no pursuit.

Slowly he turned back toward the man. There was no point in running now. He couldn't hide, he had been seen. The man in the alley stripped him of every advantage that the Packrat valued.

"What does he want?" the Packrat whispered.

The entire incident felt strange, backwards. The rapid succession of events that culminated with his holding the loaf and feeling indebted to the man in the dark was unprecedented. He felt compelled to meet eyes with the stranger who had robbed him of his rightful wrong. The more obligated he felt, the more angry he became.

Against his own will, he began to lift his eyes to see the man who held out the loaf so freely, but before their eyes could meet he spoke out defiantly.

"I don't need it."

"I know."

"*Who* knows?" thought Peter. He spoke boldly, "What do ya' want for it?"

"Nothing."

"I have to give ya' somethin'. What do ya' want?"

"Nothing."

"Why not?"

The man didn't answer. Peter reached down into his pocket. His fingers touched the bent button; now he was trapped. His neck began to warm beneath his shirt. He wished he had never ventured into this alley or spotted the brown bag. He wanted to give back the loaf and run, but the thought of facing the rodents empty-handed remedied that. He was confused. He could hear his heart beating in his chest. The Packrat's hand jerked wildly, there was a short ripping sound.

The boy shoved something in the man's hand, then he ran as fast as he could for the far end of the alley. Just as he was about to round the corner back onto the street, he stopped. He looked back at the man's face, a face he would never forget. A moment later, Peter disappeared around the corner and was gone.

The man opened his hand.

Inside was a button—not gold, but dull and black.

When Peter arrived at the abandoned wine cellar under the inn where he hid himself at night, the little ones were already asleep from hunger. He tore the loaf in half and put a piece under the arm of each child. He knew they were dreaming of bread and he wanted it to be there when they awoke. He sat down with a small piece himself. As he chewed, he thought of the man in the alley.

"What are Ya' up to, Lord? Ya're feelin' a bit mischievous these days."

He reached in his pocket and touched the bent button, then he looked down at his shirt. He pushed his finger through the hole where a black button had once been.

He leaned back and dozed off to dream of bread.

The man with the two loaves knew the Packrat—not personally, but he knew of him. He had seen him occasionally and heard of him often. There were stories about the street boy who didn't know he was poor, the dirty one who laughed when it rained and sang from the gutters. Yes, he knew the name "Packrat."

Jonathon heard how the boy earned the name because he never stole without leaving something in place of what he took. It was said that the Packrat called it "tradin'," not stealing. Jonathon knew the boy was too young to understand that the criterion of trading was mutual consent; such things meant nothing to him.

When the street people gathered at the firecans at night, the name Packrat came up often. There was always a new tale of the boy's mocking a nobleman, his making a game of misery, or helping a lost little one.

That's how Jonathon knew there was a better-than-average chance that the bread was not just for him. There was talk of how he looked out for other urchins.

The fact that the boy took no thought that he was helping was one of the most endearing things about the Packrat. That was why Jonathon gave him the bread. Since he worked at a bakery, he had enough for his needs.

"If what they say is true, the boy will be lucky to have any left for himself after he shares with the unfortunate others he looks out for."

Jonathon couldn't help smiling when he opened his hand to reveal the black button where the bread had once been. Here was proof that the stories he had heard were true. It made him laugh.

As he studied the button in his palm, Jonathon evaluated his trade; he considered it a good one. He was pleased to have the chance to share his bread with the Packrat. Only one who has gone without bread would understand what it meant to have bread. Jonathon understood.

Speak Ye Comfortably

IT WAS NEARLY NOON WHEN THE DISTANT CARRIAGE WAS heard coming up the dirt lane toward the manor house. In the quiet of the valley, the distant clatter of the wheels could be heard several minutes before the actual arrival.

Thick, gray, easterly-driven clouds draped the sky. From the manor house at the rise of a small, central bluff the entire surrounding valley could be viewed in its fullness. In the diffused light of the overcast day, all nature seemed melancholy and still. The day was as it appeared: a day of mourning.

Near the open north window of the parlour stood the Lord of the Manor, Baron Kilmanseck. He stood in silence, gazing out on the reach below. The Baron was a rich man of sorts, well known to all—including royalty.

He was described as either prolific or plump, depending on how well one knew and respected him. He was esteemed among the noble because of his social stature, but he was characterized by his nervousness. He was known as a jittery man, a foot tapper. The Baron always suffered from indigestion. It was said that his propensity towards worry was better suited to a baroness.

In spite of any hearsay or disparaging jokes, however, everyone knew he was a player. The Baron had something for which most could only wish: he had the ear of the new King. Having a personal relationship with George of Hanover instantly made him somewhat a dealer in destinies. If one had need of the crown, the Baron's name was not one which went unconsidered.

He received many gifts, mostly from those in need of a favor. Not only did the Elector of Hanover like the Baron, he listened to him. On several occasions, George had requested that the Baron come to Hanover to consult and discuss English politics. Consequently, the Baron was invited to all the royal functions and was confided in at each of them. It was not unusual for the King to seat the Baron near him so that he could inquire of him concerning the personal dealings and political opinions of his guests. The Baron made it a point to know the goings-on and gossip of English society in order to answer accurately any and all questions put to him. His mind was in constant anxiety over the question he would not be able to answer.

Handel knew all of this. He also knew that when the Baron traveled, he often arranged his schedule such that he could attend the opera, including Handel's operas. The Baron even attended some of the small concerts Handel performed in London.

The two had spoken on occasion concerning the common interest they shared in Hanover. Handel had properly readied his relationship with the Baron. Perchance at some point, he would have need of him. The Baron had wisely done likewise. He had questioned Handel's loyalty to his employer twice before, but Handel did not heed him. Now, those warnings seemed prophetic. The time of reckoning had finally come.

Still, the Baron was tolerant of the artist's frailties and shortsightedness. There was no denying Handel's gift. In spite of his better judgment, the Baron took a liking to the Saxon and desired for him to stay in good graces with George the King.

He fully expected a visit from the errant artist. He was neither surprised nor displeased when he heard that a carriage had entered the estate. He remained uncharacteristically calm as he contemplated Handel's predicament.

The Baron was well into devising a plan of clemency in the Saxon's behalf when he was roused from reverie by voices in the entryway. Momentarily, the parlor door opened; into the room stepped the head butler.

"Sir, if I might interrupt. Mr. George Frederic Handel is here to see you. Shall I tell him you are presently indisposed?"

Before the Baron could respond, Handel walked past the house servant and into the room. He bowed low.

"My lord, Baron Kilmanseck, I am in desperate need of your help. You are a loyal patron of the opera..."

The Baron turned to Handel, who immediately recognized the impropriety of his actions. His words trailed off as the Baron measured him with his eyes.

At long last, the Baron nodded to the butler to leave. Handel considered this an invitation to continue.

"I have acted in poor judgment. I should have returned when summoned, but I was compelled to stay in London. Surely you understand."

The Baron turned his face back to the window; he spoke low.

"Please reverence our quietude. We are in mourning."

Handel moved closer, his voice rising and falling in nervous whispers.

"Yes, m'lord, indeed. The Queen was generous, kind-hearted—a lover of music like yourself. That is why I'm here."

The Baron waited, knowing that Handel needed no acknowledgment to continue.

"You are a personal friend of our new King, the Elector of Hanover."

"Your employer," reminded the Baron.

"Yes, I was his Kapellmeister."

"You are his Kapellmeister."

"Yes, of course. He was kind enough to give me leave to come to London."

"But you never returned."

"How could I?" Handel answered, his voice tainted with impatience.

"You had obligations."

"Yes, I know, but they love me here. Queen Anne herself granted me an annual stipend, commissioned operas. How could I leave?" Handel was not asking, but telling. The Baron turned again from the window. Upon seeing the earnestness in the Baron's face, Handel recognized his error. He knew he had gone to the brink of losing a possible ally. His miserable temper had nearly gotten the best of him again. He spoke in desperation.

"I could lose everything—everything I've done here. Please speak to him, plead my cause."

After long consideration, the Baron turned back to the window. He had already made up his mind to help, in spite of Handel's impertinence. His love of music outweighed his contempt for insolence. He understood that artists were temperamental fools who could not be expected to understand the delicacies of dealing with royal egos. Baron Kilmanseck upheld Handel in spite of his shortcomings. He had schemed a scheme.

He glanced back at Handel one last time as if weighing the consequences of the course he was about to take.

"It may take some time. Do you have someplace you can go, away from London until I send word for you to come?" asked the Baron.

Handel thought momentarily.

"My mother is ill at Halle."

"Go."

Handel started toward the Baron, his hand extended. The Baron raised his palm in reproach.

"Mourn your Queen."

Handel bowed, but the Baron didn't notice; Handel was already gone to him. As he was backing out the open door, Handel opened his mouth to speak, but no words escaped. Quietly he left by the same door he had entered. He was gone before the butler could see him out.

Comfort Ye

THE HORSES BREATHED LONG STREAMS OF STEAM IN THE early morning air. Sweat foamed around the leather belly cinches and collars of their harnesses. They had pulled eastward through the long night without a change of team.

The German countryside was just beginning to wake up in the blue of pre-dawn. Birds sang their songs of morning. Fragments of dirt softened by a brief shower the evening before peeled off the spinning wheels. Droplets of water clung precariously to blades of grass along the edge of the road. A lone driver sat atop the carriage.

Inside, Handel dozed in the early light of morning. As the carriage rattled over a stone bridge, Handel woke with a start. He looked out the window to ascertain their position. He rapped on the ceiling with his brass-handled cane.

"How much farther?"

"What's that, sir?" The driver asked.

Handel leaned out the window and yelled up to him.

"How much farther to Halle?"

The driver slowed the carriage to a stop and leaned over the edge of the coach. "Excuse me, sir?"

"Why are we stopping?"

"To hear, sir. You asked a question!"

"How long before we reach Halle?" Handel demanded.

The driver thought for a moment. "Mid-morning should do it, sir, if we continue at present speed."

"We have no present speed," snapped Handel. "Perhaps you would be so kind as to remedy that."

Handel leaned back in the carriage and rapped the ceiling with his cane. The driver reigned the horses; the carriage rolled on toward Halle.

Inside, Handel's thoughts turned to music. From memory, he replayed over in his mind an aria from the second act of Matheson's *Cleopatra*. He had stowed the melody away in his memory for a future performance. It was a skill that he put to good and regular use.

Handel had an uncanny way of remembering everything that he heard. He could reproduce a piece after a single hearing from a year before. His brain was a virtual library of music which he categorized and called up as needed. If he played a piece, he could remember it almost to the note. He was known by his contemporaries as "Handel: The Great Borrower" because he often took another's idea, expanded on it and made it better. He could hear a melody line from a piece, build a structure around it, then incorporate the reincarnation into his own work. He did it so well that even the original composer could hardly recognize it. Handel could easily rationalize borrowing the idea by saying that he was only doing what should have been done in the first place.

Ideas were ever coming and going. No piece was ever completely finished to him, since he never stopped considering new ways to turn an old phrase. When a new spin would come, he would find the closest instrument on which to try it out. Once played, the music was sealed into his memory forever. Each note of it became part of his repertoire, to be called up and embellished as needed.

Handel was in deep meditation when a familiar smell permeated the carriage compartment. He raised his eyes to look out the window. To the west stretched the Saale, the river of his youth. He had grown to love the river in every season, but none so much as spring. He loved the yellow poppies that grew near the bank, the song of the larks singing in the morning air. The high water of spring runoff lapped against the green reeds near the top of the bank.

Looking downriver he could see the Saale sweeping away down the valley to its confluence with the Elbe.

Upriver, a league before him, he could see the church steeple of Halle rising out of the low-lying fog. Every Sunday morning, his parents would usher him into church amidst a blanket of fog, only to emerge from service an hour later to perfect sunshine and clear blue sky.

He loved Sundays. He was exposed to more music on that one day than the others combined. He listened intently to the prelude, the postlude, and any other-lude in between. When the choir sang, he hummed along. He joined in the congregational hymns with great enthusiasm.

The steeple rising before him stirred in his soul rich feelings of nostalgia and warmth; and yet there was something amiss. The church was the one image of Halle that was most recognizable to him, but something was different. The shape of the steeple was familiar, but the steeple itself was not as he remembered. It seemed to be in a different location. Then he recalled his mother telling him by letter that the church had burned down and the spire had fallen. The thought of the church not being where he remembered saddened him. He fondly remembered playing the organ there as a child.

A new church was built, but there was no mention of the remains of the prior for several years. It was only the month before that she had written that the church had been restored and was now serving as a children's hospital.

Through thin layers of swirling fog, he could catch glimpses of the green fields running right up to the brick of the town wall. A cool morning breeze blew across the river, stealing away the fragrant air surrounding every flower or field over which it passed. This was the aroma that permeated the coach, transcending Handel's deep concentration and making him all but forget any thought of music. Like the sweet smell in the wind, Handel was carried away to days younger when he and his mother would push open the windows of the house to let in the cleansing breath of spring. She much preferred the slight discomfort of a chilly room to breathing warm, stale air.

Out the opposite side of the carriage stretched rolling fields of sprouting corn. From memory, he could picture the broad Saxon plain as it would appear three months hence: a sea of huge corn stalks, which would reach the top of the carriage. He knew they would never seem so tall now as they had in his childhood.

As the carriage veered left at a fork in the narrow road outside Halle, the surrounding fields became even more familiar. They continued on that road for several more minutes over the rolling hills of Saxony. Handel kept a steady watch out the window. Finally he spotted what he was looking for.

Out in the distance, beyond an open field, stood a small cottage in a stand of large trees. When Handel saw it, his eyes glowed with absolute wonder. Through the small portal of the carriage window, he was gazing into his childhood. Memories of his youth swept over his mind like a stream over moss, washing away any doubt and anxiety. His face became a visage of complete contentment.

He looked down at the winding dirt path leading up to the house. He recalled the day when he was ten and had chased his father's carriage down this same path on his way to the ducal court at Weissenfels, where George's half-brother Karl served as valet. So intent was young Handel to see his half-brother that when his father denied his request to join him—because he "thought one of his age an improper companion to go to the court of a prince"—young George followed the carriage on foot. He chased along behind for several miles before his father finally gave in and allowed him a place at his side.

As Handel viewed this path now, he considered how his life had changed by virtue of his persistence, for it was in Weissenfels that the Duke heard young George playing the organ in the palace chapel and inquired concerning him. Upon finding out that it was his valet's younger brother, he provided princely encouragement to both the boy and his father, who until then had discouraged his son's musical interests.

The carriage rolled past the thick trunks of the trees leading up to the Handel home and stopped in front of the cottage. While the driver untied the ropes securing the bags on top, Handel slowly opened the door and stepped down from the carriage. He stood motionless, looking on his childhood home with profound richness of soul. Every detail of the house was as he remembered: the ivy crawling up the northern exposure, the moss under the eaves, the red geraniums lining the window boxes. As he stared at the small home, he suddenly felt as though he had never left.

The driver hurriedly went about his task. He lowered Handel's travel chest to the ground and then jumped down alongside it.

"I believe that is all, sir."

Handel did not answer.

"Mr. Handel, sir; I'll be going now."

"What's that?" inquired Handel.

"I'm leaving, sir."

"Good."

The driver's head cocked to the side. He scratched his chin and murmured some indiscernible words under his breath. He spoke again.

"Are you forgetting?"

Handel glanced at the chest, then at the small travel case that he kept with him.

"No. Everything is here."

The two men stared at each other briefly. Handel was first to speak.

"Were you not paid?"

The driver nodded.

"Are we not here?"

The driver nodded again.

"Are we not finished then?"

"It is customary that when one's service exceeds the norm, one might receive a gratuity."

"Did your service exceed the norm?"

"We drove through the night with no rest. The horses are tired and thirsty."

"Feed them!" was Handel's curt reply. The driver's head lowered; he stared at Handel from under furrowed eyebrows.

Handel got the point. He sighed, then reached in his pocket and pulled from it a small purse, which he held out to the driver. He did not watch him take it. His eyes were back on the house.

"Thank you," said the driver once the purse was in his hand. He reached to close the coach door but was unable to; Handel stood directly in front of it.

"Sir—," the driver stammered. He remembered the frequent tongue-lashings he had received since the two-day journey began. "Never mind."

He walked to the horses and, with a push on the rump, nudged them forward until the door was clear of Handel. He hustled back to the open door and slammed it closed. He climbed as quickly as he could to his place on top, reigned the horses, and was off.

The carriage rattled down the lane, leaving Handel standing exactly where he had stepped from the carriage. A man came out the front door of the cottage. He talked as he walked. Handel recognized him immediately as a physician. His own father, Georg, had been a physician. Handel had seen the same attire and concerned look on his father many times.

Georg Handel had been a highly respected barber-surgeon who practiced in Leipzig and in the court at Weissenfels. In his youth, young George had watched his father walk out that same door in the same manner on his way to the infirm.

The father was stern with his young son who bore his name. He had high hopes for young George. He pressured the boy incessantly to study law. "A profession of honor," he called it.

Young George had aspirations musically, which caused considerable consternation in the Handel home. It was only after the duke's vehement insistence that George develop his talent that his father was forced to make concessions with regard to his son's musical pursuits. He allowed it, but was no more the happy about it. Handel remembered the disappointed looks his father would give him while he readied the carriage to go tend to the sick. Perhaps, that was why Handel now viewed the man approaching him with mild contempt.

"Mr. Handel? I was told you were coming," the man called.

Handel all but ignored him. He surveyed the overgrown gardens in front of the cottage.

"The grounds are in need of care. Who helps with the gardening and pruning?"

"How much do you know?" the physician continued.

Handel looked at the house.

"The cottage hasn't changed much."

Two voices were talking, but, of the four ears present, none had yet listened.

"She seems to be in a lot of pain."

Now he did have Handel's full and undivided attention. The physician continued with marked uneasiness.

"The fever is constant. Smallpox perhaps, but the symptoms are somewhat different. Until we are certain, she is quarantined. You should take precautions."

Handel's unbending stare made the physician acutely aware that his diagnosis had been all but sympathetic. He went on, this time more compassionately. He spoke now of the patient, not just the ailment.

"She will not know you are here. She is seldom fully awake and yet never completely at rest. She has not had a moment's peace since she's been in my care."

Handel nodded. The physician watched Handel's gaze drift back to the cottage and up to the small window in the hayloft above the house.

Handel entered the front door carrying a small case under his arm. He stopped just inside the door as if he had walked directly into an invisible wall. He scanned the room from left to right. A thousand remembrances moved across the stage of his mind. He saw the open door leading to his mother's bedroom. From where he stood, he could see the bottom half of a bed but not the face of the person filling it.

He moved slowly toward the door. With each step the old oak floor creaked under his weight. As he drew closer to the threshold, more of the room opened to him. The ceiling, which seemed so high when he was young, felt uncomfortably close. He lowered his head as he walked, not so much for clearance, but out of reverence.

As he reached the doorway into the bedroom, he stopped. He looked upon the face of his mother for the first time in many years. He said nothing. Words could not express the feelings that he had as he looked upon his mother's face after the long absence. His face showed the love that his heart held. He stood in that position for a long time.

Finally, he stepped into the room, the case still under his arm. He laid it gently on a nearby chair, then looked at his mother. Dorothea was restless, unsettled. Her eyes moved rapidly under her eyelids. The muscles in her hands were tightened into fists. Occasionally, she would let out a moan between heavy breaths.

Her son reached to her and tenderly brushed her cheek with the back of his hand. He kissed her fevered brow. He pulled a small wooden chair alongside her bed and sat down. He snapped open the three clasps along the outer edge of the case and pulled from it a violin. Deftly, he lifted it to his chin and then took the bow into his other hand. As the hairs of the bow touched the strings of the instrument, a pure strain of perfect sound filled the air. Softly and sweetly he played from memory the melody of the minstrels—the *pifferari*. It was the one melody that she had specifically asked him to learn for her. For hours, young George had sat at his mother's footstool, playing this song she loved best. Now he sat at her bedside, playing for her again, transforming her pain into sweet memory.

Within a few moments, Dorothea became tranquil. Even in her sleep, she knew her boy had come home.

Throughout the rest of the day, Handel played each time Dorothea became restless. He stayed at her side until the sun was gone and the chill of night had settled on the earth. A crescent moon could be seen, but it did not give much light. Every star in the firmament was visible in the dome of black overhead. From a distance, the outline of the house could not be seen at all. Had it not been for the single square of light where an oil lamp burned in the bedroom window, it would have seemed that the violin music that sang through the air wasn't telestial, but a gift from the heavens to mother earth. It was the pure music of God—the sound of angels, the song of perfect love.

The cottage became quiet. Dorothea slept. The only movement in the house was a dark form with a single candle in hand, ascending the steep narrow staircase.

Through the slats of the closed hatch in the floor of the attic, thin blades of light grew brighter. The small door swung open, letting in the full influence of the candle in Handel's hand. His head appeared through the entrance in the floor. He held up the candle to see. Dust curled around him. He searched the loft as if remembering something from years past.

He ascended the last steps of the stair and stepped up to the A-framed room. The smell of dust and hay was sweet and pungent, but he did not sneeze. He had conditioned himself to the dust and smell and was long since immune from any effects.

He walked carefully, so as not to make a sound, across the open room to the southeast corner, where a small window looked out to the front lane leading up to the cottage. There, lying on the floor in the corner, partly covered with hay, was an old furniture sheet. He lifted it and affectionately folded it into a neat roll. He laid it under the window. His eyes closed. His right hand slowly raised away from his body. His fingers began to move. Somehow, unseen by anyone but himself, an imaginary instrument appeared beneath them.

In time, Handel returned to the chair at his mother's side. Long into the night he watched her, pondering the sweet memories of youth. Of all the faces in Handel's memory, Dorothea's was most cherished.

Handel laid his head on the bed next to his mother's hand. When his eyes finally did close, the last thing he saw was her face.

Down in the farms along the valley floor, the roosters were starting to crow. The sun had not yet crested the tops of the surrounding hills, but the distant bluffs to the west were already steaming in the morning light.

Within the cottage, no one was as yet awake. Dorothea had slept through the entire night for the first time in weeks. Even now, she slept on, a peaceful smile on her lips. Her son George lay asleep in the chair at his mother's side, his head on the bed near her outstretched hand. Lying on the bed next to the footboard was the violin, the bow laid next to it.

The morning passed, mother and son each sleeping and dreaming of the person just inches away.

When sunlight came through the window, Dorothea's eyes opened. She looked on her son asleep in the chair. She didn't see the face of a grown man, she saw the face of a little boy on her bed—the boy who had been everything to her.

George's birth had come when she desperately needed something in which to lose herself. At the time, she was still grieving the loss of another son, born only a year before, who lived but an hour. It left her nearly broken, and her husband had been less than comforting. While he was stern, she was compassionate. He was dogmatic, she, provisional. He was platonic, she longed for affection. The many differences became all the more apparent when the child died.

Dorothea needed something. She prayed for intervention, and God heard her prayers. She was blessed with another boy. Not just a boy, but a boy who possessed her heart. This little boy with the locks of gold was golden to her, every whit. George filled the immense void left by her lost child.

Every morning and night, she sang to him the songs that she had loved as a child growing up in the Austrian countryside. Even before her George could use words, he could mimic a phrase of melody. He learned language through song; he learned song at the foot of his mother's chair. He developed an ear at a remarkably young age. He could find pitch and tempo by the time he was two. The mother knew that this gift was a thing to be nurtured and not hidden away. Even against the behest of her husband, she gave the boy a clavichord. The father would absolutely not allow any lessons or instruction of any kind. He would not so much as allow it to be in the house, but Dorothea would not be stopped. If she couldn't have the instrument in the house, she would keep it hidden just outside the house; she moved it to the hayloft above the cottage.

This boy and his music had given her joy in the deepest reaches of her soul.

She looked at him now, fully grown, asleep at her side. She glanced at the violin at the base of the bed and knew immediately that the music of her dream had not been a dream. He had played the music of the minstrels, the melody that somehow had a power to calm her like nothing else. It reminded her of Christ and Christmas. Once, when George was young, they were in Italy at Christmas. While there, the minstrels came down from the mountains to play the *pifferari*, the shepherd's song. When she heard it, she asked her son George to learn it for her.

The notes of the music had come quickly, but the heart of the melody had come with age. As he had grown, so had the soul with which he played. What she had heard in her sleep was the voice of God speaking sweet peace to her restless spirit.

She looked back at her son. Her eyes moistened, but she quickly blinked the tears away. She gently touched his hand and whispered, "In my dreams I could hear the melody you played as a child while I worked in the house."

George's eyes opened.

"The shepherd's song," she whispered through a soft smile. She lifted up slightly, then settled back in her bed.

"How are the English?"

"How is my mother?" he asked, his head still on the bed.

Dorothea smiled again. She was aged and tired, weakened by the illness, yet she was still alert and sharp. She was not a woman of worry; she had no use for whining or dim-wittedness. The things that put her off most were sloth and hypocrisy. She had no tolerance for either. She could chastise if necessary, but every scolding was followed by an outpouring of affection.

She sat up in the bed as best she could. Her son listened, but only partly. He fully anticipated the interview he was about to receive.

"You're still Lutheran, aren't you? If they somehow converted you to the King's church, it had better be for a good cause…not for some damnhell woman or wife or whatever the excuse Henry had for changing things around. Never could understand all that re-arranging of the church and sorts over a woman. What a damn mess they made of things."

The son endured the quiz patiently. Dorothea's strength seemed to come back steadily as she vented.

"Men are lazy, but women meddle. You have no time for such nonsense—they're nothing more than a distraction. There is nothing more ghastly than a female who can't imagine a man putting anything else ahead of her."

George knew this might be his only chance to turn the lecture into a conversation. He spoke while she breathed.

"I'm still Lutheran. They have been kind enough to accept me as I am and still allow me to play in the cathedrals and churches."

"At least they're not stupid, the English I mean," she said as her physician walked into the room. She rolled her eyes towards the intruder. "More than I can say for our stock!"

The doctor had not heard enough to be offended. He stopped at the credenza, quite overwhelmed at the surge of strength displayed by his patient.

"I see that having your son here is good for you," he said.

"Someone should be," she shot back. She looked at George and continued with a nod toward the doctor.

"Thinks I have the smallpox. If I did, I'd be dead now, wouldn't I?"

"We took the necessary precautions," the physician defended. Dorothea shook her head in disgust.

"Damnhell precautions—why not just bury me now as a precaution against dying."

The physician had had his fill; he left as quickly as he had come in. While Dorothea was still mumbling, Handel probed further.

"Are you weak? Have you any strength?"

"What little I have is used up on him. Having him look after me is like having a meddlesome woman around!"

By this time, her strength was indeed giving out. She lay back into her pillow, exhausted. Carefully, George adjusted the pillows behind her head and straightened her covers.

"Get some rest while you can. I won't leave."

Her eyes were still on him when her lids closed over them. Handel picked up the bow and violin from the bed and laid them in the case on the floor. He quietly sat back in the chair and watched her doze off into restful sleep.

For the next several days he was there by her side, tending to her every need. He played for her each day. None of the songs ever required even the smallest part of his skill, but they were the melodies that she loved. He would play for hours at her bedside. Sometimes she would sit with her eyes open, sometimes she would sleep, but always she was listening.

As he would play, she would lean back into her pillows and fall back into the past. There was nothing that brought her more joy than to hear him play. As her ears filled with song, she thought back to the happy days of mothering, when she would perform the chores of the house with a lightness of heart and step, accompanied by her young George. She knew then he had promise, but to hear him now was, for her, prophecy fulfilled.

He sat by her side whenever she was awake and never left until she was safely and fully asleep. Then he would quickly tend to his own needs so he could be back in place before her eyes opened. He made the meals, changed her bedding, fluffed the pillows, and cooled her hot face with damp cloths. But most of all, he played for her. Never had he played for such an adoring audience as this. Seldom does a mother have the opportunity of seeing her children attain the glorious heights she imagines for them, but Dorothea witnessed the fulfillment of her highest hopes and yearnings each day her boy put violin to chin. She could never have dreamed that illness could be so merciful. She thanked the God that made her for the blessing of infirmity.

On a particularly clear morning, Handel determined that his mother needed some blue sky and fresh air. He emerged from the cottage carrying her in his arms. He laid her down on a makeshift bed of blankets, which he had fashioned under the tree. The sun sparkled in the leaves above her head; the blues and greens of spring rejuvenated her and gave strength to her tired limbs. While she waited, Handel imposed on the physician to help him carry the heavy clavichord from the cottage to the place under the tree so he could play for her.

"Higher! Lift it up. Higher!" Handel shouted. "How can one who makes a livelihood of restoring the body have so little use of his own? Lift, man!"

The physician lifted, but little happened. Handel was forced to shoulder the greater part of the weight. His helper really just balanced the instrument as Handel carried it.

Once they arrived at the tree, his assistant quickly disappeared to avoid having to endure more hardship or ridicule.

Handel played. Dorothea leaned back into the blankets as music filled the valley.

So passed the days in Halle—the son caring for the mother who had spent so many years caring for the son. They were peaceful days, filled with a richness of spirit only possible to those who are of the same heart. Every shared memory was healing, every conversation, edifying. For Handel, it was a diversion from the present; for Dorothea, it was a journey into the past. The childhood years provided the structure and framework of their relationship, but age and experience had dressed the house. Time apart filtered and refined the gold of love and loyalty they had for each another. The son honored the mother; the mother adored the son. Even though Handel knew it was only for a season, he never said so. Intuition told Dorothea what her son didn't say, but she chose not to mention the inevitable, either. What neither of them fully realized was that each day the son was home would make it all the more difficult to leave again.

Upon Them Hath the Light Shined

FOR THE MOST PART, THE EVENT WENT UNHERALDED. IT was not newsworthy. *The Spectator* had no announcement, as it often did when nobility was involved. There was no fanfare. Very few people knew anything had taken place at all. For most of London, the day came and went as every other day. But for Jonathon and Rachel, never had there been a day like this.

So few were invited to the ceremony in the little church on the west end of Cheapside that the doors to the chapel were left open for passersby who wanted to pray. There was no choir, no wedding march, no wedding dress nor flowers. There was no exchange of rings at the end to signify their love; their lives of devotion would do that. Neither the bride nor the groom had family to attend, only a small circle of friends from their respective places of work. Aside from this tiny circle, only the priest and God knew that anything had taken place at all. It was a pauper's wedding, short and simple.

The ceremony was scheduled around the bakery's business hours. The doors were closed for less than an hour during the mid-afternoon lull. Not a single customer was inconvenienced. Jonathon worked that morning, baking extra to cover for his absence in the afternoon.

Rachel was given a half-day leave from her seamstressing, but that was all. Both the bride and groom knew they would be at work again in the morning, but what did it matter? Their wedding had been the grandest event that either of them had ever been a part of—not because of the grandness of the event, but the grandness of their hearts. They were in the truest and deepest grip of love. Now that they had shared covenants, Jonathon could not think of anything in life that could give him more joy.

As he looked into Rachel's eyes, tears streamed down to his chin. His eyes revealed what his soul felt. He did not know what he had done to find such favor in the eyes of God as to be worthy of her, but he gratefully thanked his Maker for it.

He hoped for nothing more than to protect and keep his Rachel from harm and to give her the best life that he possibly could. From the moment she consented to marriage, he lay awake for hours at night formulating plans for her happiness.

Their courtship took place over three years. So careful was Jonathon of not overstepping his bounds that it was almost four months from the time he first saw her before he spoke to her. He fell in love with her from afar. He watched her come into the bakery in the late afternoon for weeks before he dared wander out from the ovens to work behind the counter. He would schedule the last batch of rolls to come out of the oven at the same time she usually came in. While he would stack bread for display, he would watch her. He knew her walk, the slight turn of her head when she became embarrassed, her sunny smile, and, most of all, how her luminous auburn hair fell in thick tresses down past her shoulders.

Occasionally, through the spaces between the loaves, their eyes would briefly meet. Her dark brown eyes would shyly glance away, but that brief encounter was enough to make his hours of work pass by as if they were but a moment. Rachel was indeed beautiful.

Jonathon was not alone in his appraisal of her beauty; others also noticed. Rachel was careful to keep herself hidden from the wanton eyes of those beyond her tiny circle of influence. When she was in the street, she wore a dark hooded cape and walked with her head down so she could go completely unnoticed. When she entered a door, she would courteously pull back the hood to reveal her face and hair. Eyes would dwell on her much longer than was polite. Most of those who beheld her beauty were elevated by it; some were not. Regardless of one's motives, she was captivating.

As lovely as Rachel was outwardly, it was her spirit that made her shine. She was beauty that did not regard itself as beautiful. Her face was radiant. Her eyes shined with purity. Rachel was sublime both within and without.

Jonathon was meek, which had nothing to do with his physical strength—he was manly throughout. But somehow, he learned as a young man that he need not be of the world to be in it. He seldom reacted out of anger, which was, more often than not; the way of the street. Mr. Wheelock, who owned and managed the bakery where Jonathon worked, saw something inherently good in the boy and hired him. For eight years Jonathon worked every day except Sundays—especially Easter—and Christmas.

Although he was lean, he developed great strength. When Jonathon first began working, he would drape a heavy mitt across his collar so he could shoulder the heavy trays full of bread. He had a long pale scar across his lower neck from a time when Mr. Wheelock absentmindedly backed into him while he was pulling the tray from the oven. Rather than burn his employer, he spun the tray away from the man's head and took the blistering metal himself. In spite of the searing he received, Jonathon did not drop the tray.

Through the first year, he would take a tray cleanly from the coal-burning ovens with two hands. After several years, his hands and arms became so strong from kneading the thick dough and lifting the heavy trays that he could easily hold a tray in each hand.

When the bakery was slow and the work was finished, his fellow workers would bet one another on how long Jonathon could hold a full tray of bread in each hand. They knew he would never go long enough to lose strength and let bread fall to the ground. For minutes he could hold the trays, arms outstretched. For the first two or three minutes his arms were steady. After three minutes his muscles would start to quiver, but still he would hold firm. Others tried, but just above four minutes was the longest that anyone else had held the trays; that record cost a few loaves that fell to the ground. Mr. Wheelock put an end to the contesting until the challenge was put to Jonathon; then he consented again, knowing his bread was safe.

At first, no one even considered a bet above five minutes. Mr. Wheelock himself enjoyed several early wins before the others adjusted their bets upward. Jonathon had long since proven any bet under five minutes to be short-sighted. Each subsequent time they put Jonathon up to it, the numbers rose. The most recent bet was for just over six minutes, which he surpassed by three seconds. While the winners celebrated, Jonathon immediately went back to work. No one was very surprised that Jonathon never bet on himself.

Jonathon was kind to those he worked with. He never put his own interests above theirs. His loyalty to his employer was unmatched. Whatever was required was done without so much as a murmur. He was eternally grateful to have bread himself and would do whatever necessary to help the man who supplied it. He thought himself blessed in every way conceivable under God's gracious eye. There was nothing that he lacked or wanted—until the bell at the door rang, and he glanced from his work to the hooded stranger who entered the bakery.

At first, he thought nothing of it; but when the stranger pulled her hood back from her face, his soul yearned. It was not her beauty alone that caught his eye, but there was a sweetness about her that enchanted him. He could think of nothing else. He longed to know her name, to touch her hair, to look into her dark eyes for as long as she would let him. He loved her as gently as soft rain in summer and as purely as the scent of pine in winter. He could not imagine life without her even if it meant no more than the brief sight of her in the late afternoon.

He remembered every detail of the day they first spoke. She pulled on her hood to leave and turned just as the bakery door was swinging open. The door struck her arm, spilling the contents of her basket to the floor. Jonathon jumped to her aid before anyone else realized what had happened. As he looked up from the ground, their eyes met. Something passed between them; it was unseen by anyone else. He replaced the fallen goods with fresh ones. As he handed her back the basket she said, "Thank you." Those simple words from her lips kept his spirit soaring for several days. After that, they began to speak regularly, always exchanging greetings, both coming and going. Slowly, they got to know each another, quickly they fell in love.

Giving themselves to each other in marriage did not feel like a sacrifice but a rebirth; they did so gladly and completely. No words ever crossed Rachel's tongue which were more heartfelt or solemnly sincere than, "I do." Jonathon could hardly speak when his turn came. The priest interpreted his tears and nod as affirmation, and the ceremony continued. No two souls had ever come together in such humility and utter devotion. They belonged to each other. Everyone present knew it had always been so.

Yet Once a Little While

THE BUILDING WAS NOT FIT FOR USE, YET IT WAS BEING used. The south wall of the church had crumbled when the fire raged through it. It was here that the fire blazed the hottest. The mortar radiated so white-hot in the conflagration that it cracked and exploded outward in a spray of chips and dust. The clay bricks of the wall fell in charred heaps once the mortar was gone. Fortunately, the destroyed wall belonged to an outer room. The nurses had since boarded off the doors to the south room and simply worked around the debris. It was unquestionably an inconvenience, but since the building was given to them they closed their eyes to any annoyances.

The fire had ignited near the boiler in the south corner of the church. Fortunately, the fire worked its way outward more efficiently than inward.

Thus, the main chapel was fairly well preserved, along with the foyer and the large meeting room, which was restored into a kitchen area.

The pungent smell of smoke still hung in some areas of the church, but no one seemed to notice. It was another small annoyance that went unheeded by the new occupants.

The steeple, which had stood at the southeast corner of the church, stood no longer. When the south wall fell, it compromised the base of the steeple in such a way that it fell also. Miraculously, it did not impinge on the main structure, but fell parallel to the south wall in a long pile of red bricks. The gardens were partially buried beneath it, but the greater part was not.

The yard and grounds recovered quickly; the grass and flowers around the church returned the next spring. Lush moss and lichen grew on the north side of the heaped bricks. The only dirt sterilized by the intense heat was directly next to the south wall, where the steeple fell. The other beds and gardens were, in fact, revitalized by the ash. Yellow and red tulip bulbs which, some had worried, might have been destroyed by the fire, came back heartier than before. Around the outer wall, perennial flowers stood tall and erect, the petals strong. Even the blue and purple lobelia flourished in the ash that fell around the outer wall. The stark contrast of the beautiful reds, yellows, and purples against the blackened bricks was striking. The path around the church gardens was a favorite Sunday walk for the townspeople of Halle.

The apparent viability of the remaining structure depended completely on which direction one looked at it. From the south and most visible side, the church looked as if it could fall entirely with the next burst of wind. The outer wall was more fallen than erect. Black bricks lay in piles, along with the charred remnants of wooden beams and fallen joists.

From the north, the church looked relatively unmarred except for the charred bricks around the perimeter of the doors and windows, where the intense heat had blown out the glass and flames had licked the edges of the jams and sills.

The east and west walls stood completely intact; one had to look closely to see that new mortar had been chinked between the bricks. That was the only indication of any change from the original building.

After the fire, the building waited several years before being reemployed. Although the church carried great sentimental value, most people agreed that it was quite unusable. There was some talk of tearing down the eyesore. Many felt it was unsafe.

No one wanted the half-gutted building until the nuns stepped forward. Some townspeople were even against their taking it over, reasoning that it would always be a black eye. However, most of the town welcomed the idea and supported the effort every way that they could.

The nuns promptly replaced the wood and glass needed to enclose the interior from the elements. They spent weeks getting the inside ready and cleaned. They hauled out wheelbarrow after wheelbarrow full of bricks and burned rubble.

They carried out the charred and burned pews, swept up the ash, and brought in as many beds as they could fit. All this was done for the children. The sisters restored the old church into a children's hospital. It took them over a month to get the building ready for occupancy. The city officials in Halle gave up the building on the condition that the hospital would maintain charity status to avoid any undue tax pressure on the townspeople.

The need for a children's hospital was great. In the first few days more than forty children were placed in their care. Some were broken, others ill—all suffering. The nuns and nurses were cheerful. They shared all that they had with the unfortunate little ones. They embarked on a full-scale solicitation for support from every local business and family to donate whatever they could. The outpouring of generosity in behalf of the children was tremendous. Many of the townspeople brought goods from their farms; services were rendered, book-readers and well-wishers were numerous. But the gift they received on that perfect spring day was a rare treat that even the nuns could not have expected or imagined.

When the cart carrying the clavichord first arrived, the nuns were certain it was a mistake. The head nurse argued with the lead porter all the time he and the other delivery men were carrying it in, but they did not heed her. Disappointing whoever dispatched them was far more frightening than the rebuff of any ten nurses or nuns, and the men set the instrument down in the center of the main hall. The head nurse's face was changing colors for the third time when the visitor who arranged for the delivery finally arrived. Now that he was there, how grateful they were for the persistence of those he sent before him!

The gift they received was unlike any before or after. The children who were able sat on the floor on blankets around the instrument. Those constrained to beds were pushed as close as room would allow. The chapel area was in complete disarray, but no one cared. The doors of the hospital were thrown open. Children from outside were invited in for the special concert. Within a few minutes, the hospital ward was completely full.

For well over an hour, Halle's own George Handel sat at the clavichord playing songs for the children. As he played, he looked from child to child, eye to eye. He smiled and winked at the sick ones. After he played all the songs the children could think of, he told them a story while he played narrative music on the instrument, paying special attention to all the dramatic highs and lows.

As the story neared the climax, the children looked and listened, completely enthralled. There was not so much as a fidget as Handel's voice softened to a whisper.

"So back on his tail the German mouse sat..."

Handel's right hand tinkled the keys.

"'Dat big, fat, English cat can't take my hat.'
So while the cat slept,
The little mouse crept,
Until he stood, his hands on his hips,
Directly beneath the sleeping cat's lips..."

Handel paused. The children's eyes widened as he played a nervous ditty on the clavichord. Little heads leaned forward in anticipation.

"Carefully, quietly, without making a peep,
Up the cat's nose, the mouse did creep."

Handel played each mouse step ascending up the scales.

"He took his hat from off the fat cat,
Then slid down her ear,
On his tiny mouse rear."

Handel leaned low, looking across the keys at the children. Suddenly he stopped playing. He put his finger to his head as if thinking.

"He paused for a breath,
Thought maybe to kiss her—
But instead, gave a tug,
On her big, fat cat whisker."

Handel's right hand came down on the keys in a blur, playing the lively scales of the mouse's flight.

"The mouse took afoot like a shot from a gun,
No sooner than that, the cat took the run."

Handel's left hand joined in, playing the ponderous chords of the big, fat cat. The children giggled and clapped.

"Under the chair, the two did go—
The quick, little mouse and the cat, who was slow.
Back and forth, in and around,
The mouse led the cat—like a fox and a hound.
He remembered each trick his mouse parents taught him
For outsmarting cats whose wits had grown dim.
When safe in his hole, the mouse finally stopped,
In through the opening, the cat's nose popped."

Handel's right hand slowed to a thoughtful pulse. He raised his eyebrows and put his left finger to his chin, pensively.

"The mouse gave a sigh, he eyed the cat's whisker—
Then to her surprise, the little mouse kissed her."

Handel's hands whirred through several bars of grand finale. The children clapped with joyful delight as the music retarded into one long sustained chord. Then all at once, Handel's hands lifted and came down on the keys for the final chord. He jumped to his feet, his hands high over his head; the children who could, spontaneously rose with him, their arms and hands stretched high. Then in one great wave, with Handel leading, all their arms came down together with one excited explosion of cheers. A huge smile shone on Handel's face. He loved these children and they loved him. He adored how their little faces were such clear and simple conduits to their hearts. There was no guessing with this audience. He could look in their eyes and know they were with him. The children were guileless. Here, he was neither composer nor artist, he was simply a friend.

When Handel had first heard from his mother that the church was restored into a children's hospital, he immediately began planning for this moment. It was everything he had hoped it would be. With the single exception of playing for his mother, he could not think of a performance that brought him satisfaction equal to this. For the first time in many years, Handel's mind was on something other than himself. Never had he been more happy.

While the nurses moved things back into their proper places, Handel went to each bed performing magic tricks for the patients. The last bed he approached was occupied by a small boy with mangled legs. Handel sat down on the mattress alongside the boy. One of the boy's legs was twisted outward at the ankle; the other was broken below the knee. The flesh around the bones was still bruised and blackened. Handel's first compulsion was to turn the errant limbs into their correct position. He reached out a hand for the boy's knee, but the boy let out a short yelp when Handel touched the joint.

"The nurse tries to pull it straight for a few minutes each day," the boy volunteered. "It hurts," he added frankly.

Handel was impressed by the innocent honesty of his young friend.

"Your story was good, Mister," the boy said.

Handel's gaze met the boy's for a moment, then ventured back to his legs.

"They don't look very right, do they?" said the boy. "The nurses say I'll be able to use a walking stick."

"I use a walking stick. I quite like it."

"Do you have to use it, or is it just for fun?"

Handel didn't answer. He turned to a nearby nurse helping another child.

"How did this happen?"

"I was in the street, getting my little sister," answered the boy.

"A carriage went over his legs. The driver never stopped to see what had happened," the nurse told him.

The little boy spoke up. "They must have been in quite a hurry to get somewhere."

Handel took the little boy in his arms and put him on his lap. He smiled at the youngster.

"That good story you were talking about—what part of it did you like the best?" Handel asked.

"The chase, that's what I like best. My sister and I take turns chasing each other down the walk."

The head nurse stepped close to Handel. He reached in the pocket of his vest and handed her a small cloth purse of coins.

"It's not very much," he apologized. "I wish it were ten times that—a hundred times."

The nurse wrapped her warm hands around his hand and the purse. "You've already given us so much!"

The boy thanked Handel as the musician laid him carefully back on his bed. Handel retreated outside. He walked to the south end of the church and disappeared through the fallen outer wall and into the three-sided remains of the south room. He leaned against the cool bricks, his face to the wall. Nearly an hour passed before he reappeared.

Get Thee Up

IT WAS QUIET IN DOROTHEA'S ROOM WHEN THE KNOCK
came at the door. She slept soundly, while her son George watched from his
chair at her side. Eight weeks had passed since he arrived in Halle. During
that time, there had been marked improvement in both the mother's health
and the son's well being. In hindsight, the time had passed far too quickly.
There were still things Handel wanted to do. He hoped to go back to the
children's hospital, to take his mother to see the Saale, even to plant a small
garden so she would have summer vegetables to enjoy.

There were things to be done which he had not anticipated when he
left London. He knew they would probably remain undone if he continued on the path which brought him here. He had come to Halle to hide,
but instead he found home.

When he heard the horses' hooves outside the house, he immediately knew what it meant. He was warned that his time with Dorothea was growing short. For the past week, he had felt premonitions that this day was coming. When he heard the knock, he rose to his feet and looked at his mother's face; it was calm, peaceful. There was a second knock, this time louder and more urgent. He turned from her and noiselessly walked to the door. He moved quickly so there would not be another knock that might possibly wake up Dorothea. He swung open the door with his finger already at his lip to quiet the visitor. Before him stood a courier with an envelope in hand.

"Mr. George Frederic Handel?"

"Yes, yes. Speak quietly, please." He looked back into the room where his mother slept. The courier presented an envelope to Handel.

"I have a letter for you, sir."

Handel took the letter from the courier's hand and turned it over to look at the seal: Baron Kilmanseck. The next sound he heard was the pounding of hooves trailing off down the lane. He walked back into the house and gently pulled the door closed behind him. He returned to his seat at his mother's side and laid the envelope on the bed before him.

It was not that he was afraid of what it might say, but for the first time, he wondered if he really wanted that which the letter contained. All of his life, he had pursued the thing that awaited him in London, and yet Halle had made him question the dream. Reflection had been self-revealing, and now, as never before, he wondered if he were truly ready and willing to embrace the life he had worked so hard to obtain. Two paths were laid before him: one leading to London, the other, home.

The days in Halle had been kind to his spirit. For the first time in years, his heart was calm, his soul unburdened. He didn't realize how weary he had become of the fight until he was removed from it. Now he was not certain if he could embrace it again with the same fervor with which he had pursued it across all of Europe—nor was he certain he wanted to.

He looked into the sleeping face of Dorothea. Until then, his thoughts had only been on himself and what he wanted. As he looked upon the peaceful visage of his mother, the decision suddenly became clear. He would do according to her will.

He opened the envelope, read the letter, then put it back inside. His face was emotionless as he pondered the meaning of the communiqué. At long length, he took his mother's hand and kissed it, then slowly walked to the bedroom door.

Dorothea's eyelids opened. Her eyes went straight to the letter in her son's hand. There was no question in her mind about what the letter contained—she knew. She said nothing. She watched him walk out the door of her bedroom and stop near the table in the next room. He gathered up the sheets of music spread there and put them under his arm, then disappeared from her view. For the second time in her life, she let him go.

April 14, 1737
Mr. Edward Holdsworth—Richmond

Dear Edward,

Since receiving your letter, I have come home to Gopsal for some desperately needed solitude. I have, of late, been preoccupied with a certain scriptural wordbook, a libretto possibly, which I will tell you about in detail when it is finished. For now, it sufficeth to say, I put a great value on it as it has come with sacrifice enough to make it noteworthy. As it could involve Handel, I confess considerable curiosity at your interest in his whereabouts.

I received a letter from our Mr. Handel two weeks prior. It seems that he quite unexpectedly determined to visit his ill mother in Halle. As we both know, there were other pressing reasons for him not to be in London during the Royal Change of Guard. I thought it convenient that matters in Halle would be so pressing as to need his immediate attention with all that is happening in our part of the world. He stated quite clearly that he is intent upon returning, although vague as to the time and circumstances whereby that would take place.

It has been almost two months since our Saxon King arrived in London, and Handel has still not presented himself at the Royal Court. Consequently, I have been made privy to a plan to bring Handel back to London and, God willing, back in good graces with his employer, the King. A quite ingenious plan really—Baron Kilmanseck, the author.

Your most humble friend and confidante,
Charles Jennens
Gopsal

The Lord, Whom Ye Seek

I̲T WAS AN ACCIDENT. THE PACKRAT MEANT WELL. BUT, AS is sometimes the case, things did not turn out as they should have. It was one of those curious ironies of life when the best of intentions fall prey to the worst of circumstances. Consequently, the outcome rendered was completely opposite of what was hoped for.

Peter wanted to help. He believed he was doing the right thing, but when tragedy came, he was at the heart of it. It happened in the spring, during the season of Lent. The incident involved James, a well-known vendor along the river streets.

James was a crusty sort with a broad, defined face. He had a prolific nose and thick black hair that made him seem more imposing than he actually was. His face was wide for his body, for he was a fairly narrow man—not overweight but not under either. Were it not for his severe facial features he would be hardly noticeable. His nose and protruding black eyebrows made him otherwise.

He lived alone in a tiny flat near the docks where he was close enough to the river to hear the sea-going boats come up the Thames from the coast. Inevitably, long before sunrise, he was one of the first on the boardwalk to make his bid for the freshest catch.

At one time, James was a fisherman. He went out on his boat early each morning to fish. In a terrible storm he lost his boat and nearly his life. With what little he had left, he purchased a small cart on which he would carry his fish from the wharves to the open street market to sell. Even though he missed being on the water, his new business proved more profitable than the old.

It was a small cart on which he could fit only a small number of fish. At first look, the humble enterprise did not seem sufficient to support him. Most vendors worked in bulk, marking up their wares a little and selling a lot.

But this small cart provided enough for James not only to take care of himself, but to live with some comfort. James had been given a gift: he understood the flesh of fish like few others. Even though there were countless vendors who sold fish on the street, James sold the very best. His reputation was based solely on quality. He was a fish broker of sorts—buying low, then selling high.

He developed a method of testing the fish before he would purchase them. This quality test became an intrigue and quite legendary on the street.

First he would negotiate a price. If a fisherman would not agree to a number, he would move on. After years of saying the same overused and painfully obvious cliché, he needed only to smile at the fisherman to let them know what he was thinking: "There are other fish in the ocean."

Once a price was established, he would proceed with the test.

He carried a razor-sharp blade with him to the docks. With this, he would cut a small sliver of flesh from the tail of the fish. He then used the sample to determine the quality of the meat.

He would roll the thin slice of raw fish into a small ball. As he would roll it with his fingers, he could assess the oil content of the flesh. He knew precisely the texture which would render the best taste. He would smell the shiny fish oil on his fingers, then rub his fingers together to feel its viscosity.

After this, he would smell the ball several times, turning away between each sniff to fill his nostrils with fresh air to avoid becoming habituated to the scent. Most samples never made it this far. If the fish was still up to his standards, he would plop the ball in his mouth and push it from side to side with his tongue to get a taste for the meat.

Finally, he would gently press the raw meat between his teeth to test the tenderness of the flesh. If he then swallowed the morsel, the fisherman knew he would be buying. If he spit out the ball, he would move on to the next seller's basket without a word. If James got as far as putting the sample into his mouth, the fisherman knew their product was good since few fish ever made it that far.

Those fisherman who were willing to go farthest from the coast were usually those most pleased with the outcome of the test.

Occasionally, fishermen would raise their prices after he swallowed the sample, knowing that he too would be marking up his sale price. But at this, James would smile, shake his head, and move on with a laugh. He believed if a man raised the price based on his appraisal, the fish would sour for him as quickly as his assessment of the deal.

"Money changers," he called them. In a sermon he had heard those words from the Bible in reference to those who bought and sold in the temple. He figured that was a good name for anybody who would change the price after it was set. He made it a point to give those fishermen a second chance at honesty, but never beyond.

The other buyers watched him closely. If he purposely skipped one boat's catch, others would do the same. James esteemed few things more highly than fish; he made no allowance for those who took advantage of the riches of the sea.

Quite often, the vendors who followed James would buy those fish that almost made it into his mouth. Fortunately for many, James's cart was small. Others tried to duplicate his method in order to learn the art of selection, but to no avail. James had a gift; everyone knew it. All those who bought from him were the benefactors of that gift. Because his fish were of the highest quality, he could sell his product for a higher price, thus making his profit considerably larger.

It was usually early—a little before noon—when James's cart would empty. He could have made a second run each day but didn't feel it necessary. His one cart was big enough to take care of his needs and he felt no urgency to aspire beyond that.

The day the accident happened, James came from the docks with his cart of fish like every other morning. Soon he was surrounded with buyers. Usually the servants of the rich and noble were the first to meet him, as they could afford to spend a little more for quality.

On this day, the Packrat veered from his normal habit and decided to work the streets near the docks. He was pleased to see the fish-man who never had to shout out a sales pitch to get customers. Peter couldn't help but notice how there were twice the number of buyers surrounding James's cart as the other fish vendors. The Packrat found great pleasure in watching house servants try to barter with James in behalf of their rich bosses. To Peter it seemed fool-stupid to haggle over a few pence when their employers could easily pay double and not care one whit.

With a holiday coming, there were more people than usual on the street buying food in preparation for the celebration. James was met by many, all wanting the contents of his cart. Peter had never met James personally but he had heard of his gift and thought it impressive. As he watched all of this, he wondered aloud.

"What's my gift, Lord? Surely there is somethin' Ya' saw fit to give me. When shall my gift be made known?"

He thought for a moment, then laughed.

"But I do have a gift—takin' other people's gifts from them." He glanced back at James and his customers. That's when he saw it happen.

James was so busy with the faces around him, that he had not eyes to see all of their hands. He had just finished selling a large cod to a willowy woman in the noisy crowd surrounding him. So intent was he with helping the others, that he simply asked the woman to put her money in the canvas pouch that was nailed to the side of the cart. The Packrat trained his eye to always follow money when it was changing hands. He watched as the woman's hand went into the pouch with a few coins and came out with more. None can spot a thief better than a thief. Had the offender been a beggar or an orphan, Peter wouldn't have thought twice about it, but since it was a representative of the wealthy class, there was no hesitation.

"Robber! Thief!" screamed the Packrat.

Everyone and everything stopped in that instant. All heads turned toward the urchin who stood several paces away in the street. Peter's hand was raised; his finger pointed in the direction of those standing around the cart of James. Several, including the guilty, looked around innocently and wide-eyed, wondering about the commotion.

Peter waited. He fully expected her to run, but she didn't. He couldn't understand what she was up to. Why didn't she run? That's what he would have done. He suddenly wondered if he had made a mistake; maybe his eyes had deceived him. His head cocked to the side curiously.

"What is it, boy?" James's voice rang out. "Thief, you say? Where, boy?"

Peter stepped forward. He tried desperately to recreate in his mind exactly what he saw. Her hand went in, then came back out with more, of that he was certain. Surely, the proof would be in that hand. He looked at the woman who had looked so guilty to him moments before, now she had an angelic expression of hurt on her face. She pointed a finger of pained disbelief towards herself. Again James's voice broke the silence.

"Well—where is the thief? Show me, boy."

Peter was hesitant, unsure.

"I thought—I thought I saw somethin'. Not for certain, but yeah. Your purse there, her hand went in and then out—there was more."

"More what?"

"More money. She took your money."

"Who?"

"Her!"

Peter was close enough now that his finger pointed to the houseservant woman who stood closest to the cart. She appeared stunned that he would dare falsely accuse her. James looked at her right hand; it was closed tightly into a fist. Her left hand held firmly to the bottom hem of her apron making a sling in which she carried the heavy fish. James took hold of her free arm and lifted it up; her hand didn't open. James tightened his grip on her arm. The veins in her forearms began to show through the white skin. Her hand quivered as her fingers began to unravel. When her hand finally opened, to everyone's surprise, her palm was empty.

James immediately released his grip. White creases were left in her skin between the red imprints of fingers. James's eyes shifted back to the Packrat, who was more shocked than anyone.

"I saw her! She put in her hand and took out more."

Peter approached her, staring at her open hand; he looked up into her eyes.

She looked down at him pitifully. Those who stood close were touched by the woman's compassion on the urchin boy after being wrongly accused, but Peter saw something else. Behind her eye Peter did not see pity but contempt. He had seen that same look before on the cruel women who used him to beg for them when he was a small child. Under threat of beating, they would make him sit on the ground at their feet while they begged. Nothing was more pitiful than a mother with starving children. Many pedestrians who would normally pass by without a second thought couldn't help but take compassion on a destitute mother. It was a lucrative asset to have a brat. But none of the aid received was ever given to him. Until he was old enough to jump away before catching a kick to the head, he had been used by several such women.

As the Packrat looked into this woman's eyes, he instinctively put his hands over his ears and shied his head away from her. He quickly moved out of reach.

"I'm very sorry. There has been a mistake," said James. "Please take another fish as a token of my apology."

James held out another smaller cod to her. She turned from the boy smiling and opened her apron to receive it with the other fish.

"Liar!" Peter screamed as James dropped the fish into her apron. She whipped around and glared at the Packrat, forgetting to compensate for the extra weight of the second fish. The apron slipped through her grip; the sling fell open spilling her fish onto the ground, along with several coins, which tinkled loudly as they hit the cobbles. As all eyes turned down to the money and fish, the woman bolted. But Peter's eyes had not followed the crowd; he watched her. The instant she moved, he lunged at her. His shoulder drove into her side sending the two of them tumbling over the cart.

Peter crashed into James, throwing him back against the building wall. As he plummeted into the wall, James's body rammed against a large, loose nail in the stone wall which secured the countersupport chain of a heavy wooden shop sign hanging precariously overhead. The jarring was enough to bend the nail up and release the chain. The full weight of the sign came swinging down before anyone had a chance to duck out of the way. It swung safely above Peter and the woman who lay sprawled on the ground with the fish from the overturned cart. But James was not so lucky. The sharp, squared corner of the sign struck him in the temple in full swing. There was a dull knock as the wood impacted against his skull. His legs went soft. He collapsed to the ground as blood gushed from the open wound on the side of his head. The entire street surged in the direction of the accident. The guilty woman used the commotion to crawl into the bowels of the moving snake and disappear.

Peter was dumbstruck. His head swirled at the sight of the red ooze coming from James's head. The boy tried to get to his feet but he couldn't. His head was spinning. He rolled onto his side; his face rubbed against the slimy, slick skin of fish. The thick odor of dead fish filled his nostrils; his stomach turned. He could taste the vomit push up the back of his throat. He knelt briefly with his head between his legs, then leaned back for a long breath of clean air.

Out of the corner of his eye, he saw a man jump from the crowd and bend down near the lifeless body of James. Peter could hear ripping sounds. He looked again to see the man pushing a torn sleeve of cloth into the gaping crack in James' head. Peter tried to blink away the drops of sweat streaming from his forehead into his eyes. Through the salty film he thought he recognized the man huddled near the wounded. The world began to darken to the Packrat. He looked up once again before losing consciousness. The man turned his face to him. Peter recognized the face—then blacked out.

The Packrat awoke to loud pounding. The shopowner whose sign had fallen had a hammer in hand and was pounding the nail straight so the chain could be re-attached. The Packrat looked around at the aftermath of the incident. The crowd was still dispersing. James had been taken away to an infirmary. The woman was gone; she was free. The cart was standing upright, but the fish were also gone. The sidewalk was stained red in the place where James had fallen. Peter resolved at that moment to never step on the pavement where the blood stained it.

A local merchant who knew James wheeled off the cart to keep it safe for him. When Peter sat upright, the few remaining witnesses of the tragedy glanced his way, whispered to one another, then walked away. Somehow, their looks made him feel ashamed, as if he had done something wrong. One man leaned down close to him and said in a low voice, "You've done enough damage here today. Move on now."

Peter wasn't sure exactly why, but he knew he was not welcome. He slowly rose to his feet and stumbled away down the street. He could feel eyes on him as he walked. He wondered why he felt so guilty about trying to help. His first thought was never to do that again, but then he remembered the face of the man who helped James. Until that moment, he had completely forgotten about him. He had recognized the face but couldn't remember how or why. The Packrat walked for blocks working over in his mind the face of the man who helped and where he had seen him. All day long it haunted him. Finally that night, just as he was about to fall asleep, it came to him. He sat upright and whispered aloud, "The bread man."

Weeks later, Peter heard that James was back on the street with his cart. He was greatly relieved at the news. He sneaked over one day and watched the street where James usually worked—to make sure. He was pleased to see him pushing his cart full of fish along the street. No one seemed to recognize the Packrat or pay him any heed; that also pleased him. He did get close enough to see the ugly dent in the side of James's head, but he figured a dent was better than dead.

It was a few months later when the Packrat heard about a fish vendor whose eyes were going dark. Peter anxiously asked around to find out who it was. It made him sick when he found out it was the one with the gift. James' head endured the blow, but with each passing day, he was losing the use of his eyes.

The news weighed heavily on the Packrat. He asked every day for word about James. He heard that the docks were no longer safe for him. James continued to go every morning until one day he drove his cart off the side of the wooden platform. He and his cart plunged into the cold water. Had someone not been there to rescue him, it's certain he would have drowned. As it happened, two dockworkers heard the commotion and snagged him from the cold deep with an oyster hook. That was the last day James pushed his cart to the wharves.

After a few more weeks, James lost all sight. He found a spot near where the accident took place, where he could sit against the wall and eke out a meager living. Between begging and the small pittance the other vendors would give him to test their fish, he somehow lived.

The landlord took his flat away, but the shopkeeper whose sign had inflicted the blow allowed him to sleep in the standing room of his underground coal bin. It was close enough to the furnace to be warm in the winter and it kept the rain off in summer.

Occasionally, Peter would go that way and watch James from afar. He got close enough to speak to him one day, but the shop owner recognized him and moved him on.

"He blames you," he said. "He holds you to blame for his blindness. I'd watch myself if I was you, boy. If he gets his hands on you, you'll be a sorry lot. Now move on. Go away before you do more harm."

Peter ran. He dared not go back again. He felt somehow responsible, so he continued to get news of the blind man when he could. Often he would give pence to his little urchins and watch from a distance while they would go to James and make his cup ring. It was a bitter experience for Peter—bitter because there was no apparent reason for it. He could find no learnable lesson in what had happened. It was a damned shame, nothing more. So pointless was the terrible consequence of his effort to do the right thing that Peter couldn't help but question God's motive in allowing it to happen. Certainly He could have stopped the sign. Was it possible James was being punished for something Peter had done? It didn't make sense. If God could stop it, why didn't He? Was it God's will or just a bad thing that He allowed to happen? The Packrat did not understand, but he determined, at long length, that he must accept it and move on. Still, he could not help but wonder if God knew what had happened, or if God even knew or cared about him. He pondered aloud the one question that he desired most to know: "Do Ya' know me, Lord? Do Ya' know the Packrat?"

Her Iniquity Is Pardoned

THE SUN SPARKLED ON THE WATER LIKE SWIRLING CURRENTS of white gems. The reeds that lined the banks of the Thames were tall and still. The evening before was overcast, but the coastal breezes stole the clouds away, leaving in their wake a sky of purest blue. After a long week of inclemency, the bright morning felt like a call from the world for her children to take a holiday. The King himself answered the call.

Weeks before, he had planned a day on the river. As if in adherence to the King's mandate, nature obeyed. Even the Queen and courtiers were shocked at the stunning beauty of the day. All London came out to worship the glory of Spring in all her majesty. Parks were full. Sidewalks were crowded. Word of the King's flotilla spread through the city. The banks were lined with spectators out to witness the royal barge.

There was only one person in all of London who was unhappy about the change of weather. The King's son, Frederick, the twenty-three-year-old Prince of Wales, had futilely hoped that the dreary days would continue. It was not so much the floating that he detested but the fact that the King had ordered it. The son and father were at odds long before coming to occupy Windsor. The crowning of George did nothing to help the relationship; on the contrary, it strained it further.

King George believed that young Frederick would become the central focus of opposition to his kingship. He never trusted him and made no excuses for his inexorable dislike of the Prince. Frederick returned the favor by doing his best to erode the ground on which the King stood.

As it was, the King had ordered a royal float on the Thames to Richmond and back. All the preparations were made, and the King's barge was readied. King George and his wife, Caroline, were accompanied by several invited guests on the royal barge, along with a small string ensemble. Baron Kilmanseck was among those on the King's boat.

The royal barge was surrounded with several other boats for courtiers, gentlemen, and ladies who were asked to join the royal flotilla. A smaller barge was also prepared for Prince Frederick and his entourage. The King ordered it; Prince Frederick reluctantly obeyed.

The main body of boats stayed close together as they meandered downriver to Richmond. Much to the King's dismay, the Prince and his minions opted to float a fashionable distance behind the rest of the company.

As the procession progressed, King George became increasingly irritated at the breach of etiquette by his heir. He searched the river for the Prince's boat. Caroline cared little about the politics of the float. She thoroughly drank up the glory of the day, but the King could not keep his mind off Frederick. Like a tiny burr in the collar of his shirt, the conspicuous absence of the louse became a nuisance. The music played by the string ensemble did little to calm him. Baron Kilmanseck stood close to the King, waiting for a chance to approach him. But the appropriate time to do so had not yet presented itself. When the King stood to look around, the Baron made his move.

"Majesty, does the music suit your liking?"

King George searched the river for Frederick.

"Where is Fretz? Baron, can you see Frederick and his foul flock?"

Somewhat amused with his little pun, the King chuckled as he repeated "foul flock" several times to himself and the courtiers who stood close until everyone got the joke.

"The Prince of Wales is directly behind, Your Majesty, surrounded by several smaller boats," answered the Baron, knowing this revelation would incite an angry earful. Even though he knew it was something that the King detested, the Baron was obliged to call Frederick by title. King George despised the fact that Frederick received title by virtue of blood only. He heard the words "Prince of Wales" as an insult, a word of offense. He bristled every time it was said in his company. The Baron, caught between propriety and the King's hot temper, chose the latter. George's anger was out of his control, being guilty of insolence—the volatile sin of pride and presumption—was not.

The King looked aft to see the entourage that the Baron had described. He wanted to make sure Prince Frederick was close enough to keep an eye on. Now that he knew where he was, he could not keep his eyes off him. He shook his head in disgust.

"Popularity always makes me sick, but Fretz's popularity makes me vomit."

The King turned to Caroline, who peacefully looked out on the water. He walked to her side and plopped down into his chair. He leaned close to her ear.

"Two babies are born, one to a king, the other to a pauper. One has royal blood, the other—nothing. Does God choose?"

His voice rose in pitch along with the amount of blood in his face.

"Does God choose? Does he look on the spirits of premortal men and ordain the great ones to be princes, heirs to the crown, the kings of England?"

He stood to his feet. All the boats nearby quieted at hearing the King's raised voice. The musicians stopped playing. The only sound was the nervous tapping of the Baron's foot and the distant laughter from the Prince's party. The King looked back to see Prince Frederick, somewhat drunk, conducting an imaginary orchestra. Caroline spoke softly in an effort to calm him.

"Freddy is still angry you broke off his marriage plans with the Prussian princess."

"I did not think that ingrafting my half-witted coxcomb upon a mad woman would improve the breed," snorted the King.

Seemingly calmed, he began to sit down in his chair, then jumped to his feet and shouted across the water for all to hear.

"Our first-born is the greatest ass, the greatest liar, the greatest canaille, and the greatest beast in the whole world, and we heartily wish he were out of it!"

The boats were quiet. Water lapped against the gunwales. Even the distant laughter of the group behind was gone. The King took a deep breath. Caroline did not so much as glance up as George sat down next to her. He motioned to the musicians to play.

Within a few minutes, all had forgotten the outburst—all except Frederick. The Prince remembered every word, as did those who were with him. He stared back scornfully at his father-King. He could endure private scolding and closet criticism, but public humiliation was intolerable. He joined the King's excursion out of obedience; to be forced to endure unprovoked ridicule was more than he could ignore. As he simmered, the woman who stood nearest him watched his fury fester with great interest. She could see in his face indignation sufficient for her to exploit—if done so carefully.

Madame Hervey was a crafty, middle-aged woman who aligned herself with young Frederick by virtue of his acerbic derision of the King. She meddled for meddling's sake. She endeared herself to the Prince because his rare combination of contempt and position made him an object worthy of her designs.

Frederick confided in her. He respected her. Through the past year, she successfully fostered in him a sick addiction to her approval. She mothered his acrimony by carefully nursing his resentment with the milk of malevolence. She helped navigate him first through the waters of self-pity, then resentment, and now to the brink of retaliation. She had been waiting for an opportunity such as this. Now she needed only identify the perfect moment to plant the seed that would turn emotion into action.

In addition to Hervey, Addison and Steele of London's newspaper, *The Spectator*, were also aboard the Prince's vessel. Madame Hervey insisted that they might be helpful to the Prince's cause, should he ever determine to take a stand against his father. What he could only do privately, they could do publicly in their editorials each week. By joining company with Frederick, Addison and Steele were in a position to learn the private and public goings-on of the royal family. They knew well that disparaging inside information was good for circulation.

The collective venom of the Prince and his colleagues packed poison enough to strike a formidable fang at the King. Nervous as he was about such allies, the Prince succumbed to the Madame's wishes, against his own better judgment. He found himself surrounded by an army capable of inflicting damage on whatever foe they united themselves against.

At length, the Prince turned to his people, who anxiously waited for him to spill his mind.

"How is it that an obstinate, self-indulgent, miserly martinet with an insatiable sexual appetite can wave his hand, and we spend the day afloat," said the Prince.

"He's the King," Hervey observed.

The Madame determined to dip a measuring stick in Frederick's angst to test whether it was deep enough to continue. She could not have scripted the Prince's next words more perfectly.

"When he meets with any opposition to his own designs, he thinks the opposers insolent rebels to the will of God."

"Where do you stand—with regard to the will of God?" she asked coyly.

Their eyes met. She had trumped him and now waited for his next play. Addison and Steele were curious to see how he would respond to the pricking of his ego. There was a moment of indecision as the Prince considered the consequences of his next words. He wavered momentarily; then fear of disappointing this predatory peer group outweighed conscience. His gaze shifted back to his father. He spoke more for their ears than for right.

"I need a way to get at His Eminence—an angle."

Madame Hervey smiled. Her boy had taken the bait. Her gaze shifted back to the King. She savored the opportunity that had surfaced so unexpectedly. She dared not waste it on anything without a back strong enough to piggyback on for a long and lively ride. She pondered the possibilities.

Now that the King had thoroughly vented his mind of Fretz, he was more disposed to enjoying the float. He sat back in his chair, inhaling the breeze coming up river. The long winter had stretched so far into spring that he had forgotten how fresh and new the morning sun could feel. He relaxed as the Baron paced.

Baron Kilmanseck always paced, but today the King noted that he paced with purpose. What the King couldn't see was that the Baron was intensely interested in something happening on the west side of the river. A barge had just pushed away from the dock as the flotilla passed. The Baron followed the progress of the uninvited boat as it moved parallel with the King's boat. From a distance, rows of passengers could be seen.

Gradually it started to close the gap between them. The closer the boat veered towards the procession, the more nervous the Baron became. The King mused at the Baron's anxiety.

"Baron, rest yourself. You pace like an expectant father. Come, sit. It seems I recall an inquiry, about the music, methinks. Isn't that right?"

Not waiting for an answer, the King began to hum along with the string ensemble that played on his barge. The Baron's mystery boat now floated at the edge of the royal procession. There was sudden movement among the several rows of passengers. Bright highlights shone off metal and polished wood. In unison, instruments were raised and readied. A single hand was raised high in the air above the mystery boat; when it came down, the Baron answered the King.

"I was asking m'lord, if you were enjoying the..."

"Wait!" The King interrupted.

King George turned his ear to the sky. He leaned into the breeze. There was sound in the wind. He waved his hand for all aboard to stop talking.

"Hush, quiet! Do you hear that?" the King queried in a whisper.

"Hear what, m'lord?' inquired the Baron.

"Be quiet! Listen."

The King's ensemble began to play with more spirit, encouraged by his insistence upon everyone listening. King George slid to the edge of his chair and emphatically waved his arms for the ensemble to stop playing.

"Stop! Stop that...that—whatever. Be still."

The entire company became hushed and quiet. Then, all at once, every ear heard it at the same time.

Music.

Music filled the air. It echoed across the water as if coming up the river on the wind. As those in the King's procession listened, they were moved. This was not the overstuffed ceremonial music that usually accompanied royalty; this was a joyful sound, a celebration of life. Horns sang, strings joined. The entire river was full of song. It seemed to be in the very breeze that blew in their faces. Its very presence made the spirit rise and exult the day.

Some in the party searched for the source, while most simply accepted the gift and contented themselves to listen happily. Enraptured by the strains echoing up and down the Thames, the King gripped the Baron by the arm and whispered.

"Do you hear that, Baron? That is music. Music that feels for you, like a child nuzzling for its mother's breast. Feel it seize your soul—ennobling it, clutching it. That is the realm of genius."

Elated, the King savored each new phrase of sweet melody. Where the day was once beautiful, it was now glorious. No one thought to break the spell of the song with speech.

At length the King could see a small group of courtiers pointing and looking at something. His eyes followed the path of their turned heads to a barge of musicians floating at the perimeter of the flotilla. The King stood and beckoned the barge to come close. He took the Baron with both hands and pulled him close.

"Fetch me the man who fills the air with sound—such beautiful sound as this. Whoever he is, he is more now."

The King took his seat alongside Caroline. While the music continued, the barge rowed alongside the King's boat and was anchored to the cleats on the royal barge.

The Prince's boat also closed in.

A man stepped across the tied boats. The Baron approached the King to introduce the summoned musician, still unseen by the King.

"Your Majesty, I ask leave to present to you as one too conscious of his faults to attempt any excuse for it, but sincerely desirous to atone for the same by all possible demonstrations of duty, submission, and gratitude, could he but hope that His Majesty..."

The King's patience was exhausted.

"Baron—the man!"

Into view stepped George Frederic Handel. All eyes, including Frederick's, were riveted on the King. Everyone knew that Handel had dared not show his face in the King's court since George of Hanover had arrived in London. The politics of Handel and King George were well known.

The King rose to his feet as he uttered aloud.

"*Der Verlorener! Mein Herr* Handel."

Handel bowed low.

"Your Majesty."

"You abandoned me."

Handel paused pensively. All awaited his answer.

"Your Majesty, I beg forgiveness. I am what I am, a simple-minded musician, nothing more. My heart was taken captive by London. I have no other excuse."

The King sat down, leaned back into his chair and pondered. Handel had made no better excuse than the absolute obvious and plain truth; that fact was utterly apparent. The King's position swiftly changed from prosecutor to judge. Handel had laid himself on the altar of the King's wishes. He publicly bared his neck to his Monarch.

"My dear Saxon, you forsook home and patron. Your heart should choose its loyalties more prudently," the King declared.

"Oft misguided, yes; but my heart has been and always will be yours, Majesty."

The King thought momentarily. His stern eyes softened.

"What do you call it?"

"Majesty?"

"What do you call it?"

The King rose from his chair and approached Handel earnestly. He snatched the score from Handel's hand.

"This. What do you call it?"

Handel was caught with his guard down. He was in such a hurry to write the music that he had not considered what it should be called. He fidgeted as he tried to stammer out an answer.

"Well, it's called, something I think…something I think you will like."

"What something?" the King demanded in a loud voice. Handel quickly looked around—to boat—to river—to boat—to shore. Water lapped against the side of the barge. Sun danced on the riffles of the river. Handel's face suddenly brightened as he declared proudly,

"*Water Music! Water Music*, m'lord."

A broad smile stretched across the King's face. He looked around at the courtiers, who were all smiling and nodding their affirmation. He held up the music.

"*Water Music*, yes. So it is. I adore your *Water Music* more than I despise your annoyances."

Handel smiled as he looked around at the faces of the admiring crowd. The King became serious; he glared at Handel indignantly. Handel's face grew sober. A hush fell on the group. Respectfully, Handel dropped to one knee in front of the King and humbly bowed his head. King George waited unmercifully long before speaking again. He rubbed his chin and shook his head like the father of a misguided child he loved and yet knew required discipline. He glanced around the group, smiling his amusement at this last bit of punishment he was imposing upon the misguided artist. When he could no longer endure the guilt of making Handel suffer, he took him by the arm and raised him to his feet.

"Would that my offspring were so penitent. You are conditionally pardoned. *So tretenwir uns zusammen vor!*"

The King raised his hand to Handel; all applauded. The King shouted over the clapping.

"Now, my conditions: You shall receive an additional two hundred pounds with your annual stipend."

Once again, the company cheered.

"My next condition:" he paused until it became quiet. "You must play it again."

Again the group cheered their approval.

The Prince witnessed all of this. His eyes moved back and forth between the King and Handel. As the *Water Music* began to play again, Madame Hervey laughed out loud. She bent close to the Prince and spoke in low tones, articulating every word.

"You want an angle, you get a wedge. A very noisy one at that."

The Prince stared at Handel.

"This Handel—I only know of him, not about him. What kind of man is he?"

"Same as any man," she replied.

"Does he have any vices, habits, glaring improprieties? A mistress, perhaps?"

Madame Hervey shook her head.

"No mistress, no wife, no depravities, no perversions. He does, however, have a temper and a voluptuous ego." Hervey pondered momentarily.

"If memory serves me correctly, you attended *Cleopatra* the night of the altercation. That is your man."

Frederick's eyes fastened on Handel. Steele, who to this moment had restrained himself, could no longer resist the opportunity to add his piece.

"Obviously, he doesn't pass up any opportunity to eat."

"We will use what we have," said Frederick.

Madame Hervey leaned even closer and whispered into the Prince's ear.

"He has but one passion, one love: music. If you want to be rid of the man, be rid of his music. But be patient, Your Highness. You can't simply take it away, you must ease it away, note by note, carefully, gently, until it's completely gone before he even realizes it."

Frederick looked in her eyes.

"Lead it away as the Devil leads men to hell." she whispered.

Frederick's eyes shifted back to the King and Handel standing side by side. He watched as the King put his hand on Handel's shoulder and laughed out loud. The Prince sat down and closed his eyes. Madame Hervey smiled at Steel and Addison as the boats passed down the river.

May 17, 1737
Mr. Edward Holdsworth—Richmond

My Dear Edward,

Concerning politics and Handel, I fear that the sliver of enmity started on the river will fester into an infectious boil. Mr. Handel may find himself precariously caught between father and son—worse yet, King and Prince.

Why the King should so intensely dislike his heir is not certain, but as we have seen before, reviling one's first-born is a royal privilege, if not prerequisite, of the crown. Albeit our new King is a lover of music, he is still of the House of Hanover and not without faults. Our dear Mr. Handel served as his Kappellmeister at Hanover until he was given temporary leave to visit London. When he never returned, the Elector followed him here, to be crowned King. Handel dared not show his face at the court, and rightly so; for kings, as we have seen, do not deal well with insolence or neglect. That is when Baron Kilmanseck devised his plan for Handel's clemency, which worked perfectly. Now we must wait and see what the King has in mind for Mr. Handel. I durst not believe it will happen without some opposition from the son.

Your most humble servant and friend,
Charles Jennens

Make Straight in
the Desert a Highway

THE CARRIAGE RATTLED OVER THE COBBLES OF LONDON.
Inside sat Handel, still ecstatic from the miracle on the river. Baron
Kilmanseck had done the impossible. In one stroke, Handel was not only
pardoned, but exalted. His stipend was increased, and surely the King had
things in mind for him to do. After all, Handel had been invited to St.
James that evening to dine with the King and his guests. Handel knew
what this could only mean: the King intended to commission an opera.
Handel's mind was swirling with possibilities when the carriage, which
the King had provided, turned the corner onto Brook Street where he
lived. He could not get home fast enough. He took hold of his walking
cane and was about to rap the ceiling, when he noticed the King's seal on
the inside of the door and thought better of it.

As the carriage approached his two-story apartment at 25 Brook Street, it began to slow down. Before it had completely stopped, Handel was out the door and up the walk to the entrance. He turned the door handle, but it was locked. He banged on the metal door plate with the brass head of his cane.

"What is this? I can open the King's eyes but can't open the door. Mr. LeBlonde! Open up."

Enraged at the inconvenience he pounded even harder.

"Who are we trying to keep out? Peter, open the damnhell door before I pound it to pieces."

He started to rap again just as the door swung open. Peter LeBlonde, Handel's servant, stepped to the side to avoid Handel's cane.

"Have a good nap?"

"I didn't expect you this soon, sir."

Handel handed Mr. LeBlonde his cane and coat, then turned abruptly. His loose-fitting wig shifted on his head.

"Who were you expecting—thieves? murderers?—with the door bolted shut in the middle of the day?"

"Purely habit, sir."

Handel marched down the hall as if looking for something. He threw open the doors to the parlor and strode into the room. Mr. LeBlonde followed. A large tray of pastries sat on the table. Handel devoured shortbread and butter cookies while he talked.

"Is there any drink in this house?" His wig shifted on his head. He carelessly tossed it aside; it fell behind a chair. Peter made no effort to retrieve it.

"Were you able to perform, sir?"

"It was brilliant—I was brilliant. The King could not resist. He increased my stipend, invited me to St. James for supper."

"You must be eternally grateful to Baron Kilmanseck. The barge and musicians must have cost him greatly." Handel did not hear him.

"The King is going to commission an opera tonight, I'm certain. He's a music lover. Of course, that's it."

Handel took another large bite of shortbread.

"What time is it? The carriage is returning at six o'clock. I must hurry. He'll want me to play a concerto for his guests—something bright, I think."

As he walked to the door, Handel started humming. He returned to take the tray of food. As he pulled the plate from the table, some of the cookies slid off the edge and shattered on the hardwood floor. Handel looked at the mess, then at Peter. He turned straightway and disappeared out the door. Peter had not moved from his place. He heard Handel's feet ascend the stairs. The humming continued. When Peter heard his master's heavy steps traverse the hall, followed by a door slamming shut, he knew Handel was in his study.

Peter bent down to pick up the broken fragments of cookie from the floor. A moment later, harpsichord music echoed through the house. It was the same tune that Handel was humming when he left the room.

Hours passed. Handel's voice boomed in the hall outside the parlor door.

"I can't leave like this. Where did I put the stupid, silly thing?"

Peter LeBlonde's voice was calm.

"In the parlor, sir."

"The parlor? Of course, the parlor—the place where you were napping when I arrived home."

The door burst open. Ill-humored, Handel released the knob and walked into the room. He became more and more irritated as he went about pushing chairs and tables around while searching to find the missing item.

"Damned thing! Peter, where is it?"

Handel dropped to one knee and looked under the furniture. He spotted the lost article behind the chair where he had carelessly thrown it hours before. He reached under the chair and pulled out a white wig of curls. He spotted another wig near the hearth. It too had fallen and was laying in some blackened ash. He retrieved both wigs and compared them side by side. The one found near the fireplace had a thick, black streak up the back. He flopped the clean one atop his head and hurried out the door.

He Shall Come

THE DINNER GUESTS OF THE KING CHANGED FROM EVENING to evening depending upon the politics of the day. Usually, for the King, supper was the dyspeptic hour. No matter what else was served, the King knew he would receive a generous helping of societal woes. Whenever possible, he would excuse himself from supper because of a sour stomach, which, more often than not, was the truth.

Caroline enjoyed the social aspects of the dinner hour with its conversation and gossip, but King George had no use for it. Just a fortnight ago, Prime Minister Walpole had cornered the King for nearly two hours concerning the imminent threat of Polish succession. The King could hardly put up with Walpole's anxieties for a minute; two hours were pure torture. By the time the discussion was over, George was willing to let the Poles go and take Walpole with them. Were it not for Caroline's trust and confidence in the Prime Minister, the King would have little to do with him.

As it was, the only evenings the King genuinely enjoyed were those when he was asked by one of his patronizing guests about his own war heroics. He could reminisce ad nauseum about the battle of Oudenarde and his exploits on the field. But as of late, even Caroline had begged off hearing the same cobwebbed stories again. Thus, the King was subjected to whatever topics were of most concern to his guests. He endured their agendas, their whims, and their complaints for no other reason than abject duty. For the most part, he could not have been more disinterested.

This night, however, there was something planned that the King was actually looking forward to. Before dinner was to be served, Mr. Handel would favor them with some music.

The King's sitting room was full of guests. Even Prince Frederick was present, as he was expected to be. The guests were seated around the organ to listen to Handel, who played a concerto he announced as "Happy We." The title seemed unusually apropos as it not only described the listeners, but also the player. Those sitting behind Handel could see his pleasure by the shake of his wig.

It was obvious to all that the King was pleased with both the music and himself. He had acted in kingly fashion that day on the river. His judgment had been merciful, and his country was blessed for it. He knew that Handel would be a great aid to him in soothing some of the discontent that Londoners felt about having a German king. There would be some who would criticize him for his surrounding himself with other Germans such as Handel. *The Spectator* boys would have a field day with two fat Saxons, but he was certain that when they heard Handel's mastery and unmatched artistry, even they would applaud the King's wisdom in securing him for England. All in all, King George could not have been more happy with the day's events and the prospects that lay ahead.

When the music ceased, the guests applauded vigorously. As far as the King was concerned, Handel was already useful by giving his guests a topic of conversation other than unrest. The King beckoned Handel to his side. While Handel made his way through the crowded room, ladies snickered. When Handel drew near, the King's eyes drifted to the top of his head. Handel knew precisely what it meant. With a quick flick of his head, his wig shifted straight. There were more snickers. Prince Frederick just shook his head in disgust.

"*Mein Herr* Handel, my, but you are gifted," smiled the King.

"Your Majesty, I sing your praise."

"Never has praise been so pleasing to the ear," said King George. He knew that Handel was now his most loyal subject. Had the King not extended forgiveness so generously, Handel's allegiance would not have been so firm. The King purchased Handel's loyalty with mercy.

"I am delighted, Majesty. I thought you would like it," exulted Handel. The Prince cleared his throat.

"I wish to commission an opera from you, to open the season at the King's Theatre in the Haymarket," said the King.

"I promise the very finest, Majesty."

Again the Prince cleared his throat. Those closest to him tried their best to ignore his impudence. Handel continued.

"You will not be disappointed, Majesty."

Again Frederick cleared his throat. Several of the nearby gentlemen glared at the prince. He reacted by feigning to defend the King's honor.

"Given the company, I believe a certain degree of humility would be fitting." Frederick declared in a loud voice.

"Who speaks? Did someone speak?" The King demanded, searching the room.

The Prince stepped forward.

"Yes, Majesty—the heir to the crown," said the Prince, certain to get a reaction out of the King.

Frederick knew that his father would not recognize him by his given name or title. In circumstances such as this, Frederick could usually count on the King's saying something regrettable in front of his guests. Thus, the Prince took great pride in provoking his father into saying something less than noble. Unwittingly, King George turned the teeth of the situation back on his son by simply asking a question of the group at large.

"What did he say?"

"That a certain degree of humility would be more fitting," said Frederick.

"That's absurd." Handel said indignantly. "Should not the finest music be presented to His Royal Highness?"

Frederick did not expect this. He had simply lobbed an ill-timed dart in the direction of his father, and now the roles had reversed and he had become the target. What was worse, the King had a spokesman who was not bashful by any standard. Frederick suddenly felt the ground beneath him become unstable.

"The music is not in question, sir," he said.

"What then, sir?" demanded Handel.

"Inappropriate arrogance for the occasion."

"That is not for you or me to say, sir."

"On the contrary, it is for me to say," said the Prince. "Your vanity is in poor taste, sir."

Gasps and murmurs echoed around the room. The Prince challenged both the King and Handel. His accusation created a strange enigma for his father. On one hand, if Handel defended himself, his self-posturing could be misconstrued as blatant casualness for King and crown. Being German complicated the issue since their relationship was already the subject of considerable scrutiny. On the other hand, if Handel apologized and admitted arrogance, the Prince would have defended the King's honor in his own home. The thought of Fretz being praised for standing up in defense of the crown made King George nauseous. Surely, word of that would spread through London by morning. The King stood in silence, not wanting to consider what that outcome could mean to his enemies.

The guests in the room dared not even whisper for fear of inadvertently taking a stand with one or the other.

Handel was confused for a brief moment, then to the amazement of all present, he broke out into spontaneous laughter.

"Ahh, my vanity. I am greatly relieved, I thought you spoke of the King."

Handel never even considered the political predicament that was so apparent to everyone else present. In his naiveté, he turned the situation back onto the unsuspecting Prince, who stared aghast at the King.

"Your Majesty, I wouldn't...I shan't assume to mean...you can't believe I was speaking of you! There has been a mistake."

The King scowled at Frederick. When he could restrain his amusement at the unexpected turn of events no longer, he, too, burst into hearty laughter. All in the room joined in except Frederick.

The more laughter he was forced to endure, the angrier he became. His face became pale white with a bitterness that can only be created by the utter humiliation of being the brunt of a joke. He looked upon Handel as the embodiment of his most bile-ridden contempt. He hated with his entire being what the musician had done.

Handel's next words to the King drove the blade even deeper into Frederick's open wound.

"Majesty, I beg forgiveness. If I boast, it is in adulation of you," he laughed.

"You will be forgiven when I have heard the opera," declared the jubilant King.

"'Tis glorious penance I pay. May I never be pardoned."

The Prince could stand no more.

"Perhaps some competition would inspire you to greater heights."

The King turned around to see Frederick standing not one full stride in front of Handel. The two stared at one another. Handel did not move a muscle. The King was about to intercede, but the Prince spoke before he could get out a word.

"I propose a competing opera at Lincoln's Inn. Let the people decide who is gifted and who is fluff."

"No person of quality would demean themselves by setting up factions of fiddlers," said King George. But Frederick did not back down, nor did Handel. This was a challenge directed straight at the man who, a moment before, had embarrassed him. For a brief minute, everyone else in the room disappeared to the two men who faced off against each other.

The King stepped to the side of Handel. As he did, Handel gave a nod to Frederick. Handel spoke to the King in their native tongue in a show of unity.

"*So tretenwir uns zusammen vor.* I am the King's humble servant."

Before the King could respond, Frederick blurted out, "Done."

Seconds after the word had escaped his lips, he was gone.

As soon as Frederick left the room, the dinner party once again became relaxed and pleasant. The discord between King and Prince was so strong that no one was completely at ease while Frederick was present. Now that he was gone, even the King was more amicable. He had enjoyed the music immensely, and so had his guests. He had provided them with such a treat that their conversations centered on art and beauty rather than injustice and inequality. What a welcome change it was for the King and Caroline. They mingled with their guests freely, enjoying the festive atmosphere of the occasion.

Of all those present, Handel was the most popular. He was the King's guest of honor. People were still talking about the river and how ingenious it was for Handel to seek forgiveness through music. Handel never mentioned that it was not his idea at all, but that Baron Kilmanseck was the imaginer. Whether he chose not to tell to protect the Baron or elevate himself was never known. What was clear, however, was that in the morning Handel was in exile; by nightfall he dined with the King.

At one point during the evening, His Majesty implored Handel to sit down at the organ and play the "Allegro Alla Hornpipe" from the *Water Music* for those who were not on the river to hear. Actually, the King wanted to hear it again himself and simply needed a good excuse. Handel obliged happily. When the music ceased, again Handel stood and bowed to the King's guests, many of whom were surprised at his social finesse and etiquette, a distinction for which the Germans were not well known. He was both astute and tactful in his manners while still maintaining a generous enough portion of himself that he might not become too homogeneous with London's nobility. He effectively walked the thin line between capriciousness and convention.

The time that Handel spent studying in both Hamburg and Italy not only trained him in music but also in the social graces. He learned courtesy in Hamburg and charm in Italy.

Wit had come from his mother, Dorothea. His thick German accent came by heritage. A combination of these acquired talents made Handel quite an amusement at social events. Londoners loved how he was so enchantingly able to strangle the English language. Handel knew this and used it as a means to ingratiate himself to those he met. He had that uncanny ability to engage whatever tools were necessary for any circumstance—tools which worked well in the short term but could not endure repeated use.

While Handel was not at the organ, the King did some scheming of his own. He took Mr. Handel by the arm and led him toward three ladies standing apart from the others. Handel did not afford any resistance as the King led him to the small circle of admirers. He rightly assumed that these were ladies whom the King hoped to impress. He would do his best not to disappoint him.

"I have some guests I've been wanting to introduce to you," exclaimed the King.

The ladies blushed.

"Ladies, I am pleased you are all here." George turned to Handel: "Have you ever seen such beauty?"

Handel knew what to do.

"Ladies, I am sure Aphrodite sleeps poorly knowing there is such beauty among mortals."

The women swooned.

"Whom do I have the honor of beholding?" he asked.

As the King introduced each, Handel bowed low, graciously kissing each hand.

"Lady Grenwall, Lady James, and this is Lady Collingwood."

Handel stepped back as if to view them all at the same time.

"My, but you honor your husbands with your grace and beauty. I should be pleased to meet them and express my greenest of envy for their good fortune."

Lady Grenwall curtsied as she spoke.

"Thank you, sir, but you needn't worry. We will remind them ourselves—excepting Lady Collingwood, who has no husband. She is quite single and quite available."

King George put out his arm to escort the other two ladies away.

"We thought you might enjoy a small diversion, Handel. Come ladies, let us leave these two for a moment."

Handel immediately began to feel drops of sweat form on his brow. Lady Collingwood waited patiently for him to engage her.

"Well, m'lady—you are indeed a Lady?"

"Indeed."

"But you are not married. When His Majesty said, 'Lady' while introducing you, well naturally, I assumed that you had, or were soon to be—as it were...."

"My husband was killed in the fighting—the Spanish."

"They are like that—the Spanish, I mean," stammered Handel. "I am sorry. Then you are alone. Do you like that?"

"It's lonely. No, I do not like it. Do you?"

"Yes, indeed. It's quiet. No fussing really, no distractions. Men are lazy, but women need attention."

"I shan't distract you any further. Good evening, sir," she said. She intimated a curtsy, then left him to join the other guests. So unskilled was he in the art of romancing that he was not sure if he had offended her or not. He had little time to wonder as other guests surrounded him. As they inquired regarding his plans, he glanced around the room for Lady Collingwood, but could not find her.

Arise, Shine

THE TRUNK OF THE TREE WAS VERY LARGE AND KNOTTED, easily wide enough at the base to hide the Packrat three times over. He used it often when he took occasion to watch the people in the park.

On Sunday afternoons, families would go to the park to picnic on the grass. Peter would hide behind the tree and watch the children and parents from afar. He couldn't help but notice how clean and white the children's shirts were, and how their mothers always brushed the grass off their knees when they fell. He watched what they ate and how it was eaten and how adults always touched their faces with napkins after each bite. Peter thought them very clumsy eaters to have to keep cleaning up their faces so often.

He watched how the mothers coddled the children while the fathers read the newspaper. It was in the park that Peter learned that being a mother was a busier job than being a father. Fathers watched and read. Mothers worked. Children played and sometimes obeyed. That is what being a family meant to Peter. He knew these were not the families of the very wealthy, but of merchants, homeowners—those who earned a living, but were well paid for it. These he respected because he could see that they were responsible for their place in the world. Most of those he observed were not The Given.

Occasionally the very weathly would venture into the domain of the ordinary, but they stuck out like pocks on a sick child's face. As hard as they might try to fit in, it couldn't be done. They walked as if they were in carriages, upright and tall.

Even though it was difficult to refrain from chiding them, Peter made a silent oath to leave them alone on Sunday. Ridicule, which seemed appropriate on other days, felt oddly foul on Sunday. He did not attribute the feeling to God or observance of the Sabbath day, but simply excused it as another of his strange personality traits. That alone was sufficient reason to obey, for he was content enough with himself to heed his own premonitions.

Peter found himself particularly interested in the children, especially young children. He was intrigued at how different their lives appeared to be from what his had been. The smallest act of being picked up from the ground and comforted by an adult was something completely foreign to him. It was hard to even imagine. To have the dirt and grass wiped off was incomprehensible. He watched the mothers do that innumerable times for their small ones, and it still befuddled him.

The Packrat watched one little boy fall a dozen times in as many minutes. Each time the mother was there to help him up. Fortunately, every time the boy fell, he tumbled closer to the tree that hid the Packrat. The child was now close enough for Peter to hear the mother's voice when she picked him up. Peter expected the little boy to receive a scolding; instead the toddler was praised for his efforts, with kind words spoken in loving tones.

The Packrat imagined those words being said to him. He remembered the things which he heard the good mothers say and repeated them in his mind when the pangs of loneliness gnawed at him in the night. Even a mother's words were better than no mother at all.

When the little boy toppled within several feet of the tree, his knee hit a protruding root from the huge tree where Peter hid. The boy cried out. The mother was instantly there, picking him up in her arms and holding him close. She whispered words of comfort in his ear. Peter was close enough to hear every word.

But it was not the words that touched him; it was the sincerity of the words. The mother truly ached with the child. She did not try to minimize the hurt, she fully empathized with the child. To the Packrat, it seemed that she miraculously took upon herself the child's pain.

It was only a few moments before the child's tears were dried and the soreness was gone. The entire scene was so captivating that Peter was careless. He leaned far enough out from behind the tree that he was no longer hidden. The mother spotted him over the shoulder of her child. Their eyes met. The Packrat felt a flush of embarrassment redden his cheeks. He expected a quick look of disdain that he had dared invade their privacy, but no grimace appeared. The mother simply smiled at him—a smile far better than any words could have been. Peter smiled back.

The mother went back to her family, the Packrat went back to his. Much passed between them in that brief encounter. Perhaps the event transpired as it did because the two had similar responsibilities. Perhaps they instinctively recognized the role of caregiver in each other. Regardless of what prompted the exchange, they each determined to do their duty better. Their individual reasons for recommitting were different, but the outcome hoped for was the same.

And I Will Shake

THE THEATRE WAS PACKED TO OVERFLOWING. EXTRA CHAIRS were put at the ends of each aisle to create additional seating. There was great anticipation concerning the opera which was to open the season at the King's Theatre in the Haymarket.

Aaron Hill, the theatre manager, gave the general text to one of the staff poets, Giacomo Rossi, who had provided the Italian libretto for the opera. The piece, *Rinaldo*, based on the story of Rinaldo's being freed from the amorous snares of the sorceress Armida, was taken from Tasso's *Gerusalemme Liberata*.

But it was not the libretto that was long awaited: it was the man who had put that libretto to music. Handel received his commission from the King himself, and now it was time to hear what the Saxon had done.

All the elegant and influential of London came en masse to hear the new exotic and irrational entertainment called opera, which had been introduced to London just a few short years before. Until now, the Italian opera was unrivaled. The Italians were comfortable atop the European music scene, but Handel was billed as the one who could possibly lead London to the forefront of the operatic world. After all, he had spent years in Italy learning the craft from the masters, writing for the most renowned castrati and sopranos in Florence, Venice, and Rome. Italy had been the final leg of his journey of learning that had taken him through nearly every musical venue in Europe.

Early on, he had studied under the magnificent and renowned composer and performer, Friedrich Wilhelm Zachow in his hometown of Halle. From Zachow he learned the secrets of the aria—line and shape. He learned the fine points of orchestration and choral writing, with particular emphasis on the beauty and power of strong intrepid bass lines. He learned the intricacies of instrumental coloring, which later became such an integral element in his own style.

But possibly the greatest lesson gleaned from Zachow was a solid foundation in harmony. Zachow provided the young musician with scores of examples from his vast library of music, from which Handel began his journey into the art of harmony.

In Hamburg he studied alongside two other gifted contemporaries: Telemann and Matheson—the same Matheson who regretfully invited Handel to perform in his opera *Cleopatra*. Telemann and Matheson graciously allowed Handel to join in their efforts, whereby he was able to observe and study each of their strengths. Later, as he traveled throughout Italy, he would reflect back to those co-authoring days in Hamburg and apply the valuable lessons he mastered under the tutelage of his friends.

It was in Rome that he met Arcangelo Corelli, the orchestra leader at Cardinal Ottoboni's Palazzo della Cancelleria. The Cancelleria staged operas for the likes of Giovanni Bononcini, Alessandro Scarlatti, and Francesco Pollarolo. It was in the paths of these masters that Handel had walked. From these he learned framework and structure.

Corelli was instrumental in teaching Handel control of the orchestra and to demand of them nothing short of perfection. Handel watched the ensemble rehearsals wherein Corelli stopped the music mid-bar to correct an irregular bow. He demanded that all the bows in the string sections move up and down in perfect unison. Handel learned well Corelli's intolerance of laziness and mediocrity in his performers. Corelli would not tolerate anything less than perfection, nor would Handel.

Now his schooling was over, Handel was in London on the errand of the King, and all the influential of the day waited anxiously to see if he could deliver on the magnitude of a full opera. Adding to the excitement was the promise that Aaron Hill had spared no expense on the engines and effects that would be employed in the performance. Word spread quickly that the librettist, Rossi, had been hard pressed to stay ahead of Handel who had scored the opera in just two weeks—an unprecedented feat.

Handel had a reputation for having enormous creative bursts, but a full opera in two weeks was unimaginable. This, combined with Hill's securing the finest actors and singers available, guaranteed a full house long before the tickets and wordbook ever appeared at White's Coffee House.

The performance was all that it was hoped to be. The cast and chorus were impeccable. The words were enchanting. The music: astounding. As the opera moved into the final act, success was already well in hand. Handel stood proud atop the conductor's stand vigorously waving his arms through the final chorus of *Rinaldo*. The audience had been polite and courteous throughout the performance.

By all indications, the opera was triumphant. There were a few noticeable flaws in the choreography and set changes, but even they were easy to overlook in the grand scheme of the show. To measure in full how the performance had been received, Handel needed only to finish and then appraise the applause. As he conducted the last several bars, his wig bounced on his head like bubbles in a boiling pot.

The King sat tall in his royal box, expectantly waiting for the finale to end. He leaned forward on the edge of his seat where he could peer over the railing at the people below. He had been criticized by the English for his lack of taste concerning the arts. His efforts to bring one of the most gifted and promising musicians in Europe to London would certainly silence the critics.

While the orchestra sustained the last note of the finale, the entire audience rose to its feet in one great wave. The music ceased. The King stood as Handel turned from the stage and bowed his gratitude and respect to His Majesty. The crowd cheered while King and composer exchanged waves and smiles. *Rinaldo* was a success; the night had been won.

By mid-afternoon the following day, word of Handel's triumph had reached deep into London's nobility. Performances of *Rinaldo* were scheduled intermittently through the next three months. The King was pleased beyond anything expected. He found occasion to attend an additional two performances himself. There had been some mild criticism of the opera, but even that had been overshadowed by the tremendous uproar the opera created. The only criticism that received any notice of significance appeared in *The Spectator*. Addison and Steele couldn't resist the opportunity to ridicule the ostentatiousness of *Rinaldo*. Their editorial read:

"The opera of *Rinaldo* is filled with thunder and lightning, illuminations and fireworks, which the audience may look upon without catching cold, and indeed without much danger of being burnt. Indeed, at one point in the 'delightful grove' of Act I, sparrows flew over into the pit and befouled those beneath."

But even Steele and Addison couldn't dampen the overarching approval which *Rinaldo* received. Handel had not the time to accommodate the invitations that were now presented to him. Almost overnight, he found himself in huge demand. Foppish youth began to wear black streaks in their wigs to emulate the flamboyant fad adopted by their heroic conductor. Little did they know that the ash-streaked wig Handel wore on occasion was worn in desperation when he had been too careless in tossing aside a clean one and could not find it.

The King commissioned more operas. He openly praised the efforts of his fellow Saxon. Handel greatly enjoyed the benefits of success. Each week he received his stipend along with a percentage of the receipts from the performances. Without fail, each week he wrote a short note, accompanied with five pounds, and put it in an envelope to be sent to Dorothea Handel, Halle, Germany. He had sent something each week from the day he left home for Hamburg.

When his father died prematurely, he took the responsibility to care for the temporal needs of his mother. She was much younger than his father and required assistance for many years following his passing. It was a duty which her son took on gratefully. He did not consider supporting his mother an obligation but a blessing. He also took occasion to send anonymous gifts to the children's hospital.

Many followed Handel's early successes in London with great interest, some for good, others for ill. Of the many, none were more diligent than Mr. Charles Jennens.

Jennens was an eccentric; everyone knew it. He had wealth, which brought with it considerable prominence among the aristocracy. He was the heir of Gopsal, a large estate in Leicestershire. He was a learned man, a dilettante of sorts, dabbling in everything from politics to the arts. He was outspoken to a fault, often resulting in heated debates.

Edward Holdsworth, Jennens's most trusted friend, was also passionately interested in the arts: literature, painting, architecture, and, especially, music. Both were faithful followers of Handel. They each subscribed to all of his works, beginning with the publication of the opera *Rodelinda*. These two held strong to the supremacy of Handel and his music.

Jennens was quick to perceive that his wealth afforded him the luxury of speaking his mind whether the opinion was popular or not. He knew that he may have to endure criticism, but it did not affect tomorrow's meal; so he persisted. It was well known that he had the propensity of making everyone else's business his own business. He was not afraid to go on the record and believed that everyone had the right to know where he stood in regard to an issue. He did so with regularity, much to the dismay of his increasing circle of enemies.

Mr. Jennens would often print replies or editorials on handbills in response to newspaper articles that were contrary to his views. Addison and Steele at *The Spectator* were well acquainted with Jennens. They knew him and disliked him. He had written and printed several scathing rebuttals to articles penned by the editors. Subsequently, they would often write with the specific intention of provoking him. History had shown that Jennens was not one to let a sleeping dog lie. They learned exactly what soured his stomach and how hard he would return a stiff volley.

Jennens's latest and perhaps most controversial stance was with regard to the writings of Shakespeare. With a strong dose of gall, Jennens took the liberty of rewriting those works of Shakespeare which he believed had been attended to carelessly. It was not a direct attack on Shakespeare himself, but the disappointing prognosis that perhaps there was some sickness in his body of work. To say the least, it was a difficult pill for most to swallow. The mere mention of such a thing was inconceivable. Steele and Addison salivated openly. They could not have coaxed a more unpalatable utterance from Jennens's lips with sugar cubes. If they could have scripted Jennens into a mire, they could not have done better. It was perfect.

Attacking Shakespeare was so wholly unexpected that it had to happen twice before they dared believe that it was intentional. Jennens was caught in a gummy flypaper from which there was no escape. Finally, they had him, and what was even more delectable was that he had put the sword in their hands. They cut him into tiny pieces with sharp satire and biting editorials. So outrageous was Jennens's folly that the public was entirely unsympathetic. In fact, the on-going skirmish was quite amusing. Opposing articles were read aloud in pubs. In melodramatic style, people cheered one moment and booed the next. Jennens and Addison contended with one another on a very personal level. The battle went on for months.

Whenever there was no news worthy enough to preempt some good old-fashioned slander, Addison preyed on Jennens. There was no end to the mileage in a mishap such as this. Jennens did his best to take the argument back to its original premise, which was curiously innocuous, but *The Spectator* boys would have no part of it. The pen was open and the pigs were out. The more Jennens sputtered, the more guilty he appeared to be.

He decided at long length that this was a dung heap he was forced to ignore. The more he kicked at it, the worse it smelled. As difficult as it was to do, he determined to respond no more. He virtually went into hiding concerning the matter. He would neither speak nor write of it. When he was publicly called to arms with regard to it, he simply turned his back and walked away. The game was no longer any fun, and soon the articles lessened. There were a few flagrant jabs here and there to see if he would come back out to play, but Jennens maintained his silence.

What no one else knew was that his silence was temporary. Indeed, he had a plan. The first step in that plan was to lull his enemies to sleep. Only after they were convinced the war was over would he make his move. Until that time, he contented himself to work on more ennobling pursuits, including the scriptural wordbook, which he intended to give Mr. Handel.

But Who May Abide
the Day of His Coming

THE ROOM WAS DIMLY LIT. THREE LONG CANDLES FLICKERED
in the corner of the study—which was all the light for the entire room.
Prince Frederick knew that on the other side of the closed curtains, the
sun was probably just now setting, but he didn't open them to witness it.
He looked around the room in silence.

The shelves of books were in perfect alignment. It was clearly more
important for the spines to be even than the books to be used. The air in the
study was motionless. It was heavy and thick, not just from countless old
books and stained woods but more from perfume. The scents of varied flowers filled the room. Smelly pools of stagnant air hung suspended in the stillness. The smells seemed to be distilled and preserved from days long past. In
a room designed to make one feel at ease, he was anything but comfortable.

When Frederick considered what was about to happen, he wondered how many like schemes were given birth in that room. The more time he was alone, the more his anxiety grew. He became less trusting of this specious undertaking as the minutes passed. He began to seriously question his motives under the gaze of the many books and the truths that he knew they contained. The sweet and pungent smells of perfume grew rancid to his nose. Fragrance gave way to foulness. The walls began to close around him. Doubt filled his mind. He reconsidered the consequences of the journey upon which he was about to embark. His heart faltered under the weight of guilt. He felt he was drowning in the darkness of the room.

Suddenly he could think of nothing else than to get the curtains open and see the influence of the sun on the countryside; then he could think more clearly. He moved toward the window as if driven there by his last remaining surge of will. As his hand reached for the curtain, the door swung open. Into the room walked Madame Hervey, followed by an Italian.

Prince Frederick quickly turned around before his hand could pull back the curtain. No sunlight ever made it into the room. Madame Hervey stepped close to him, took his hand, and led him to the man who had entered with her.

"May I introduce Giovanni Battista Bononcini," she announced. "And likewise, I present to you, Frederick, the Prince of Wales."

Bononcini lifted one foot forward and bowed while taking the Prince's hand in his and putting it to his forehead.

"M'lord, it is my sincerest and deepest pleasure—"

"I am told your operas are unequaled in Italy," the Prince interrupted.

Bononcini stood up, somewhat taken back by the Prince's unritualistic frankness.

"You are kind, Your Grace."

"And what of my question?"

"I have enjoyed much success in Italy."

"You studied in Italy."

"Yes, Your Grace."

"How many operas have you written?"

"Fourteen, Your Grace."

"And performed at the Cancelleria."

"Yes, Highness."

"Do you know of Handel?"

"Yes m'lord, from Rome. We worked together on occasion."

"Is he all he thinks he is?"

"He is gifted, yes, but—"

"Yes?"

Bononcini glanced at Madame Hervey, who directed his attention back to the Prince with her eyes. Bononcini spoke carefully, "No man could reach the elevation he thinks of himself."

Madame Hervey leaned close to the Prince and spoke in his ear.

"Now we will see if opera is better served Hanoverian or Italian."

She began to laugh, Bononcini nervously joined in. The Prince didn't laugh, nor did he speak. He thought long and hard before he cautiously nodded his affirmation. He ventured a look back at the closed curtains behind him. He thought one last time to flee this dark place and be gone from the sweetly stinking room and all that it contained, but it was too late. The words he had spoken in anger on the river bounced back and forth between his ears. He was committed. His trajectory was set. Nothing could have been more frightening to him. He took Bononcini's hand in a firm grasp and held it long before speaking.

"Are you more skilled than he?"

"I dare not say, but this I will say; he is German, I am Italian, opera is Italian. One is ale, one is wine."

The Prince stared deep into Bononcini's eyes. He could see that his arrogance was well grounded, but he also saw an unmistakable hint of doubt. At that moment, he knew it would take more than Bononcini to defeat Handel.

Never a city to back down from watching a good fight, London welcomed the idea of competing operas. There was considerable talk among the aristocracy concerning the generals of each operatic army. On one side were the Saxons—the King and Handel; on the other was the Italian—hosted by young Frederick. Most people thought it insolent for Frederick to be so bold as to challenge his father, the King, to a duel of artists. Quickly, sides were taken and musical ranks marshaled.

The King entrenched himself with Handel and their faithful in the King's Theatre in the Haymarket. Frederick and Bononcini hurled their flaming musical arrows from Lincolns Inn Theatre. At first the Prince's efforts seemed futile. Bononcini raised his baton to an orchestra which outnumbered patrons. Madame Hervey, Steele, Addison, and the Prince were in attendance at every performance. So alone were they, that curious people began to come to witness the spectacle—an audience of only four. Once there, these same curious people soon realized that Bononcini was a talent to be reckoned with. Word began to spread that the Italians had come to take back what was rightfully theirs: Italian opera.

Handel continued to flourish with the established opera-goers, while Prince Frederick and Bononcini began to draw a new, younger audience. Many of the youth who were first to jump in line behind Handel months before, were just as quick to desert him for the more faddish Frederick. Their allegiance and loyalty went only as far as was fashionable.

The Prince took every occasion to invite people to be his personal guests at the opera. He mingled with the attendees openly in the foyers and sat among them, rather than in his royal box. He was witty and charming with the ladies. He listened to the idealistic bantering of the men. Frederick availed himself to the audience in every way; they responded with their patronage.

While the Prince made himself accessible, Madame Hervey had ushers positioned in the lobbies to keep lists of those who attended performances. These same people were then invited to social gatherings where opera tickets were passed out as party favors, so patrons could bring other acquaintances and friends. Whenever these socials took place, the Prince and Bononcini always favored the group with a fortuitous visit. Madame Hervey's courtyard became known affectionately as, "the other Lincoln's Inn ticket office." It was joked among the patrons that a season ticket to Lincoln's was the same price as only one performance if one made a point of meeting the Madame.

Handel, on the other hand, was complacent. He expected London to attend his operas out of loyalty to the King and appreciation of his craft. He firmly believed his work was superior and expected London to respond for that reason alone. In actuality, the presumption was true, but the anticipated outcome was not. Over the course of many months and several operas, interest in Handel and the King's Theatre began to wane, while the opera at Lincoln's Inn readily increased. Handel did not seem to notice the empty seats that began to appear. When the theatre manager, Aaron Hill, pointed them out, Handel became belligerent, insisting that London had no ear at all.

"The ears of London are mere flaps of flesh intended to keep wigs aright and hats aloft," he barked.

Instead of trying to appeal to the audience on their level, Handel went to war with them, openly challenging the listener to raise their musical comprehension to where he was. While the Prince congratulated and rewarded audiences for their patronage, Handel berated their lack of taste and understanding.

Audiences at the Haymarket began to diminish; receipts became harder to secure. Handel finally resolved to bury the competing opera with one powerful stroke of superiority. He determined to approach the King with a proposition that would allow him to bring the world's finest talent to England and the King's Theatre. King George thought the idea ingenious, and the Royal Academy of Music was established.

The King literally poured money into the Academy. Handel used those funds to travel to Europe where he could engage the most talented and expensive divas and castrati to come and perform in the Academy's productions. He went to Venice, Nice, Rome, and Naples in search of the finest singers in Italy. He returned with sopranos and castrati unequaled on the stages of London. It was an unprecedented move that seemed untouchable.

At first, the ploy worked perfectly; the Academy flourished. Handel again took the upper hand as the dominant force in the music world. The sheer prowess of his featured singers was impressive enough to fill the theatre, but again, in time, seats began to vacate.

In a decidedly risky move, Handel determined to do the unthinkable: perform operas in English. He abandoned the conventional Italian paradigm for a more accessible English version of opera in an effort to play down to the tastes of London. The people had always complained that they couldn't understand the Italian librettos, so Handel and the Royal Academy obliged them by producing several operas in the native tongue.

The move proved tremendously successful. People could finally understand the story behind the music. Customers queued up en masse to attend the new "English" opera. The reception astounded even Handel.

The idea had been born out of desperation, but now it seemed nothing short of divinely inspired. The Prince and his entourage all but disappeared for months while Handel and the King enjoyed absolute success. Through several operas there was no disruption in attendance or enthusiasm. But again their enemies made fuel from air. Madame Hervey orchestrated a purist's effort by openly criticizing Handel and the Academy's disregard for established tradition. Handel was disparaged by the vocal minority for his manipulative efforts to erode the Italian form with a harsh and less lyrical language. The criticism started as isolated sparks thrown on a smoldering pile, but Steele and Addison were able to raise the temperature of the controversy with one very witty and biting verse:

"Another King, most stout, turn'd English operas out,
Which Britons first admired, but now, alas, are tired."

The editorials were highly effective in putting a new wedge between Handel and Bononcini. The armies of each composer were again aligned on the side of their hero. Bononcini led those holding out for the pure language of opera. Handel stood strong with his followers under the banner of his English opera. The pile of smoldering discontent was fanned into a conflagration of fiery tempers and harsh words. No dispute between the Tories and Whigs could have been more hotly debated. The theatre became a battlefield. It seemed that one could not attend the opera without taking sides.

The younger audience was clearly on the side of the Prince. It became more and more difficult for supporters of the King's Theatre to endure the mudslinging of the mutinous youth. For those who were loyal to Handel and the King, a night of entertainment became a night of revilement. The Prince's younger constituents actively sought opportunities to verbally sully Handel's older patrons. Some even stooped to throwing garbage on those waiting in line to get in the theatre.

Handel's elderly patrons were simply unwilling to endure a night of derision for the sake of opera. As a result, Bononcini's operas sold out, Handel's dwindled. The support of the community seemed to shift toward the Prince and company.

Addison and Steele did not let up in the least. Like wine, their writing seemed to improve with age. The longer the war waged on, the smarter and more economical was their satire. Readership increased steadily.

Subscriptions reached an apex at the same time that the editors' pencils were the sharpest.

"Some say, compared to Bononcini,
That *Mynheer* Handel's but a ninny;
Other aver that he to Handel
Is scarcely fit to hold a candle;
Strange all this difference should be
'Twixt Tweedle-dum and Tweedle-dee."

Handel needed a lift. He was convinced that he needed a celebrity of sorts to bolster his upcoming opera. Once again, he looked to Italy. Again, he traveled there for the sole purpose of securing a diva who could drive up the ticket sales. He needed a marquee name to lure back the citizens of London. He found one in Francesca Cuzzoni. Like all divas, she was large and ill-tempered; unlike most others, her very name guaranteed receipts.

She agreed to come to London for the full run of Handel's Italian opera, *Ottoné*. When the opera-going public heard she would be singing in Handel's upcoming series, they came. She was, by all accounts, magnificent. People were dually impressed with her ability and control of a note. Her voice had such power as to fill a room. Handel's critics laughed about how doing so was no great feat, "Since she fills half of the room herself."

Frederick and his cronies mounted a full-scale attack on Handel and Cuzzoni. She was Italian. *Ottoné* was Italian. Handel, the giver of English opera was now going back to the language to which the Prince's Bononcini had remained loyal. Frederick's stable of supporters pounded Handel for his indecision. He was accused of knee-jerking just for the sake of receipts. They mocked his apparent money grubbing over his desire to maintain the integrity of the art form. They fought their case persuasively, but it did not appear to have any effect. For weeks ticket sales held strong. But by the end of the thirteenth week run, receipts once again began to fall off. Frederick's team began to win by attrition.

When the final performance came, the house was only slightly over half full. Handel stood at the podium, leading with an empty stare. His mind was elsewhere. The King sat quietly with his daughter, Princess Caroline, in the royal box. There was little to applaud, and few to muster applause from. When the opera concluded, the King and daughter slipped out the back to avoid having to endure the critiques of the other ticket holders.

One man, however, did see them leave: Antonio Paolo Rolli, the Director of Italian Affairs for the Academy. He was a narrow man, with small, deep-set eyes. His protruding brows shaded his eyes from light. His voice was thin and irksome. It bore upon the mind of the listener like water dripping from a leaky faucet. He spoke in hidden verse—never actually saying what he intended, yet always intent upon the saying.

Through the past year, he had watched the movements of Handel and the King with great interest. When Handel was first commissioned an opera, Rolli was reduced from opera director to his current position. Before he ever met Handel, he was jealous of him. His blood ran even hotter when the King insisted that all those associated with the Academy support and supply Handel with whatever he wanted.

Rolli was instrumental in the effort to secure Cuzzoni. He made the necessary concessions to entice her to make the journey to London. He put together her travel itinerary. He attended to her unreasonable wants and wishes. He was faithful in fulfilling his obligatory duty of listening to her countless complaints. He spoke flattering words. He transported her to and from the theatre. He was in charge of all her temporal affairs—including food, which in and of itself was a daunting task.

All this he did while secretly hoping that Handel would stumble. When he saw the composer stub his toe, he was quick to get out from under him, thereby accomplishing two things: he would not be crushed by Handel's fall and he would be in a perfect position to help pick him back up.

When Rolli could see Prince Frederick's opera poised once again to take the upper hand, he schemed. Handel would be the carriage that would carry Rolli to his highest aspirations.

First he carefully pointed out Handel's faults, always under the oft ill-intended guise of constructive criticism. He covertly went about eroding Handel's reputation with sarcastic gossip and scurrilous sniggling, particularly to the other Italians. He feigned himself a friend of Handel and the Academy, when in reality he was posturing himself to make a play in the great game.

It was not that Rolli disliked Handel because he was less than purported; on the contrary, he was one of the few who truly recognized the artist's superiority. Rolli's jealousy was birthed in the furnace of pride. He desperately desired what Handel had. He wanted to be equal with Handel, to be known and esteemed on the same plane as Handel. There was only one way possible for that to happen: Handel must fall. Until now, the dream seemed impossible, but suddenly the goal appeared within reach.

When he saw the king leave, Rolli stalked the stage, waiting for an opportune time to approach Handel. He did not want to speak to him with others present. Handel left before the stage fully emptied. The opportunity was gone. Rolli knew he must wait for another chance.

Then, miraculously, Handel reappeared back on the stage to collect his music from his stand. The theatre was empty, the lights dim. The circumstance was so perfect that it felt entirely arranged. Rolli walked up behind him; his voice startled Handel out of his meditation. "Sir, I may be able to help, if you will allow me, sir."

Quite surprised, Handel spun around and looked at him suspiciously. Rolli continued.

"Yes, I believe possibly we can help each other. As Director of Italian Affairs, it has come to my attention that you wish to secure the Diva Bordoni—Faustina Bordoni—to sing with, or as egos are wont to be involved, *against* Cuzzoni."

"Antonio Rolli, isn't it?" Handel queried. Rolli could only summon a stupefied nod. Nothing Handel could have said could have cut him any deeper. As closely as Rolli was involved with the arrangement of Cuzzoni, Handel still did not regard him of such stature as to make it a point to fully remember him. Rolli did his best not to let his face betray his thoughts. Handel went back to his work of collecting music. He thought for a moment before responding.

"An interesting idea."

"I believe it could generate some interest," Rolli continued. "I have the ear of Faustina, but of course, I would need incentive."

Handel glanced up from his music. Rolli stepped closer, his voice almost pleading.

"I am a librettist first. Allow me to write for you, share in your genius, have part in the glorious work you do."

He held out a leather folder to Handel.

"Librettos. Take them, see for yourself." Handel studied Rolli's face before taking the folder.

"You believe you could persuade Faustina to join us here?" asked Handel.

"I am certain of it."

Handel's eyes went to the folder. He grasped the handle and started for the door. As he walked, he said but three words, "Do it then."

Who Shall Stand

THE KING WAITED IN HIS EMPTY COURT. ONE MOMENT HE was on his feet, pacing, the next he sat, bent over, rubbing his forehead in his hands. He mumbled under his breath. No distinct words came out, only guttural noises from deep in his chest. Deep creases were etched in his brow. He was poor at waiting.

At length, the door at the opposite end of the hall opened: across the threshold stepped Frederick. King George shouted from the far end of the room.

"There you are, impertinent swine! Is there no level of baseness to which you are not willing to descend?"

His words rang out into the foyer where guards and footmen stood ready. The door slammed closed behind the Prince as the valet was quick to dam up the royal rantings.

"Why so bent upon the ruin of one poor fellow so generous and good-natured as he?" the King stormed.

"Good morning, Your Majesty," smiled Frederick.

The King was not amused. He continued with slightly less volume, "A scheme such as yours does little honor to the undertakers whether it succeeds or not. The better it succeeds, the more reason you have to be ashamed of it."

"You speak of Handel?"

The King gazed at the Prince with an unbending stare. His eyes bore down on the Prince with utter disdain. He looked upon him as one looks at an insect about to take a bite of flesh.

The Prince, who to this point had appeared unaffected, looked into the face of contempt. He grew solemn.

"It was your hand, sir, that stood the man up on a pedestal. If he falls from that place, it will be by his own hand or the one that put him there, not mine."

Their eyes did not break from one another. After several seconds, it was the King who first glanced away, perhaps from a fleeting thought of regret. The moment he saw it, the Prince whirled in place and walked across the hall to the door. His footsteps echoed through the hall and the King's empty soul. The door opened, then closed tight. Frederick was gone.

The street outside the theatre was a traffic jam. Carriages were lined along the walkways and sidestreets. A long line of people started near the door and wound back down the steps and around the corner of the theatre. Never before had an audience in London seen the likes of what was about to take place.

Rolli had delivered as promised. The two divas, Cuzzoni and Faustina, were both scheduled for that night's performance. No theatre in London had ever boasted two talents such as this on the same stage at the same time. Handel had carefully reworked the score in order to give each of the sopranos the exact number of solo bars.

The rehearsals came and went with little disruption, aside from mildly obtuse efforts from each diva to move upstage of the other.

Handel knew that there was not a stage in London big enough for the two of them to share happily, but it was not their happiness which he sought. He purposely kept a safe distance from each of them to avoid complicating the situation with anything of a personal nature. He was stubbornly demanding through rehearsals. He had no patience for their haughtiness. His actions demonstrated no preference for one or the other. He considered them both prima donnas and treated them as such. It rued him deeply to think that he was reliant upon these self-centered sopranos to fill the house. He hated them for the exact reason he needed them.

His frustration was vented upon those in the orchestra and chorus. Playing and singing at the Kings Theatre under Handel's baton was no longer an honor, it was drudgery. It was often said in quiet conversation that nothing was worth the price of working for Handel. Some actually left the company citing as their reason that life was, indeed, too short. But the enthusiasm of opening night felt promising even to the cast and orchestra. They forgot most of the misery and hoped that a good debut would take the starch out of Handel's collar.

The theatre was crowded and noisy. Seating was disorderly. Several arguments broke out in the audience over rightful seats. A general feeling of confusion permeated the crowd.

Although the King was not in attendance, his daughter, Princess Caroline, did make a showing. In an effort to capitalize on the same ploy that Frederick used so effectively, the Princess sat in the audience. This added to the problem, since some came in hopes of speaking with—or to—the King. The audience was more orderly and polite when the King was present. No one cared much if Princess Caroline was there or not. Princess Caroline was not thought of as much more than a royal brat. Her presence could quiet no one.

Rolli watched with great anticipation from the librettist's box. As the guests were seated he conspicuously stood on several occasions to observe the filling of the theatre. This was the moment he had desperately longed for. Between Handel and the presence of not one, but two of the most renowned divas in Europe, this performance promised to be remembered and recorded as one of the greatest ever. His name would fill the enviable place of librettist. His future as a marquee writer was assured.

As Handel rose his baton to start the concert, the crowd only partially quieted. The orchestra was several bars into the overture before the noise became tolerable. Curious heads turned this way and that to try to determine the cause for so much commotion, but there was no apparent reason.

There was little change in the atmosphere of the opera until it became time for the sopranos to enter. Their entrance was simultaneous. The audience immediately shushed.

The ability of the two divas was truly impressive. Both had a command of voice, pitch, and breath that was astounding. The audience was stunned to hear two voices of such quality on the same stage. Each would pick up where the other left off in an ascending display of virtuosity. Hearing the two divas juxtaposed directly against each another created a truly unusual opportunity; they could be compared directly.

Some preferred the roundness of sound and strength of Cuzzoni, while others leaned towards the clarity and absolute purity of Faustina. There was much discussion in the audience as each patron shared their observations and preferences with those around them. The discussion created no small stir as people traded opinions with those nearby. Cuzzoni and Faustina began to sense the growing controversy with each new entrance and stanza. They stood on opposite sides of the stage singing their separate yet equal length bars of music. At the end of each solo, the growing factions applauded the skills of their favored diva.

On one entrance, Faustina stepped forward, upstaging Cuzzoni by almost a yard. Her supporters responded with cheering and applause. Not to be outdone, Cuzzoni stepped forward of Faustina on her next entrance while her followers cheered their approval. The divas worked their way forward step by step until there was no stage left in front of them. Faustina nearly slipped into the pit, sending the audience into hysterical laughter.

As events on stage escalated, the separate factions in the audience became more vocal. Soon, those in the crowd became more involved with one another than even the singers. Like a tug-of-war it went on, each side cheering for the diva on their side of the stage. Handel became aware of the division and exploited it. He accentuated the controversy by creating opposing sections in the orchestra. As the situation heated, so did tempers. Instead of simply applauding their favorite, the opposing sides began taunting the other diva. One faction began whistling over Cuzzoni whilst the other side clapped over Faustina.

Handel called for drums and timpani to underscore the battle. People rose to their feet and shouted obscenities at those across the aisle. Catcalling continued among the patrons until tempers ignited into several fights in the audience. The entire scene finally erupted into a nasty catfight between the two divas. Faustina and Cuzzoni tore at each other's hair and dresses. As they hideously clung to one another's hair, Handel arrogantly continued without any thought of intervention.

The audience became a brouhaha of arguing and yelling. Wigs were pulled from heads and wordbooks were tossed back and forth across the audience.

Princess Caroline tried to bring order to the chaos but was completely ignored. Appalled, she ran from the hall amid scoffs and jeers.

Rolli watched bitterly as pieces of torn wordbooks fell from the balconies in a shower of confetti. He could not believe his eyes.

Unseen by Rolli, a woman entered his box from the rear. She whispered something in his ear, then handed him a folded card. He opened and read the words delivered to him. He turned, but no one was there. He read the card a second time before folding it. It was then that he noticed the Prince's seal. He stuffed the paper into his shirt and disappeared out the back of the box.

There was more harm done in that single episode than could be recovered from. The damage was done. Handel, the one person who may have been able to avert the final catastrophe, aided in it. The end was inevitable. Not even the King could turn the tide against his countryman after the treatment that Princess Caroline received. It was over. All but the few most loyal of followers left him. In spite of the harm his enemies had inflicted over the past years, it was his own hand that had dealt the worst blow.

The Voice of Him
That Crieth in the Wilderness

THE RAIN FELL SOFTLY ON THE MARBLE SILL OF THE LARGE
library window. It rained all day and into the night; the sky showed no
signs of easing. Dim light shone through the rain-streaked glass.

Inside, Charles Jennens sat at his large walnut desk writing by lamplight. His large shadow darkened the wall behind him. So intent was he
upon his writing that he had not noticed the rain. On his desk lay several
pages of handwritten manuscript and an open Bible. Under his quill was
but one sheet of paper on which he now wrote. He gently laid down the
quill and picked up the paper before him. He quietly read the words he
had written.

William Holdsworth—Richmond

Dear William,

I am dearly afraid that Handel may be all but gone. Ahh, but I long for things as they were: countless operas, theatres filled to overflowing, London, the musical center of the world with Handel at the heart of it. Alas, but for divine intervention, his enemies have succeeded. Even the King's presence cannot offset the public's indifference. The taste of the town is so depraved that the vulgar and bawdy Beggar's Opera triumphs over the Italian one.

I regret that the indecencies and general disturbance occasioned by the partisans of the two celebrated divas has given the satire plenty of material from which to draw. Faustina has gone. Cuzzoni remains, although I don't know why. Rolli, his librettist, is average at best. Handel is at the brink of complete ruin. If his next opera fails like the past several, I don't believe he will pursue it further. His health lessens. I hope he has strength remaining for what I intend to give him. I could say more, but it grows late and I must defer the rest until I write next—by which time we will know concerning his opera Deidamia.

Your devoted colleague,
Charles Jennens.

Postscript: William, I believe Handel's enemies are closer than he knows. Though I'm not sure who, I am quite convinced the Prince has found himself a Judas.

Shall the Lame Man Leap

THE MONTHS PASSED FROM SUMMER TO FALL. HANDEL WAS no longer the man he had once been. He no longer had stipends, parties, or patrons. The King's Theatre was given over to the satirical *Beggar's Opera*, which enjoyed tremendous success. Handel's failed operas provided enough themes to give the *Beggar's Opera* plenty of fodder from which to profit.

Once out of the King's employ, Handel was in the precarious position of having to finance his own endeavors. He continued to perform and produce operas but on borrowed funds. He promised success to his investors, but to date, had not yet performed on those promises. He found himself in the cannibalistic cycle of trying to pay for past failures with the assurance of future success. This spiraled him downward until nothing short of landmark proceeds would provide enough to get him out of the financial predicament in which he found himself. He had already used up any favors he could secure at the hands of his faithful. He pushed friendship beyond what it could endure.

In desperation, he took loans brokered to him from unknown sources. He accepted the funds on the weak rationalization that it came from supportive admirers, but there was a foulness about the money that he couldn't deny. Now even that was all but gone. He had borrowed himself into unrelenting bondage.

Finally, when all else had failed, he approached John Rich, the theatre manager at Lincoln's Inn, for one last opera with the promise of filling the house for a long seven-week run. Rich himself was struggling and in dire need of financial bolstering. The Prince and Bononcini had long since vacated Lincoln's for the larger theatre at Covent Garden, but, once Handel faltered, even their efforts slowed as the public grew weary of opera without the muse of competition.

Handel gave Rich his word that he would succeed. Foolishly, he personally guaranteed the theatre's money. Since Rich had nothing better slated for the mid-winter run, he agreed, against his better judgment.

Rich scheduled rehearsals for *Deidamia* to begin in the late fall for a post-Christmas premiere. Along with Cuzzoni, Handel was successful in drawing a few additional singers who were as desperate as he was. Rolli was responsible for the libretto that Handel put to music. Of the several librettos that Rolli did for Handel in the months following the divas' onstage fight, none proved great.

Rolli was the recipient of considerable criticism and was oftentimes named as one of the principle reasons for Handel's fall. His bitterness grew stronger in the months following the Faustina-Cuzzoni incident. Rolli was supremely proud of the work that he had done for Handel; he was supremely disappointed with the reception his work had received. Rolli was certain that Handel had given only mediocre attention to his very best efforts. Each time the two combined on an opera the results were less then desirable.

When Handel made a deal with Rich at Lincoln's Inn, no other librettist stepped forward. Rolli was brought on by default, but he still believed the composer put most of the blame for their failure on him. He interpreted Handel's detachment as derision.

When it came time to rehearse for *Deidamia*, Rolli watched from a seat near the back of the hall. Each day he distanced himself more from Handel, while doing his best to get close to those most able to hurt Handel.

He watched while Handel accompanied Cuzzoni from his seat at the harpsichord. As she labored through a series of sixteenth-note scales, Handel shouted instructions.

"Sixteenths, madame! Stay up—you're losing time. Do your Italian directors allow such laziness? Time! Time!"

He stopped playing.

"Would you like us to wait until you catch up?"

"Your aria is unsingable," she sighed, exasperated.

"Unsingable?" he roared.

"I won't sing it. It's not like the Italians'. Opera is Italian. You could learn some things from them."

"I studied four years in Italy and often wondered how so great a culture could be followed by so little fruit."

"I won't stand for this. You have no opera without me. This is an outrage. I won't sing it!" Cuzzoni bellowed as she walked off the stage.

At this point, Rolli stepped in to quell the conflict.

"You will need to change it."

"Another Italian!" shouted Handel. "What do you suggest?"

"Make it more singable."

Handel's fist came down on his stand. The baton in his hand splintered, falling to the floor in pieces.

"Stay out of it! This doesn't concern you!"

"As secretary of Italian Affairs and librettist I must say your conduct—"

"Librettist? Is that what you are? You call this a libretto? A child's rhyme has more depth than this...this drivel."

Hatred glowed in Rolli's eyes. Cuzzoni stopped near the edge of the stage and turned back to Handel with her hands indignantly braced on her hips.

"It's unsingable. I won't sing it!"

"You will sing!" Handel shouted, purple with rage.

"I'd rather die first," said Cuzzoni.

"Fine."

Handel threw away his chair; it tumbled across the stage floor. Members of the chorus had to jump to get out of its way. Handel marched toward her. He grabbed her with both hands, dragged her screaming to the window, lifted it open, and proceeded to squeeze her large body through the opening. Everyone stared in utter disbelief, none willing to stand between the lion and his prey. Bystanders on the street looked up in horror at the huge woman hanging from the second story window, screaming. Handel held her in a firm grip with one hand while pushing her out with the other. It took several good shoves to get her midsection, the greater part of her, through the window. She began to feel herself slip once her hips were through the portal. Her screams intensified. At first she had screamed in anger, now she screamed in utter terror. Rolli grabbed at Handel's arm to try to stop him.

"Have you lost your mind? Stop!"

With one mighty thrust, Handel threw him to the floor with his left hand while still clutching the diva with his right. So strong was Handel that Rolli flailed to the floor like a rag doll. Handel pulled the face of Cuzzoni close to his.

"Diablesse, would you still rather die than sing? What do you say now, diva? Will you sing the aria?"

Her weight was well outside the window. If he let go now, she would fall two stories onto her head. She no longer screamed, she begged for her life through broken sobs.

"Yes, yes. Please—yes."

"You will sing it?"

"Yes, I'll sing it. Please!"

"All right then." With one powerful tug, Handel pulled her back through the opening and stood her up on her feet. She collapsed the moment he let go of her arm. Rolli ran to her aid as she sat on the floor muttering through tears. Handel walked back to his place at the harpsichord, talking to himself. He sat down at his seat, then looked back at the woman.

"Are you ready?"

Cuzzoni didn't hear him. She sat in a large pile on the floor, rattling out Italian between sobs. Rolli stood to his feet and raised an accusing finger toward Handel.

"She is not ready, nor am I."

Handel shook his head in disgust.

"I didn't ask if you were ready, nor do I care. You've proven yourself to be unready with amazing regularity. Why should today be any different?"

"You will wait, sir," Rolli demanded.

"So be it. Perhaps we should proceed with something more worthy of our time."

Handel turned to the remainder of the group. An unexpected look of contrition passed across his face.

"No more today! We'll practice again tomorrow."

John Rich, the manager of the theatre, entered from the back of the theatre. Handel spotted him and promptly disregarded the group. He hurried up to Rich while he was still coming down the center aisle.

"I need an advance, from the receipts."

"There are none," said Rich.

"Surely there is something!"

Rich couldn't believe his ears.

"It's insignificant, certainly not what it should be! It belongs to the theatre."

"Whatever you can spare," insisted Handel.

"What's it for?"

"I have need." Handel was urgent.

Rich rubbed his forehead, sighed, then led him to a room at the back of the theatre. As they left the hall, Rolli knelt down near Cuzzoni.

"I'm finished with him," she said. "He's mad! He can find another to sing his aria."

Rolli took her by the arm to help her get her feet beneath her. Most divas were stout, but until then he had falsely assumed that their size was part of the image. As he lifted, he realized that she indeed filled the full immensity of the dress. It required tremendous effort to lift the woman. He tried his best to be polite and not appear to overexert, but failed miserably. Standing her up was a multi-step process. By the time she was fully vertical he was holding his chest and panting. She left him and walked toward her dressing room. When she reached the side curtain, she stopped and turned back to Rolli who was still bent over and breathing heavily.

"You should consider finding someone else to join with. Approach the Academy, before it's too late."

She beckoned him to come close. He readily obeyed. She leaned in and whispered in his ear: "Don't wait too long, or you'll be dragged into the same pit you've been digging for him. You can't fool me, Antonio. You may finally get what you have been hoping for!"

As Rolli watched her disappear behind the curtain, he pulled from his pocket the worn and folded card given to him the tragic night of the fight. He read it again very carefully, then left by the back door.

Thou Shalt Break Them

WHEN PETER LEBLONDE ENTERED THE STUDY, HANDEL was already sitting at his desk, his head in his hands. Peter watched as his master kneaded his head with his fingers. He recognized it as one of the unconscious actions that the desperate do when they begin to lose hope. The language of his master's body reflected the burdens of the soul. Peter had witnessed this same behavior many times over the past months. He had become well acquainted with Handel's movements: how he pressed his thumbs against his cheekbones and wrung his forehead with his fingers. Peter had learned to say things twice, knowing that Handel would probably not hear him the first time. He could come and go without even being noticed by his master. So random were Handel's thoughts that Peter wondered if he was ever fully aware of the goings-on around him.

Peter watched as Handel's hand drifted back to the paper before him. He picked up the quill and continued briefly, then held the pen aloft and read to himself.

"Sir?" interrupted Peter.

Handel's hand went back to the paper. He wrote a few more words, stopped, laid down the pen, then folded the paper over several pound notes. He slid the money and letter carefully into an envelope.

"Sir?" inquired Peter a second time.

"Yes, yes. Please make sure this gets to my mother."

Peter took the envelope and began to leave. Handel's voice stopped him.

"There is a small children's hospital in Halle."

"I know," said Peter.

"I can't remember the name, but it's quite well known. It was restored from a fire gutted church on the north end of the township. See that they get this."

He held up a small purse of money. Peter hesitated before reaching out to take the pouch. Handel did not look up. It seemed to take all the strength he had to hold up the small purse. Peter obediently took it from his hand. "Do you have a note to send with it?"

"No, nothing else."

Handel went back to the papers on his desk without another word. Peter walked out the door and into the hall, where he stopped and turned. His master's hands had returned to his head.

They Shoot Out Their Lips

H USHED VOICES ECHOED DOWN THE LONG HALL. ALTHOUGH he could not discern words, it was clear from the different overlapping pitches of voices that several men were present. The only other sound was the tapping of his hard leather soles on the marble as he walked. The voices grew louder as he drew near the room bearing the title "The Hall of Judges."

At the sound of his approaching footsteps, the voices inside quieted to whispers. The man proceeded toward the open doorway at the end of the hall. He paused to take a deep breath before entering.

At the opposite end of the room was a massive mahogany table. The surface of the table reflected the blue light from the tall, square-paned windows that lined the walls. Behind the table sat seven mature men in heavy black gowns. Sitting on the table in front of the center judge was a leaded glass inkwell and a quill. Out of the visitor's sight but etched into the base of the glass inkwell were the words "Royal Academy of Music."

The whispering stopped when the judges became aware of the dark figure standing motionless in the open doorway. The chief judge nodded; the visitor walked forward through the door toward the table. His footsteps sounded loud and strident in the vacuous silence of the room. This added to his apprehension regarding the task he had been sent to perform. Upon reaching the table he stopped and bowed low to those before him. He took from under his arm a large leather folder and untied the tassels that held it closed. He took from the folder several manuscripts, then slid them across the table to those sitting before him. They each carefully studied the handwritten librettos they were given.

The visitor, Rolli's personal scribe, waited for their verdict. After several minutes, the manuscripts were handed back to him one by one, with the exception of the libretto which lay before the chief judge. The scribe was excused to a small chamber while the panel had a short discussion. Each of the seven jury members made a brief comment, which the scribe could not hear. He was then invited back into the room.

The head judge reached forward, took the quill from the inkwell, and wrote something at the bottom of the libretto before pushing it back across the table to the scribe. The scribe hastily put the libretto into the folder, bowed again, then walked back the way he had entered. As he emerged from the room, there was a subtle change in the voices behind him. Quiet whispers became subdued laughter. The scribe's steps hastened away from the sound as quickly as possible until it faded into oblivion.

The Lincoln's Inn stage was dark with the exception of a broad shaft of warm light spilling onto the hardwood floor from a small room at the rear of the stage. The doors of the theatre were closed for the night. The stagehands had all gone, leaving the theatre still and silent.

From behind a side curtain, a shadow appeared and walked across the front of the stage toward the lighted room. As in the Royal Academy, the sound of footsteps echoed through the empty hall. Again, the shadow paused in the doorway of the open chamber before entering.

Under his arm was the dark silhouette of a large leather folder. He glanced down to a stack of wordbooks piled outside the open door where he stood. The light from within the room streaked across the cover sheet of the top book; it had but one word: *Deidamia*. A voice from within the room spoke.

"Well?"

The man stepped through the doorway. The room was small. Inside was a square desk, on which burned a single candle. Against the side wall of the room was a floor chest with a hinged lid; next to it stood a small wooden chair with no arms. The square chamber was stark with no windows. No ornamentation hung on the walls. There was little air.

On the desk were several more wordbooks—the same as those piled outside the door—along with several loose sheets of paper and a short pile of books, all open and lying on top of one another. The influence of the candle revealed what was already known: it was the same man who had approached the judges. Behind the desk, with his back turned toward the scribe, sat Rolli. It was his voice to which the scribe had responded by entering the room. Rolli inquired a second time:

"Well?"

The scribe was slow to answer. He laid the leather folder on the desk. Slowly, Rolli turned around, his eyes on the scribe. Without looking away from him, he peeled back the cover of the folder and took the top manuscript in his hands.

"All the operas for the upcoming season have already been commissioned" said the scribe in a hushed voice.

"What about next season? They did recognize them."

"Indeed, they were familiar with all your work."

"But accepted none. What reason did they give?"

The scribe glanced down at the libretto in Rolli's hands; Rolli's eyes followed. The judge's writing at the bottom of the page was shadowed. Rolli held up the page to the light. Handwritten were the words, "Rejected: December, 1740." Rolli laid the libretto down on the desk before him; his eyes rose back to the scribe.

"What reason did they give?"

"No reasons in particular. Nothing really. Just a few passing comments, nothing much."

Rolli waited.

The scribe continued with marked uneasiness. "They said they have no need of old librettos—especially failed ones."

"There was more," Rolli surmised.

"Yes," surrendered the scribe. "They said, "If Rolli's librettos can turn London against Handel and the King, God Himself with a cast of saints and angels, couldn't fill the balcony.'"

At this, the scribe stepped back, fully expecting Rolli's fury to be released upon him. But there was nothing.

Rolli waited.

The scribe shuffled back to the desk. He hesitated, loathing what he was about to say. Rolli's stare was unyielding, the scribe succumbed.

"They said that God would certainly judge Handel mercifully, for his generous attempts to carry one so thin. They said that with Handel, you are second-rate; without him, you're nothing."

The muscles in his jaw quivered as Rolli's teeth closed and ground together.

"They mock me," he whispered.

"They call you 'George's word lackey,' 'Handel's goady toady.'"

"They laughed?"

The scribe began wringing his hands. He closed his eyes before speaking, "Yes."

With a tortured groan, Rolli swept the desk with his arm, dashing the manuscripts across the room. The candle hurled against the wall, then fell to the floor, dead. Rolli rose to his feet in the darkness. Words boiled from his lips.

"Handel—*L'Alpestre Fauno*, if I must fail, I will do all in my power to destroy you. Though I should burn in the depths of hell, I will drag you there with me."

The People That Walked in Darkness

HANGING ABOVE THE DOOR OF A SMALL SHOP ON A NAR-
row backstreet off Cheapside was the sign that read, "S.R. COOKE—
Merchant/Druggist." In small lettering in the bottom corner of the large
front window of the same mercantile was another graph which read,
"Barber/Surgeon Guild 1731."

Mr. Samuel R. Cooke was shorter than most men. He made a mod-
est name for himself as a shop owner and part-time surgeon. He made his
living doing the first; he entertained himself by doing the latter.

His store inventory included much of nothing and a little of everything. It had no particular theme—not just groceries, not simply furniture, nor shoes, nor clothing. And yet he had some of each of those items
on hand. He simply sold the things that people wanted and needed, even

if they didn't realize they needed it until they saw it through his store window. He made his living by providing. That was the long and short of it.

There were two rooms in Cooke's store: the front showroom where he displayed his wares and a back room where he kept his things—along with special order items—which were not for public display. It was in this room that he performed the few barber/surgeon duties he was called upon to do. Although the use and appearance of the rooms differed dramatically, they were divided only by a thick fabric drapery hung on two nails above the arched doorway between them.

The showroom was well lit from a large, south-facing window. On clear days, the sunlight would shine through the window into the fore area and brightly illuminate the room. In spite of the room's being crowded with merchandise, it was fairly clean and generally in good order.

The aft room was dark. There were no windows and, therefore, no ambient light. The drapery over the doorway swallowed up any light which might have otherwise seeped into the rear area from the front window. The air behind the curtain was hot and musty. Two oil lamps burned almost incessantly, giving off both the stench of oil and humidity of smoke. The back room was cluttered and filthy. There was no clear path through the debris. The only ventilation came from a small round pipe that protruded from the ceiling. It was half blocked by ceiling plaster. Were it not for the half that remained unimpeded, there would have been no circulation of air at all.

There was a door in the back that was used only by Cooke and those few who came for his surgical services who wanted to remain nameless and faceless.

The narrow doorway between the two rooms separated the light from the dark, the open from the hidden. Quite simply, it was the line between good and evil.

Mr. Cooke sat on a short stool in the back room of his shop with a lamp on a crate next to him. Standing directly before him was a sizable man partially disrobed from the waist down. The fine, white linen shirt that the man wore clung to his wet chest. Under his arms were long, sweat-darkened arcs. Drops of perspiration glowed on his forehead as he clenched his cuff in his teeth and tried his best to be still.

Working by the yellow light of the burning wick, Cooke was performing what most would consider repulsive surgery on the quaking patient. Cooke didn't appear at all disquieted by the baseness of his task—on the contrary, he appeared somewhat gratified. The surgeon was clearly more intent upon the wounds than the wounded. His patient's moans seemed to give him all the more pleasure.

Cooke's lower lip was swollen with quid. When the man standing would jerk away from the pain, Cooke would spit into the tin urn on the floor between his legs. As the man stepped back within reach, Cooke glanced up, smiling.

"You might want to take the edge off of the next pop—it's a good one."

The man scowled at Cooke's apparent enjoyment of the sickening surgery. He pushed something in his mouth and chewed it into pulp. He washed it down with gin while Cooke picked up an ice pick-looking instrument from the floor near the urn and wiped the spittle droplets off it with his sleeve. In one swift move he thrust the sharp pick forward, then pulled away. The man writhed in pain.

"Aaagh, aren't you finished yet—filthy sores."

"The price of promiscuity," said Cooke.

"I even have them in my mouth now!"

"Amazing how hidden indiscretions always ooze their way to the surface."

"Shut up and hurry, wretched beast."

Cooke worked quickly. He did not look away from his work nor did his patient move out of reach. Cooke paused only to wipe the sweat from above his eyes with the back of his hand. While he worked he spoke, his voice taut.

"How many young ladies are now suffering because of your philandering?"

"I don't care. Shut up and mind what you're doing. Be careful that you don't—"

Before the man could finish, Cooke lanced an especially red and swollen boil. The patient groaned as he buckled over in pain. While he was still bent over, Cooke stood from his stool, turned, and laid the instrument on a nearby table. He spoke with his back to the man.

"The pus from your lesions has a foul stench. Is it the infection or the profession?"

The man to began to gingerly tuck in his shirt. The tension in his voice began to ease.

"What do you have against solicitors?"

"Nothing—except what they do!"

The solicitor looked around the dark room.

"So what are you exactly? Surgeon? Shopkeeper? Druggist?"

"A profiteer in people's needs, wants, or miseries—it doesn't matter, it's all the same to me," said Cooke. "I sell whatever people will pay for!"

"You *do* have my opiates?"

"As I said: whatever people will pay for."

"It's the only escape from the wretched pain."

Cooke turned to him with a wicked smile curled on his lips.

"You have to have me, so, you see, I have you. Unless you want your secret known," he taunted. "Who knows? Sometime I may have need of you."

"You're the worst kind of filth," hissed the solicitor.

"Worse than an opium-eating bedpartner with a syphilitic secret?"

As Cooke laughed, the bell at the front door chimed. Cooke quietly moved to the curtain and peered out one of the many holes which he had rubbed threadbare for times such as this. Through the thinned fabric, he could see out—but no one could see in.

The front door slammed shut. He watched the customer approach the counter. He recognized the face immediately.

Rolli rang the service bell repeatedly, then paced back and forth in front of the counter. Cooke stepped back from the cloth, primped himself, then walked out to meet him. The lawyer, numbed into a stupor, sat down in a chair in the back room. When Cooke came through the drape he was instantly amicable. Rolli spoke the moment the shopkeeper appeared.

"Is it finished?"

"It turned out quite extraordinary, perfect dovetailing—a beautiful gift if that's what you intend," remarked Cooke.

"Did I say it was a gift?"

"Well no, sir, I just assumed—"

"Where is it?" Rolli interrupted.

Cooke walked back through the drape into the back room, then returned a few moments later with something wrapped in oiled rags. He laid it on the counter and began to carefully unwrap it. Rolli couldn't wait for him. He eagerly peeled back the last layer to reveal a beautiful hand-crafted olive wood box with a sliding lid. The corners were seamless. The dark but-terflied olive grain veneer on the lid formed a diamond-shaped pattern in the center. The light outer corners were the color of pure amber. On the upper edge of one corner of the lid were the letters G.F.H.

"It's perfect," whispered Rolli through his teeth.

Rolli did not even look up when the bell at the front door chimed again. Cooke glanced up—then looked again when he recognized the pauper couple coming through the door. The woman wore a long hood, which covered her face. Cooke could tell by the way that she carried her-self that she was heavy with child. Cooke became so preoccupied with the woman that the husband at her side went entirely unnoticed. He quite forgot about all three men in his store.

The couple walked to the oak cradle sitting near the front window. Cooke watched as the woman reached up and pulled back the hood. Her face was revealed first. It was radiant. Every feature of it seemed to exude a luminous shine outlined against the soft glow of the window behind her. Last to be revealed was her hair. As the hood fell back she shook free the long waves of auburn hair, dark as coffee. Cooke was spellbound. He lusted after what his eyes beheld. While he stared longingly at her, she and her husband stared longingly at the cradle. She saw him and innocently smiled at him. Cooke's face did not change. Rolli jolted him out of his stare by stashing some money into his hand.

"Here. Wrap it back up."

Cooke's hands obeyed, but his mind was elsewhere. Rolli's eyes fol-lowed Cooke's to the couple near the cradle.

"Shopkeeper!" he demanded with a loud voice. "I'm in a hurry!"

"Excuse me, m'lord. Yes—here you are. Let me get the balance."

Cooke pulled back the drape in the doorway, then disappeared behind it. Before his eyes could adjust to the dark, he walked directly into the solicitor who was standing just behind the curtain. He had obviously been watching the entire episode going on in the adjoining room. Cooke was irritated by the fact that the solicitor had used his spyholes to watch him. He shook his head in disdain as he pulled a drawer from an old chest where he kept a clay jar filled with money. His patient stepped behind him, his voice hushed.

"I saw how you looked at her. It's her, isn't it? The girl you say should have been yours."

The solicitor walked back to the curtain. He watched Rachel throw back her hair and kneel next to the cradle. He felt Cooke come up alongside him.

"Consider a trade. I get rid of him, you satisfy my appetite," the solicitor whispered while watching her through a threadbare spot in the drapery. Rachel turned her face in the direction of the curtain.

"She is quite stunning—for a pauper girl. She's probably never had anyone but him!"

Cooke's hand thrust up into the solicitor's throat. He fiercely pushed him away from the curtain back and against the wall. The man's head thudded as it rebounded off the plaster. Cooke raised up on his toes and stared him in the eye.

"You touch her, you lecherous scab, I'll tear out your lesions with a hound's tooth."

"Listen to me. You want him out of it, give them the cradle," the solicitor choked out.

Cooke's grip on his neck eased just enough for him to continue.

"Do you want her or not?" he stammered.

"What are you saying?"

There was a shout from the front room. Rolli was growing impatient.

"What's going on in there? Hurry up, I'll be late."

Cooke's stare never broke from the man in his grip.

"Tell me."

"Give it to them. Tell them to pay when they can. Leave the rest to me."

Cooke's hand loosened more as he began to understand. His hand finally fell from the solicitor's neck. Cooke walked to the doorway, pulled back the curtain and walked into the light of day. He dropped several coins into Rolli's open hand but he did not look at him. He did not even realize Rolli was gone until the door slammed him back into consciousness. His listless gaze shifted over to Jonathon and Rachel. She looked at him and smiled. The curtain moved ever so slightly behind him.

The Ears of the Deaf

ABOVE THE STREET HUNG THE GRAY, MOLTED SKIN OF COAL and wood smoke, holding in both soot and sound. Every fireplace in London bellowed the black stuff into the air. The mixture of particulate haze and fog was so stifling that people would scarcely dare go outdoors without a handkerchief held to their mouths to filter out the impurities. Nearly all the lights in London were extinguished early.

In the late hours of the cold December night, a faint glow came from the window of 25 Brook Street. Handel could not sleep. His thoughts careened back and forth between desperation and *Deidamia*. He fiercely needed it to be a success. He sat at his desk working until his eyes could no longer focus on the paper before him. Several times he had to pick up the quill, which fell from his ink-stained fingers during brief blackouts. He had pushed himself to utter and complete exhaustion, until the very smallest of efforts was painful. Holding a pen, turning a page—these required all the will he could muster. He rebuked himself for his weakness. When he no longer had the strength to hold his eyelids open, he determined to retreat to bed but not without a severe scolding from himself first.

It was an agonizing effort to rise to his feet and carry himself to his bedchamber. His eyes would not open; he walked from memory. It seemed to him to take several minutes to get to his destination. When he arrived in his room, he never thought to undress; he simply fell on his bed and pulled a blanket over himself. He slept poorly for several minutes before his mind took away any desire to surrender to sleep. Even though his body could go no further, his mind would not rest. Like a noisy tenant next door, it chased sleep away.

At first he tried to disregard and ignore it, but the dull pricks of doubt were like distant gunshots in the street: not loud, but enough to create imaginings of fear. He wished he could clear his mind and find sanctuary in peaceful sleep, but he had trained himself not to give way to his enemies. Tonight his enemy was fatigue. He attacked it with what little energy he had left. That had always been his answer to adversity: assault it with every possible weapon he could muster. If failure were the foe, he would attack the source of his anxiety and wrestle it until the foe became more tired than he. He knew in the depths of his soul that his strongest offense was simply to outlast anything or anyone who crossed him. For years he perfected the art of beating his adversity into submission.

Sleep was no different. It was a necessary evil, which he endured but never embraced. He viewed it as a weakness of body and, frankly, a damned waste of time. He had no patience for those who prized sleep. He considered them doleful and lacking gumption. He did not trust sleep because it rendered him defenseless and vulnerable. When his body cried out for it, he would chastise himself for his weakness and create some mild discomfort so that he could not sleep too comfortably or too long.

One thought crossed his mind before he finally did doze off: "I don't have time for this."

Within the hour he was stirring in restless delirium. He was never fully awake yet never fully asleep. He tossed in his bed, becoming more and more angry at the nocturnal purgatory he was caught in. His thoughts were of injustice and betrayal—the foulest of sleep partners. The longer he lay, the more frustration he felt.

Finally, when he could endure no more of the timeless void between sleep and semiconsciousness, he got up to work.

In the blackest hours of night he sat in his cold study, working under the influence of a small candle. Again, as so many times before, he questioned every creative decision he had made in the score. He had fought with *Deidamia* for several weeks. On every page there were musical elements—sometimes entire bars—scratched out and rewritten. More often than not, that same bar would be recorrected to its original scoring.

For hours he sat shivering in the night, rewriting this, reworking that. Beneath the guise of trying to give London what it wanted, he was questioning himself. He could not and would not accept the possibility that he was, in fact, doubting his own ability.

The hours passed slowly. Even though he realized with the rest of the world that the dawn must surely come, it seemed everlastingly harsh in its waiting. And yet, the moment his window began to gray with light, he felt a surge of strength from having conquered the night. He worked through the morning hours with haste. He tried to second-guess what would appeal to the opera-going public.

Through the past weeks, he had gone to every form of musical entertainment he could find in the city—not because he felt there were lessons to be learned, but to see what the audience was responding to. Truth was, there was frighteningly little which was successful. London had grown tired of opera and the Italians. They wanted something of their own. The *Beggar's Opera*, which satirized Handel's work more than any, was the only musical medium that was followed with any enthusiasm. It was an irreverent romp, which poked fun at the very heart of serious opera. It was the poor man's opera, and what damage it didn't do in pulling audiences away, it did in belittling the ostentatiousness of formal opera. The game of satire was closed to him for he was the brunt of it.

In his efforts to outguess the whims of London, he rewrote several parts of *Deidamia* only to find that when he looked at it again, it lacked the precision and expertise he had worked for years to develop. He scribbled out the changes he made on one piece the night before and shouted in exasperation, "Replace the sixteenth-note scales with something singable? Aye—why not take the singing out all together? Perhaps something with a beat...something which shall hit London right on the drum of the ear."

Peter LeBlonde entered the study. He had heard Handel's frustrated shouts from the hall. He came in quietly, not wishing to disturb him. He stopped just inside the door and watched his master in silence.

Peter knew his place. His was a life of service. He was a gentle man of sound understanding. Although he was a servant, his mannerisms and language were not coarse, but trained and refined. Through the years he had come to know his master: Handel, the man. He knew well the successful Handel, the man who had written scores of operas in just the past few years alone. He knew the Handel of renown, the Handel of *Rinaldo*.

But the Handel he looked upon now was a man unknown to him. The proud Handel of years before was gone. This was a man nearly broken yet still large to view, simultaneously demanding both pity and veneration. He spoke while going about his chores in an attempt to lift his master's spirits.

"What great notes fall from the pen today, sir?"

"Changes, rewrites, transposing this and that, and all with less than a week before performance." Handel never looked up from his work. At length he stood and walked to the harpsichord. He spread several sheets of handwritten music before him.

"Peter, tell me what you think of this."

He began to play a rewritten aria, which he had labored with all morning. He lifted his eyes to Peter expectantly.

"So, what do you say?"

"Master, you know my ear is not trained."

Handel played louder.

"Is it pleasing to you?"

"All your work pleases me."

"But this work particularly: is it lesser than previous efforts? What do you say?"

"I don't dare say. I am not qualified to say, sir."

"Certainly you can judge."

"I am no judge. I regret that I do not know."

Handel slammed his fists down on the keys.

"All London knows. I can go out on the street and get an earful of opinions. Now I ask and cannot get one. I can't keep up with it all. First A is trump, now D."

Peter stood in humble silence.

"Speak, man! What do you think?" Handel shouted.

Peter considered long. He did not speak until he was sure he knew the words to express what his heart felt. He responded in a quiet voice, each word distinct and clear.

"It is a triumph, m'lord, but I fear that few shall hear it. The Thames runs deep, but the surface is frozen over with ice. So it is with London."

The two stared at each other for a long time. Handel looked back regretfully at the music before him. Peter knew that what he had said pierced deep into Handel's heart, but it would have been more painful had he been patronizing. Peter, who moments before had spoken as a confidant, once again assumed the role of servant.

"I'll get you some tea, sir."

Peter left the room to retrieve a tray of tea, which he had left on a small sitting table in the hall. His footsteps seemed to awaken Handel from his reverie. He picked up a sheet of music from the harpsichord and held it close to his face. As Peter reentered the room he heard Handel speak to himself.

"London, you adore, then despise, with but a breath between the two."

Peter put the tray on a table and turned in time to see Handel lay the music down. Handel's hand slowly raised; his eyes closed. Almost imperceptibly, his hand began to move as if leading an imaginary orchestra. The rhythmic movements continued for almost a minute. Then, suddenly, his hand dropped to his side. Lines of worry began to crease on Handel's wide forehead. Peter stepped forward.

"Here you are. Some hot tea should suit you nicely."

Handel opened his eyes. Peter poured water from the steaming pot. Handel spoke in quiet introspect.

"We made quite a noise for a time, didn't we."

"You did indeed, sir."

"I should be content to have ever had such times." Handel paused for some time, then continued. "Perhaps I sin in my desire. Perhaps God frowns on my ambitions."

Peter stepped close to Handel and handed him a hot cup. Handel looked at him as he took the cup from his hand.

"From my infirmities, I learn patience; from adversity, diligence. From failure—?"

He considered a moment, then spoke with firm resolve.

"From failure, I learn nothing. I will not be tutored by failure."

Peter walked back around the desk. He picked up the urn and began to pour another cup very slowly so his eyes would be busy while he asked the question that lingered in his mind.

"Do you believe God wills it?"

Handel did not react as Peter had feared. There were times in the past when Handel viewed Peter's questions as insubordinate. Peter had paid severely for it in chastisement. He expected nothing less today. But, instead, Handel was calm, thoughtful. He stared into the swirls of steam rising from the cup he held tight in his hand.

"When I was a boy, my father forbade me from playing. He regarded civil law a far greater pursuit than music. 'Though music may be a fine amusement, as an occupation it has little dignity, as having for its object nothing better than mere pleasure,' he would say. Thus, he would not allow any musical furniture in the house. We obeyed. My mother and I moved the clavichord from the house to the hayloft. Yes, we deceived him. But you must understand, it was not resentment. I was afraid—afraid that if I turned my back on the music, it would go away."

Handel stared at his hands.

"Oh the joy of those days, playing for hours while my mother worked in the house and yard. When my father would leave, I would practice. Nothing short of cutting off my fingers could have prevented it. Mother would do my chores so my father would never suspect otherwise. When she saw his carriage coming, she would hurry to the front door and slam it several times to alert me. She would stall my father until I could climb down from the attic and busy myself, but it wasn't enough.

"At night, when I knew he was asleep, I'd sneak to the hayloft with a small candle in hand. I'd climb up to the attic and pull away the sheets from the keys. Of course, I couldn't play, for fear of waking him. So gently, without making a sound, I'd lay my hands on the keys—to touch them, feel them. It was quiet at first, then, little by little, music would come into my mind, flowing forth like a mountain spring. Music. Music

I'd never heard before. Like dew it came from some unseen source and yet undeniably here," he lifted his hands to his heart.

"A passion, a gift. It seemed as though touching the keys completed a link between heaven and earth."

Peter watched as Handel held out his hands and laid them on the keys of the harpsichord. As they touched the ivory, Peter imagined music. At first it was distant—but surely, he was certain it was heavenly music that filled his soul. It was not the impressive scales and flowery lines of opera, but a sweet melody of perfect clarity. It seemed to reach deep within him, lifting him from out of the temporal and into a higher place. It was as though he was somehow blessed with the vicarious hearing of what was in Handel's mind. The melody was simultaneously sad and transcending. It was music he had never heard before. This was not the music of the world—this was God's music. He whispered reverently.

"Do you still hear it?"

Handel's eyes opened. He lifted his hands from the keys. The music in Peter's mind faded as Handel spoke.

"I have spent an entire life working—developing every idea, every possibility—for one reason: to find my music—what I love."

"Master, turn back to the God who gave you that love."

Handel looked at Peter then at the harpsichord. When he spoke, his voice sounded harsh.

"We need more practice, more work. We won't be ready for opening night. We must double the rehearsals."

Handel picked up the score before him and returned to his work. Peter left the room. He pulled the door closed behind him.

When he heard it close, Handel gazed longingly at the keys. He reached forward, resting his fingers on the keys. He waited in silence for something to happen—but nothing. Frustrated, he pushed down hard. The noise shattered the quiet. Downstairs, Peter turned up his ear to hear the overture from *Deidamia* echoing through the house. It was nothing like the music he had heard in his mind a short time before.

The Brightness of Thy Rising

CHARLES JENNENS SAT AT HIS DESK WRITING ON THE PAGES of paper laid before him. The Bible on the desk was open to a well-worn and marked page. He reached for the Bible and looked at the page in the book of Isaiah, following down each verse with his quill. The pen stopped at the eleventh verse of the fortieth chapter: "He shall feed his flock like a shepherd, and gather the young ones in His arms; and gently lead those who are with young."

He thought long before putting his finger in the Bible to hold the page while thumbing through the thin onion pages to another passage. His turning finally stopped in Matthew, chapter eleven.

"Come unto me all ye that labour and are heavy laden and I will give you rest. Take my yoke upon you and learn of me; for I am meek and lowly in heart: and ye shall find rest unto your souls. For my yoke is easy, and my burden is light."

He flipped back and forth between the two references, pausing each time to reread the marked verses. He began to write on the page before him. There was a loud knock at the manor door. As he wrote, he heard footsteps in the entry hall. The lock in the front door clicked open, and he recognized the voice of his butler.

"Can I help you, sir?"

"Is this Mr. Jennens's place—Charles Jennens?"

"Yes."

"Would you tell 'im 'is handbill has been printed and posted?"

"I'll see that he gets the message, thank you."

"His critics will have some interestin' readin' tonight, I'll bet."

"Yes."

"You know, he could save on printin' bills if he'd take odds with some lesser-known writer!"

"His motive was not to save money."

"Well it's 'is money, he can do with it what he wants...but rewrite Shakespeare?"

"If it pleases him."

"It sure don't please anyone else!"

The messenger began to laugh. If no one else was amused by his commentary, at least he was.

At this, Jennens got up from his place in the study and opened the door to the entry. When the messenger saw him, he excused himself.

"M'lord—I was just leavin'. Good day!"

While Jennens and his servant watched the messenger tail away down the street, they spoke.

"You heard, sir?"

"Yes. It will be interesting to see what comes of it. I've been quiet long enough."

"How do you hope it will be received?"

"Objectively—that is all I hope for."

"I'm sure that some will have something to say about it. Do you believe there will be any retaliation?"

"Indeed. Addison and Steele will sputter like stuck fish. They dislike me as much as they dislike Handel."

"Handel, sir?"

"They've never liked him. They don't like having a King with an accent or his musical kraut."

Jennens walked back into his study. The servant followed him as far as the door.

"You are faithful to him, sir?"

"I'm certain my political future will suffer for it, but I have an errand for him. I've been working on a libretto which I intend to give him—a scripture book of sorts."

Jennens sat down at his desk and picked up the Bible.

"You put great value on this, sir," observed the servant.

There was no response. Jennens's mind was elsewhere. The servant closed the door.

He Hid Not His Face

ANOTHER REHEARSAL, ANOTHER DISAPPOINTMENT. HANDEL
walked home through the cold street muttering to himself. It was an
amusing habit that everyone was aware of but him. He would talk to himself openly on occasion, voicing his derision of a weak performance days
after the event had transpired.

Tonight, he reviewed in his mind the rehearsal that had just ended.
He despised the libretto, but it was too late to change librettists. He was
unsure of his music, but he dared not question himself. He needed a new
soprano, but none was available. He hated Cuzzoni; she had left him
midway through rehearsals. The only one who had power to hold her to
her contract was Rolli, but he released her from it on account of
Handel's threat to end her life. He knew the incident at the window was

a terrible mistake. He could have dreamed about her plummeting to the ground a thousand times without external consequence, but, instead, he had acted out the crime the first time it entered his mind. No one liked the diva Cuzzoni, but his temper had gotten the best of him. His actions cost him the trust of his cast and orchestra; worse yet, he had lost their respect. Now, the more he demanded, the more tentative they became. Rather than performing with confidence and boldness, they played and sang as if fearful of making a mistake. Like the abused child who dares not speak for fear of the whip, their music was apathetic. He had emasculated them, and in the process he had seriously jeopardized his chance for success. The more tentative they were, the harder he bore down on them. He exploded into a rage at nearly every rehearsal. So preoccupied was he with the possibility of failure that he lashed out at the very people who could help him. He hid thoughts of inadequacy behind actions of obstinacy.

As he walked home from rehearsal, he was rewriting, editing, talking himself through every stanza of a score and questioning every creative decision once again. If there were a way to improve upon it, he would run it through his consciousness enough times to come to the answer. In days past he could easily recognize the right answer when it came to him. Now, his mind was only a maze of questions with no clear beginning or end.

No piece concerned him more than the soprano aria near the end of Act II. It was in that aria that the leading lady proclaimed her undying love for her soon-to-be husband. More than any other piece, he wanted it to be right. As much as he despised her, Cuzzoni stirred in him a deep longing for her elegant voice—which fit the piece so well. Now he was not even certain who would be singing it, but he was certain it would need to be simplified. He could see in his mind the score, and hear the music in his ear. He rambled as he walked.

"Finish the duet in F major. Pick up with C dominant. No! B-flat sub-dominant, pick up at bar five."

He stopped mid-thought. He urgently glanced around him for a street sign. He was still several minutes from home, but he wanted to hear it now. He tried to think of the closest church that would have an organ, but he had gone home a different way and was not so familiar with the surroundings. As he thought of somewhere close that might have an instrument, his eye happened to notice a lamp just going dark in a second-story townhouse window across the street. He ran across the cobbles and up the short walk to the porch and began pounding on the door.

"Open up, please! Open the door. Come sir, I know you are not asleep, I saw your lamp. Open, please."

He stepped back from the door to see if the lamp had been retrimmed. The window glowed. With renewed vigor, he began pounding again.

"Open up."

The lock turned. The moment the lock clicked open, Handel fell through the door, almost knocking down the man of the house, who was in his bedclothes. The man's bewildered wife looked on from the staircase.

"Do you have an instrument—a clavichord perhaps? Anything? Where? You must. I just need a moment. Hurry, man."

Befuddled, the man pointed toward a dark doorway of an adjoining room. Handel hurried through the portal and into the darkness. The woman pointed in the direction Handel disappeared.

"Was that...?"

The man nodded affirmatively as music began in the next room. The man looked back at his wife standing stupefied on the stair. He listened for a moment, then shrugged his shoulders and started back to bed.

"Aren't you going to make sure he leaves?" she asked.

"Why? I somehow think we'll know of his whereabouts."

He climbed past her, over the top stair and back to the bedroom. She followed in resigned disbelief.

They lay in bed for several minutes, listening to the music echoing through the quiet house. Finally, he closed his eyes. He fell asleep first; the wife listened as her companion's breathing became long and slow. She looked at her husband lying next to her. A faint smile was on his lips. In that smile, she saw the handsome young man she had fallen in love with years before: his strong, pronounced chin, his deep-set eyes. She took his hand in hers. She listened a little longer, then turned on her side and closed her eyes.

"I suppose it can't hurt anything," she said before nodding off.

Even for Thine Enemies

In the parlour fireplace, the flames burned low. Oil lamps glowed in the corners of the room, giving off some light but not enough to fill the shadowed areas. On the sofa in the middle of the room sat the Prince with Madame Hervey. Addison and Steele sat opposite them in two large, overstuffed chairs. Another man stood near the hearth, his face to the dying fire.

"We may, at long last, finally see the end of him," said Hervey, smiling.

"We should be ashamed—ruining a man's life simply to humiliate another," the Prince said with his head down. There was a noticeable tone of regret in his words. A concerned look crossed Steele's face as he glanced first at Addison, then at the Madame. She also felt the twinge of

Frederick's faintheartedness. She did not allow his comment to sit longer than was absolutely necessary. She laid her hand on his arm as she spoke; the Prince's eyes rose to meet hers.

"The toll is considerably heavier when the prize is the King. Are you having reservations?" she asked, a slight edge of sarcasm in her voice. The Prince thought briefly before answering.

"On the contrary, I said we should be ashamed!" affirmed the Prince. He looked from face to face for approval. No one disappointed. He leaned forward in anticipation.

"Now, what is our plan?"

"I've planned an irresistible party to conflict with opening night, and I've invited all the usual opera-going nobility," said Hervey, rising from her seat and walking to the person standing near the dying fire.

"Ahh, but you are so deviously suave," remarked Addison.

Madame Hervey rewarded his observation with another revelation, "The truly nasty business falls to our darling Antonio."

The Madame leaned in from behind and took the man's earlobe in her teeth. She bit him softly before sliding her teeth off his skin and walking back to her place on the sofa. The shadow standing at the hearth turned to face the others. The flickering light from flaming wicks shone on the near side of Rolli's face as he addressed the others in the room.

"I've employed a certain gentleman. I don't believe he will disappoint. He has a sinister way of making himself very unwelcome."

The Prince's face tightened. Steel and Addison also seemed surprised at Rolli's announcement.

"What sort of man is this?" queried the Prince.

"I believe ruffian would be the term best suiting him," answered Rolli.

"A ruffian," exhaled the Prince..

"He will make things quite unpleasant for *Il proteus alpino* and his opera. I also have some personal touches planned."

"Is all that really necessary?' asked the Prince. "It seems so malicious. Our intent was simply to use him; we don't want to injure him."

"I do!" shot back Rolli. He put aside all illusion of decorum. "I want him to feel every stinging hot prick of failure. Your business is with the King; mine is with Handel."

When the prince turned away, the Madame shot a severe glance at Rolli to remind him where he was and to whom he was speaking. He understood, but his tone and tenor did not alter. The Madame teased him in an effort to relieve tension.

"Ironic really. If he fails, you fail!"

"You climbed aboard a sinking ship," added Steele.

"It didn't have to be," snarled Rolli. "When I joined him he was incomparable! We all know that no talent equals his. But he would rather expose the mediocrity of my libretto than allow me to share in his eminence. Now I am blamed for his failure!"

Rolli avoided eye contact with the Madame. After a brief pause, he continued. "But when the end comes, I will be the one left standing. My name will be spoken in the same breath as his. He will make me immortal."

"You're quite certain of that?" asked Steele.

"I have a gift for him, a lovely gift." Rolli smiled. "Once *Deidamia* fails, what little life he has left in him will fail also. Handel will fade as a dried leaf plucked from the vine. Shortly after the funeral, they'll search through his personal artifacts for that which gave his life meaning— music, memoirs, letters. Instead they will find something far more precious: an elegant box."

Rolli spoke as a demon. His voice seemed to bleed from his hollow throat like the last whisper of a dying man. The Prince felt his skin bristle at the sinister sound. Rolli went on, "'What a fine piece of craftsmanship,' they will say. 'Surely he must have held this piece in highest esteem—his most valued possession.' How will they know the piece belonged to him? I've made certain there will be no doubt. It will speak to them as if it were his own voice crying from the grave." Rolli turned his face back to the glow of the red embers. "Carefully they will slide off the lid of the box to find the master's treasure," he said. "He will do far more for me in death than he ever could alive. He will make me immortal."

The room was silent. Prince Frederick was first to break the dark spell.

"He must feel the end coming!" he said. Rolli was quick to respond.

"Like a noose around his neck. He's just not sure whose hand is holding the rope."

Like a Refiner's Fire

THE DAY HAD BEEN GLOOMY. WHATEVER EVIDENCE THAT
the sun had actually risen somewhere that day had passed hours before.
Night fell hard on the earth as if pushed down and slammed against the
ground, holding the world in utter blackness. There is darkness that hides
and darkness that blinds; this was the latter, brought on by both the lack
of moonlight and the cold.

London was locked in the deep freeze of the coldest winter in memory. The Thames was frozen over and littered with boats and ferries listing in the ice pack. It seemed a great, ghostly white highway stretching
through the bottoms of London.

No one dared go near the edge as there had been talk of unfortunate
sailors and docksmen who had slipped and fallen through the frozen

crust. Their bloated bodies were purged and spit up through cracks in the ice days later, their eyes open, the terror of death frozen on their faces.

The wind swept down the full reach of the Thames, becoming colder and more biting with each bend in the river. By the time it reached the streets of London, the chill in the wind was deceptively bitter. Nothing could withstand the icy arms of the night.

The homeless without shelter froze in their sleep on the street. They would dream that their lives were scraped and scratched away from them by cold, ashen fingernails, and, try though they may to wake up, the nightmare could only fade to complete blackness. Days would usually pass before the frozen corpses were dragged away to be piled up until the ground would thaw enough to dig graves.

The streets of London were silent. What little light that did seep from the small, frosted windows of taverns and inns did not fall far from the window. Any light in the street was swallowed up by the cold. Only those street lamps that stood in the protection of a nearby building had any chance of holding a flame.

Clouds of steam rose from open sewer grates and coal cellars. Cancerous smoke from countless chimneys fell downward to the street, unable to pierce and escape the blanket of cold.

No one could remember a winter such as this. No one ventured out unless it was absolutely necessary—except one man.

He moved through the streets randomly, stopping for a moment here and there at announcement posts and public sign boards. Each brief stop was followed by a series of pounding sounds. He would then move with haste a short distance to another post where he would repeat the same action. John Rich, the Lincoln's Inn manager, had no other thought than to finish this nasty job and get indoors. Occasionally, a hustling pedestrian would pass by and wonder what cause or fear urged him forward with his loathsome task, but no one cared enough to stop or ask. He was just there, and tomorrow's light would reveal his cause.

He continued up the street, his feet crunching through the crusted snow until, finally, only the sound of occasional pounding could be heard through the fog and darkness. In his wake were several playbills nailed on every available post and notice board. A closer look at the posted announcement revealed the valuable information that warranted a sacrifice such as being out on a night like this. The message was simple; it read:

"*Deidamia*: An opera by George Frederic Handel to be performed January 10 at Lincoln's Inn Theatre."

One of the playbills fluttered in the wind on the most visible posting board in the street. Whenever something new appeared on this board, it was common for a considerable group of readers to encircle the post through most of the following morning. It was the one place that you could count on your message being read. Rich was especially careful to make sure that the playbill posted there was secured on the nail.

Suddenly, out of nowhere, a small, cold-reddened hand ripped the playbill from its nail. In the shadow of the post stood a small boy. His dirty fingers folded around the paper. He stepped from behind the post into the blue glow from the snow and smiled. The Packrat jammed the playbill into his coat pocket already bursting with other playbills. He looked around anxiously to see if anyone was watching—nothing, no one.

With a shake of his head and a laugh, the boy was off again, pulling down playbills wherever he could spot them. The Packrat moved spryly, not seeming to mind the cold. He went about his mischief with a skip and a smile. The playbills, posted with such effort, were torn away with reckless abandon. The boy seemed especially gratified when the bills tore away from the post and didn't just pull off the nail. It was a game, which he delighted in winning.

In the middle of his romp, the Packrat stopped in his tracks. He peered around the streetscape. His eyelids tightened into slits of blue that pierced the veil of fog that masked the street. He stood motionless for several seconds. When he broke from his stance, he did so without breaking an ice crystal beneath him. Peter stole swiftly into the deep shadow of a nearby building. Crouching down under the brick sill of a low window, he disappeared into the darkness.

The Packrat watched. A minute passed. He glanced around the street as he waited. That's when he saw it: a fallen playbill lying in the snow below the post where he last stood. In his haste, it had somehow dropped from his pocket without his noticing. It lay upside down in the snow; only a torn corner fluttering in the breeze would give it away. His first thought was to leap and rescue the paper back into his pocket. His fingers twitched—but it was too late. Someone was coming.

At first it seemed only a phantom of darkness against a gray palette of fog, but little by little, the outline of the image began to sharpen as the mist thinned around it. The boy knew he was hidden from the approaching phantom, yet there was something disturbing about this intruder that rendered him breathless. He didn't dare move. For the first time that night, he felt cold.

With each step, the phantom grew in stature and size. The Packrat cowered backward into the alcove as the image continued straight toward him. Just as Peter knew he must exhale, a man appeared out of the fog not thirty steps from him. Vapor streamed out of the boy's nostrils and into the open air. Again, he wanted to reach out and pull it back, but he kept still.

The man was large, formidable. There was a heaviness about him. He walked with his head lowered, his back arched as if somehow burdened. His steps betrayed a hitch, perhaps a paralytic tic in the hip.

Peter knew he could outrun the stranger if the need arose.

The man kept coming. His gloved fist was wrapped around the brass head of a walking cane. The Packrat measured it in his mind so he would know how far to stay from the man.

The stranger had not looked up. Peter began to hear a muttering voice. He looked around for someone else who might have stumbled out of a pub door, but the sidewalks were empty. His eyes moved back to the man in the street. He could barely discern the words through the thin night air:

"We need more time. They want too much. More rehearsals—more time. We have no more time."

The boy was so intent on trying to hear the words that when the stranger stopped it startled him. He stood not ten feet from the sill under which the Packrat was wedged. Peter's foot accidentally slipped against the ice sheeted wall.

Scrape.

Peter watched as the stranger's head tilted in his direction. Soft blue light wrapped around the man's cheek. The boy saw his half-lit face. His

eyelids widened; nothing else moved. He kept absolutely silent. The stillness was broken only by the bark of a dog several streets away.

The man's eyes did not shift from the place where the boy sat
hunched in the shadows. The Packrat squinted, not wanting the whites of
his eyes to be seen. But he didn't look away; there was something faintly
familiar about the man. His mind reached to remember, but nothing
came. He nervously moved his fingers, which were buried deep in his
pocket. His fingers touched a metal piece at the bottom of the pocket of
his trousers. The cold of the metal sent a sudden chill up his back, but he
remained motionless. The dog barked again.

Slowly the man turned his head downward. Until that moment, the
boy had forgotten about the lost playbill.

The man stared at the ground. With great effort, the man reached
down and grasped the fluttering corner and pulled the paper from the
snow. A heavy sigh of steam rose from the man's mouth as he pushed the
playbill back on the shining nail. The boy breathed aloud as he wondered
why anyone would care about some fallen playbill.

Again, the man looked into the darkness that hid Peter. The Packrat
felt as though his eyes were upon him even though he knew the man's
gaze could not penetrate the darkness. A moment later, the man was gone.
He walked away, just as he had come. He disappeared slowly into the fog
until the phantom was no more.

Peter stepped from his hiding place and back into the street. He
walked to the post and stared at the large footprints in the snow. He
placed his cracked leather shoe inside the imprint; it was not quite half.
The boy turned in the direction of the stranger and wondered, and again
he touched the piece of metal deep in his pocket. He shrugged as he
looked up at the playbill flitting in the wind. He tore it from the nail,
held it high, and shouted.

"Try to rob a robber? Ha!"

The boy laughed as he ran off down the street into the cold night.

At that same moment, a shadow crossed the *Deidamia* set on the
Lincoln's Inn stage. Without warning, a hand with a sharpened letter
opener began slashing at the canvas facades. Huge gashes were hewn in

the painted backdrops. Props were thrown wildly. Long sections were ripped from music scores. Sheets of paper covered with music were shredded and hurled across the stage. Costumes were slashed and torn.

The menacing shadow ravaged through the orchestra pit, throwing down music stands. Like a possessed demon, the shadow moved, leaving havoc in his wake. When he reached the harpsichord, he picked up the stool and crashed it down on the keys sending splinters of wood into the air. The shadow stood for a moment, panting. He reached to his neck to straighten his cravat, then disappeared behind the curtain.

Be Not Afraid

THE SMALL WINDOW OF THE TAVERN WAS NEARLY FROSTED over. The corners and edges were white and opaque. In the middle was a small spot still barely clear enough to see through. The Packrat peered through the small hole into the dark, smoky tavern. His breath fogged the glass, obscuring the one section he could see through. He stepped back from the window and kicked the snow, frustrated at his stupidity in getting too close. He rolled his eyes to heaven before taking a deep breath and striding confidently through the door.

The wall of smoke nearly pushed him back out the door he had entered. He swallowed back a cough as he waited a moment to allow his eyes time to adjust to the darkness. He thought it was dark outside, but in here was no better. He began to move around the room, pausing to check each table's occupants. He boldly looked into the faces of each person he passed, searching for the one he sought. He noticed that many of the customers did not want their faces to be seen. They would lean into the darkness or cover their faces with their hands if they did not want to be recognized. Peter thought it quite humorous that oldsters, by nature, acted so guilty. To torment them, he would sometimes stare until they either revealed themselves or yelled at him to move along. After one such scolding, the owner of the establishment started his way, but Peter quickly moved along.

He glanced back several times to make sure he knew his way back to the door. He didn't like being this close to so many oldsters. He memorized his path to the entrance in case he needed a quick escape.

For the most part, he had no use for grown-ups or their world. What he did savor were their smells: tobacco, ale, money, and opportunity. As he passed each table, he could feel their eyes follow him. He was sure they hadn't seen a boy so young in the tavern before. He tried to act as though he belonged, but it was futile. He stood out like the moon in the midnight sky.

His face was flushed. His eyes were keenly alert, detecting the nervous twitch of every card-holding finger—a talent acquired from countless nights on the street.

He measured each man he passed. He would mentally categorize them according to what kind of threat he thought they might pose. Some were drunk; others were handicapped with false or wooden limbs. These did not worry him. Some were strong; others had callused and dirty hands. These he needed to stay clear of. He knew that those who barked would not leave their chairs, while those who were silent would.

What he watched the closest, however, was their eyes. He was most careful of those with black, shadowed eyes—those who stared directly back into his eyes. These eyes made him shudder. He knew that they had not come to that color by chance.

He continued past the huge stone fireplace wherein a small fire burned. He thought to stop and warm his hands, then noticed that there was little if any heat coming from it. As he looked up from the embers, he realized that he had now moved into another room, which was darker than the first. The little light there was from lamps seemed to die before it could reach into the void where he now walked. He bumped into someone, but he dared not look. He spun away before the offended had time to react.

He stepped into a corner near where a small candle was burning low. As he stood in silence, the walls and the smoke seemed to close in around him. He felt the darkness of this room begin to get the better of him. This was not like the darkness outside—that was God's darkness. This was different. This was man's darkness, and it terrified him. He tried to spot the door, but he had come too far into the room. It was lost behind bodies and smoke. He told himself not to panic as he began making his way back to the fireplace—that was the first leg of his escape. Fear seized him. As he carelessly hurried around chairs, tables, and bodies, a strong hand caught him by the arm and pulled him down. He landed in a chair that he hadn't even seen.

Across a small square butcher block table sat a man, his face in the shadows. A voice spoke.

"Bloody cold out. Worst winter ever. Snow makes travel nasty, 'specially to the theatre," the voice laughed a sinister laugh, which gave Peter goose bumps. Wafts of smoke blew from shadowed lips into the Packrat's face. The man leaned back in his chair and spoke in a hushed whisper so only the Packrat could hear.

"Your mischief, along with a little ruckus on openin' night, and I'm afraid it'll cost poor Mr. Handel dearly."

"Handel?" Peter asked, forgetting where he was.

The voice enunciated each word, "George Frederic Handel."

"Never met 'im," quipped the boy.

The man's face leaned from the shadows into the dim light and close to Peter's. The boy recoiled at the sight of him. The light raking the man's face revealed deep pock marks. He bore a long thin scar above his left eye. His eyes were black.

Peter did not like being this close to one he trusted so little. He turned away, as if looking around the room. The man took hold of Peter's collar and pulled his ear close to his mouth.

"Of course you 'aven't met him! But somebody 'as, and they don't like 'im."

"What's he done?"

"No matter, but the somebody's willin' to pay to 'ave him gone."

"Dead?" asked Peter as indifferently as he could sound.

"For some there's worse 'an dead: ignored, forgotten."

The man laughed again. It made the hair on Peter's neck stand on end. The man let go of the Packrat and settled back into his chair. "Dead too, perhaps, but that ain't my job."

"It's all the same to me—long as I get mine," Peter popped off in a haughty tone.

The ruffian grabbed the Packrat again, this time pulling him over the table to his face. Peter felt his feet leave the ground.

"Remember that, mind you. Don't go gettin' a conscience."

When the ruffian released his grip, the boy's feet landed flat on the floor with a slap. Several heads jerked around at the sound. Eyes pierced the darkness in their direction. A flash of misgiving swept over the man's face as he glanced around the room self-consciously. Peter saw this. He knew from experience that the most callused of criminals would often bristle at an offense to a child. Peter knew that even the vile belly of a tavern could mean his salvation if the patrons thought this man was taking advantage of him. Hard men will forgive a murderer long before they will condone the abuse of a child. It was not unusual for those who are most critical of another's abuse to be guilty of the same crime. Peter realized that control of the situation had shifted to him—if he played his hand right. He began emptying his pocketfuls of playbills onto the table. Nervously, the man pulled the playbills under his arm.

"Fool! Not 'ere!"

"You said to bring proof," said the Packrat.

The ruffian calmed himself.

"Ahhh—that's right. Yes, I do remember now."

He reached in his pocket and held out his filthy hand to Peter. He dropped several coins into the boy's small hand.

"I'm givin' ya' extra to finish the job—where they won't be found." One more belated coin fell from his hand.

The Packrat stuffed the playbills back in his pockets, then put out his hand for more money. The ruffian looked confused as Peter held up the last several playbills in the other hand.

"I am most clumsy...'twould be a shame to drop these 'ere," the boy whispered.

The man looked sideways at Peter. At length he pulled more coins from his pocket. As the boy reached for them, the man grabbed Peter's hand in a viselike grip.

"Watch yourself, rodent," he warned.

The man opened the boy's hand with his powerful fingers and laid the coins in his palm. The Packrat's hand closed around the money. He stood to his feet, then laid something on the table in front of the oldster. He pushed the object toward the man. The ruffian picked it up and gazed at the item: a woman's broken hairpin. While the man studied it, the Packrat stepped quietly to the next table. He spoke with full voice to the two men sitting there.

"Sirs—the man yonder thought these might interest ya'."

He dropped several crumpled playbills on the floor next to them. As the men reached down to retrieve them, Peter snatched the money from off their table and bolted for the door.

Peter ran through the dark tavern, negotiating corners and tables from memory. Before anyone realized what had happened, the Packrat burst out of the heavy tavern door and into the street. The moment he emerged from the smoke filled room, he felt at home. He scanned the street for refuge. For once, he was truly grateful for the harshness of the night. He knew that no pursuer, especially an adult, would stay out in this misery any longer than necessary. Any pursuit would be short-lived. Behind the black door of the tavern he could hear voices closing in fast.

Peter spotted a Charley asleep in his nightwatchman's box. On numerous occasions, he had watched the obnoxious young aristocrats—with nothing better to do than drink boasts to one another—parade out of the pubs late at night. Often they would challenge one another to topple a Charley between his callings of the hour.

Although he had never stooped to doing the deed he now considered, Peter had seen it done many times before with indescribable results. With a Herculean effort, inspired by the angry voices loudening behind the tavern door, he trounced the stand and toppled the Charley box, sending the sleeping watchman face first into the street.

The Packrat didn't wait to see the result. He was already in a full sprint by the time the Charley's face planted in the snow. The furious watchman climbed out amid a string of cursing, his pants singed and smoking from the toppled can of coals he used for warmth. Meanwhile, the incensed ruffian and several others poured from the tavern door. The ruffian spotted the boy running down the street just as the Charley spotted the ruffian, standing in the exact spot where the box had been moments before. Dragging his scorched leg through the snow, the watchman barked at the ruffian.

"Hey, ya' bloody sot! Get over 'ere! I've seen ya' before. Don't try to get away, or I'll really have somethin' on ya', ya' damned drunkard. Get over here!"

Seething, the ruffian could only watch as the Packrat disappeared around the corner at the end of the block. He breathed through clenched teeth:

"You can't hide from me, rat! Another day!"

"What's that ya' say? Damned drunks need a sound thrashin' or a night in the lockup. That'll teach ya'. You're comin' with me."

The Charley grabbed the man's arm and led him away. The ruffian only slightly resisted as he stared in the direction the boy had run.

The Packrat continued in a full sprint for much longer than usual. Fear inspired him to keep up the pace for several blocks. At last, he slid around the corner of an alley and waited in the shadows. From here, he could see several blocks down the street in both directions. After a long count to one hundred, he realized the chase had stopped before it got even started. The Charley plan worked. Relieved, he stepped into the light of a street lamp and opened his palm. Several coins glistened in the golden light from the flame. He started to laugh.

"May I never grow old..."

He looked heavenward and spoke aloud.

"Did ya' hear me, Lord? Call it a prayer if Ya' want. May I never be a grown-up—fools with years of experience."

He dug through several layers of shirts and pulled out a little cloth pouch tied around his neck. He put the money inside, then stuffed the pouch back down his shirt against his skin. It didn't feel cold. He picked up a nearby stick and began digging in the snow and dirt; he laughed again.

"And may I never 'ave a conscience—good for nothin' but guilt."

He dug and prodded for several minutes in the snow and frozen earth. When the hole was little more than a crater, he ripped the playbills from all of his pockets and dropped them in. Even though he had no intention of ever seeing the man in the tavern again, duty compelled him to keep his word and dispose of them as agreed. He stomped the playbills into the depression, then tried his best to cover it over.

When he was convinced that he had done his minimal best, he touched the bulge of money next to his chest; he couldn't help smiling.

"'Tis not my business to know the dirty doin's of oldsters—but they do pay good."

He reached down and picked up a handful of snow and packed it into a ball. A rustling to his left startled him. He slowly turned and peered into the darkness. He breathed easier when he spotted an alley cat rummaging through some rubbish heaps about twenty steps away. He patted the snowball, wound back, and hurled the hardened ball. It pelted the cat squarely in the side. The ill-tempered feline screamed and hissed as it tumbled over into the snow. The Packrat laughed as he ran away, leaving the playbills behind—half-buried in the dirt and snow.

Keeping Watch

Good evening, sir. Mrs. Delaney has been expecting you."

"Ahh, yes. I am late," sighed Handel. "I expect we shall both be scolded for it."

"I'm afraid so, m'lord. She has no tolerance for tardiness."

Mrs. Delaney's head butler took Handel's long coat from him and put it over his arm. He did not ask for Handel's cane; he knew from prior visits that Handel preferred to keep it with him.

Handel followed the butler to a large glass door, which opened to a sitting room. Inside, Handel could see Mrs. Delaney reading in her chair.

She was a tall woman, quite sturdy of frame. In resting position, her face appeared stern, which was contradictory to her natural disposition.

Her tendency was toward kindheartedness and benevolence. Although she was a woman of stature, she was unassuming. It was often said that to be in her good graces was to be in God's, for their judgment was similar.

She was described as merciful by her friends and just by those who found themselves at odds with her. In spite of her reputation for generosity, she did not shy away from controversy. On the contrary, she could be intensely loyal and would fight tooth and nail for what and whom she believed in.

She was a great admirer of Mr. Handel. They had become friends during his early days in London. She attended his operas religiously, subscribing to each and every run that he produced. During those years, she invited him to her home often. Over time, the visits became a weekly ritual. They would sit for tea each Tuesday night, discussing matters of music and musicians late into the evening. She thoroughly enjoyed the company and conversation; he thoroughly enjoyed the friendship and food. She became a source of valuable insight and inspiration. She was faithful when others waned. When so many others abandoned his swamped and sinking ship, she put reinforcing fingers into the leaky walls of his confidence.

She was Handel's elder by just a few years, but she took it upon herself to counsel him, both in triumph and failure. She earned his most trusted confidence and respect—not because she patronized him but because she was so painfully honest. He fondly recognized in her many of the mannerisms of his own mother, including her intolerance of sloth. Her criticism was usually correct—her suggestions, timely. She had the uncanny ability of keeping one finger on the pulse of society and another on his, thus divining whether the two hearts were beating synchronously or not.

Handel listened to her like few others because he knew that she sincerely had his best interest in mind. Finding a person of such qualities was rare indeed. He did not treat their conversations lightly. She was a skilled listener. She was given the gift of being able to recognize genius and the wherewithal to enjoy it. She held no secret aspirations to produce the sound herself. She was perfectly content to have tea with and listen to the person from whom genius did readily flow.

Handel, on the other hand, filled her life with pleasure, something of which she had little. She had no children to give her joy. Her husband,

Mr. Delaney, was a busy man who did not appreciate the commodity of leisure time. He would busy himself to excess. If his wife wanted to fill her time with recreation, as he called it, she was usually obliged to do it alone. On occasion he would indulge her artistic whims, but more often out of duty than for personal pleasure. Mrs. Delaney needed someone with whom she could share her love of music; Handel needed someone with whom he could share his mind. She was good for him, and he for her.

Handel wanted to be at his best when he came to visit. He always tried to paint optimistic pictures—no matter how blanched the colors of his personal palette were. Usually he could muster more positivity than he actually had, but when he arrived that night he was simply worn out, both body and soul. Given the choice, he probably would have passed on the visit, but his respect for her far outweighed any fatigue he might have felt. Even though he was late, he knew he must keep his appointment.

The butler opened the door.

"Delinquents—that's what you are, the both of you. Juvenile delinquents. Must I keep a constant watch on you?"

"Good evening, m'lady. I am most sorry. I fear rehearsal has delayed me again."

"You would let those scoundrels make you late for me?"

"They know not what they do. They are ignorant, and I, insolent. Please forgive us both, madame."

She smiled. He always made her smile; it was one of the things she appreciated the most about his visits.

The butler returned with a tray of tea and butter cookies. She always made sure that there were fresh butter cookies on hand since they were Handel's favorite. While the servant poured tea, she noticed Handel did not reach for the delicacies. She watched his face with keen interest; his thoughts were obviously elsewhere.

"Will there be anything else?" asked the servant, handing them each a cup and saucer. The hostess shook her head, and the butler quietly left the room. Handel didn't realize how long he had been thinking until he looked up to see that tea was poured, the butler was gone, and the room was quiet.

"I'm very sorry," he said. "I'm afraid I've been impolite. Forgive me."

"No need. Now tell me, how are rehearsals?" she asked.

"Encouraging. The singers are most earnest. Never have I had a more willing group."

"But will they draw?"

"If London will have something new."

"Who are they—your principals?"

"Reinhold and La Francesina."

"And the rest?"

"New people—from the chorus."

"Is no one else available?"

"They have...prior commitments."

"Beelzebub, I dare say. Half-fledged songbirds flittering about in mediocrity when they could be singing for George Frederic Handel."

"You are kind."

"I am correct."

She waited a moment to calm herself before continuing.

"The librettist?"

"Rolli."

"That snake. Why? A dozen librettos—none great. His words are a millstone hung about the neck of your music."

"He made himself available."

"Then tell me, will this opera be received better than *Imeneo*?"

"I can only speak for that which I've seen."

She smiled.

"Now you scold me—one of your most loyal patrons. You know I relish every note you put to paper."

"Would that the King had the same character flaw."

"Flaw? Nonsense. It's true; we both know it."

Handel leaned forward as he pondered her words.

"I'm afraid that I've taxed the ears of London. They seem to prefer hearing that which requires little effort." He took a deep breath, then stood to his feet.

"I regret I must go. It is, as always, a great pleasure to see you."

She did not get up from her chair. "We must celebrate the opening. You'll join us? Tuesday next?"

Handel bowed his gratitude to her. He understood her exact intent. Her purpose in hosting a party had little to do with celebrating; it was intended to rally support. In times past he may have offered some mild protest, but not now. He desperately needed any help he could get. He was thankful that she recognized his need without his having to ask. She could not have been more genuine in her efforts; she was guileless in her desire to be of assistance in any way that she could.

Handel found his way to the door. The butler heard the door open and close from his place in the kitchen. He hurried out to his employer to ascertain what he had missed.

"Mr. Handel has gone?"

Mrs. Delaney leaned back into the chair and closed her eyes.

"He'll be back."

Shame and Spitting

JOHN RICH WAS THE FIRST TO DISCOVER THE SABOTAGED set. He had arrived early to open the theatre, and his heart sank at the sight of the destruction. He sent word to Handel, who arrived not long afterward, and rehearsal was postponed for several hours while the hired stagehands tried to clean up the chaos.

Music stands were easy to pick up, but it would take days to repair costumes and shredded backdrops. There was neither time nor money to consider making new ones.

Handel did not respond as Rich thought he would. Rich expected him to stomp around the stage in a furious fit of screaming. Instead, Handel was silent. He took off his coat and went right to work. He worked twice the speed as any of the stage crew—righting set pieces, reassembling scores, picking up stands and chairs. Within a few hours, the cast and orchestra were in their places. The rehearsal began.

The singers in the chorus rubbed their hands together to keep them warm. For the first hour, the new soprano, Reinhold, struggled through the same twelve bars of her opening aria. In the meantime, the rest of the cast danced from one foot to the other to try to keep their feet from going numb. The theatre was nearly as cold inside as out. As Reinhold sang, her breath curled above her in ribbons of condensation. Handel's fingers were blue on the keys—partly from the cold, and partly from the broken blood vessels from his incessant pounding. Reinhold was the only person in the hall not freezing; she was hot with anxiety, doing her utmost to meet the unrealistic demands of the impatient conductor. It had only been a few days since Reinhold had been hired to fill the space vacated by Cuzzoni, and she was still unfamiliar with most of the score. She was brought to London from Worcester on short notice.

Handel had a tantrum when he heard that Cuzzoni had quit. So fed up was he with the divas that he cursed the Italians in front of Rolli in every language known to him. He hired Reinhold without any thought of consulting with Rich beforehand, and Rolli didn't find out until she was on the stage rehearsing.

Handel took out his frustration with the divas on Reinhold. He rose to his feet while he played. The more difficulty Reinhold had, the harder he would strike the keys, as if he could correct her by drowning her out. She finished one phrase—Handel played through a small bridge before her next entrance. As she joined him, he stopped playing.

"Intonation, madame! It is not here—" Handel opened his arms to their full breadth. "It is here!" He brought his hands together with a clap. "You do not go out looking for the lost pitch like a wayward child. It must be here," he raised his index finger and held it unwavering, near his chin. His voice intensified.

"Command it. Take control of it, or it is not. Again!"

He played through the bridge into her entrance a second time. She came in on the beat and continued as Handel improvised on the harpsichord. The other soloists squirmed as the intolerant conductor again berated Reinhold.

"Don't be timid. Sing! More—even more. Project. Not from your head, open your mouth. Does the Devil possess it? Sing, madame!"

She tried her best to follow, but much of it was sight-reading. Handel became more intolerant with each passing bar. When she missed another entrance, he fully erupted.

"Is this the way you praise God in Worcester?"

Reinhold stared back at him. She could not speak.

"God is very good and will no doubt hear your praises in Worcester, but no man will hear them in London," Handel shouted.

At this, Sandie, the baritone enlisted for the opera, stepped forward in defense of the woman.

"What do you expect in these circumstances, taking over the lead at such short notice! Extra practices, missing music, and the cold—why not just rehearse out in the street? And your pompous accompaniment—what singer could follow your impromptu? Perhaps I should jump down on the harpsichord."

"Oh, let me know when you do that, and I will advertise it. For I am sure more people will come to see you jump than to hear you sing," Handel scoffed.

While Sandie stood dumbstruck, Rich and Rolli entered the back of the theatre and walked toward the stage. Handel glanced their way in disgust, then began playing again. Rich stepped close and tried to speak to Handel through the music.

"Perhaps we should not open."

Handel ignored him. Rich persisted.

"Perhaps we should postpone."

"Postpone? We can't afford to," shouted Handel over his own playing.

"We jeopardize the theatre's money as well as your own. You haven't secured any singers who fill houses. I must do what I think is best for the finances of the theatre."

Again Handel ignored him and continued playing, cueing Reinhold's entrance as if nothing had been said.

"Work with this!" He held one hand to his chest while the other played. "It will come if you will concentrate on it."

Rich stepped closer, trying to reason with him.

"Much could be lost if we close early."

"More if we never open," Handel shot back.

Rich frowned and shook his head in disbelief. He had taken a big chance on Handel. He alone knew the precarious financial position of the theatre and, thus, himself. He looked back at Rolli.

"It's your libretto. Can you afford another failure?"

When he heard this, Handel's face turned purple with fury.

"No! Not failure. Success! Can you afford success?"

Rich was stunned. He stepped back as if blown from his place by the sheer force of Handel's voice.

"Backdrops ruined, music missing, costumes, cold rehearsals.... Who else paid for a key to the theatre?"

Rich couldn't speak. He no longer saw a man before him, but a monster. The defamation of which Handel was accusing him was completely unexpected. Feeling betrayed and disparaged, Rich turned and walked away without a word.

Panting, Handel watched him walk up the center aisle toward the door. Rolli observed all of this without so much as a blink. Halfway up the aisle, Rich stopped. He spoke without turning around. "There are only three keys."

Handel's gaze shifted from Rich to Rolli. When his eyes met Rolli's, the librettist quickly turned and hurried up the aisle towards Rich.

Handel turned back to the group on stage. He contemplated for a moment, then lifted his hand to Reinhold as if nothing had happened. His cast stood in shock. Outwardly, he appeared completely unmoved by the incident.

"Pick it up at bar sixteen, count three—the entrance of the quintet."

He began to play the introduction as the other four singers took their places on stage with Reinhold. The group nervously began to sing.

"Late! Be ready! Again!"

As the music developed, Handel glanced back to see Rolli talking to Rich. The two left the auditorium—as did Handel's thoughts.

Hours later, the stage was deserted. The cast and orchestra had happily gone home for the night. The foot-candles were extinguished. All of this transpired unnoticed by Handel, who still sat at the keyboard.

He was hapless—exhausted in both body and spirit. He knew it would take nothing short of a miracle to save him. For hours he reasoned every possible avenue his mind could muster for angles to pursue in search of receipts. In time, he rose to his feet and listlessly walked around the backstage area picking up loose music.

As he stooped to pick up a fallen wordbook, he heard footsteps. Rolli appeared from behind a backstage door. He walked across the front of the stage, not expecting anyone to still be there.

"Antonio!"

Rolli spun around to see Handel standing behind him.

"Who have you spoken with?" Handel asked.

Rolli stared at him as though he had spoken a different language. Handel didn't wait for an answer.

"You have the ear of influential people. Have you been speaking with them?"

"Spoken…about what?" Rolli stammered.

"Invited them! Asked for their support!"

When Rolli finally understood, he smiled.

"Oh, yes—absolutely. Yes, indeed. We will have their full support, you have my word."

Rolli proceeded across the stage toward the door. Handel continued as he walked.

"I've been invited to Mrs. Delaney's home for a Christmas gathering the evening before we open. Perhaps you should make an appearance—it may help our cause!"

"I'll consider it. Perhaps that could be useful."

Rolli hurried away.

Handel resumed his picking up of the papers strewn across the stage. When he reached for one loose page near the backstage curtain, a cold breeze blew it out of reach. He knelt where the music had been. In the gap between the bottom of the stage curtain and the floor he could feel a cold draft. He pulled back the curtain to reveal two large windows left wide open. He walked to the windows to close them against the cold. As he glanced down at the snowy street, he saw the theatre door open below. Rolli appeared through the threshold, took a key from his pocket and locked the door behind him. He hurried off down the street toward a waiting carriage, which Handel could barely see in the low fog. Rolli disappeared into the fog; a moment later, Handel heard the carriage rattle away.

For Thy Light Is Come

Is HE HERE?" INQUIRED THE ANXIOUS YOUNG LADY RICH.
Mrs. Delaney knew precisely of whom she spoke. No name needed to be
mentioned, for this was a gathering of the Handel faithful. Invited were
all those who supported the artist in spite of general sentiment. Never
had there been a need like now for Handel's friends to rally around him.
There was nothing secret about his desperation or predicament.
Everyone—both friend and enemy alike—knew *Deidamia* had to be a success, or Handel would most likely be finished.

Mrs. Delaney sensed the urgency more than anyone. In his weekly
visits, she witnessed the decline at close range. She was afraid for Handel.
She hosted this gathering as a final show of support before opening
night.

It was an elegant party. Christmas garlands and wreaths hung on every banister and door. There was great excitement in every conversation. A chamber orchestra played at one end of the spacious banquet room. Mrs. Delaney stood with Lady Cath and Lady Rich, two of Handel's most enthusiastic young supporters. When no answer came to her first question, Lady Rich inquired a second time.

"Is he here?"

Lady Cath was more oblique in her approach, though no less excited.

"I understand you've invited a special guest tonight."

Mrs. Delaney smiled—that was all the response she could give before Lady Rich usurped the balance of her reply.

"Shall we meet him? Will he play? Is he here?"

Mrs. Delaney laughed.

"I shall answer each question in order. Yes, you shall meet him. Yes, I'm sure he will provide something for the ear. And the answer to the third question is not certain—I've not yet seen him, but that is not to say he is not here."

A commotion broke out among the musicians playing at the far end of the hall. A musical duel of sorts seemed to be taking place between the two masked keyboard players on either side of the orchestra. One played the organ while the other accompanied on the harpsichord. The organ player improvised first, followed by the harpsichordist matching the interpretation through the next few bars. Mrs. Delaney was about to stop the players, then she noticed that her party guests were clapping with each new improvisation. For several minutes it went on as the two players jousted their craft to the utmost delight of the audience. Ladies Cath and Rich turned to Mrs. Delaney as if to ask if she had planned this for their entertainment, but she was as surprised as anyone.

Ultimately, the other musicians in the ensemble ceased playing, unable to keep up with the increasing difficulty and speed with which the duelists endeavored. With each passing improvisation, the second musician began to take the upper hand. The organist played as if chased in a game of musical follow-the-leader. His hands scampered this way and that, leading his pursuer through a minefield of music. But it made little difference; the second was on his tail, pushing him forward relentlessly. The first tried every difficult trick known to him, but still the other was there, right behind him by only a single bar.

Twice the harpsichordist purposely slowed down, allowing the other some room to get in front and make a break. The moment the spectators began to think the organist had dodged him, he would race back into the organist's draft in one long flurry of notes, to the utter amazement of all. Finally, when the first was completely exhausted with nowhere else to run, he jumped to his feet. He pulled his mask from his face, and exclaimed with a loud voice:

"Ha—I've been bettered! It has taken me until this moment to realize by whom."

The organist slowly bowed and made the sign of the cross to the man sitting at the harpsichord. The room fell silent. All eyes were on the second player, still masked and seated. The organist spoke again. His voice started low, then crescendoed with each word.

"My mentor, Scarlatti, never spoke your name without crossing himself. Unmask sir, for you are either the celebrated Saxon or the Devil himself."

The harpsichordist rose to his feet. His hand reached for the mask. He began to take it off, then waited momentarily. The spectators held their breath. In one swift motion he lifted the mask from his face—

It was Handel.

The crowd burst into spontaneous cheering and applause. Handel's face was at first serious. He gazed out from under furrowed brow at all those present. His solemn eye moved from person to person until the cheering stopped and a hush fell on the room. Like the consummate conductor he was, so eminent was his very presence that he could dictate the atmosphere of the room with a mere look. There was one, however, who was not intimidated.

"Cheer up, you pompous blunderbuss," scolded Mrs. Delaney. Guests ventured looks at one another to confirm that their ears had not betrayed them. Everyone waited to see how Handel would react. His lips became stretched and thin; the corners began to slide upward. All at once, his face brightened into a huge smile, which even made his ears rise. Again, the guests cheered and applauded. Over the clapping, the organist shouted, "Play, Saxon. Play!"

While still standing, Handel played fifteen bars of splendid improvisation. When he finished, he raised his hands in the air. A roar of cheers filled the room. His ears rose another inch. He hurried down the risers to those guests waiting to greet him. Mrs. Delaney made her way through the crowd encircling him.

"We are honored, Mr. Handel," she smiled. Before he could answer, Mr. Stanley intervened.

"Madame Delaney is a great admirer of yours. There is not a note you play which she does not adore."

Handel took her hand in his.

"She knows me less well than the critics, yet I am honored."

"You shall pay for it," she said, smiling.

"Take what you will, but I beg you leave me that which covers the essentials."

There was a great swell of laughter as Mrs. Delaney led him away from the circle to two ladies standing nearby. They curtsied respectfully.

"Sir, I'd like you to meet Lady Rich and Lady Cath."

"My Ladies, you are—?" He faltered, "Please pardon my asking, but—are you both married?"

They were both quite taken aback.

"Yes, quite," volunteered Lady Cath. A great smile of relief washed over Handel's face. At once, he became more engaging. He bowed low to them and lifted each of their hands to his lips.

"I should like to express to your husbands my greenest of envy."

With eyes fluttering, they cast bashful glances at each other. Several other guests had come up from behind and hedged Handel in. He was their prisoner. In rapid fire, questions were thrown at him. He answered as quickly as he could.

"So which of the sopranos do you favor?"

"Ask, and I will tell."

"What of Bordoni?"

"Faustina? Beelzebub's spoilt child."

"What of the Castratti, Senesino? They say he can sing a full opera with but one breath."

"If only his chest were full of ale instead of air."

"What of Cuzzoni?"

Handel's face began to redden. He worked himself into a lather.

"*Je sais bien que vous etes le diable meme.* She is a she-devil, as ugly to view as she is beautiful to hear."

"So did you in fact hold her to the window and threaten to throw her to the ground below?"

"And would have gladly, but I was not willing to clean up the mess she would have made."

The group began to laugh until they noticed that Handel had grown somber. Those closest to him likewise grew sullen. Handel continued pianissimo and finished forte.

"Imagine the distress of the pedestrians nearby—had she survived the fall."

He smiled a grand smile. The rest of the company responded in kind with relieved laughter. Lady Cath's voice rose above the others.

"Every night we should be so well entertained."

Handel answered while holding his hands over his large belly: "I regret that neither my calendar nor my middle can afford to expand—though I wish with all my heart that they could."

Laughter filled the room.

At this moment, one of the guests excused himself through the crowd surrounding Handel until he stood in the inner circle facing the artist and Mrs. Delaney. Handel saw him coming. The smile on his face leveled. When the guest stood in front of Handel, he held out something to Handel.

"Please accept my humble gift, to celebrate our upcoming success."

Rolli handed Handel an elegantly wrapped package. Handel's face did not change. He started to speak, but the words were drowned under the noise of guests urging him to open the package. He unfolded the corners of wrapping hiding the gift. He peeled back paper to reveal a hand-crafted olive wood box. Handel silently mouthed the letters which were carved in the corner of the sliding lid. Mrs. Delaney watched without a word.

"Show us," called the crowd. Handel held aloft the gift. The company gasped in unison as the olive box was held up for them to see.

"What does it say?" asked Lady Cath.

"G. F. H.," answered Rolli with pride.

"His initials—George Frederic Handel," was whispered around the room.

"Show us again," urged Lady Cath.

"Yes. Show us," pled other voices in the room. Handel held it up again for all to see. Cheers rang out when people recognized the carved letters on the box. Above the din of voices, Rolli shouted for all to hear.

"It contains handwritten librettos of the operas wherein you've honored my words with your music…"

Applause.

"…that they may not be forgotten," shouted Rolli. "May they find place with your greatest works and live on forever."

The volume of approbation crescendoed. Mrs. Delaney eyed Rolli suspiciously. She made no effort to hide her distaste for the man. Handel's face remained stolid. His eyes wandered back and forth between Rolli and the gift, which he held loosely in his hands.

At one point, it began to slip from his grip. There was a gasp from Rolli as he jumped forward to seize it before it could fall. Handel looked down at the box as if he were not quite sure what happened. He looked up into Rolli's face, which was tight and rigid. Hints of anger sparked on Rolli's face, but they flared out before Handel was certain what he saw. He felt Mrs. Delaney squeeze his arm once then release it.

"Back to the hall! Our guest will be along shortly," coaxed Mrs. Delaney, not taking her eyes off Rolli. Rolli averted his eyes in spite of her beckoning stare. The moment Rolli felt liberated from her gaze, he exited.

The guests gradually dispersed to follow the hostess into the supper hall. When Handel turned to follow, Mr. Stanley and Mr. Coot intercepted him.

"I'm told you're considering more oratorios," queried Mr. Stanley incredulously.

"I've considered it, but it's an unproved medium," answered Handel.

"It would finally allow you the luxury of dealing with singers less stubborn than yourself," chuckled Mr. Coot.

Handel looked at them with a stern face; the jovial Mr. Coot smiled nervously. After a moment of uneasiness, Handel boomed out a loud laugh.

"The Devil. You flatter me. I thought my reputation was getting soft."

As Handel walked away, still laughing, Charles Jennens appeared in the open doorway in front of him. He had heard every word.

"Will you be doing more oratorios?"

"Charles! I had no idea you were here. It's very nice to see you."

"And you, Mr. Handel. How are you?"

"Tonight—I am well. Tomorrow remains to be seen."

"What are your plans after *Deidamia*?"

"I don't know. I weary at the thought of it."

"Have you been approached by any other theatres?"

"It seems they are all too busy to give ear to me."

"I have something that may interest you."

"A commission? An assignment perhaps?"

"A libretto. I believe it's worthy of your attention."

"An oratorio?"

"It exceeds all else I've done."

Jennens handed him a stack of parchment paper, distinctively wrapped.

"It seems that everyone has a libretto for me tonight," mused Handel. "If only the King had a libretto for me." He grinned at Jennens. Jennens did not counter.

"Thank you. I'll see what I can do," Handel said, bowing and excusing himself. As he walked toward the table full of food, Jennens added, "You will not be able to ignore it!"

Handel turned around and watched him leave.

With Jennens's words still ringing in his mind, Handel walked to where there were tables filled with food. He stopped and absentmindedly began sampling each item. When his mouth was completely full, a curtain behind him opened to the dining hall where everyone at the party was seated. Handel tried his best to smile with his mouth full.

"Tired of waiting for the rest of us?" Mrs. Delaney asked. With a few words, she diffused what might have been an embarrassing situation for her guest of honor. An insignificant few were appalled at Handel, the vast majority laughed and thought nothing of it. Some actually thought that the incident was planned in advance as a practical joke.

The party lasted late into the evening. Just before the guests began to leave, Handel played the overture of *Deidamia* on the organ—at Mrs. Delaney's request. It proved to be a grand idea as many who had been undecided about attending the opera were pushed over the fence. The music was wonderful. Perhaps it was because of the lovely circumstance, perhaps it was the simplicity of hearing it played on a single instrument. Regardless, to those in attendance, music had never sounded so sweet.

The guests left for home, filled both body and soul. The emotion of that night would certainly carry over to opening night. Mrs. Delaney's highest hopes for the event were realized.

When the guests had all departed, Handel sat for a few minutes in the parlor with the hostess. For several minutes nothing was said. Neither felt the need to speak—their thoughts were of like mind. Finally, Handel stood and walked through the door into the entrance hall. Mrs. Delaney followed. She personally retrieved his coat and held it open for him to put on.

"M'lady, I should serve you," he smiled graciously.

"You have."

She opened the door; he passed through it. As he walked down her path to the street, she spoke reassuringly.

"It will be a success—you will see. Bravo, *Deidamia*."

For Unto Us

THE PACKRAT STAYED CLOSE TO THE BUILDINGS AS HE walked. The overhanging eaves provided minimal shelter, but it was shelter. The snow came down around him in swirling sheets. In reality, it was not snow but frozen rain; it would freeze just above the street, masking everything in a ghostly blanket of ice. Peter tried to protect his face with his hand as he walked along the abandoned street. When he would turn his eyes outward to establish his position on the street, the crystals would bite into the bare skin of his face like angry horseflies. As he walked, his thoughts were of the little ones; he hoped that they would be in by now and not trying to make their way home in this madness.

The Packrat knew every crack and hole in the street, yet even he became disoriented at times. Street signs were covered. House fronts all looked the same. The street itself was buried. So thick were the sleet and snow whirling around him that he could hardly see the next step in front of him. Just a few minutes before, he had walked right up to the backside of a nightwatchman; he hadn't seen him until his face was planted in the back of his long wool coat.

At times he would hear the dull pounding of a passing carriage in the street near him. He didn't dare venture out beyond the edge of the walk. He knew going in the street could mean being flogged to death under the hooves of horses without the driver of the carriage ever knowing. From a driver's perch, he would only appear a shadow against a flying sea of white. The driver would think him no more than a chunk of dark ice under the snow.

Peter used the dark building walls to create contrast in the flying snow. He stayed as close to the wall as he could. This helped him keep himself oriented. When he looked straight into the storm and focused on the chaos swirling around him, he became confused.

He came within a step from falling headfirst into a coal pit, which he didn't see until it was almost too late. He had to cling to the mortar between the bricks in the wall to keep from falling in. He was disgusted that he had allowed himself to get so far from home when he could feel the bite of an oncoming storm in the air earlier that same day.

He picked up his pace, knowing he still had a long walk ahead before he would be safe in his hole. He fantasized that a carriage would stop and pick him up for the long walk, but the dream didn't last long. It was too outrageous a thing to even pretend.

He was anxious to be out of the cold and under the inn where he had hollowed out a habitation—and where the fireplace above radiated heat down into the basement below. That was a dream he could wrap his hope around. Just the thought of it made him feel warmer and gave him strength as he plowed through the snow.

He put out his hand and slid it along the glass window of a haberdashery as he passed by. He had been yelled at countless times for smudging the glass with his "grubby mitts." Tonight there was no yelling, no one to stop him. He turned the corner and soiled the window next to the one he had just streaked.

He began to count windows as he walked. He made a bet with himself on how many windows he would have to pass before he would be home. He set his bet at forty-three and started counting. His hand was just sliding across number fourteen when he stumbled upon it. So preoccupied was he with counting windows, that he never saw it until he nearly stepped on it. He jumped to the side to avoid tumbling over the dark mass huddled against the wall directly in his path. His skin went to goose flesh before his feet again touched the ground. He spun around, fully expecting an arm to be thrust at his neck. But there was no arm; the shadow didn't move. Peter dared not go closer. He had no curiosity about things he could not discern. His habit was to give a wide clearance to anything that he had not fully ascertained. Still, there was nothing about the shadow that seemed ominous or threatening. He figured the best thing to do if he didn't know what to do was nothing. He moved on.

It was then that he heard the cry. So mournful and desperate were the sobs that his feet froze in place. Seldom had he heard real pain vocalized. The cold of the night chilled the Packrat's body, but this sound made his heart shiver. It pierced through him and rang in his ears.

He took a step toward the dark mass against the wall. It didn't move. He took another step closer; his foot cracked the ice underneath. He drew back startled, but still it didn't move. The cries subsided. He was certain his presence had been detected. All at once, he thought to flee, to get away from this place and into the safety of shelter.

He turned and started down the street at a run, past windows fifteen and sixteen, but there was no pursuit. His pace slowed. As quickly as he had been off, he circled and headed back to the shadow. There were two things he knew with absolute certainty: whoever or whatever it was, was in pain, and it would never last until morning without shelter.

As he drew close and again began to distinguish the dark mass against the wall, he determined that regardless of what might happen, he would help if he could. Fear left him in that instant. No longer did he feel threatened. He did not approach with apprehension, for he had given himself over to a higher cause. All thoughts of himself and his personal comfort and safety gave way to a force even stronger than fear: charity.

Without hesitation, he knelt down in the snow near the shadow. His eyes were instantly drawn to the ground. Around the mass were dark, discolored veins of blackness in the snow. The packrat leaned down to the ground for a better look. He scooped into his hand some of the black and held it in the dim light emanating from a lantern burning low in a shop window. The snow was not black but red. He looked back at the thing huddled before him. He knelt back down, reached out and touched the huddled mass. A tattered wrap opened and two eyes looked at him. Just as he was about to speak, a heavy hand landed on his shoulder.

Peter did not turn around.

His breathing quickened, but his body was motionless.

The grip on his shoulder eased and lifted. He could feel a presence kneel down alongside him. Peter was not afraid. He spoke with certainty.

"What's wrong? Why is she bleedin'?"

"She's in pain—the baby is coming."

Peter didn't stir. He somehow recognized the voice, but he was not thinking of that right now. He continued to stare at the eyes under the wrap. So soft and mournful were they that he couldn't look away. He felt as though every deed he held in his heart, every thought, was opened to the eyes that now rested upon him. Suddenly, the eyes closed as the woman's body folded in pain. Peter's heart yearned within him when he heard each soft cry of agony. He knew not who the woman was, but for the first time in his life he longed for a mother.

The person at his side reached for her. Strong arms wrapped around her to comfort and warm, but neither was possible under the circumstances. Only now did Peter see the face of the man. He recognized him the moment he saw him. It was the man who had once given him bread.

The man spoke with quiet urgency.

"I've tried to find a doctor, a midwife, someplace warm to take her, but the doors are all closed and locked. No one answers."

The woman cried out as her body contracted. She fell down in the bloodstained snow. Like a shot, Peter was up on his feet, knocking frantically on every nearby door. Few doors opened. Those that did were slammed shut. Peter screamed from the street.

"Open up, please. We need help, the woman is 'avin' a baby. Open up, damn it!"

Peter ran back to the couple, panting.

"Where do ya' live?"

"Cheapside—more than two miles from here," the man answered.

"What if she has the baby 'ere?"

"The midwife felt the child two days ago. The baby's feet are down. Without a midwife, the baby will die during birth."

Peter raced back to the nearest door and pounded with all his might. A window above him cracked open. A woman's loud voice shouted down at him.

"What is it?"

"There's a woman here—she's 'avin' a baby and needs help."

After a moment the voice shouted again.

"What kind of woman?"

Peter glanced at the dark figure huddled in the snow; he looked back up at the window.

"A woman in pain."

The window closed. Peter waited anxiously for a minute—then another minute. He pounded again and again but the window never opened again.

"It's no use," Jonathon shouted through the flying snow. "We need to get home, or the baby will die in the cold. You lead the way."

Jonathon turned away from the Packrat and picked up Rachel. He turned back to Peter to help him, but the boy was gone.

With Rachel in his arms, sobbing with pain, Jonathon started down the street. Going was difficult in the deep snow. Her long dress dripped a trail of blood.

The Packrat continued down the street banging on doors and windows, but still no answer. He stopped to give his mind time to work; he heard the dull pounding of a carriage rolling over the cobbles behind him. Without a moment's hesitation he was in the street.

As the carriage came near, Peter jumped in front of the horses with his hands held high. The animals reared back in fright almost hurling the driver out of his seat to the ground. When he steadied himself, he shouted down at the Packrat.

"Fool boy! You should be dead; get away from there."

Seconds later, the Packrat stood at his side in the carriage. So quick and agile was he that he had scaled the ladder to the driver in less time than it took for the driver to figure out what had happened.

"Little wretch, get down from—"

Before he could finish, Peter reached deep down into his shirt and pulled out a small bag hanging from a string around his neck; he shook the metal contents in front of the driver's nose.

"I need ya'—now!"

The wind ripped by Jonathon as he carried Rachel along the sidewalk. Every step was difficult in the deep snow. He slipped several times, once falling to his knees on the ice, but he never dropped Rachel. In his heart he thanked God in prayer for giving him work that would prepare him for this all-important moment of his life.

He kept going. As he trudged headlong into the beating wind and snow, he began to tire under the weight of his beloved burden. His legs were getting weak from both the effort and the cold; he needed to pause and regain his strength. His foremost thought was of his wife's pain, and he fought back fatigue and moved on. His foot caught a chunk of ice, which he had not seen. He fell forward, quickly rolling himself to the side so that he would take the brunt of the fall. He somehow managed to get his body beneath Rachel as they plummeted to the ground, but Rachel still let out a cry as the two fell in the snow. She folded into fetal position as her body contracted again. Jonathon tried to lift her but it only intensified the pain. He determined to wait until after the contraction before continuing. He held her in his arms, protecting her face from the falling snow. He could feel her muscles tighten into knots with each swell of labor. Within her heavy and broken breaths were deep, almost inaudible moans of torture. He knew that were it not for something deadly wrong, the baby would have already been birthed.

He felt her body begin to relax. His first thought was that the present contraction was over and that she could move. He then realized that he was feeling something much different; he sensed that her life was slipping away from him. His arms tightened around her, but the more desperately he held on, the more tangible were his thoughts of losing her. Her arms, which before were wrapped around her belly, fell limp at her sides. Jonathon struggled to his feet. The moment he got his shoes planted beneath him, he stood, lifting her in his arms. He leapt forward into the snow, feeling that the race he now ran was not just to save the baby, but to save his Rachel. His legs blindly felt for safe footlandings. Rachel cried out as another pain-filled contraction literally tore her insides apart. This time, Jonathon did not stop. His strides increased in speed and length. In his agony of hearing his beloved's mournful sobs, he couldn't help but close his eyes and cry aloud himself.

"Please, God—help us."

When he heard a droning sound in his ears, he opened his eyes to see a large dark image appearing out of the fog and snow. He stepped backward as the image grew larger before him. He recognized the dull pounding of an approaching carriage. He turned his back away from the street to protect the one he carried from the ever-dangerous wheels. He looked back over his shoulder to see the hulking shadow coming straight toward him. He leaped for the wall, protecting Rachel with his body. As he sheltered her from harm, he heard the carriage stop just a few feet behind him. He glanced back as the carriage door swung open. Out jumped the Packrat.

"Hurry—tell him where to go."

Jonathon did not ask questions—he quickly lifted Rachel inside the compartment. While the Packrat tried to help get her comfortably seated, Jonathon shouted instructions over the blizzard to the driver. Moments later, the door slammed shut. The carriage lurched forward. Inside, Jonathon tried to calm Rachel.

"We're almost there. Hold on! Hold on, dear Rachel!"

Rachel made little sound once the carriage was moving. She could not sit up, but rested on her side as they bumped over the cobbles and ice. Jonathon could hear her holding her breath, then letting it out in long streams. Her face was pale, her eyes shut tight.

As the carriage began to slow in front of a small streetside flat, the Packrat jumped out the door and ran. He hit the ground while the big wheels were still turning. His feet slid out from under him and he tumbled over twice and got right back up without losing a step.

"Do you remember where to go?" Jonathon shouted, his head sticking out the open door, but Peter didn't hear him; he had already disappeared behind the white wall of swirling snow. Jonathan carefully picked up Rachel and lifted her out of the carriage and through the narrow doorway of their tiny home.

When he laid Rachel on the bed in the dark room, she made only a whimper. Jonathon set about to light the small lantern.

Outside he could faintly hear the dull crunching of carriage wheels in the snow get fainter and fainter. When the wick of the lamp took flame he was back at Rachel's side. He took her head in his hands and leaned gently over her ear.

"Don't worry, he will come, he will bring help," Jonathon whispered. Water filled the corner of his eyes as he held Rachel's face close to his. He wished there were some way that he could take her pain upon himself. He felt utterly helpless as he held Rachel in his hands. All of his hope dangled precipitously on the head of a small urchin boy. He whispered again.

"Please come. Please come back."

A group of people began to gather at the door. It was not often that a carriage came this way, especially at this time of night. Their curiosity may have been only slightly stronger than their discomfort, but it was stronger. There were several that braved the cold to satisfy their gnawing nosiness.

With a loud shout, the Packrat cleared a path through the gatherers for the midwife to get through. The path closed before the Packrat could follow her inside.

"Is she bleeding?" the woman asked as she made her way to Rachel.

"For some time now," answered Jonathon.

"We must hurry. Help lift her legs, the baby may already be coming!" She pointed to the oil lantern.

"I need to see here. Fetch the light and close the door, or we'll all freeze."

Jonathon glanced at those standing in the doorway as he reached for the lantern. Nothing needed to be said, they understood and backed out the door and into the side alley where a firecan had been lit.

The Packrat tried to see through the legs of people standing in the doorway before it closed, but there was nothing to be seen. He went to the window and stood up on the pile of snow which had slid off the roof and drifted near the wall. From here, he could just see over the windowsill and through the muslin curtain. He could not see things clearly through the frost, but he could make out bodies as they darted around the room. He could hear the voices inside through the glass.

"The baby will die if we can't get it turned!" the midwife said. "Help me here."

Peter saw a large figure step alongside her. He could hear the mournful cries of the woman on the bed. He had never seen a child born before. He wondered if every baby born required this much hurt.

His thoughts were shattered by a cry of agony from within the house. He could bear no more of the woman's pain. He jumped down from the heap of snow, ran across the street, and sat down under a small overhang from where he could see the house. It was not until then that he realized that the storm had nearly blown itself out.

Light flakes of snow now dropped vertically from the black sky. Peter watched those at the firecan who held their hands out to warm them, but he had no desire to join the group. He didn't want to hear their banter and speculation about the goings-on inside the flat. He considered their chatter to be like the sparks that rose above their heads and quickly flickered out into nothingness. All he could think about was the woman whose cries seemed to wrench his very heart. Her pain made him feel empty inside. He couldn't stop thinking about her eyes. That was all that he had really seen of her, yet those eyes had called forth feelings from deep within him unlike any he had felt before. He had only seen eyes like that once; he vaguely remembered them. It was the last remembrance he had before entering the orphanage for abandoned children. It was his earliest memory—one which he never really understood. He could not remember whose eyes they were, but, when he looked into the eyes of the woman huddled against the wall, the memory came back with force.

As he sat in the cold, he wondered if it was painful for his mother when he was born.

"No wonder," he whispered. "Who'd want to keep somethin' that hurt you so much to have."

He watched the glow in the window across the street for a long time. Finally, he leaned his head back against the cold stone wall and closed his eyes. He silently asked God for a favor in behalf of the woman—a favor he felt he had rightfully earned.

The firecan had burned down to glowing coals when the door to the house opened. Only a few of the people who started out around the can still remained. Jonathon stepped out into the street and closed the door behind him. One of the few by the can approached him; they spoke briefly. The man reported to the others what Jonathon had told him, then they all went home.

Jonathon gazed long down the street in one direction, then the other, but the street was empty. He looked upwards. Through holes in the clouds he could see stars shining above him. While he watched, the clouds opened even more. Then, as if prompted, he stepped farther into the street. He continued his steps until he stood on the opposite side of the street from his home.

At his feet, huddled against the wall, was the Packrat. He sat motionless with his head between his legs. Jonathon stood over him. The boy could feel someone near. He opened his eyes and looked up into the face of the man before him. A large hand reached down for the Packrat. Peter looked at the hand; it was the same hand that had held out bread to him in the alley. Peter reached up and took hold of it in a tight grasp. Jonathon pulled the boy to his feet and led him across the street to the narrow doorway.

When Jonathon pushed the door open, Peter stepped back. He didn't dare look at what might be in that room. He subconsciously began to move his head from side to side. He looked up at the man, who just nodded and smiled softly. Peter trusted the man who had given him bread even though he still didn't know his name.

Jonathon walked through the door and disappeared from Peter's view. When Peter had called up the courage to walk to the threshold and look in, he could see the man kneeling at the side of the bed, the woman's hand in his. Lying on her stomach was a tiny, sleeping baby. When Jonathon saw Peter at the door, he leaned down and whispered in the mother's ear. The Packrat could not hear what he said, but he watched as the woman pulled his hand to her lips and kissed it, then laid it alongside her cheek.

The father rose to his feet and stepped back from Rachel. The mother's eyes moved from him to the boy, who stood motionless in the doorway. Jonathon closed the door behind him to keep the warmth in. Rachel's hand lifted from the bed; she beckoned the Packrat to her side. Again he looked at the man, who nodded his permission for the boy to approach. Peter stepped toward the bed until he stood just inches away from her. The mother's eyes seemed to remove any fear he might have felt. She spoke to him in a weakened but kindly voice.

"You're the one they call Packrat."

Peter smiled. It pleased him to think that she would somehow know of him. His gaze moved to the sleeping baby on her stomach. The child was wrapped in a warm cloth, but the tiny face was open towards the boy.

"It's a baby girl: Christina. She's sleeping," said the mother.

"Christina," whispered the boy.

Peter had never seen anything so perfect. He counted her tiny fingers and toes. He stared in amazement at his own fingers, then at hers, comparing how small yet complete the baby's were. As he looked on the child, his face shone. A holy hush seemed to glow in his eyes, as if he were looking at the baby Jesus Himself. He reached to touch the child, then stopped. The mother gently took his hand and moved it forward to the baby. He touched the soft palm of the baby's hand. Her little fingers closed around his finger. A look of purity beamed on the boy's face.

"See the small mark below her ear?" said Rachel.

The Packrat touched the dark mark on the skin just under her ear on the side of her little neck.

"She'll always have it. It's a mark placed by God to remind us that her life is a gift to us. Christina—our Christmas gift from God."

Rachel smiled at Peter, who smiled back. Rachel took the Packrat's hand from Christina's neck and held it gently in her hands. Peter felt to do something he had never done before. He wanted to reach out his arms to this mother and hold her. Even more, he wanted her to hold him.

Instead, she opened his hand and put something in it. As she let go of him, he opened his hand to reveal a thin brass chain with a single golden locket. He looked at Rachel as she folded his hand around it. Until that moment, he had only one thing in his possession that he truly cherished—a gold button. Now he had two things.

He touched Christina once again on the birthmark and whispered, "Christina."

He squeezed the mother's hand one last time before slipping quietly to the door.

Jonathon noticed that the midwife was preparing to leave.

"We're grateful. Is there some work I can trade for your service? Baked goods possibly?"

"It's taken care of," she reassured him.

Jonathon was confused. He looked curiously at the midwife. She said nothing, but glanced up toward the door, which the Packrat had just pulled closed behind him. At first Jonathon did not understand, but little by little the blanks filled in. He walked to the door and looked out. Way off in the distance he could see a small boy running down the middle of the icy street.

"Thank you," he said, but only God heard.

And Gross Darkness the People

———————

THE STREET WAS DARK AND DESERTED. IN THE DISTANCE could be heard the long tolling of the clock tower. Twelve times the forlorn bell echoed through the streets of London. The muted chant of a nightwatchman calling—"Twelve o'clock!"—slowly faded into nothingness. Moments later there was the slightest movement in the shadows. Unless one was looking directly at the dark image, it would never have been noticed. White rims of black eyes shifted back and forth, peering up and down the long street. When he was certain that the street was empty, a man dressed in black stepped from the shadows into the street.

One minute later, out of the fog appeared a richly ornamented carriage, which proceeded toward him until it came to a stop next to him. The door cracked open. A man's voice spoke from within in hushed tones.

"Did you do it?"

"Just as you said," answered the man in the street.

"And they're disposed of?"

"Just as you said."

"So you expect payment?"

"As you said."

Inside the carriage, a woman laughed. The door closed. There were whispers inside. The man in the street cleared his throat. The door of the carriage cracked open again.

"Do you know what to do now?" asked the man from within.

"Yes—make things unpleasant."

There was more whispering inside. In time, a silk cuffed hand appeared out the crack.

"Take heed: forget where you were tonight."

The hand condescendingly began to peel off coins one by one with the thumb and drop them into the hand of the man standing in the street. The voice of the man inside the carriage spoke as he paid.

"I'll wager blood money spends well with your kind."

At this, the man in the street grabbed the cuffed hand and squeezed it until it loosed and dropped all the coins.

"Not as well as with yours," he hissed.

The woman inside began to laugh again. The man outside clenched the cuffed hand for several seconds before releasing it. As soon as he did, it was quickly retracted and the door pulled shut. There was a dull rap on the ceiling of the carriage. It pulled away from the man and disappeared into the fog. When the black-clad man turned, the light of a street lamp raked across his pocked and scarred face. As quickly as that, he was back into the shadows and hidden by the night.

It was very late when Rolli slid the key into the hole and turned the large lock that secured the back door of Lincoln's Inn. He entered, then closed the door and locked it behind him. As he walked across the back of the lobby, he could hear the distinct sound of organ music. He walked to the open door at the rear of the main hall. Sitting at the organ, playing by candlelight was Mr. Handel, keeping watch over the theatre through the night. Rolli watched as Handel played several bars from the *Deidamia* finale. Handel was bent over the organ, barely able to keep himself from falling on the keys. Handel exhaled long streams of gray steam across the top of the organ, where droplets of water had formed. He had been about this night vigil for several hours. Through the minutes that Rolli was there, Handel never looked up from the organ. In time, Rolli exited by the same door he had entered. As the lock clicked closed, Handel's head tipped toward the sound, but that was all.

He Was Bruised

E̲VERYTHING WAS READY. INSIDE THE THEATRE, FOOT-
candles were lit, the hall warmed. Rich started heating the theatre
hours before the show was to begin to make certain that it would be
comfortable for the guests. The furnace was stoked with enough coal
to last through the long performance and beyond. Backdrops had been
repaired as best they could be; costumes had been sewn back together.
The sabotage of several nights before had been remedied under the
watchful eye of Handel himself. He took hold of a situation that might
have closed any other opera and put it to his advantage. Where there
were gaping holes in the backdrops that could not be repaired, holes
were ripped in the opposite backdrops so the set would appear sym-
metrical. The stage appeared to be designed that way.

If the sleeve of a costume was missing and could not be found, the other sleeve was torn off to match. For those who knew what had happened, many of the scars remained, but for the audience, it had all been made to look as if planned. The resulting style and art direction was, if nothing else, original. Handel had a reputation for trying new things; with *Deidamia*, it was stage design. It was another piece of leather for the critics to chew on apart from just the music.

Even the cast and orchestra were amazed at what their exacting conductor had salvaged from what should have been devastating. His resiliency inspired them. They all got caught up in the energy of the premiere performance and momentarily forgot the difficult path they trekked to get there.

Outside, the night was cold but clear. The stage was set, both inside and out, for a successful opening of *Deidamia*. Even Handel himself was amicable. He took special care that day to give words of encouragement to his principals. During the final warm-up rehearsal, he had been almost approachable. Reinhold had completely missed an entrance in her duet with Sandie, but Handel was encouraging rather than demeaning. He allowed her try it again; the second time she was punctual, and he was pleased. There were wagers among those in the chorus about whether he was, in fact, becoming tolerable or just too tired to care any more. All of those who had sung in his prior operas agreed that fatigue would never render him apathetic. The mere thought of it was completely absurd. For that one day, the beast was tame.

As the hour of truth approached, coaches began to arrive carrying opera patrons. Albeit this was not like the overwhelming crowds that Handel had enjoyed with earlier operas, it was shaping up to be very respectable. People began to queue up at the main door into Lincoln's Inn. Conversations were light. Attitudes were positive. Most of the guests from Mrs. Delaney's party earlier that week waited in line, hopeful of a grand performance.

Just minutes before the doors were to open, a stately coach pulled up in front of the theatre. The door opened and the elderly Mr. Coot started to climb out. Inspired by Mrs. Delaney's gracious efforts to rally the Handel loyal, he had determined to attend Handel's opera. As he carefully lowered himself down the steps, out of nowhere appeared a drunken ruffian, who bumped into the door of the carriage. The impact jarred Mr. Coot's foot off of the step; it slipped to the ground. Had he not had a firm grip on the handhold of the carriage door he would have fallen backward into the blackened slush. The drunk laughed as the mature gentleman gathered himself and straightened his coat.

"Pardon me, m'lord. I didn't see you there." The foul-smelling drunk leaned close to Mr. Coot. "You noblemen are hard to see in the dark. It's so dark no one could tell the difference between you and me."

The ruffian leaned back and laughed again. While he laughed, two others of like kind joined him on either side. Mr. Coot walked around them and back to the carriage, being careful to stay clear of them.

The three ruffians surveyed the area. The one on the right hissed a few things under his breath and pointed to those in line. He was their leader and the darkest of the three. He and another headed off in different directions. They began moving through the theatre patrons, wreaking havoc wherever they went. The youngest of the threesome stumbled among the people waiting in line near the door. He stunk of rum and smoke. Every time he came close to a woman he would lean close and breathe his stench into her face.

"Give us a kiss, love," he would exhale at them. He recklessly fell into people, knocking off wigs, pushing people to the ground. A few of the more timid patrons wanted no part of this and left discreetly while the foul men tormented others. The leader of the three stayed near the back of the line, besmirching those who were still coming.

As Mr. Coot attempted to politely assist his daughter out of the compartment, the same ruffian leaned over him again, draping his arms over his shoulders.

"What's this? Another wig? Pardon me, madame!"

When Coot threw the stinking arms off his shoulders, the ruffian pushed him away. The wretch turned his attention upon the shrinking young woman left standing on the footboard. When the ruffian stumbled towards her, she backed through the door and sat down on the seat. The drunk leaned his head through the carriage door.

"Who's this? Come out, m'lady, let me see you."

"Out of the way—you're drunk!" said Mr. Coot, pushing the ruffian from the carriage door. The ruffian grabbed Mr. Coot's arm and wrenched it behind his back, then sent him sprawling into the side of the carriage. The horses reared and jerked. The driver climbed down and laid a hand on the letch's shoulder to turn him around. The ruffian spun, his fists ready, and landed a punch to the driver's chin. His head jerked back and the driver dropped to his knees in the snow.

"Stay away. This woman wants me. She'll be the entertainment tonight."

The drunk reached for the handhold and began to pull himself up into the carriage.

"You'll have hell to pay first," said the brave father taking hold of the thug's filthy coat and pulling him back from behind. When the ruffian's foot touched the ground, he whirled around wildly, belting Mr. Coot in the bone of his cheek. The elderly man buckled and fell face first in the snow. When he hit the ground, the ruffian planted his boot in his side. Mr. Coot coiled up onto his knees and elbows, gasping for air. When the ruffian saw him choking, he grabbed him by the chin and pulled his head back and laughed in his face.

"Hell is paid off cheap."

His dirty comrades joined in the laughter.

"You came for a show—enjoy it," shouted the leader of the group, as he groped his filthy fingers over those at the rear of the line. Every time he would touch someone, they would groan in disgust. Several of those patrons closest to the commotion hurried away to their carriages.

The ruffian at the carriage again put his head inside the door and his eyes fell on the girl. She cowered into the darkest corner she could find. Her muffled cries pleased the ruffian as he leaned his dirty face farther into the carriage.

"Now, come out and play with me."

He reached into the carriage and caught hold of a fold in the girl's dress.

In terror she clung to the handle inside the carriage as he tried to yank her out. He grew weary of the tug-of-war and put his foot up on the footrest for leverage.

With a loud curse he heaved.

The girl screamed.

There was a ripping sound as the ruffian fell back from the carriage, his hands full of shredded cloth. Inside, the girl's leg showed through the torn hole. His lecherous eyes saw it before she could cover her bare thigh. A wicked smile crossed his face. He threw the ripped piece of dress into the face of the girl's father, still lying in the snow gasping. The ruffian climbed again to his feet. Mr. Coot reached around his leg to try to stop him, but another kick to the side of his head sent him reeling into the snow.

"Now I shall have the daughter of a nobleman."

The brute staggered back to the carriage and put his head inside.

He stared at the bared leg of the quaking girl. She choked out whimpered words of prayer between breaths. He reached for her foot, but she quickly pulled it away. He leaned farther in and groped for her with his vile hand. It brushed against the bare skin of her thigh as she pushed away from him with her legs. When he touched her, he changed his mind about pulling her out.

"If you won't come out, then I will come in. Either way, it don't matter for what I 'ave in mind for you."

As he raised his foot up to the step, he heard a loud voice behind him.

"Hey, ya' bloody ugly bastard."

The ruffian stopped mid-step. His head tipped just a click. The voice shouted again.

"That's right, you 'eard me. You're one bloody, ugly, drunk bastard."

The ruffian's lip twitched. His stare slid downward from the girl. He turned his body slowly toward the source of the sound. The instant his head came around to see who dared speak the words, a rocket-thrown ice ball slammed into his face. The force of it knocked him off the footstep. He groaned in agony as he tumbled back against the carriage wheel, then slid off the side to the ground. Shards of ice blinded him; he covered his eyes with his hands. Blood burst from his nose and trickled through his fingers and down the length of his arms.

While he rolled in the snow, moaning, Mr. Coot seized the chance to climb into the carriage and slam the door shut. The carriage rolled away with the young woman watching out the back window. She waved to the boy from whose hand came the sphere, but he never saw her; the Packrat was too busy packing another handful of ice.

When the ruffian rolled up onto his knees, Peter's lightning arm unleashed another ball. Rock-hard ice tore into the soft flesh of the ruffian's ear. Blood exploded from his torn earlobe. His nose and ear bled profusely as he fell forward into the red snow, screaming in pain.

All at once, like the shock of cold water down his back, the Packrat realized the gravity of what he had done. He had reacted to a situation with no thought of the consequences of interfering. He knew what men like this did to those who got in their way. The thought of what would happen to him if he were caught made him sweat in the cold. Instinct took over. He began to back away, hoping beyond hope that the ruffian hadn't seen his face before the ice blinded him. He was certain he didn't want to give the villain a second chance when his eyes cleared. On impulse, Peter turned to run—directly into the arms of the leader.

"Where you off to? You don't want to miss the show."

The Packrat looked up into the man's face. He immediately recognized the thin scar above the brow, the pocked face. The Packrat's thoughts shot back to the tavern...the handbills...the stolen money...toppling the Charley into the street.

His mind then shifted to the most recent events. He had come up the alley at the side of the theatre—that's when he saw the bully accosting the woman in the carriage. He never looked around to see if the brute had accomplices; he had simply reacted to someone's need. Now he was in trouble.

"Packrat! I had hoped we would meet again. We have unfinished business," the man snarled, pulling the boy up close to his face.

"Do ya' remember me? I sure remember you."

His fingers wrapped around Peter's neck like a tightening vice. The boy's airway squeezed shut under the clamp of the ruffian's powerful grip. Peter's feet barely touched the ground as he groped for air. The man looked around. The few remaining opera patrons scattered.

"Look!" he said, still clenching the boy's throat with one hand and holding him by the nap of his coat with the other. The Packrat gasped for air as the man thrust his face forward. "You still work for me. I was hoping to create a disturbance—you've provided me with one."

"Will I be paid?" sputtered the Packrat.

At that moment, someone grabbed Peter's arm and severed him from the leader's hold. Skin from the Packrat's neck peeled under the fingernails of the leader's hand as he was torn away from its grasp. The boy winced as blood oozed through the exposed white skin. A foul hot stench in his face shocked him back to reality. The blood-drenched face of the ruffian who had been hit by the ice balls was only inches in front of him.

The man held Peter out with one hand, then crushed a fist into the side of the boy's head with the other. The Packrat's eyes rolled white and his legs folded underneath him. He dropped flat on his back, face up. The bloodied ruffian stomped his heavy boot on the Packrat's chest. Had the deep snow not given below him, the boy's ribs would have been crushed under the blow.

The Packrat's small frame folded around the assailant's foot. The ruffian jerked it away with a kick to the boy's mouth. The Packrat's teeth drove deep into the soft flesh behind his lip. His mouth filled with blood.

The ruffian stepped back from his helpless victim. He wiped the blood still dripping from his nose on his sleeve and looked at the wet shine on his shirt. He stood hulking over the boy as if trying to determine the best way to finish his brutal task.

"You'll bleed a cup for every drop you cost me, rodent."

The ruffian's foot coiled back from the Packrat's head. The boy ducked and covered his face with his hands in anticipation of the blow.

A loud crack peeled through the air.

Peter felt someone fall over him and land at his side.

He heard another loud crack.

Peter looked up, just in time to see something crash across the leader's back, hurling him to the ground. Above the Packrat stood a large man holding a thick, wooden board in his hands. Never had anyone looked so immense to him before. The man stood over Peter like a mother over her young.

"Be gone, now—or receive another!" shouted Handel, towering above the ruffians. His deep voice echoed down the length of the street like thunder in a canyon. The leader climbed to his feet and faced Handel. The Packrat scrambled behind Handel's legs. The ruffian took a step forward, the board in Handel's hands rose above him. The wretch stopped short of the reach of the board. The two men stared into each other's eyes. Peter could not see the face of the man standing over him, but he could see the shadowed eyes of the thug. Peter shuddered when those same eyes shifted down to him. He hid his face behind his rescuer's leg. When he snuck a look back, the ruffian was surveying the area. The last few coaches were just leaving, the others had all abandoned the opera for safety. The ruffian began to laugh.

"Fine, we'll go. We're finished here."

He picked up his companion to leave. The third drunk joined them as they stumbled down the street. When they were halfway down the block, the leader stopped and called back to Handel.

"Where's your audience? They must not have enjoyed the performance, old fool."

Shrill laughter reverberated up and down the narrow street, but it was not the leader who laughed. He stared with black eyes at the Packrat, still sitting on the ground behind Handel. His eyelids tightened as his gaze shifted back up to Handel. His eyes went even more black.

"Another day, Mr. Handel. I am finished tonight, but I'm not finished with you. We will have another day, you and me. You too, 'Rat!"

The three disappeared into the darkness.

A large hand was extended to the Packrat. Peter reached for it without hesitation.

"Are you hurt?" asked Handel evenly.

Peter shook his head, although he felt as though his chest was caved in. The Packrat saw Handel's eyes follow the last carriage down the street. He looked at Handel's face for signs of emotion, but there was nothing. The big man was silent in every way. It was Peter who spoke first.

"Everyone's gone."

Handel did not answer.

The Packrat's face was bruised badly, blood dripped from his lip. Handel looked at the boy's face with concern.

"It's all right," said Peter. "It'll scab."

Handel looked again down the long street. His thoughts seemed distant, faraway. As Peter watched him, he began to understand.

"You're him. They were all here for your show."

Handel's face did not change.

"What'll ya' do now?"

"Word travels quickly. We'll have to see."

"Will the people come back?"

"I don't think so."

"If your show's good, then maybe..." Peter hesitated when Handel looked at him.

"Why do they hate ya'?" Peter asked.

Handel thought for a few moments but did not answer. The board slipped from his hands into the bloodstained snow.

"It's finished. No more operas," Handel sighed.

He walked to the theatre door. Peter followed. Handel spoke to him without looking back.

"You're welcome to come in and warm yourself. It's a little better than this."

The Packrat tipped back his head to consider. He saw eyes watching him from the window above the doorway. Rolli leaned forward to watch Handel enter the door below.

"No. No, thanks," said the Packrat. "This suits me fine. I'm leavin' now."

Handel walked through the theatre door. The Packrat looked up again at the window. Rolli stared down at him. Peter ran away as fast as he could.

In the Land of the Shadow

HAD THE SIGN NOT BEEN SO PAINFULLY CONSPICUOUS, very few would have probably noticed. But as it was, it made quite a conversation piece as passersby speculated on the future of both opera and Handel. Enemies of Handel directed their carriages far out of their way to view the Lincoln's Inn marquee firsthand; they were not disappointed. One simple addition to the marquee said it all. In huge block letters over the top of the theatre billboard was one word: "CLOSED."

Steele and Addison took special occasion to mention it in *The Spectator*. Beneath a scurrilous cartoon of a fat pig sitting at the harpsichord was the caption, "The Great Boar."

In the subsequent article it stated that *Deidamia* had closed after only two performances. Nothing was said of the unfortunate skirmish on opening night. Somehow, the editors neglected to mention any word of it. Only those who actually witnessed it acknowledged that anything out of the ordinary had happened at all.

When the mishap did come up, it was met with skepticism. It sounded so implausible to think that anyone would stoop to such brutal tactics, that the story seemed preposterous. The subject was usually met by scoffing and laughter.

The day following the announcement, the last remaining stagehands who were willing to work for half-wage were busy striking what was left of the set. Little, if any, of what remained could be used again. Considering that most of the backdrops and props were already distressed in varying degrees, most of it was thrown out to be burned. Even the wardrobe department had little use for what was left.

Rich, the theatre manager, told the crew, "Get rid of it—all of it." The workers, who were being paid little, were not careful about their business.

Handel watched all of this from a seat far back in the theatre. He had a blank stare on his face as hinges folded and wood snapped, bringing the painted canvas backdrops crashing down. The workers were no more careful with Handel's jarred ego than they were with the set. Each time a piece dropped, jokes would drop also.

"The walls fall slower than the show."

"Perhaps people would pay to see us tear it down."

"Better chance of that, than payin' for any bloody opera."

"We should try it; can't fail any worse 'an 'im."

"Silence," a voice boomed. "That is enough."

Handel rose out of his chair, his eyes fixed upon those before him.

"Either stop this instant, or I shall tear your limbs from your mindless bodies and beat you with them. I will hear no more of it."

He could not stand fully erect, and yet he could not have seemed any more imposing. They shrank before him like beaten dogs. None of the workmen said another word until well after Handel left the stage for the solitude of his small dressing chamber.

He packed the last few personal items from his room. He straightened and stacked the loose sheets of score, then slid them neatly between the folds of his leather carrier. He broke off the last inch of candle from his small silver candlestick and wrapped it in a torn shawl that he had pulled from the rubbish heap near the back stage door. When all was done, he silently looked around the room.

He had never noticed the absolute bareness of the walls until that moment. It was curious to him that he hadn't been aware of the starkness of the room. He was a lover of art, and yet the absence of it had gone unnoticed. Now he wondered if he had ever really looked at the walls of the small cubicle. He turned full circle, staring at each crack and nail hole in the plaster. Typically, he would have given no thought to such trivial things, but with the weight of his financial obligations so taxing, even mindless musing provided some solace. If nothing else, it was a brief retreat from the worries that plagued his every thought. So burdened was his brain that it sought refuge in the insignificant as a recess from the inevitable.

He pulled on his cloak and walked out the door. For the first time ever, he saw the walls of the hall. He heard his empty steps echo along the dividing corridors. He saw his shadow shorten then stretch as he passed by open doors with lights within.

Finally, he came to Rolli's chamber at the back of the stage. He paused a moment; a sliver of light streaked out the slightly open doorway. He knocked softly. He knocked again, this time loud enough that he could not be missed. There was no answer. He took hold of the knob and pushed open the door. He walked into the square room and up to the small table Rolli used as a desk. A single candle burned brightly on the corner of the table. At the base of the candle was a silver letter opener. Light from the flame sparked highlights off the shiny steel onto the gray walls. Handel took from his leather folder the original libretto of *Deidamia* and laid it on the desk in the soft light of the candle.

Handel then looked up. He couldn't help but notice that Rolli's walls were bare also, with the exception of a small portraiture hanging on the rear wall. He had been aware of it before but never taken the time to really appraise it. He leaned close to the canvas. It was an artist's rendering of Rolli sitting at a desk with quill in hand. Behind Rolli was a window looking out on a cityscape that was clearly Italian. Handel knew that particular creative decision was not by chance. A heavy sigh confirmed that he thought the piece rather pedestrian.

As he walked back to the door, he watched his shadow from the candle grow smaller on the interior wall of the chamber. His shadow passed over a large chest, which Rolli had pushed against the wall. As Handel emerged through the doorway he slowed to a stop. Something about the chest was not right. Handel would not have given it a second thought had there not been the corner of something sticking out from under the lid of the chest that caught his eye. His face grew taut. Slowly, he backed into the room.

Snagged in the closed lid was the corner of a piece of paper. Handel's fingers closed around the folded corner, and he pulled. The corner ripped away from whatever was left inside. On the torn corner of the paper were notes of music. Handel recognized them instantly. He lifted the lid, expecting it to be locked. It creaked open. The light of the candle could not reach over the edge of the chest; he couldn't see the contents. He tipped the chest toward the light so he could see inside. It was full.

Handel began pulling from it several loose sheets of music, dozens of wrinkled playbills and numerous mangled wordbooks. Underneath were costumes, torn and stomped into the bottom of the chest. He found props that had been missing—violin bows, shoes, cravats.

Just then, Rolli walked into the room. He didn't see Handel kneeling in the corner. Handel let go of the open lid. Rolli twirled at the sound of the lid slamming shut. Out from the darkness lunged Handel, catching him by the loose fabric of his sleeve. He dragged him to the chest and threw open the lid with his other hand.

"Liar," Handel screamed. "Liar! It was you all this time. You betrayed me! You betrayed all of us. Stinking, filthy liar."

Handel grabbed at the contents of the chest. He pulled music, handbills, and costume pieces out and hurled them into Rolli's face. Rolli threw up his hands to shield his face from the onslaught. Handel reached through Rolli's protecting arms and grabbed him by the throat.

"I trusted you. What a fool. I should have known not to trust you. You're a waste—a damn waste. You'll never know greatness, never. You're second rate, mediocre, nothing—you're nothing!" roared Handel, his face twisted with rage. He pushed Rolli against the opposite wall with a mighty thrust. Rolli's head rebounded off the wall, and he fell forward to his hands and knees. He scrambled behind the desk, out of reach. He felt the back of this head; when he pulled his hand back and held it in the light, his fingers dripped red. Drops fell onto the libretto laying before him. When he tried to wipe them from the paper, he was too late. The ink was already softened; his hand smeared the wet words across the page. Rolli's head lurched back violently, his eyes gleamed with a maniacal shine. At that moment, roles of prey and predator changed. Rolli lunged forward, grasping the letter opener in his fist. Fire flickered off the side of the shiny metal as he raised it over his head. The black shadow of the gripped blade rose high up the wall above Handel.

"It is you who are nothing, your music is dead. You are dead. You have nothing left. You're a rotting carcass that no one wants or cares about. You stink of failure. You had a gift, but you've lost it. You failed. Do you hear me? You are the failure!"

Rolli's voice reverberated back and forth through the halls of the the-atre. Rather than diminish, the sound strengthened with each echo. The words were no longer Rolli's; it seemed to Handel as though countless voices bellowed the words down the open corridors and empty chambers.

Handel stood panting, out of breath. With each exhale, his height lessened. Sadness engulfed him. Without thinking of Rolli, his head dropped in silent agony. He wrung his hands pathetically. Rolli's blade hung over Handel's bared neck. It was not pity that kept him from strik-ing, but contempt. Handel leaned back against the wall, his face in his hands. With a wave, he dismissed Rolli.

"Go! Go away! Leave!"

Rolli slowly withdrew his raised hand. He gathered the things left on his desk, then walked past Handel to the door. When he was safely outside, he spoke in a hushed voice.

"To want a gift and not receive it, that is a life of torture. To have a gift and lose it—that is eternal hell."

Handel's eyes closed.

For as in Adam All Die

H ANDEL DID NOT TRY HIS HAND AGAIN AT ITALIAN OPERA.
He sought other media, but none of his ventures were successful enough to make any dent in the debt that he had accumulated. Creditors were losing patience. Theatres would not engage him. Even singers and musicians were wary of his contracts as he tried more and more to negotiate to give them a share of the receipts rather than wages. Payroll was reliable; the box office wasn't.

Those who were faithful to Handel found their loyalty even more burdensome after the failure of *Deidamia*. Patrons were openly ridiculed whenever the subject of music or opera was mentioned. Public sentiment turned away from both opera and Handel. Defending Handel was a lonely endeavor.

What complicated things further was the distrust many felt for royalty, especially German royalty. Handel, being German, became a whipping boy for those at odds with the King. The very association, which had launched him into London's music scene, was now a curse. If one liked the King, one tended to tolerate Handel; to those who did not like the King, Handel was despicable. The vast majority of people were more pleased than disappointed at the premature closure of *Deidamia*.

Many nationalists went so far as to view the demise of opera as a rekindling of patriotism, since opera was, in fact, Italian. The Italians had rubbed their opera in the faces of the Londoners from the start. When Handel failed, and others alike, few tears were shed. Now that the days of opera were waning, loyalists categorized it as a fad, a trend that lasted far longer than it should have.

There was little change in Handel's day-to-day routine following *Deidamia*. He spent the days at home with the shades pulled shut. He busied himself with writing, but notes never appeared on paper. At night he would walk, but only after the watchman had called the hour of ten. By then, the streets were empty and most of the lamps had been blown out. Often he would walk past the home into which he had intruded for the use of an instrument. He stared at the black window in hope that a new phrase of music would come—some creative color upon which he could improvise—but nothing ever came. For minutes he would wait, even hours; still the window remained dark, and he had no reason to make it otherwise. Night after night he walked away empty, his head bowed low. He would walk well past midnight, then return and retire to his chamber.

In the morning, his bedsheets were seldom wrinkled. He spent most nights either standing near the window, as if watching for someone, or sleeping in the chair. Each day his mind became more numbed by inactivity. So preoccupied was he with failure that he could not clear his mind for creativity. The sad irony was that the only thing that could save him was exactly that which held him captive: his music.

He went to the Academy on numerous occasions to plead his cause. Repeatedly, his inquiry ended the same way. One of the jurors would stand, hand him back a manuscript, then shake his head.

Against his own edict, Handel presented the idea of reprising *Rinaldo*, but it was not accepted. The Academy closed their ears to him.

With increasing regularity, collectors would knock on his door. At first he was obstinate, later apologetic, then finally apathetic. As time wore on, he no longer answered the door. Ultimately, it became the oppressive responsibility of his servant, Peter LeBlonde, to deal with creditors. He did so out of simple necessity, not by any desire of his own. Often those who came collecting would carry balance sheets to push into LeBlonde's face. He knew desperately little of the details surrounding the agreements that Handel had made, but needed little knowledge to understand the desperateness of the situation. As the pressure increased, even LeBlonde began to let calls go unanswered.

As Handel disappeared from view, *The Spectator* spoke of him more often. The less threatening he became, the more Addison and Steele sank their editorial teeth into him. There was no element of his life they declined to malign. They took particular delight in his corpulence. Cartoons portrayed him as any and every prodigious animal that they could think of. The Great Boar was the most popular of all the names given him. At first, Handel bristled at their flagrant attempts to defame him. But as time passed, he stopped reading the newspaper.

He literally took himself out of society. Early on, while he was still fresh on people's minds, he put on a brave appearance and accepted invitations to gatherings so he could be seen out and about. But as the weeks passed, he attended sporadically at best and, subsequently, not at all. Even his visits to friends became less frequent as he begged off for any inane reason he could concoct.

In spite of her best efforts, Mrs. Delaney was unable to slow the cocooning of Handel. He quietly slipped into oblivion—not by any single event but by countless small events. Even though *Deidamia* was the most recent failure, it was not the only failure. It was the last in a long line of disappointments.

It was not until Handel watched from his upstairs window as two lackeys carried away his vanity and a favorite painting that he was shaken out of his stupor. The realization that he had allowed himself to fall that far was hard to accept. He decided right then that it was time to try to get back on his feet. He racked his mind for any avenue he thought might still be open to him. He could think of only one.

Her Warfare Is Accomplished

THE FIRST FEW MONTHS OF 1741 SEEMED LIKE A YEAR.
Although the bitterness of January had passed, the weeks leading up to
the equinox bleakly languished on. Night came early; morning late. The
sky and ground alike were gray with ash and coal residue.

The landscape was colorless, as were the faces of most Londoners.
It was during those endless rainy days of late February and March that
society sought refuge in gatherings. Often there could be as many as three
or four engagements each week, if one availed oneself to all of the social
opportunities presented. So frequent were the socials that those of high
stature were often forced to choose their loyalties carefully.

One of the most active hosts was Madame Hervey. The staleness of
the interior air of her home in the waning weeks of winter was comparable

to the staleness of the conversations. Her gatherings were little more than formalized whining sessions with food. Attendees bickered and moaned about everything from politics to personals.

Prince Frederick was a regular participant in the disgruntlement. Close associates were so conditioned to his casualness that they no longer couched their words in his presence, even when the topic of criticism was his own family.

As the weeks dragged on, the gatherings themselves began to be the topic of discontent as the noble began to dispute the decorum expected at socials. The most significant and heated of ongoing discussions concerned the traditional reception line for such events. It was customary for the host to form a reception line to give proper greeting to the most auspicious guests. Some argued that it was time to do away with such convention, whereas others believed the custom of formal acknowledgment needed to be given greater ceremony. The point was argued incessantly over several weeks of parties.

Other topics of conversation included street paving, government, traffic, the royal family, and even music. *Deidamia* and Handel provided conversation text for several weeks, but even that had grown moldy. Those intent on discussing Handel were forced to be discreet, as the audience for it grew thin and weary. Talk of opera became a hiss and a byword. Handel was old news. Those who dwelled on the subject disproportionately long were regarded as chronic. Rolli had to be the most careful, as he was also the most suspect.

Long after the subject of Handel's disappearance was out of fashion, Rolli doggedly retrieved it back to the forefront. He was obsessed by it. Finally, the Madame had to pull him aside and caution him concerning his offense. To salve his need, she would excuse herself and the Italian to another room where Rolli could vent openly. In the same way that she exploited the Prince's derision of the King, she continued to nurture Rolli's hatred of Handel.

As the party lingered on, Madame Hervey caught Rolli by the arm and led him away from a relieved group he was boring with talk of the Royal Academy's shortsightedness. She led him past the Prince, who pandered with the ladies, to a small alcove under the staircase. Once they were alone, she pursued her business straightway.

"What has he been doing since?"

"Nothing. He does not even come out."

"Has he solicited help from the Academy?"

"Many times."

"And?"

"They won't touch him; he is too heavy a burden to carry."

They both laughed out loud at the pun. Some of those close enough to hear turned towards the laughter. The prince was among them. Hervey continued more discreetly.

"What of his debts."

"They continue—with interest."

"He has no plans for performing?"

"No house will have him."

"Is he writing?"

"If so, it will never be heard."

"The fire is burned out?"

"Completely. He is finished, forever."

"You're quite certain of that?" asked a voice from behind.

Unbeknownst to both, the Prince had joined them and had heard their conversation. Initially, the voice surprised them, but once they realized who it was, they were both relieved.

"Yes, quite certain," answered Rolli. "*Mein herr* Handel is no more. The Saxon has pounded the last nail in his own coffin. No one will have him now—not the academy, not London, not the King. He is finished."

Rolli laughed again; his voice small and empty. To the Prince, Rolli was suddenly disgusting. He no longer seemed a man, but some loathsome creature.

"You enjoy this too much. It is time for this to end! Our intention was to use the man, not destroy his life."

"That was my intention, exactly. There is no hell low enough for him to go that would satisfy me," Rolli said with a grin.

Frederick couldn't speak. In one sentence, the true nature of the librettist's intent became everlastingly clear. The Prince thought back to the premonitions that he had received along the way. He was given warnings, but he did not heed them. Now, he understood the gravity that to which he had been party. He looked at the silly smirk on Rolli's face, the conniving grin that Hervey wore. The words of his father rang in his ears: "Why so bent upon the ruin of one poor fellow? The better it succeeds, the more reason one has to be ashamed of it."

A thousand thoughts ran across Frederick's mind. Was he a dupe? Was he a foolish pawn in a bigger scheme to which he had closed his eyes? As he looked on the Italian with whom he allied himself, he was sickened. Rolli was utterly detestable to him. To think that he had allowed himself to join arms with one so vile was unforgivable. In his desire to get revenge on his father, Frederick had sunk to the foulness of a man as detestable and odious as Rolli. He viewed the creature Rolli as a dark reflection of himself. For such men, baseness was expected, but for a Prince, born with the blood of kings and queens coursing through his veins, pettiness was inexcusable. Frederick realized he was—or at least should be—better than that. He despised Rolli. The Italian was tangible evidence of Frederick's lack of integrity; he could not look on his face any longer.

"I am through with you. I want no more part of this."

The Prince threw a hand in Rolli's direction, then walked away. Before leaving the room, he turned back to Rolli.

"You may have walked in his footsteps, but his feet were so much larger."

Frederick disappeared out the door. Rolli looked at Hervey with a pained face as if to say, "What did I do?" Hervey started laughing. She couldn't stop. The more Rolli looked to her for reinforcement, the harder she laughed. She went on uncontrollably for several minutes until most of her guests stopped their conversations to watch. Rolli felt stupid standing next to her. Everyone in the room stared at him with blank faces. Madame Hervey composed herself, but tears still streamed down her face. She leaned over and kissed the Italian on the cheek.

"If nothing else, Antonio, you are entertaining."

His Glory Shall
Be Seen Upon Thee

THERE WERE FEW THINGS THAT TRULY CONCERNED THE
Packrat. He had no use for worry; for he viewed worry as "the pastime of
grown-ups who 'aven't the gumption to do somethin' about what bothers
'em." He saw things simplistically and couldn't find any reason to complicate things that didn't require complication.

There was, however, one thing that vexed him. Something for which
he had no clear answer. Hardly a day went by that he didn't think of it
and wonder what was the right thing to do. It bothered him to think that
he was falling into the usual traps he had seen adults fall into so readily.
Did he feel guilt? He wasn't really sure. Did he feel ashamed? No—
because he didn't say one thing and do another, he was straight. Maybe

he was just bothered—not because he was unwilling to do something to help, but because he just didn't know what to do.

James, the fisherman, haunted him. Peter hadn't meant for anything to happen. He had even tried to be of help, but his help rendered the man sightless.

Peter wished he could take back that day and do things differently. He would have just stayed away. How much better things would be now.

"Eyes is worth a whole lot more'n coins," he said to himself.

If he had it to do again, he would just walk on by and then take it upon himself to even things up later. But because he got involved, everything was all wrong. No matter what he did to try to help the situation, it only seemed to get worse.

At first he tried to help by having his kids leave pence for James. What little he could give would never be what James had earned before. The effort seemed to benefit the Packrat and his conscience more than the intended receiver. He sought other ways to try to understand what might be of help to the blind man.

Peter wanted to know how James felt. He walked through the streets with his eyes closed to try to imagine what life was like for him, but it never lasted long. As soon as he heard something that startled him, or tripped over something he couldn't see coming, he would open his eyes. When he cheated, he talked himself into believing that James was only mostly blind and that certainly he could see something.

Sometimes he would sit against the wall on the same street as James and wait with his cup out and his eyes closed to see if people would actually donate a coin or two. He had no intention of keeping the money, but did it only as a test to determine what James might be getting in his cup. He made a point of being close enough to the blind man to get an accurate assessment of the neighborhood, but not close enough to chance getting nabbed by someone who might recognize him. He kept a safe distance for a long time just to be sure, but as the weeks and months wore on, his boldness increased.

"Grown-ups can't remember their manners; how'r they gonna' remember me?"

Peter decided it was time to try something new. He used the money from his cup to buy a small loaf of black bread. He quietly laid it next to James, well out of reach. He waited until all those around him seemed preoccupied, then he rolled the round loaf next to James's leg. When the loaf bumped against his leg, the blind man caught hold of the bread. His head turned in the direction from which it came. The man's motionless eyes stared right at the Packrat. Peter dared not move. So unflinching were James's eyes that Peter was certain he could see him. The eyes did not blink nor glance away. The penetrating stare was so stark and severe that Peter panicked. He leapt to his feet and ran as fast as he could into the crowd to hide. As he darted through legs, a voice rang out above the din of the street.

"Thank you."

The Packrat did not wait to hear if there would be other words. He didn't even turn to see who had said it, but he knew it was James; his heart told him so.

The following day Peter did the same thing. This time he did not run. Instead, he made faces at the motionless eyes, but they did not change. He laughed to himself about how stupid he must have looked running away the day before. He didn't realize he had squeaked out a sound until there was a slight head adjustment from James towards him. The shift had been minimal, but, like a dog catching a new scent and altering its course slightly, James's face turned a little more directly upon Peter. Again the boy was frightened, but he didn't run.

"He heard me," mouthed the Packrat. "How could he have heard me with all the noise of the street?"

Peter picked up a small pebble and tossed it to the other side of James. The moment the tiny stone clicked the ground, James's head turned in the direction where it landed. This astounded the Packrat. He considered himself to be a "bleedin' good list'ner," but this topped anything he could do.

For the next several days, the Packrat either slid something to eat near James's leg or dropped a pence in his cup. Each day there was a "Thank you." The boy began to feel a shine for the blind man like few others he had ever known. He dared not speak to him, for he was certain that James must hate him like no other. But still, he could not leave him alone. At first his conscience had driven him to the man; now, it was a strange kinship which kept him coming.

After several weeks of frequenting the wall against which James leaned, Peter became careless. In a hurry, he tossed a coin towards the cup, but missed the mark. Rolling his eyes with disgust, he reached down to the ground to pick up the errant coin. The second his hand touched it, James caught hold of his arm. The old man's hand darted so fast that Peter had no time to even react. The boy was certain he had been caught the same way a thousand fish must have been snatched from the water. The man's fingers wrapped around the boy's arm tightly. Peter was shocked by the power and sheer strength of the man's grip. He tried in vain to pull his arm away, but he did not gain a single pore of skin. He knew he could not escape without an equalizer of some kind. He searched the ground for a rock with which to beat the hand that seized him. He was not quick enough, for before he could find a weapon, he was reeled in closer.

Terror swept through the Packrat. The hair on his neck bristled up like frozen needles. James reached out with his other hand and grasped the boy's opposite shoulder. Peter tried to reach up and grab the arm that held him, but the fingers on his shoulder tightened, the boy's arm fell to his side, numb. Never had he been so absolutely and inescapably captured.

The man who held him could have his way with him, and Peter was powerless to stop him. He was at the complete mercy of the man from whom he had taken sight.

James pulled him close to his blind eyes and seemed to stare at him. Peter wondered what he saw. The boy shuddered in his grip, careful not to make a sound. His only chance was that James would not discern his identity. Anonymity was the boy's sole ally. He hoped that the blind man would think he was trying to steal from him and that was all; he would scold him, slap him, then throw him back to the street. The boy was already promising himself never to venture within a block of this corner again—not even if open purses were hung out on the clotheslines.

"You're him," James said, with a voice from deep within. "You're the rat-boy."

All hope evaporated. He was discovered. Somehow, James knew his identity, and it didn't matter how. Fear filled Peter's veins with an icy chill. Only once before had he faced a situation with absolutely no possibility of escape. Intervention saved him then, but for salvation to come a second time was incomprehensible. The boy fell limp in the man's hands.

Then to his utter amazement, the grip on his arm eased. He could feel blood rush back into his white hands like a thousand ants biting him.

The mighty grip, which had held him bound, was released. Instinct took over; the Packrat was away before James could reconsider. He started into the crowd—then stopped. Peter's face flushed at the next thought that came to his mind. He stood motionless, wrestling with the idea. Then, taking a deep breath, and going against all that he had learned from living on the street, he turned and walked back to James.

As he stood hesitantly above the blind man, then took another deep breath and sat down right next to him. Peter leaned back against the wall and closed his eyes.

"I know you," said a voice next to him. Peter fought back the temptation to open his eyes. He was astounded at how loud and clear the voice seemed, even though he knew that James was talking in a normal voice. With his eyes closed, Peter became aware of much more sound around him. The street seemed louder than he had ever heard it. He could hear separate noises instead of the constant cacophony of sound to which he was accustomed. James's voice startled him.

"Why did you come back?"

"I don't know—maybe to try to even things up," said Peter.

"I know you."

"What do ya' mean?"

"I know who you are."

"How do ya' know me?"

"I know you didn't mean to hurt me. I know that you do mean to help me. From that, I know you."

Peter did not understand. He could not comprehend that a man from whom he had taken so much would not want to take the same from him. Peter cheated and opened his eyes just enough to look at James's face to see if he was frowning. He wasn't. The Packrat closed his eyes again.

"Do ya' want me to be blind, too? I understand if ya' do."

Because his eyes were shut, Peter did not realize that James had turned his head toward him until he spoke again.

"No."

"I'm sorry," said the boy.

"Sorry doesn't help me see."

"I know, but I'm still sorry. I'm sorry your eyes don't work so good. I wish I could give ya' one of mine. I think that would make it right."

"Is that what you think?"

"It seems right to me."

James leaned his head back against the wall. The boy continued, "I think I could get by with one, don't you?"

James's dry, sightless eyes, moistened. "Yes," he answered.

"One is better than none, I guess," said Peter.

"I guess so," answered James.

The boy opened one eye. He spoke as he carefully looked back and forth around the street.

"I think it would be okay; it's like lookin' through a hole in the fence. Ya' can't see ev'rythin', but ya' can still see a lot."

The Packrat blinked each eye open and shut while still looking around at the people in the street. "I think I'd choose my right eye."

"Why?"

"Maybe 'cause I close my left eye when I'm aimin' to throw somethin'—maybe."

"I think I'd choose my right eye."

Peter looked over at him with one eye open. The blind man continued, "When I steer from the back of the boat, I sit to the left of the rudder and keep my right hand on the handle. If I had my right eye, I could still see almost all of the boat in front of me."

"That's a good reason," affirmed the Packrat. He leaned to the side and pretended to be driving a boat. It was true, he probably would be able to see all of a boat before him. He grinned at the blind man, again impressed by his good sense. The boy closed both of his eyes and leaned back against the wall.

"Do ya' miss your boat?"

"Yes."

"I never knew ya' had one."

"It sank."

"I'll bet that made ya' sad."

"Yes."

"What do ya' miss the most?"

"The smell of the sea; the wind in my face."

Peter opened his eyes and leaned close to James. He stared at the man's eyes for a long time. He waved his hand in front of his eyes.

"Did ya' see that?"

"No, but I know you waved your hand in front of me."

"How do ya' know that?"

"I'm not blind."

Slowly, a smile began to curl on James's face. The Packrat started to laugh; James joined him. The two sat side by side laughing out loud and long. No one who worked that part of the street could believe his ears. Not one person had heard James laugh since that terrible day the sign fell. Peter stopped laughing and looked again at the man's blind eyes.

"Can ya' see anythin'—anythin' at all?"

"I can see light. Even the blind can see light."

The boy's brow folded.

"I don't get it?"

"It's not what you think. Some day you will."

The Packrat wondered. The answer he had received was not what he expected. He probed further.

"What can ya' really see?"

"I see everything I could before, I just can't see it with my eyes."

"That's good. If ya' couldn't see anythin' at all, that would be bad."

"Indeed."

James reached over and put a large hand on the boy's leg.

"Would you help me do something? Guide me down to the docks so I can smell the wind coming off the water."

Peter stood up. He took James by the hand in a firm grasp. He leaned the whole weight of his body back to pull James up.

"Put your hand right 'ere." Peter placed a big hand on the same shoulder that the blind man had held captive just minutes before. The two walked down the street and around the corner into the wind.

O Daughter of Zion

SUPPERTIME WAS THE BEST PART OF THE DAY. IT WAS THEN that Rachel had both Jonathon and Christina all to herself. The hours while Jonathon was at the bakery went by like a song as she played and sang to little Christina; when Jonathon was home, the song had harmony.

Their living was indeed meager, but what did it matter? They had each other, and now they had Christina. Neither Jonathon nor Rachel knew they were poor, for they were only poor materially. They considered themselves rich in every other way. As long as they were able to meet the simplest and most basic of needs, they were contented.

Rachel was able to continue some sewing at home, although the bulk of the responsibility for sustaining life fell to Jonathon. No obligation could have pleased him more. He felt a tremendous sense of pride in his stewardship as husband and now father. As he arrived home each night, he thanked his Maker for his richness of life and the love of his ladies.

Rachel's recovery from labor and delivery was quick and complete. Taking care of little Christina did not tax her but seemed to invigorate her. The natural recovery process of her body was quickened by her caring for her baby. The anguish of her birth was all but forgotten in contrast to the immense joy she now held in her arms. No movement had ever felt so natural to her as the motion of rocking her little baby to sleep. She felt that every second with Christina was a treasure, every day was priceless and irreplaceable.

It was difficult to sew during the day, whether Christina was asleep or awake. Rachel didn't want to miss a single smile in the waking hours or one peaceful breath during Christina's sleep. No matter what occupied her hands, her thoughts were on the baby: her breathing, her face, her dark brown eyes.

Rachel's life was all she had ever hoped it would be. Her soul was wholly consumed in the love of her husband and daughter. Her heart was drawn out in constant, fervent prayers of thanksgiving for what God had granted her.

Rachel was busy at the cast-iron, round-bellied stove when Jonathon arrived home. He held under his arm a small brown paper bag, which he carried back and forth to work each day. Going to work it was folded into a square in his pocket; coming home, it carried two small loaves of bread.

When he came in the door, his eyes first went to Rachel, then to the bundle in the beautiful wood cradle near the bed. The cradle was the most handsome piece of furniture in the simple home. It seemed such a fitting bed for their angel, Christina. Jonathon kissed Rachel, his love, on the back of the neck, then sat down on the bed near the cradle. He reached in and picked the baby up in his arms and gently held her. He spoke to her as he stroked her tiny head with the back of his fingers.

"Well, m'lady, what did you find out today? Were you good?"

"Tell your father you were very good," answered Rachel from across the room.

"Ah, you were good, weren't you, Christina," cooed Jonathon. Rachel smiled at the little voice her sturdy husband used when he talked with his angel girl.

"We saw a horse—she liked that," said Rachel as she poured onions into the hot broth on the stove.

"Was it brown? No. White?" guessed Jonathon.

"Black!" Rachel helped.

"Black. Oh my, that got a smile. Your first horse and I not there. Life is not fair."

Jonathon kissed the baby on the forehead, then laid her back in her bed. As he leaned over the beautiful spindled side rails of the cradle and looked at Christina, Rachel remembered something.

"A man came earlier—a solicitor."

She walked over and knelt down at his side.

"He asked if you wouldn't mind going by Cooke's store and signing some papers for the cradle. He said it was nothing, just for record keeping."

"That's odd. He didn't say anything before," wondered Jonathon aloud.

"Perhaps he forgot."

Jonathon held out a hand to her. She shuffled close to him and leaned her head against his leg. He held her close for a moment, then looked back at the cradle.

"The sooner it's paid off, the better. I don't like being in his debt!"

Little Christina took hold of his finger.

"She doesn't want me to go. Will you wait for me? I won't be long," he reassured.

"Hurry please," Rachel said.

Jonathon nodded. He smiled at the baby.

"A black horse, eh? Where am I when all the good things happen?"

"I love you!" whispered Rachel.

"I love you both, m'ladies."

He reached out and held Rachel's hand for a moment; then stood and walked to the door.

"Now don't you two be going anywhere else without me. I don't want to miss anything else! Promise?"

Rachel's worried face softened into a smile. He waited for her to wave goodbye before closing the door behind him.

It was between twilight and dark when Jonathon arrived at Cooke's store. The walk went swiftly as his mind was full of thoughts of home. When he arrived at the store, there were no lights burning within. He wondered why he had been so silly as to leave home at this time of night when he was sure the shop would be closed. He had made the trip for nothing. And yet he felt an urgency to react that superseded common sense. There was something about the circumstance surrounding the cradle that discomforted him. When it arrived at his home, he was apprehensive—troubled. He did not accept it as much as he had allowed it to happen. He accepted it by simply failing to reject it. When the deliveryman explained the arrangement, it sounded fair, yet felt foul. While Jonathon was contemplating his misgivings, the deliveryman took the cradle into the flat and set it in place. Little Christina was laid in the beautiful cradle before Jonathon really knew what had happened.

Seeing her there and the smile on Rachel's face as he entered the room was acceptance enough; no words needed to be said. He remembered glancing at the straw mat where Christina had been sleeping. What was adequate a moment before now appeared dirty and unsuitable. He was afraid to take the child out of the beautiful cradle and put her back on the humble mat because he was not prepared to deal with the disappointment he would cause. He watched Rachel's face as she tenderly talked with Christina. The deliveryman left, the cradle remained.

The irony of it all was that Rachel had experienced the same anxiety but did not want to disappoint Jonathon.

Jonathon reviewed the circumstances surrounding that event every day following the cradle's arrival. He tried to remember the exact words of the arrangement that was proposed to him. He had never been party to an agreement of this kind, and it frightened him. The closest he had come to consignment was when he had offered the midwife baked goods in trade for her services. He had no experience or understanding of such things. The transaction seemed harmless, yet he was prone to be suspect; there was something hidden in the words. Jonathon rehearsed again what was said to him. As best he could recall, it went something like:

"Mr. Cooke wishes to join in the celebration of your new arrival. He saw you in the store admiring this cradle, and he wants for you to have it. Do not be concerned about paying, what is important now is that the child has a place to sleep that is worthy of her. You can pay for it when you are able."

Two lines concerned Jonathon:

"Don't be concerned about paying for it," and, "You can pay when you are able."

Ableness was the part of the transaction that seemed so odd. If you are not able to pay for something when you receive it, then you are not able to buy it. That simple formula served Jonathon throughout his life. It seemed wrong to own something that he had not purchased with his own living. He much preferred a straw mat that he unquestionably owned to any cradle that, in truth, was owned by someone else. He felt burdened by the mere thought of owing someone money for something that he considered to be a luxury.

The shine of the wooden spindles on the cradle dulled for him each passing day. Adding to his perplexity was his lack of trust in Mr. Cooke. He considered him a dark man with hidden motives. He felt a loss of spirit in his presence. Being in debt made Jonathon nervous; being in debt to Cooke made him ill.

He determined at that moment that he did not want the cradle; he would bring it back to Cooke's store the next morning. He felt relieved once his mind was made up. His heart lightened at the thought of being rid of it. A smile appeared when he thought of Christina lying on her clean straw mat. It was what they could afford, and it was without obligation or debt. Besides, thought he, the Christ child slept on straw, and He was none the worse for it.

Jonathon was like a new man. The weight that he had carried on his way to the shop was in stark contrast to the relief that he now felt. He wanted for it to end now and not wait until morning.

He looked in the window but could see little. He tried the door handle—it clicked open. The bell inside chimed. Just as the door swung open, Cooke appeared around the opposite street corner. His timing could not have been more perfect. Cooke saw a dark figure lean into the open front door of his shop.

"Hey," he shouted. "What are you doing? Get away from there!"

Jonathon jumped back from the door. Cooke ran towards him while calling out to a watchman on the adjacent street.

"Help. Stop that man. He's breaking in."

The watchman hurried across the street as fast as he could, which was not fast. The officer's panting increased exponentially with each step. When he got close and held up the lantern in his hand, Jonathon could see he was elderly. If he determined to, he could outrace him and Cooke with minimal effort. The idea flickered for only a moment, then extinguished.

"Stop him. Don't let him get away," Cooke barked. The watchman seized Jonathon by the arm. There was no resistance. It took both of the older man's hands to reach around the taut muscles in Jonathon's arm. The watchman held on tightly even though he expected the robber to land a blow to him and run, but none came. It was apparent that the thief had no intention of trying to escape. The watchman released his arm, then stepped back.

"He doesn't need stopping."

"He's a thief, anyone can see that," said Cooke coming up alongside them.

"What has he taken?"

The watchman's eyes surveyed Jonathon's hands; they were empty.

"What are you doing here?" he asked.

Jonathon appeared dumbfounded. He was taken by such surprise that he didn't realize the question was directed at him. Again, the watchman demanded of him,

"Why are you here?"

"I came to sign some papers; that is all. The door was open."

The watchman reached for the handle and twisted the knob. The door fell open with little effort. The nightwatchman shrugged his shoulders and glanced at Cooke.

"It's unlocked. Do you always leave it unlocked?"

"It doesn't matter. The store is closed, anyone can see that."

"If you're so concerned about getting robbed it might serve you well to lock the door."

"What I do is my business. What about him?"

With a point of his finger, Cooke directed the watchman's attention back to Jonathon.

"You said something about signing papers? What sort of papers?"

"I'm not certain. Papers of sale, agreement papers. I'm not really sure," Jonathon stammered.

His confusion about why he was there, combined with the frustration of being falsely accused, had his mind reeling. He took several deep breaths to calm himself, then tried again to explain himself more thoroughly.

"This man gave us a something. We did not ask for it; it simply arrived at our house, and we were told to pay for it when we could. I am not a thief. I was asked to come and sign some papers, but we don't want it. I intend to return it tomorrow and be finished with all of this. Mr. Cooke knows me."

Cooke's head turned when his name was mentioned.

"Returning what? What are you returning?" asked the watchman.

"A cradle," answered Jonathon.

Cooke leaned forward and lifted the arched handle of the lamp, which hung in the watchman's hand. The light rose until it completely filled the shadows of Jonathon's face. Cooke looked at him closely.

Jonathon could now clearly see the eyes of his accuser. At first, he was relieved, knowing that Cooke may have been mistaken as to his identity before. He hoped that the entire misunderstanding would now be resolved. But as Cooke's stare lengthened, Jonathon began to feel uneasy. His thoughts somehow went to Rachel and little Christina. For some reason he could not understand, he began to fear for them. So real were his feelings of ill that he turned his head in the direction of home and almost ran to them. When the watchman spoke, it startled him.

"Do you know this man?"

Jonathon was about to answer when he realized that the officer was speaking to Cooke. He waited for an answer, but still none came. As he looked into Cooke's eyes, he saw evil. Cooke's face grew menacing. Jonathon didn't know what ugly decision was being weighed out behind those evil eyes, but he knew that it had something to do with him. A voice spoke to his mind as real as any his ears had ever heard; it said but one word: "Rachel."

So overwhelming was the warning that Jonathon breathed aloud the word as he heard it.

"Rachel," he whispered. Cooke's eyes focused. It was as if Jonathon could see Cooke's thoughts through those eyes. Both men understood in that instant what the other wanted.

"Take this man officer. He's a thief; he's a debtor," snarled Cooke.

"That's not true—you know me," defended Jonathon.

"You owe me money and haven't paid. That's all I know!"

"That was not the arrangement. You said we could—"

"Have you brought the balance? In full?"

"Of course not, you know we don't have it!"

"Take him away, he's a debtor."

The watchman was taken back by the sudden avalanche of words. He nodded towards Jonathon.

"Do you have a debt with this man?"

"I have the cradle, yes; but he said we could pay when we could."

The watchman turned to Cooke.

"Did you have such an agreement?"

"We had an agreement. He broke it."

"I didn't agree to it."

"You kept the cradle. That is agreement enough."

"We did not ask for the cradle, he sent it. Take it back. I'll go get it right now and be done with it."

The officer thought for a moment, then turned back to Cooke.

"That seems fair to me. If he brings back the cradle, then all is as it was before."

"I don't want the cradle," hissed Cooke, his voice different than before. The watchman stepped back from Cooke. Even he began to feel uneasy about the man to whose aid he had come.

"What do you want?" the watchmen asked.

Cooke paused, knowing full well that his next words could condemn the man standing before him. Jonathon's destiny dangled precariously on the hinge of Cooke's decision. He laid himself upon the altar of Cooke's compassion.

"Please, sir, don't do this. You know I have a family. Please, think of them. They need me. I am their provider, without me they will have nothing. Please, Mr. Cooke, have mercy."

"What do you say?" inquired the watchman. "You can't wish to prosecute. It will be debtors' prison."

"Don't presume to tell me what I think," Cooke snapped. "I want him taken away—to court, to prison, I don't care. My personal counsel will make arrangements in the morning concerning any legal matters."

Both Jonathon and the watchman were shocked at Cooke's decision.

"Are you certain? Do you understand what you are saying?" gasped the watchman.

"What? Do you question me? The word of a respected merchant against that of a pauper? Now you listen to me! Either act now, or be acted upon yourself. Do you understand?"

The watchman reluctantly took hold of Jonathon by the arm. Cooke backed against the door of his shop. It swung open. Inside the bell on the door rang. The ring blended with the dull ringing in Jonathon's ears.

The watchman moved forward. Jonathon followed in stunned submission. He was certain that the entire situation would be nothing but a bad memory once he had the chance to explain himself to someone. When they passed by Cooke, the watchman spoke aloud.

"The offended seems more hideous than the offender."

Cooke said nothing.

Jonathon beseeched the officer.

"Why? What have we done? My family—someone must tell them. Please let me go home first, then I'll come. You have my solemn word."

Before the officer had time to consider the request, out of the shadows in front of them stepped a boy. He had been hiding in the dark of an alley close enough to hear everything. At the sight of the boy, Jonathon stopped speaking. As he was led past him, he looked deep into the eyes of the Packrat. No words were said; they both understood. Jonathon looked back over his shoulder until he and the officer disappeared around the corner. The Packrat took off like a shot in the opposite direction.

He Was Cut Off

DISTANT VOICES ECHOED BACK AND FORTH DOWN THE
long empty halls of the stone prison. Clangs of metal locks and the banging of chains stung through the air above any human sounds. The rough-
hewn stones in the wall and floor repelled the grim sounds, creating an
endless droning of dread. Every view, touch, and noise in this wretched
place felt harsh and forsaken.

Within the wet bowels of the ghastly quarry, there was little light
and much less comfort. The walls were lined with shiny, slick black
stripes where ground water seeped through hairline cracks in the stone
and mortar. Dark puddles rippled on the floor when water dripped from
the ceiling. In debtors' prison, it was dark and cold regardless of the time
or season.

It was early morning when those below were awakened by the loud pound of the door thrown open at the top of the stone stairs. All those within the prison recognized that sound immediately. Shadows and light appeared on the stone steps leading down to the many different chambers wherein the offenders were kept.

The debtors' prison was comprised of one large room near the bottom of the stairs. About head high, there was a small opening in the huge wooden door into the cell. Other doors farther down the hall led to those being held for other offenses. Faces filled all the small openings when light from a burning torch descended the stairs. Footsteps on the stone stairs clapped down the empty corridors. Only one voice could be heard distinctly.

"Keep moving there, don't dally now. I think you're going to like it here."

Two shadows appeared at the base of the stairs. Metal clinked as one of them scrolled through several keys on a chain. The faces in the small opening backed away as the jailer reached forward and inserted the key into the lock and turned it. There was a loud click. He then lifted two boards off the supports on either side of the door and dropped them with a loud bang to the floor. Jonathon jumped at the jarring sound.

The jailer pushed open the heavy door and peered in smiling. It was then that a third man appeared at the bottom of the stair holding a handkerchief to his nose and mouth. While he watched from the bottom stair, the jailer reached back and began taking the shackles off Jonathon's wrists. He smiled as he worked. The chains fell from Jonathon's arms to the floor. The jailer put his large hand on Jonathon's back and launched him blindly through the narrow opening.

"All right, meet your new mates, all debtors. Well, what do you think? A fittin' place for the likes a' you."

The door slammed shut with a loud boom that echoed down the length of the prison halls. The jailer leaned back and listened, relishing each reverberation of the thunderous sound. It sounded as distant cannon fire. As the echo began to diminish, the man with the handkerchief spoke.

"He shouldn't have any contact with the outside; no visitors, no letters—understand?"

"Oh, he won't, sir," assured the jailer.

"Good."

The man cringed.

"Damned sores," he moaned.

"What's that, sir?" queried the jailer.

The man reached in his pocket and slipped something under the handkerchief into his mouth and began chewing. He reached in his pocket again and laid several coins into the jailer's hand. He ascended the stairs without another word. The jailer followed, a few steps behind. Several seconds later, the door at the top of the stair shut with another boom.

His Soul in Hell

THE STORE WAS EMPTY. THE LAST CUSTOMER THROUGH the front door was gone by more than an hour. The last customer through the back door left just minutes before. Cooke was not expecting anyone else when he finished the detail of closing up shop and exiting through the front. He turned back to lock the door. He heard the lock click, then pulled the key free of the hole. When he turned back to the street, Rachel was waiting.

She stepped directly into his path; in her arms she carried the cradle. Christina was wrapped in a sling across Rachel's chest. She laid the cradle in front of Cooke and tried to catch her breath while she spoke.

"Please sir, let my husband go free. Here is the cradle, take it. We don't want it!"

She stepped closer.

"I can work for you. Perhaps there is a service which I can provide if only you will please let him come out."

"Take off your hood," said Cooke. "It will help me remember who you are."

Rachel pulled back her hood. Her hair fell in rich folds as the woolen hood released its contents.

"You know who I am," she said.

"Yes," he said. "Of course I know you. I thought you would come."

"Then you know my need."

"I know what you want."

"Will you help us?"

"I have every intention of helping you; I always have, but first, you must help me."

Her worried face broke into a relieved smile at the reassurance of Jonathon being released.

"That is wonderful! Oh, thank you, sir. I knew there had been a mistake. Thank you. Where shall I put it? Back in the store? In the front window?"

Rachel picked up the cradle. Although it was large and heavy, she lifted it with ease. She carried it toward the front door to put it back.

"I don't want the cradle."

"But it's in perfect condition. We have taken good care of it."

"I don't want the cradle."

"Then you will accept my services; that is fine, I can work. You will be pleased with my work. There are many things I can do."

She put the cradle back down on the paved walk in front of the store.

"When will you have Jonathon released? Now? There is much he can do also; you've never seen a harder worker. I promise you can trust me to do what you want. Can he come out tonight?"

"Not quite yet."

"When?"

"In time. In due time."

"Tomorrow?"

"When your obligation is met."

Rachel did not understand. Her smile leveled into a confused stare. Cooke began to move towards her; he put out his hand to touch her arm. She stepped back from within his reach.

"What do you want with us? Why take Jonathon?

"I don't want your husband."

"Then have him freed—now, please."

"I want what should have been mine in the first place. I have the power to free your husband, but you must earn it."

"I've said I can work. I promise you won't be disappointed. When shall I come? Now? Tomorrow?"

Christina suddenly cried out. Rachel folded back the layers of cloth that covered her baby's face. As with all mothers, her full attention was now turned to her child. Even though Cooke answered, she did not really hear him.

"Good, that's good, come tonight. Late, come late. I'll be waiting."

Cooke reached out and touched Rachel's hair. She cowered like a child at the flash of lightning. She felt as though virtue had been taken from her. Repulsed, she stepped back while instinctively covering the eyes of her child. When she saw how Cooke looked at her, she understood.

Her head began to move from side to side. At first faintly, then with more and more urgency. She pulled Christina close to her, clinging to her as if holding on to life itself. Her eyes began to fill with water. She could no longer see Cooke clearly through tear-filled eyes, but she could feel him near her. He reached out his arm again. She fled as though all hell were at her heels. She did not look back, nor did she stop until her legs gave out and she slipped and fell into a rubbish heap behind a pub. She held Christina tight to her breast. She bent over her child, sobbing.

A Man of Sorrows

No LIGHTS WERE LIT AT LINCOLN'S INN THEATRE. THE doors had been bolted shut hours before. It was only minutes before the calling of the midnight hour when loud knocking on the door broke the silence of the night air. At length, the theatre door cracked open with the clank of a metal bolt, and the manager, John Rich, peered out. Handel stepped from the shadows into the light coming through the open doorway. Rich sighed in relief.

"Ahhh—Handel. He who avoids the light of day."

"I need more time."

"Fine greeting for this time of night."

"You must put off our creditors for a time."

"Now you come—when it's too late."

"They will listen to you."

"They once listened to me, but, thanks to you, they have corrected their error."

"Appeal to their good natures."

"They have no such weakness. They want restitution."

"We'll give them what they want."

"You can't pay the debt any more than I can."

"There is another way."

"There is no other way! You're mad! You've lost your wits. And you've nearly caused me to lose mine." Rich suddenly remembered something. "Wait here a moment; something came for you."

Rich slid behind the partially opened door. Handel watched his shadow move across the inner wall and down the hall. Soon the shadow reappeared, followed by Rich's face in the door.

"This came by courier today."

He handed Handel a folded envelope, which Handel stuffed in his coat pocket.

"I have an idea that I think will appease them," Handel urged.

"Pay the debt—that will appease them."

"If it's drivel they want, then that's what we will give them. We'll fight the *Beggar's Opera* with a better beggar's opera."

"You have indeed gone mad. Compete with the people's opera?"

"It plays to packed audiences at the King's Theatre."

"It can't be done."

"Of course it can."

"Not here it can't."

"And why not?"

A peculiar sadness clouded Rich's face. He voice was laced with melancholy.

"I'm forced to close the doors. For twenty-three years I've stewarded the theatre, cared for it. Long before you came, I was here trying to compete with the grand houses of the city, and we gave them a run for a time. Now, if I can't find an investor to cover our losses, I'll lose the place—along with everything else."

"I have an idea for a satire," interrupted Handel.

"Did you not hear me. I have to close the theatre."

"I can be ready to rehearse in a week, two at the most."

"Listen to me!" said Rich. "It's over, there will be no next, no other. They are finished with us. They don't want me—they don't want you."

Handel couldn't believe his ears. He was first stunned, then outraged.

"If you think it's my fault, you're as foolish as the rest of them."

"What are you talking about?"

"London high society, the divas, you, and Rolli—you're all jealous. Putting the Saxon in his place. Why am I the enemy?"

"You are your own worst enemy!" Rich shouted. "You blame everyone but yourself. You alienate all around you—throwing your tantrums, mocking your singers. You don't give a damn about anyone but yourself! You're nothing more than a selfish, spoiled brat."

"What good is your empty hall without me? Do you think people come to see the seats? The plaster walls? No! They come to hear me."

"Who comes? Where are all the people you speak of? It's over. Let it go. We gave it a good try and failed," said Rich.

"It's not over! You may have failed, but not me," barked Handel. Rich shook his head.

"You've been given a gift that you don't deserve," he sighed.

"I am the gift!" screamed Handel. "Do you hear me? I am the gift!"

Handel stood purple-faced and panting. Rich was crestfallen. There was nothing left to say. Frustrated, he backed through the theatre door and closed it.

Handel left the theatre in haste, but within a few blocks his walk slowed to a burdensome plod. His feet made a loathful sound when the soles of his shoes scraped over the cobbles. His chest rattled out broken breaths. Occasionally he would stop at the confluence of the street and an open alley and pause to catch his breath.

The air was unusually cool for early autumn. A heavy mist filled the streets and although it never fully started to rain, the ground was damp and slick. The cobbles shone in the blue diffused light of the half moon that could barely be seen through sheets of mist overhead. Occasionally it would disappear completely behind high clouds. The contrast of the warm light from the street lamps and the soft lunar source made the street seem to stretch endlessly in a repeated pattern, as if huge mirrors hung on either side, reflecting infinitely the same image.

Handel noticed none of this. His eyes were fixed on nothing in par-ticular. He walked slowly, his head slumped forward over sagging shoul-ders. He moved like an old washerwoman, bent forward from years of scrubbing and unaware that her backbone had changed until she could no longer stand erect. He didn't see beyond his next step. Everything out-side his immediate view went unheeded. He walked from memory, uncon-sciously negotiating his way toward home through the night streets of London.

Either the hitch in his step had grown or the cobbles were more uneven, for the arthritic tic, which in better times was almost unnotice-able, now affected every step. He dragged his right foot awkwardly, never allowing the full weight of his body to land solely upon it. Most of the weight fell on his left foot. His cadence was uneven and inconsistent. The few who saw him winced as if it were painful to watch him walk.

When he did become aware of others nearby, he would enter an alley and lean against a wall in the shadows. One could pass within a few steps of him and never notice. If he heard footsteps approaching he would wait until they were long gone before emerging from out of the darkness. He made every effort to be invisible. There was no one he wished to encounter.

When he heard several loud voices coming towards him, he moved into the next alley and waited. It was especially dark in the shadows where he stopped. He silently waited as three dark forms appeared in the open portal to the street, then eclipsed past the wall which shadowed him. As their voices diminished, his eye fell back downward. That's when he saw it.

A few steps before him, just beyond the dark line of the shadow that hid him, was a sullied and stained corner of paper sticking up from the ground. Something about the damp corner of paper seemed strangely familiar to him. He stepped forward, reached down and took hold of the fin of paper between his index finger and thumb. The wet corner tore free. He lifted it to his eye and recognized the ink-blotched letters "*Dei.*" Handel's face reddened as blood rushed into his cheeks and forehead. A sudden hotness rose from his chest and up his throat. He dropped to his knees and began digging frantically in the crust. He clawed at the ground with his fingers.

He reached for an abandoned bottle lying against the wall and broke it on a brick outcropping. Using the broken shard as a spade, he stabbed at the hard, gray, crust until lacerations began to appear in the dirt. Once past the outer shell, the ground broke free. As he frantically groped through the clay and pulled back the dark earth, he discovered buried playbills. Each time he found a new one, he paused to read, "*Deidamia*, an opera by George Frederic Handel."

The further he dug, the more well preserved the playbills. He groaned aloud as he uncovered one thick pile of papers stuck together. His moan echoed down the walls of the alley. When he could find no more, he stopped digging. He knelt in the dirt, panting. He leaned forward and rested upon his hands.

At that moment he appeared contrite, but his thoughts were nothing of the kind. Names, circumstances, and betrayals swirled in his mind in a spiraling cyclone of contempt. Crumpled and dirty playbills laid all around him in filthy piles.

One by one he picked them up and put them in a stack. In all, there were nearly forty. He tucked them under his arm and lifted himself to his feet. He stumbled back into the darkness and leaned against the wall to rest. As he stood there in the shade of night, he tried to think of whom to appeal to concerning the wrong that had been done to him. He considered the Royal Academy, then realized that any efforts would be futile—too much time had passed. In spite of whatever efforts he might try, he knew that there was nothing that could be done.

He looked out into the street. From where he stood, he could see a single sign post standing erect in the half light of the moon. Like a forgotten dream, he began to remember being there before, but the specifics were hazy. Then little by little the details of that night came back to him. A night months before in the bitter grip of winter, he had stopped at that post. He had found a torn playbill in the snow that he had assumed had been ripped from the nail by the wind. He remembered pushing it firmly back on the nail before walking on toward home. Now, he knew that it was not the wind that had so heedlessly flung the playbill from the post. His arm tightened over the pile of handbills that he held in the crotch of his shoulder. Handel knew he had been sabotaged in the theatre, but it was difficult to imagine anyone so bent upon his destruction to contend with the freeze of winter to tear down playbills. He felt a sudden shiver at the thought of such a concerted effort to crush him. He no longer felt hidden by the night, but exposed for all to see. He wanted away from this place. He slid his back down the length of the wall toward the street and stepped from the alley toward home.

As he did, a pair of eyes followed him. A few steps deeper than he had been in the alley was a second person, hiding even better than the first. He alone had witnessed the entire unearthing of the past. He alone saw the man fall forward on his hands and knees in utter and complete despair. He saw the man's eyes, heard his rattled breath, felt his anguish. He watched everything from his place under the broken eave not ten steps from where the playbills were dug up.

The Packrat emerged from under his shelter and walked to the piles of dirt where Handel stood moments before. He recognized this as the same man who had pushed the errant announcement back on the nail that cold December night. He also recognized him from the skirmish with the ruffians at the theatre. It was the same face on the man who had saved him from possible death, certain irremediable harm. He looked to heaven and whispered softly, "This is You isn't it. You're doin' this to me. I hope Ya' find pleasure in Your messin'."

Three times Peter had encountered the man, and each time his response was different. The first was in this very place; he mocked the man. The second was at the theatre; he revered the man. The third was in this same alley again; he pitied the man. Of all the encounters, the last caused him the most reflection. The other two experiences—although extreme in both instances—were common to the street. The Packrat was well acquainted with the stinging thrill of exploitation, the adrenaline surge of a fight, but what he felt as he watched the man dig up the hand-bills was new territory. He wondered why he felt so compelled to somehow help this man he knew so little about. Rather than see the man's digging, the Packrat wished he could have just picked his pocket. But for Peter to witness what he had, rendered the man a prisoner of his heart. To turn his head and dismiss what he now felt would be a lie to himself.

A heaviness began to fall on the boy; he wondered if it was guilt. Only once before had he felt the darkness which he now felt seeping into his heart: when sight was taken from James. The man who knelt in the darkness had somehow caused him to think and feel things he had neither asked for nor wanted. And what harrowed his soul the most was a distant voice from deep within his memory that whispered something else: he had encountered the man on another occasion. But when, and where? That was the question that forced him from the alley and out into the street to follow him.

Handel's pace was slower than it was before finding the playbills. He no longer concerned himself with others who might be on the street at night. He made no effort to hide as two carriages in tandem drove past him. He hardly moved out of the way. The large wheels clapped over the cobbles only inches from his foot, yet he never looked up.

His legs moved involuntarily. He held the brass head of his cane loosely in his hand. The rod flayed back and forth with no observable meter. Had he lost his step and needed it to steady him, chances were good that he would end up on the ground.

As he walked, a lone playbill slipped from his arm and fell to the ground. Moments later, a small hand picked it up. The Packrat looked at it, then, for some unexplainable reason, he walked to a nearby posting board and pushed the sullied playbill onto a nail before continuing his pursuit. Peter tried to keep the man always in sight. His curiosity burned so brightly that he took no chance of letting the man get out of his view.

The boy silenced his steps. It was a skill he had learned and perfected as a child. He took great pride in the fact that he could walk within a few paces of his prey without their hearing his coming or going. He taught his soles to be soft; his heels to roll.

Handel stopped in the street as if he had walked headlong into an invisible wall. He turned his head slowly toward the window of a small pub at the side of the street. Loud voices escaped through the ill-fitting doorjamb and out into the open air. Handel heard something in those verbal offscourings that stopped him dead. Quietly he moved toward the window for a closer look. The Packrat closed in.

There was much movement within, but the faces were not clear. Handel stepped over the muddy curb and up to the square pane of glass. Large drops of condensation streaked down the undulated surface of the window. Handel peered in. He squinted his eyes against the glare of the fire burning in the fireplace. The room was full and rowdy. Every mouth was moving; every voice boomed. It was difficult to make out specific words, but he could easily discern the sound of laughter. That was what drew Handel in. He had heard a familiar laugh coming from the pub and he determined to investigate.

Handel looked from face to face. He recognized no one. When he was satisfied that he had seen all there was to see and was about to leave, a single penetrating voice of laughter rose above the others. Handel's skin quivered, but not from the cold. He turned back to the window, searching for the source of the sound. As if in answer to his query, the tide of motion within stopped; a sea of bodies opened before him. At the far end of the swath stood a man with a face that Handel instantly recognized. The face bore a long thin scar above the eye and a smile of absolute evil.

The ruffian leader stood staring at him through the pane of glass between them. At his side sat a man with his back to Handel. When the lead ruffian nudged him with his hand, the man rose to his feet. He stopped short of completely erect when a nerve in his back pinched and his torso contracted. He held his head cocked rigidly to the side. His feet shuffled until his head came around to face the window. Handel recognized the ruffian who had borne his perfectly aimed board across his back. Upon seeing Handel's face through the glass, the thug reached his hand behind and rubbed a knot next to his spine.

The third ruffian was brought into the circle, and the laughter in the room was soon quashed beneath the suffocating anger emanating from the three men, who stood staring at the face in the window. The fire in the hearth burned no hotter than the fury in the eyes of the cutthroats. A sinister laugh pierced through the damp silence of the room. The ruffians had but one thought: revenge. Providence had finally provided the opportunity for which they had anxiously waited. Handel knew he had but one saving chance for escape. He ran.

He nearly slipped and fell at his first step. His foot slid out from under him as he pushed off the ground with all his might. When his shoe slid sideways on the polished cobbles he caught himself with his cane which, luckily, lodged in a secure notch in the cobbles. For an instant, the full weight of his body leaned on the thin black rod of ash wood. It bent under the load, but did not break. The crutch stabilized him just long enough to gain back his footing and run. Had he fallen, there was a good chance that he would not have gotten back up. Handel knew the hoodlums were not men of mercy.

Handel ran for his life, driven forward by the clear and distinct knowledge that if caught, he would be beaten until senseless or, more likely, dead. As he ran, he considered going on the attack in a face-to-face fight. He knew that given his immense size and strength, there was a slim chance he could fend them off in hand-to-hand battle. Age was not his ally. If he did fight and eventually give way, these were the kind of hellions who would punish him many times over for each blow received. They would settle for nothing less than to inflict permanent damage, even death. He dared not risk either.

He intuitively knew they would take the greatest part of their anger out on his face and hands. Wicked men have an uncanny ability to conceive of ways to injure an enemy far more perniciously than just wounding the body; they target the soul. He was certain they would leave him ugly to view, and, worse yet, they would steal from him the use of his hands. They would take away from him his love and livelihood. He shuddered when he imagined the sound of the bones in his hand snapping under the bully's savage heel.

Handel ran as fast as his huge body could. He did not think of the pain in his hip or the soreness that would be suffered the next day. In spite of his size, his legs moved as if they could remember running through the fields of Saxony as a boy. His arms flailed wildly, handbills flew out from his armpit leaving a perfect trail of his escape. He grabbed hold of one, then fanned the others free. They flew in a spiraling storm behind him as the wind caught hold of them in his wake. When he came to the first perpendicular intersection with another street, he turned and disappeared from view.

When the three men burst through the pub door, the fallen playbills were the first thing they saw. The papers created a trail so wide and obvious that the leader bellowed. "A fat trail to a fat man. This is too easy."

Handel heard his voice clearly. He had only twenty steps lead when he rounded the corner. He could hear their steps on the stones behind him; they were closing fast. He desperately looked for someplace to hide, but he could see nothing ahead of him. His mind raced for alternatives. He tried to spot a door that might be unlocked at a late hour, but, alas, there was none to be found. He kept running, knowing full well that he would never outlast them. If he continued, his escape would be temporary. The last thing he wanted was to be pulled down from behind like the prey of a feeding lion. His options waned. He determined the only real chance he had was to fight. He tried to think of anything he might use to his advantage and could think of but one: Perhaps he could surprise them at the corner and take out one of the men, evening the odds some.

He rounded the corner of the alley, tried to stop, but far underestimated the physics of his weight and speed. It would have been easier to stop a runaway cart loaded with milkcans than for Handel to stop so suddenly. His feet slid out from under him. Handel had no time to react. The full weight of his body slammed against the stone pavement. He slid on his side and legs. He felt the stinging smart of skin peeling back along his thigh and hip. He covered his face with his hands as he rolled toward the brick base of a building that paralleled the street. His huge body careened against it, driving the air from his lungs and knocking the wind out of him. He rolled to his stomach against the wall and gasped for breath, his face pressed against the wet ground.

At that moment, the brutes rounded the corner behind him. Each footstep pounded on the drum of Handel's ear, which was pressed hard against the earth. He watched their feet get closer and closer. He was unable to fight or resist their attack as his lungs still burned for air. He felt the ground pulse against his face with each step of their feet. He cowered in anticipation of the first blow he knew would certainly come.

He waited.

The panting of the thugs got closer.

Out shrieked a laugh from the leader.

Handel's muscles tightened for the first kick.

He closed his eyes as their shoes came so close they went out of focus. His quivering lips moved in silent prayer.

"God, help me."

The ghastly wind from their bodies breathed against his cheek as they ran by him. Their footsteps trailed off down the street and echoed away until they were gone. Somehow, to Handel's amazement, they hadn't seen him. All at once, a long inhale rushed through his teeth to his imploded chest. Like an immense void, his lungs sucked in life-giving air. He sat fully back on his knees to open up the innermost cavities of his air-deprived lungs. Breath came in a raging flood of relief; his chest swelled wide to receive it. Strength flowed back to his limbs as his blood filled with oxygen.

"How did they not see me?" he whispered in astonishment. He then noticed a hard, black line on the ground next to him. The wall that he had fallen against was high enough to create just enough shade from the dim moonlight to hide him in a black shadow. The corner of the street he had rounded shielded him from the light of the corner lantern. He looked around himself at the rectangle of complete darkness surrounding him. It was just big enough for his body and no more. He searched the rest of the street for such a shadow as the one in which he knelt; there was no other. Had he fallen a few feet to either side, he would not have been hidden. His amazement was cut short by the sound of distant voices approaching. He knew his pursuers had lost the trail and were retracing their steps. This time they would not be so hasty nor would their eyes still be adjusting from the fire in the pub. He rose to his feet and ran partway back the way he had come, then off down a side street. He did not hear the voices again.

When he was several blocks away, he slowed his pace. As he did, the sharp stinging of his wounds began to speak to him. His legs were sore, his side bruised. The hitch in his step came back as before, only more pronounced. He stopped once to see if he was bleeding through his shirt and thought he heard footsteps behind him. He stood motionless for several seconds before he was certain he was alone. Only then did he turn down the narrow alley that opened onto Brook Street.

The Packrat saw none of what happened within the pub. He stood across the street and watched Handel standing in the warm light emanating from the window. Peter could hear the voices from within, but none distinctly. When Handel ran, Peter was caught off guard. He jumped from his hiding place to follow before realizing that whatever scared Handel would probably scare him too. He jumped back quickly, as if tethered to his hiding place. Just as he fell behind a heap of dead tree limbs and garbage, the three ruffians exploded out the door.

Peter was too far away to see their faces, but he recognized the voices—especially the leader's laugh. He dared not move. The foremost of the bullies struck such fear in his heart that he determined to follow Handel no further. He huddled close to the rubbish and decided to wait until everything was fully clear before moving on.

While he waited for the coast to clear, he spotted a partially eaten apple amid the rubbish. He stuffed it in his pocket for later. When he was certain he was safe and could finally leave his hiding place, he saw a shadow move out of the corner of his eye. He bent low and waited. A short while later, he saw the shadow again, farther down the street. This time he recognized the shape and the limp. He was back on the hunt.

Handel was safe. As he neared the end of the alley leading onto Brook Street, he walked with confidence. He was not so careful as he had been. He proceeded down the center of the alley, cutting every possible corner. He knew the safety of his home was only a few minutes away. Again he thought he heard steps behind him, paused briefly, then quickened his pace. The open end of the alley grew large before him. Once out, he had only to cross the street past two flats and he would be safe at home.

Without a second thought, he walked out into Brook Street in full stride.

Standing on his porch were two men. Handel was certain that two of the ruffians had found his home and were waiting while the other circled back and was coming up from behind. He retreated against the wall, hoping beyond reason, that they hadn't spotted him. He leaned close to the corner of a protruding door frame under a shop awning across from his apartment. He had no escape. His path to safety was blocked—retreat would most certainly reveal him to anyone who might be following. It was by sheer luck that he hadn't as yet been discovered. In the stillness of the night air, he could hear every word of the conversation on the porch. He tried his best to breathe silently as he listened.

"Did you hear that?"

"What."

"I'm not certain—but there was something."

One of the men nodded toward the place where Handel stood.

"Over there, I think."

There was a long silence before he spoke again. This time he whispered.

"If there is someone, he's probably seen us by now."

Handel did not recognize either of the voices. Their language was not the uncouth blather of the ruffians in the pub. He wondered who would wait for him in the middle of the night. One of the men stepped down off the porch. Handel could see that he had on a black cloak. The man looked up and down the street for a long time then stared back toward the corner shop where Handel was hiding.

"If it is Handel, he's hiding, waiting for us to leave."

The man left standing on the porch muffled a laugh with his sleeve.

"Hiding? Handel hide? T'would be easier to hide a summer hog. Do you think he can just slip into a crack in the pavement? Aye, that would be a sight."

"He could be hiding, listening to your mindless rambling."

"Where? Behind a street lamp? Under the rug? I hope not, we'll never find him," the man joked.

Handel watched as the man on the street took something from his pocket and slipped it into his mouth, all the while staring at the place where Handel stood. Handel could see that this man was more meticulous than the other. The uniform and hat on the man on the porch identified him as a constable, but the identity of the other was not clear. He was far more cautious and calculated in both his words and actions. The constable was careless, loud. He spoke again.

"You must want this debtor badly to be out this time of night."

"He's a big prize for those who sent me."

"He's a big prize all right," the constable laughed.

The cloaked man continued to gaze into the blackness wherein Handel stood. The longer he waited, the more certain Handel was that he had been seen. He grew impatient. He pushed even tighter into the frame under the awning. His leg accidentally bumped against a loose brick, knocking it free. It fell to the ground at Handel's feet with a dull thud.

The cloaked man's eyes tightened. The constable turned in the direction of the sound.

"I heard that. What was it?"

"It's him," said the other.

"What should we do?"

"It's your job to fetch him. I suggest you do it."

The constable stepped from the porch and began to walk toward Handel's hiding place. Handel felt his throat tighten as if terrible hands were strangling him. He glanced around, trying to spot a way to escape. As he searched the darkness, he saw something that sent a chill down the length of his back.

In the shadows, not ten steps from where he stood were the white rims of two eyes looking back at him. In terror, he stared into someone's eyes in the shadows—someone who held his destiny in the balance. One shout from the stranger in the dark and Handel was a prisoner. His very existence rested upon the person in the darkness. Words of persuasion were impossible. Any effort to prevail upon the person's mercy would be seen. Nothing could be communicated beyond what could be said through the eyes.

The constable came closer. He had walked to the side of the street where Handel hid himself. He stood in the light of the street lamp just two flats away. Steadily, he kept coming. The cloaked man followed the constable as far as the lamp, where he stopped. Now Handel could see his cloak and face. He could tell that he was a solicitor, sent by those he owed money. The constable paused. He looked back at the solicitor standing in the lamplight. The solicitor said nothing but pointed to the exact place where Handel hid. The constable pressed forward. He was far too close for Handel to have any chance of running. Fear shone in Handel's eyes. He was surrounded. Once again, the constable stopped, not ten feet from where Handel stood. The constable looked back over his shoulder. The solicitor pointed again.

"It came from there!" he said.

The constable turned back to the place where the solicitor's finger was aimed. Handel gazed into the eyes in the dark staring back at him. A single word from whoever was there and Handel was exposed. The constable took a long, slow step forward. He thought he could discern a dark body before him. He leaned forward to take another step.

Suddenly, a young boy leaped from the shadows behind him.

"I know what you're lookin' for," he laughed.

The constable jumped back in fear and surprise. The Packrat looked at Handel. For an instant, their eyes met before Handel's closed in hopeless despair. Peter grinned as he reached for the apple in his pocket and took a bite. With his mouth full, he raised his arm and pointed directly at Handel.

"Look right there."

Handel's eyes opened as the constable's head turned away from the boy and back to him. Like a flash, the boy's arm was back. The constable's head jerked forward as the apple pelted him in the back of the head and careened against the wall. Laughing out loud, the Packrat bolted off down the street, with the constable cursing at his heels. The boy skipped and ran just fast enough for the constable to think he was gaining ground. The last thing Handel heard before their voices trailed off was the boy laughing.

"Bloody grown-ups. Fools with years of experience."

The man in the street also heard. He did not turn to watch the chase. He stood in the exact spot he had been, staring into the darkness where the Packrat had pointed. When all was still, he spoke in a whisper.

"If you can hear me, be careful not to rest too easy. I'll be back. Oh yes, I'll be back. There are few things more entertaining than watching an arrogant man beg for mercy. I wouldn't want to miss that show. You should understand, you're an entertainer."

His last words were strained through a wince of pain. He chewed the plug in his mouth strenuously. Handel heard him take a long deep breath, then walk away until the black of his cloak fused into the black of the night.

Handel dared not move from his place. He stood motionless in the shadows for hours after the constable and solicitor were gone. He was certain that his assailants had only walked from sight, crept back through the back alleys, and were waiting for him to appear. Just as the darkness had hidden him, he believed it now hid them. He searched every black hole for movement. The very thing which had protected Handel was now most frightening to him. At one point during his sojourn in the dark, he heard a rustle in the leaves of a nearby cubby hole. After hearing nothing but his own heartbeat for several minutes, he watched a cat wander out of an alley and cross the empty street.

Handel shivered in the chilly night air, but the fear of being discovered outweighed his discomfort. Each time he considered leaving his hiding place, he imagined the ruffian just a few steps away, waiting in the dark to thrash him, or the lawyer waiting to have him dragged off to debtors' prison.

Twice, a nightwatchman walked down the opposite side of the street, stopping on the corner to announce the time and weather. Handel hoped that light from the watchman's lantern would help him see farther into the darkness, but he saw nothing, no one. When he heard the distant tolling of twelve from the tower, he considered coming out, but thought the time was too obvious for such a move. He felt compelled to wait a while longer.

Finally, when he could feel what little remaining stamina he had being completely stolen away by the cold, he determined to make a dash for the door. He convinced himself that, if he willed it strongly enough, any eyes upon him would be averted for the few seconds it would take him to get safely inside. When the need to flee screamed at his consciousness so loudly that he couldn't stand it any longer, he slid forward from his place in the shadows. He clung to the wall as he moved around the front of the house into the lamplight. He inched forward, hoping that his enemies would not see him. He made his way past the window, to the porch. His foot caught the end of the step and he tumbled to the ground, scraping the skin from his palms and shins; he didn't feel it. He was instantly up and running across the street in plain view. He ran as if savage bloodhounds were right on his heels ready to pull him down from behind should he falter. He slipped as he clambered up the short walkway to the porch. He fell toward the door, praying that by some means it might be unlocked.

Miraculously, when he came to the threshold, the door swung open, and he fell through onto the cold tile of the entry. He scrambled the last few steps on all fours as Peter Le Blonde pushed the door closed behind him. Out of breath and stumbling, he climbed up the stairs, made his way down the short hall, and collapsed onto the small couch in his dimly lit study.

Peter LeBlonde had watched everything from the parlour window. From the time the solicitor and constable first knocked on the door several hours earlier, he had kept watch. He saw the two men walk into the street. He prayed for his master's safety when it looked certain that they were closing in on him. He saw the boy throw the apple and the subsequent disappearance of the two men. Hours later, when Handel made his last desperate run, he saw him coming and readied himself at the door. Once Handel was inside, LeBlonde locked the door securely before going to the stove to draw hot water for his master.

Handel sat only long enough to catch his breath before going to the window. As he crossed the room, he pulled off his coat and tossed it on a chair. The envelope that Rich had given him earlier fell to the floor, but he didn't bother to pick it up. When LeBlonde entered the room, Handel was positioned at the side of the window, peering over the curtain to the street below. Handel heard his servant enter, but he kept watch on the street.

"How long were they here?"

"Since early this evening."

Handel turned from the window and leaned against the wall. To him it seemed that his world was in irreparable ruin. He knew with absolute surety that he was alone and looking down. There was not glimmer of light at the end of his tunnel. Through the past months, he had considered every asset that could possibly be mortgaged or leveraged. He had thought of every outstanding notice, bill, and invoice. The burden was too heavy. He had finally arrived at the last rung of despair when he realized that he was beyond his own ability to save himself. He tried to think of individuals he could call on for help—anyone with the wherewithal to allow him to escape from the miserable corner in which he was trapped. He considered what collateral he could borrow against and by what means he could possibly secure salvation, but ultimately there was nothing. If someone were to help, it would be for no other reason than compassion.

Handel thought of his very closest friends —not the occasional friends or circumstantial friends of good times, but those true and trustworthy friends who would not ask questions but simply give aid. There were only a few, and they had already been taxed beyond their limit to help further. Handel had even pushed Mrs. Delaney to the point in which she had compromised the goodwill of her husband. There was no more she could do. She dared not erode her husband's trust further by providing surreptitious aid to anyone— least of all Handel.

Handel's mind swept through names of people he could approach. One by one, he crossed off anyone who would want strings attached or whose confidence he had already lost. He tried to be logical about his situation, but after months of thinking through all of the options, all possible escapes, none could be found. He had exhausted every resource. Finally, his travail brought him to this single night—the final reckoning he had tried to avoid. If a rescue ship did not appear—literally out of nowhere—he would drown.

The realization of his hopelessness embittered him. He was not humbled by his circumstance but angered by it. The longer he thought about his plight, the more heated he became. Vengeance flamed in his heart. Self-pity quickly fanned it into a boiling rage.

"Why? Why has God forsaken me, turned his back when I need Him? Why close the door in the hour I need him most?"

Never had Peter raised his voice to Handel—he neither dared, nor was it his place to do so—but Peter could take no more. His patience could no longer be gated.

"God did not close the door, you did! You were more concerned with the honor of men than honoring God. He has always been there. You turned your back on Him. He has given you a gift, yet never have you used that gift to praise the Giver of it. Now you blame Him for giving you the freedom to squander it away. God is the very reason that you are standing here now. What are you without Him? Nothing."

Peter paused long enough to take a deep breath.

"You chose this path. You think of no one but yourself. You think you have earned redemption because you are a great man, but great men make all those around them great. They inspire men to be better than they are. You inspire no one."

Peter walked from the room into the hall. He stopped in the dark, looked back, and saw his master standing alone against the wall. Several minutes passed. While Peter watched through the doorway, Handel picked up the envelope from the floor, opened it, and began to read.

Handel's body began to quake. His eyes moistened. The legs that had born him through the long night of running, finally gave out. Handel dropped to his knees. Peter went back to the broken man he dearly loved. Handel looked up into Peter's eyes.

"She's gone. My mother is gone."

Handel's spirit was wholly broken. His head fell forward in anguish. Peter knelt alongside him but did not offer any assistance. From a distance he had watched the rise of Handel, and now he had seen him driven to his knees. He felt constrained to allow his master to walk both paths alone. He was there to render aid but not until it was sought. He respected Handel too much to assume any less. Peter waited at Handel's side.

Finally, the master leaned back and looked at his servant. Never had Peter viewed the man he saw now. He had become a man of lowliness, a man of sorrows. When he spoke, the words came from his soul.

"What do I do?"

Peter answered in a reverent tone.

"Give yourself to God; submit to His perfect will. He has given you a gift, but you must pay a higher price to be worthy of that gift. Perhaps He has need of you."

The servant's head fell forward in the attitude of prayer. He closed his eyes.

"If your soul is to find rest, you must also go to the garden—alone—in the dark of night. Walk through the gate, kneel by the rock, and submit to Him who gave you your passion. Your path is a desperate one. No, I do not envy your gift—I pity it."

Peter rose to his feet. He walked to the door, then paused for only a moment.

"Go back to the hayloft"

"What if nothing comes?"

Peter left the room. Handel was alone.

Behold the Lamb of God

THE MASTER REFLECTED ON THE SERVANT'S WORDS. HANDEL had lived his life with the shortsighted expectation that ease and prosperity was the reward for doing good. Until that night, he had never considered that the expectation of reward for doing good was, by its very nature, self-serving. He had falsely assumed that he deserved better because he was better. He somehow believed that his stature in life was preordained, as one of God's chosen, to bear the great gifts of mortality. But what of the widow, the orphan, the child born diseased? Was he so blind as to think their mortal state was punishment for lack of premortal valor? Wasn't it a simple pauper boy who had saved him earlier that night? What of him?

Handel painfully arrived at that pivotal moment of humble reflection when one's life of good or ill stares back from the mirror of memory. A life of good is its own reward. It pays back a hundred times over, just as bread cast on the water washes back in waves upon the sand. A life of selfishness is its own punishment. There are many courses that lead to despair, but only one path leading up and out; God is the author. It is on that path that the finest and purest of efforts begin. If one is to accomplish a great feat, it must come with great sacrifice. The holier and more righteous the endeavor, the more sacrifice God will require. He will purify the outcome by purifying the doer of the deed. That is how God's plan works. He will not intercede to correct the mistakes of men, thus robbing them of agency; He will correct men until they give unto Him their agency. He will try them in order to let his will and mind distill upon them. He will chastise their peace, wrench their heart, wring out their soul, until their eyes meet with His.

Throughout the history of mankind, this has been God's pattern of preparation. He does not make His will known through great men; He brings His perfect will to pass through humble men, thus making them great. Abraham, Joseph, Moses, Christ—these were God's chosen because they chose God.

The greatest of men did not start with a powerful step forward, but by humbly falling to their knees. Great deeds have always been forged in the fires of sacrifice and despair. One who lives in a bright room will hardly notice changes in the light. One who has walked in blackness will see the tiniest flickering candle in the distance.

Handel remained on his knees, his eyes closed, silently pondering the nature of God until the darkest hours of the morn. When he opened them, they opened to a small oil painting of the crucified Lord that hung on his study wall. Handel looked deep into the penetrating eyes of the Christ. He thought back to the eyes staring back at him in the darkness of the alley. He remembered the perfect shadow that hid him from the passing ruffians. As he pondered, he began to perceive the magnitude of immaculate providence by which he had been protected through that long night. As painful as his steps were, he began to comprehend the reality with which each was taken. If the events had not unfolded exactly as they did, the floor on which he now knelt might have been far more cold and hard than the oak floor of his study. As he considered each life-saving detail of the preceding hours, a thought flashed before him as real as if a flare had been struck in the black void surrounding him.

He rose to his feet and walked to his desk. Handel opened the drawer; his eyes rested upon the libretto, *Messiah*. He thumbed through several pages. He silently read the words on the page where his finger had stopped.

"He was despised, rejected of men. A man of sorrows and acquainted with grief."

Handel picked up the libretto along with the small, low-burning candlestick on the desk. He walked to the harpsichord and laid them on the stand. He sat down on the stool and stared at the words before him. He looked back at the face of the Savior hanging on the cross. He reached forward, gently laying his fingers on the keys.

Handel waited.

Long minutes passed. Still he waited.

From far away, as if wending its way toward him in the night breeze, something began to develop in his mind. It was so faint and distant that he could not recognize it but only anticipate the arrival. He waited in the stillness for the shape to take the form of sound. He imagined he could see the sound coming toward him, a veiled line of blue streaming toward him through an ocean of black.

At the moment he believed the line would finally reach his ear. The silence was shattered by a loud knock on the front door.

The Packrat had no fear of being caught. He knew, without a doubt, that he could lead the chubby constable as far as he wanted then escape untouched at any time. The pudgy man was slow and careless. The Packrat mused to himself that he could have slipped into any sliver of shadow, and the constable would have passed him by without so much as slowing down, if slowing down was possible. So easy was his escape, that for an instant the Packrat actually felt a twinge of guilt for having hit the man so squarely in the back of the head with the apple. But the thought vanished when he remembered the officer's head lunging forward, his hat flying, and chunks of fruit stuck to his hair. It was a direct hit; any doubt of rightness or wrongness of the deed was quickly preempted by his immense pride in such a perfect throw.

The Packrat led the officer down alleys and backstreets. Peter laughed and sang as he went, leaving plenty of time between verses to hear the curses of the chasing adult. Most of the boy's songs sprang from the threats being shouted at him from behind. The Packrat took the curses and names he was called and put them to melody. He sang a string of swearing back at the constable. His song was so sour it could have instantly curdled fresh milk, but the voice that sang it was happy. The ear-blistering teasing kept the officer in pursuit far longer than his stamina allowed. Several times, Peter waited for the fat man to catch up so he could lead him even farther away, always making sure that his face could not be recognized.

If the constable stopped to rest, the Packrat would stop, too, always close enough for the officer to see him waiting. This infuriated him even more. Peter would stand a short distance away, mimicking every word and action the man did. If the constable bent over, panting, Peter would bend over and pant. If the man leaned against the wall and issued forth curses, Peter would respond in like fashion. This game went on until well past the hour.

When the officer finally broke off the chase, Peter followed him to make sure he went home and not back to Brook Street. He purposely stayed close enough for the officer to see him following along, but there was nothing the man could do. His anger was utterly wasted, the boy only made sport of it. When the Packrat was certain that the adult was entirely spent and was headed home, the Packrat himself turned toward his home.

Peter's thoughts quickly shifted back to the more significant events of the night. From memory, he reviewed what had happened at each stop: the playbills, the pub, hiding on Brook Street. The face of the man who hid in the dark was emblazoned upon his memory. He could not get that face out of his mind. For some compelling reason, Peter had acted irrationally and had taken a chance by helping someone he didn't need to—an adult at that. He brushed it off as a payback for the man's helping him the night of the opera. Now that he had made things even, he could forget the face and, hopefully, never see the man again. The Packrat smiled and shrugged up at the sky.

"He's all Yours now. I'm rid of 'im. Good luck; he's a full-time job. No wonder Ya' needed my help."

The boy chortled as he skipped off down the street. He went several blocks, each a little less joyful than the preceding. The relief of forgetting Handel was short-lived. In spite of Peter's efforts to forget the man, his face came back into his mind with force. The memory of something that transpired long ago haunted him. He knew that there was a detail he had missed, but he couldn't figure out what. He tried to remember back as far as he could. He rehearsed in his mind all of the important encounters with grown-ups he could think of, but nothing rang clear to him. He stopped several times to try to piece people and places together, but it was hopeless. If anything did happen, it was long ago and no longer important.

After putting much effort into trying to remember, the Packrat was happy to get the man off his mind and move on to more important things. The face in the dark disappeared from his consciousness.

Peter thought of his urchins and hoped they were safe, since he wasn't there to watch out for them. He imagined them tucked into feathery down beds with full stomachs and bread under each arm. He tried to imagine himself next to them, dreaming away in silent slumber. The mere thought of it made him laugh out loud.

"Fat chance," said he. "My pockets is empty."

Peter thrust his hand into the depths of his pocket. His fingers touched something. He stopped dead in his tracks. The smile left his face. He remembered.

Handel was afraid. At first he tried to deny the fact that he had heard anything at all. So harrowing had been the night that he had no problem explaining the sound away as a nervous reaction to the wind. He looked toward the window; no branches were stirring outside. He again dismissed it as some other common house sound—settling perhaps. When he had convinced himself it was nothing, he looked back at the paper propped before him.

Again, he heard the sound. It was a knock at the front door. This time there was no mistaking it. He rose to his feet and stepped noiselessly into the dark hall. Peter LeBlonde sat asleep in a chair just outside his study door. Handel thought at first to awaken him to answer the door and fend off those who came to take him away, but he thought better of it, deciding it was not right to put Peter in a position to have to lie for him.

Handel slipped downstairs and into the parlour. Through the sheers over the window he saw a shadow pass in front of the house. He peeked through a thin crack between the curtains. He watched as the shadow moved across the street and into the far alley.

In the distance, he heard the toll of two o'clock. He waited, wanting to make sure that the visitor was not a decoy for others who may be waiting just outside his door. He tried from every possible angle to see the porch, but no matter where he went, there was still a blind spot. He waited several minutes before cracking the door open.

Nothing.

He opened the door a little wider and looked to the right, then the left; the streets were empty. The shadow he had watched leave was alone. Handel had no idea what the caller had wanted, but he didn't care. He didn't want to speak to anyone, especially someone calling at this hour. Whatever it was, it could wait until morning—or better yet, never. As he closed the door, he glanced downward. He thought he saw something unusual. He slowly reopened the door.

There, barely visible in the dark, was something on the outer door. A small rag, tied into a sack, hung on the door handle. Handel took the bag in his hand and lifted its string off the knob. He closed the door, bolted the lock, and stared at the ragged, cloth bag as he climbed the stairs back to his study. He could feel that it contained something, but he knew not what. He passed by Peter, asleep in the hall.

Handel sat down at the harpsichord in his study and pulled the lighted candle closer. He loosened the string snugged around the top of the bag and unfolded the cloth. When the light of the candle shone on the contents, Handel's head snapped back—he gasped at what he saw.

There, shining bright in the golden light of the candle was a big, shiny, bent button, partially severed in the middle. Handel lifted it between his fingers, holding the piece close to his eye. He studied the sharp edges where the button was split by the sword's steel edge. In the mirroring surface of the button, he saw himself. He had no idea who had brought it or how it had come to him. God had somehow moved upon the giver of this gift at the one moment in Handel's life that he was most prepared to understand its meaning. By divine intervention he had been preserved, not just that night, but many times in his life. When he looked at his reflection in the button, Handel knew that God knew him.

He also knew that the greater miracle was yet before him. Still, he was afraid. It was not fear of those outside that haunted him but fear of himself. What of his gift? What was God's purpose for him? Handel shuddered at the possibility that he had squandered away his endowment and offended the delicate spirit from which his inspiration came. He knew what his servant Peter said earlier was true; he was indeed a proud and arrogant man. The realization that he might have lost his birthright brought an overwhelming sense of shame. He felt wholly unworthy. There was no question that he still possessed talent. He was skilled in the craft of music. He had studied and developed that craft for the greatest part of his life; most certainly that remained intact. He also knew he could spend the rest of his life pounding out bars of brilliantly crafted song, but without the inspiration from God his efforts would remain damningly telestial. He was fit for this world but not beyond. How he longed to hear the music he had heard when he was a child; but it had been months—years—since he had felt that kind of inspiration.

From the time that he began to enjoy overwhelming popularity and success, he had listened less and less to the whisperings of his heart. He listened more to critics than to the voice inside him. His music became large to the ear but small to the soul.

In contrast, the music of his heart was pure and melodic; it seldom demonstrated his unequaled ability and prowess. The music of his mind was elaborate; it afforded him the opportunity to flatter people's ears with impressive and technically perfect music. He slowly had given up the one for the other. The latter suited his desires more readily.

Over time, Handel had become obsessed with showing what he could do rather than what he felt. Now he hardly dared to try to go back, for fear there was nothing left to go back to. Nevertheless, he knew he must try.

He laid the button at the base of the candlestick. Trembling, he reached forward; his fingers touched the keys.

He waited. Nothing happened.

He closed his eyes and bowed his head.

He heard nothing. There was no answer.

Then softly, like a voice from a distant source it came to him—a single violin of transcendent purity, echoing across his mind like music ringing down the valleys of Halle in the cool of the night. So distinct and clear was the melody that he could see the notes on paper as he heard them. He opened his eyes. On the page before him were these words:

"I know that my Redeemer liveth."

The words had melody, sweet as any strain that had ever come to him. As he listened, a tear streaked down his dry cheek.

Seen a Great Light

PETER LE BLONDE WAS UP EARLY. THE DOOR TO HIS MASTER'S study was closed. Peter did not disturb him; perchance he was asleep. Peter descended the stairs to the kitchen. He looked out the kitchen window onto a beautiful, late summer morning. The sky was deep blue, and sunlight was just starting to stream into the house.

To say that Peter was concerned about his master was a gross understatement. It was literally all he could do to keep from bursting into the study to ascertain the mindset of his master. He had no idea how the remainder of the night had evolved for Handel. In lieu of succumbing to the whims of his curiosity and going where he was not invited, Peter busied himself as best he could while he waited for some word or sign from Handel.

There was little cleaning to be done beyond any mess he himself made, since Handel seldom strayed out of his study. Peter stoked the stove with coal, put a kettle of water on to boil, then went out early to procure needed food for the day. He used his own money rather than asking Handel for any.

"You buy enough for two, but I see only one. Where is Handel?" the shopkeeper queried. "He's not been out on the street."

"His health lessens. His hand can barely hold the pen," Peter answered.

"How will he live?"

"He will train the other hand to hold the pen," said Peter, ascertaining the direction the conversation was headed.

"In the meantime," said the shopkeeper, "I'd like his account to be brought current."

"You question his credit?"

"I hear things in the market.... I hear your master's last two operas were no better than his health. They say Handel plays best to empty halls. Some say his time is passed."

"You hear this in the market?"

"Perhaps London expected more," nodded the keeper.

Peter could detect the slightest curve of a smug smile on the man's lips. Peter dropped the goods he had been holding onto the counter and left. Before the door could close behind him, he heard the shopkeeper call from within.

"Remind him of his debt—and give him my regards."

Peter was away only a few minutes before starting back home with a small loaf under his arm. Supplies had grown meager over the past several months as money grew scarce. Peter never complained. With the countless burdens heaped upon Handel, he would have starved before he would add to the pressure under which his master already labored.

As he entered the flat, Peter could stand the suspense no longer. He spoke loudly, hoping that Handel was both awake and close by.

"Sir, it's a beautiful sunny day."

He put down the bread and began opening the shades and curtains of every window. Sunlight poured in, drenching the room in warm, amber light.

"You must take some time this morning for a short walk, although I know that you do not fancy morning walks. You'll not notice the steps."

Peter finished with the windows on the main level. He climbed the narrow stairway, speaking all the while. Each word carried with it more air than the previous. Through the past months, the steps seemed taller than before.

"The shopkeeper gives his regards. He has missed seeing you," Peter rationalized the exaggeration. He did not tell a lie, he simply omitted the part of the conversation for which he had no use.

"He asked that I wish you good health."

Peter's words were interrupted by a loud, important knock at the door. The beats of his heart suddenly increased in speed and intensity. A flash of white blinded him. His fingers gripped the stairway banister as he felt his equilibrium begin to falter. His breathing became staccato. Chilly sweat seeped through the tight skin of his forehead. He spun around and hurried back down the stairs, trying his best to keep from blacking out. Fearing the worst, he approached the door, certain he would be opening it to the two men who had waited long into the night. He loathed being put into the position of answering their questions now that Handel was, in fact, home. He stood behind the door, trying to catch his breath, while formulating in his mind words of ambiguity rather than deceit.

There was another knock, much louder and longer than the first. Peter looked up the stairs to the landing, certain that Handel must have heard the knock. Handel did not show himself. The servant unlocked the bolt and opened the door halfway.

"Is Mr. Handel home. George Frederic Handel?"

Peter did not recognize the lone guest standing before him. His first thought was that the men had sent someone in their stead, knowing that the door would not be opened to them. Peter remained calm.

"Who should I tell him is calling?"

"I have urgent business with him."

"Concerning?"

"Concerning matters of personal interest."

"Is he expecting you?"

"No."

"May I tell him what it's regarding? He's very busy."

"I've come a great distance to see that he gets this."

The visitor held up a large cloth pouch, folded and tied shut with a broad piece of twine. Peter stared at the pouch, then the visitor. The man's clothes were common, his shoes unshined. The man's eyes were red and bloodshot, his face flushed. The inseam of his pants was wet with sweat and horsehair.

"Where did you come from?"

"Halle. Are you familiar with it?"

Peter could only nod.

"Can I trust you to make sure that this gets to Mr. Handel?"

Peter nodded again. The courier placed the pouch in his hands, then bowed and walked back towards the street. For the first time, Peter noticed the horse tied to the corner post. Dark patches of sweat rimmed the saddle. The courier turned one last time before leaving the short walkway.

"I rode through the night. I had strict instructions to be here by this morning."

"Who sent you?"

"The executor of the estate. It was the deceased's last request that this be delivered this morning."

Peter took the pouch inside and closed the door behind him.

Handel worked through the night. When dawn began to blue on the dark horizon, several pages of score lay before him, scattered across his desk. He inked the last few strokes on the paper, then sprinkled sand on the page to help the ink dry more speedily.

The notes on the page sloped forward as if written with urgency. In some places where haste had not allowed ample time for drying, the ink was blotched. The score was readable, but barely. The notes themselves betrayed the speed with which they were written. It appeared as though Handel's hand could hardly keep up with his head.

While he waited for the ink to dry on the aria on which he had worked through the balance of the night, he sat back in his chair and rested his eyes. A peaceful calm settled on him like morning dew on spring grass. His countenance was serene; his hand was steady. Even though he was weary, he was not sleepy.

After a few short minutes of respite, he rose from his desk. The jarrings and bruises of the night before had stiffened his legs. They were sore, his back and knees inflamed, but it didn't matter, his mind was on things more important than pain.

Once up, he gathered the sheets of score strewn before him and stacked them into a pile. He laid them neatly on the desk. He then surveyed the study. Sunlight was just beginning to enter through the narrow slits around the curtain. Shards of light pierced the room and rested upon the harpsichord. Handel walked to the window and pulled back the curtain; the room filled with light and color. As his servant had earlier, he too looked up at the sky of vibrant blue. The warm sunlight seemed to draw the stinging out of his wounds. His joints loosened. His face was tranquil. His mind was sure.

Handel walked purposefully about the room, putting everything in order and straightening anything awry. He was most earnest with his music and scores. These he put in a cherrywood locker he had placed on blocks in the corner of the room. After he traversed the room twice to make sure he had everything, he took the aria from the desk and laid it on top of the other manuscripts before firmly closing the lid of the locker.

He then gathered together in one arm several pages of loose paper, a quill, his inkwell, and his Bible.

Lastly, he leaned over and blew out the candle still burning on his desk. When the wax near the wick had hardened enough not to spill, he added it to the things in his arm. He exited the room and pulled the door closed behind him, wondering when the next time would be that he would enter it again.

The chair outside the study was vacant. Peter had already left for the bakery. Handel entered his personal bedquarters and laid the articles he was carrying on the dressing chair next to the vanity. He took a small traveling case from under his bed and laid it open. He thoughtfully selected several pieces of clothing he thought would be most suitable for the circumstances to which he had determined to surrender himself. As he considered each item to take, his face was staid, his hands, composed. He was not afraid of what faced him. He prepared with sober dignity, fully resolved to submit himself into the omniscient care of God.

Handel folded each article of clothing before laying it in the case. When he was satisfied with his selections, he added the items he had brought from the study. There was still considerable space available when he closed and clasped the buckles on the small case. He looked around his room one last time. He put his hand on the bedpost to steady himself while he descended to his knees. He knelt at the side of his bed, head bowed, for several minutes. He heard Peter come in the front entry and speak to him, but he remained on his knees. The next sound he responded to was the door. He slowly rose back to his feet. Handel knew his hour had come. There was a second knock, louder than the first. He heard the front door open; he was certain the men had come for him. He picked up his case and walked down the stairs. As he descended the steep steps he could hear voices out front, but could not make out any of the words. As he stepped off the bottom stair, Peter LeBlonde reentered the front door.

Peter was surprised to see Handel standing there with his case. Peter knew where his master was planning to go. He laid the pouch in his master's hands and walked into the kitchen. Handel had prepared his mind so completely to accept the unavoidable fate that he was unprepared for anything different. He had come down the stairs resolved to surrender himself to the authorities and debtors' prison.

Handel stared at the pouch in his hands, unaware of its contents or origin. He put down the case and sat down on an armless chair in the entryway. He untied the twine that secured the bag, then folded back the layers of cloth cover. When he saw what was inside, he stopped breathing.

Before him were all the letters and money which he had sent his mother over the many years. Dorothea had saved everything—hundreds of letters, nearly five thousand pounds. She had used none of what he had sent her for herself but saved it for him instead. She had loved him completely in life, now she had reached back from the grave to save him. The thought of his dear mother going without desperately needed food and warmth through the waning years of her life broke his heart. Her sacrifice saved enough money to pay his debts, enough to buy food, enough to heat his home through the long winter approaching. Here was his deliverance from the pitiless caverns of prison. Nothing short of a miracle could have saved him. Broken and hopeless, he had prayed to God for a miracle. God had sent one: his mother. The son put his face in his hands and wept.

And They Were Sore Afraid

Rachel did not see the sunrise although she was fully awake when it came. So hopeless was she that even the brightest of mornings could not dispel the darkness of her heart. Her pain was personal and individual. She had not slept at all that night, nor had not slept comfortably any night in the many months since Jonathon had been unjustly imprisoned. Her nights were long and restless. The hours never lingered on so painfully long as they did at night. Her loneliness was exhausting, yet there was no solace in sleep.

Rachel spent the long nights scheming every possible means to have Jonathon released. She implored everyone who she thought might facilitate his freedom, but to no avail. She could not find ears to hear her terrible plight. No one was interested in justice, only in money, of which she had little. Her efforts to free Jonathon used up what meager resources she could muster.

Rachel went without food for days on end to save what little she could to try and secure the services of a solicitor to review Jonathon's incarceration; but as was often the case, she was easy prey for the predators who fed on the weak and unfortunate. Rachel lost all that she had. Those she employed had all promised so believably, then disappeared so completely.

For weeks, she held vigil at the door to the prison in hopes that she might send a message to Jonathon. Finally, to her utter dismay, she was moved along and off the street. Over time, she lost strength for the race. Fatigue wrested away her hope. A day at a time, her spirit and body were weakened until she no longer could produce milk for Christina. Her body literally dried up. She could endure the pangs of hunger herself because of her love for her husband, but she couldn't endure the cries of hunger from her child.

She sewed as fast as she could, but without Jonathon's pay, she could not keep up with the obligations which fell solely upon her. She asked those she knew for help, but they were too desperate themselves to assist. She tried to get additional work, but no one wanted her service with the additional baggage of a "brat." Finally, she begged on the streets, but few hearts that passed her were softened.

The ugliness of her plight became even more hideous as she began to perceive her two greatest desires at odds with each other. She could not see a way to earn enough to support her and her child and have any hope of earning what she would need to have Jonathon released. In her wretched state, she could not see how God would give her the miserable mandate of choosing between the two things she loved the most. The mere thought of one without the other made her soul ache within her. It would have been no more painful to have her heart ripped in half.

Night after sleepless night, she debated the ugly predicament in her mind. After one bitterly long night, when the light of morning filled the room, her agonizing decision was made. No course could have been more wretched. She had nearly given up her life to bring Christina into the world; now she was nearly giving up her life again to keep her in the world.

When morning came, the tiny baby lay asleep in a tattered blanket on the small straw bed on the floor. Rachel knelt on the wooden floorboards, bent to the ground at Christina's side. Rachel hadn't moved from that position for hours. Her knees were callused and swollen from countless nights of kneeling. Her silent prayers had but two themes: one which lay asleep next to her, and one who waited beneath the wet stones of debtors' prison.

Her eyes were swollen. They were perpetually wet from the miserable combination of grief and fatigue.

Now that her mind was made up, the reality of her resolve made her ill. Her tired eyes gleamed with fresh tears. Hushed cries of despair laced every breath she took. As she looked at the perfect smile of peace on the sleeping child's lips, her misery deepened into her lungs. It was hard to breathe. She felt as though her chest would cave in under the strain of her broken heart. The very womb that had nurtured her baby during pregnancy felt as though it was wrenched and torn within her. Her cries became sobs. Rachel could not bear the thought of what she had determined to do. With trembling arms she reached out for Christina. Those arms that would have faltered under the weight of a loaf of bread, lifted the child with ease. She pulled the baby to her breast.

"Oh, Christina. What else can I do. Dear God, help me. If only I had milk enough for my baby."

Unconsciously, Rachel began to rock back and forth from knee to knee. She buried her face in the coarse wool of the child's blanket.

She did not move until she felt something gently touch her face. The child had awakened. Tiny fingers reached for her mother's cheek and touched it. Rachel pulled her face from the wet spot in the blanket and looked into Christina's brown eyes. She could see her reflection in the dark glass of her baby's pupils.

Somehow, it was reassuring to Rachel. She stroked her baby's face with her fingers. She leaned close and whispered in Christina's ear, hoping beyond reason that the child would understand and forgive her for what she was about to do.

"What I do, I do for you—though it breaks my heart."

Rachel kissed the child on the neck, then on the cheek. Christina prattled at the touch of her mother. The small birthmark on Christina's neck was wet.

Rachel bundled up the child and once again held her close. As she stood up, she almost fell back down; her knees were frozen in position. She slowly straightened her legs until the blood circulated back through her joints so she could stand erect. The sting of her legs coming back to life was easily endured as it briefly postponed the awful task that awaited her.

Finally, when she could walk, Rachel cradled her bundle in her arms and walked out into the street.

She hurried through the streets of London, trying her best to avoid any contact with people. She did not stop, nor did she slow. She looked at no one. She walked for over an hour.

Three times she came close to her destination only to turn down another street and delay the inevitable. She approached the fourth time, closed her eyes and kept walking forward. When she opened them, she could see a large wooden gate before her. She stopped. Her eyes lifted from the bottom of the enormous weathered oak door to the top. She had seen the place before, but never had it seemed so impenetrable as it did now.

She listened for sounds on the other side but could hear only birds in the trees above her. She glanced at the blackened words carved into the wooden gate:

"Foundling Hospital: For the maintenance and education of exposed and deserted young children."

Near the letters was a small turret in the gate, supported by two heavy brass hinges. The small hatch door on the turret was approximately the size of an infant. Rachel reached out and pushed open the turret door. When she pulled her arm away, the hatch fell shut. The loud knock of the door hitting against the solid wood of the gate scared her. She retracted from it and shielded her baby from the threatening pound.

When she looked back up, she saw a broad, stained rope at the side of the turret. She touched it. She could hear the faint ring of a bell on the opposite side of the gate. Her hand tightened around the rope. She did not pull on the rope, but eventually her arm lost strength; it fell to her side, her hand still clutching the rope. She heard a sharp ring from the other side of the wall. She leaned against the broad gate and waited, her face buried in her child's rags. Moments later, she heard a quiet voice through the opening in the door.

"Is someone there?"

Rachel did not look up. Her grasp on Christina tightened. Through the thin shroud in which the mother's face lay, muffled words escaped. Only the person on the other side of the opening in the gate heard her.

"Dear Christina, I give you into the hands of the Lord Jesus."

Rachel lifted the child with offering hands and carefully pushed open the small door of the turret. The hatch swung inward. She lifted Christina through it. Once the baby passed under the wooden door, the hatch fell down on Rachel's extended arms. At that moment, the child became irretrievable. Rachel cried out when she realized what she had done. A sickening pall of shame pierced the deepest recesses of her soul. She began to pull back as if to retrieve her baby back through the passage, but it was futile. The sharp edges of the wooden hatch dug into her arms. The harder she pulled, the deeper the black splinters sank into her forearms. There was no escape. The more she tried the more severely her arms were wedged. She cried out in desperation.

"Please, dear God—help me!"

Rachel felt a gentle hand touch hers. Someone, whom she could not see, put a reassuring hand on hers and was helping to support the child in her arms. Gently, the warm hands led Rachel's hands inward, releasing her from the turret door that bound her. The pressure on her arms eased. The hands tightened again around Rachel's. She no longer feared. She was no longer alone. Someone—unseen, but felt—knew her plight. Rachel felt something touch the back of her hand. A cheek brushed her skin leaving a streak of wet where a tear was brushed away from the unknown face. For as long as she could endure, Rachel held on to Christina. At no time did the hands leave hers, nor did they attempt to pull the child from her. The hands would not take the child, she had to let her go.

Little by precious little, Rachel released her grip on Christina and gave her over into the arms of the one within, but not before softly crying one last time.

"Oh, Christina. My dear, Christina."

She released her baby into the care of another forever. As Rachel's arms emptied of the child, the hands that held hers lifted her open palm and kissed it. Rachel felt the door lift from off her arms. She pulled them back through the open hole. For a brief moment her eyes met the eyes of the woman in whom she had put all hope.

The woman on the other side saw Rachel's eyes, which she could only describe as "windows to suffering." The woman's heart swelled at the brief sight of Rachel's eyes. They were eyes that she would never forget— a mother's eyes.

The turret door closed. Rachel's strength gave out. She fell in a heap to the dusty ground at the base of the heavy door.

He Shall Gather the Lambs with His Arms

A SLIGHT CREAK REVERBERATED OFF THE COLD STONE walls of the apse. An aged priest entered by a side door and walked across the front of the chapel. His shoes clicked on the smooth slabs of stone floor as he walked. The only other sound was the quiet murmur coming from the few people who had come early to offer up their devotions to God. The few who were there sat apart from each other, as if each possessed a small plot of earth within these walls of prayer. The priest knew each of them—not by name, but by where they knelt, which was always the same.

He noticed that the women who came early to pray were especially devoted and predictable. Their time of arrival was seldom off by more than a minute, or their place of prayer off by more than an inch. His early morning flock was few in number but bounteous in faith. He loved them.

Over the long years of performing the morning ordinance, he had learned
of them. He knew them by their bowed heads, the fold of their hands, the
tone and timbre of their whispered words. He could kneel at the altar, listen to the gentle murmur of humble utterance, and know exactly who was
there, and where they were sitting.

He earnestly prayed for these, his people, petitioning God for their
souls, their families, to ease their hardships. He considered these few to
be in one of two groups: his most faithful or most hopeless. Why else
would they be here at this early hour? It would be far easier to be like the
vast majority of his congregation and save their prayers for Sunday. For
that reason, he felt unusual devotion to these who were most devoted.

When the priest reached the altar at the center of the chapel, he
knelt and faced the crucified Lord. He folded his thin fingers over one
another and rested them on the altar. He bowed low and began offering
up his prayer on behalf of his people. While he prayed, he heard an
unusual sound.

A single voice penetrated his ear above all the rest. He did not recognize the voice. From the back of the chapel came the gentle sobs of someone inconsolable. It was a voice of absolute suffering. The barely audible
cries of agony were deafening to him; they echoed in the deepest canyons
of his soul. He had felt suffering like he now heard only once in his life,
when he saw his father and tiny sister crushed under the cruel wheels of a
nobleman's carriage. He had watched his father run into the street to save
his only daughter from the wheeled giant, but neither escaped. His father
caught hold of his precious little one just as the killing wheel went over her
fragile back and his bared neck. They died in the terrified grip of each
other. When the cowardly owner pushed his head out the carriage window
to see what had happened, he cursed them both for making him late, then
shouted the driver on. The priest witnessed all of it. Nothing in this world
could heal him. Peace had only come through the atoning blood of Christ.
He enjoined himself to the priesthood in gratitude for his redemption
from hatred. He believed there was nothing else for him to do.

As he knelt at the altar, he could think of but one thing: the voice
behind him. Words of prayer were lost to him. He stood up from his place
at the altar, crossed himself, then went in search of the sufferer. He found
her near the back, huddled into a fetal ball, weeping. He entered the pew in
front of her, leaned over, and laid his hand on her quaking shoulder.

The granite spires of the cathedral stood tall and erect like huge thorns piercing the blue sky. Rachel did not see them. She walked with her eyes to the ground. All that gave her cause to look upward and rejoice was gone. When she came to the steps of the church, it had been twenty-four hours since she had given little Christina to the Foundling Hospital. Losing Jonathon broke her heart, losing Christina broke her spirit. She had no will to go on. She wanted only to disappear from off the earth, to be swept away into oblivion.

As she wandered, she had no clear thought or view of what to do or where to go. Her face was expressionless except for frequent tears, which she made no effort to wipe away. Even as drops ran in streams down her face, her expression did not change. Anyone who knew her well would swear she had aged years in a single day.

When she arrived at the door of the church, it was by sheer accident. She had wandered onto the path leading to the entryway of the cathedral without realizing where she was. When she reached the doors, continuing forward required less energy than stopping and turning, so she entered. Her momentum carried her forward past several pews before she finally gave up. She stumbled into a long, narrow aisle between two pews and collapsed on the bench. Here she remained until she felt a warm hand on her shoulder.

"My child—are you lost?"

Rachel didn't stir. The priest waited, then continued, thinking that perhaps she needed to confess a transgression.

"My child, what is the terrible burden that you carry? Give it to the Lord Jesus and find peace."

Rachel raised her head. With tear-swollen eyes she gazed into the compassionate face of the priest. At first she did not understand. She had forgotten what it felt like to have someone truly care about her. Yet in this stranger's face, she saw benevolence—a virtue grown strange to her. There appeared in her eye a look of childlike wonder. Perhaps here was someone who could understand, who could help. As her mind caught hold on that thought, a tiny flame of hope began to kindle in her heart.

"It wasn't a burden which I gave. She was light in my arms. I gave Him my joy, my longing, my very soul."

The words fell like wet snow on a fledgling fire, nearly dousing all hope completely. She felt a stinging chill as she said aloud what she had done. Until now, she had rationalized that she was doing what was best for the child, but even as she said the words, the finality of it suffocated her in a sea of shame. Any chance of restitution or recovery seemed impossible. She could hold back no longer. Her words spilled forth in rattled sobs.

"They've taken my husband. He did nothing, and they took him to prison. Now my child—my only child, I cannot care for her. I have given her to the Foundling Hospital. She is no longer mine. I have given her away to hands that I do not know. I had no milk for her. My body went dry. She was hungry. I couldn't bear her crying. Please, don't let her cry."

Rachel could speak no more. Although she made little sound, her thin body convulsed with each choked sob. The priest stroked her trembling hand.

"She's now in the care of God. He will feed her." The priest's voice was calm and assuring. Rachel's breathing began to soften and she opened her eyes and looked at him. He spoke with certainty.

"'He shall feed his flock, like a shepherd; and gather the lambs with his arms.'"

Rachel's rigid body relaxed, blood began to find its way to her cheeks. The priest spoke again.

"'Come unto me all ye that labour and are heavy laden and I shall give you rest. Take my yoke upon you and learn of me, for my yoke is easy and my burden is light.' That is His promise to you."

The priest's voice spoke to her heart. Rachel heard every word and cherished them, but still she did not understand.

"My child's gone, I am alone. Where is there rest for me? I'm beyond God's sight, in a place where his eye doesn't see."

"God sees all of his children."

"Then He watches only, His hands do not help. When I called for Him, He hid Himself. He takes from me the only joy I have ever wanted."

"No, not so. He did not take your child, you gave your daughter freely, as He has given His life for you. There is no greater love than to give your life for another. This you have done."

Something swelled within Rachel, like a fire burning in her soul. She could not hold back the tears. She tried, but they could not be stayed. The tears came not from her eyes, but her heart. Her face turned upward.

Long, steep shafts of sunlight streaked from the high windows to the floor. One small refracted beam found its way to where they sat. She watched the soft light stream down through the dark hall.

"Peace, child," whispered the priest. "'For the Lord seeth not as a man seeth; for man looketh on the outward appearance, but the Lord looketh on the heart.' God has seen you. He knows your need. You will see the fulfillment of it with your own eyes."

Somehow, beyond all worldly reason, she believed him. Rachel lifted his hand to her cheek and held it. She stood on her feet, kissed the back of his hand, then left quietly. The priest watched her leave, then knelt where he was and prayed.

He Shall Speak Peace

Peter LeBlonde waited in the kitchen until he heard his master's footsteps going up the stairs. He knew that whatever had come from Halle was from Dorothea, and he did not want to intrude upon personal matters. Now that his master was back in his study, he continued with the preparation of their simple breakfast.

He drew hot water for tea, then set about a tray with bread and cheese. When he passed through the hall to the stairs, he saw the pouch lying on the table with a note. He put down the tray and picked up the note. The instructions were simple:

"Peter, please do with this as necessity dictates. As I intend to be predisposed for some time, I wholly give you charge of it. Thank you."

Peter opened the pouch to find the money and letters. He recognized his own writing on the addresses of most of the envelopes. He put down the tray and retreated to the kitchen closet where he often went for private prayer and closed himself into the darkness. He reappeared minutes later. He left the pouch where it was, picked up the tray and climbed the stairs. He knocked on the study door, but there was no answer. He knew then that Handel was either in deep meditation or writing. He opened the door. Handel sat at his desk, working. Peter put the tray down on a table near him, and without saying a word, he exited the room straightway.

He left the door slightly ajar so he could look in on Handel without disturbing him. He looked in one last time before going downstairs. What he saw was remarkable. Handel worked with a sureness that Peter had not seen in years. His hand was steady, his face, intent. Peter watched the quill between his fingers flick and bob vibrantly. Handel seemed young to him, as if vitality had been poured back into him like water into an empty urn. His master worked with purpose. He had not even noticed Peter's entering and leaving. It was not a gesture of rudeness; his mind was simply elsewhere.

Handel did not see Peter watching from the door. His servant could have remained for hours without being detected. So intent was Handel upon his work that the hours passed like minutes.

Spread upon the desk was the libretto given to him by Charles Jennens. Handel read the scriptural text before him:

"'Every valley shall be exalted, and every mountain made low. The crooked straight, and the rough places plain.'"

He read the words again. He picked up the quill and began making marks on the empty page. Soon it was full—then another, and another. His course was set. Handel flipped through the pages of his Bible, cross-referencing with Jennens's libretto. He read aloud words from Isaiah:

"'And the glory of the lord shall be revealed. And all flesh shall see it together.'"

Handel recalled a piece he had written years before that seemed to fit perfectly. He took a page from the libretto over to the harpsichord. His memory was flawless. He played it while forming in his mind the separate choral lines.

Peter listened from his place in the kitchen. The notes resonated through the halls of the house and out the open windows. A gentle breeze from outside blew the lace trim of the kitchen window curtain in time to the music. The genial dance of the curtain hem was in such stark contrast to the events of the previous eve that Peter couldn't take his eyes off it. While he watched, he saw something move beyond the white lace.

Peter's focus reached through the curtain to outside. Behind the house, sitting on a short stump underneath Handel's window, was a boy. Peter did not recognize the boy as one of the local children who played on Brook Street in summer. The youth's dress betrayed him as one of the street. Peter watched the urchin boy, at first with anxiety, which soon softened into curiosity. The boy did not stir; he sat still and quiet, seemingly engrossed with something near the house. The situation didn't make any sense to Peter. If the boy meant to thieve something, why allow himself to be seen in broad daylight? If he had business with the house, why not come to the door? If charity were the aim, why not beg in the street where that business was usually performed or knock and solicit help? The whole circumstance was quite odd to say the least.

What was most disarming was the boy's intrepidness. He sat on the stump as if it were his property. A casual observer would never have guessed him a trespasser. There was nothing in his mannerisms or actions to give any indication that he was anything less than the lord of the house. It was not that he was self-posturing; he just had a casual attitude of belonging that communicated an uninhibited nature. He sat on his stump with far more ease than George of Hanover sat on the throne.

What was most curious to Peter was the boy's preoccupation to the extent that he didn't seem to care that an adult was watching him. There was no question that the boy saw LeBlonde through the window on several glances, yet he made no attempt to hide or leave. Handel's servant determined that he should have a better look.

He expected the boy to make a run for it when he came around the corner of the house, but the boy hardly acknowledged him. The servant was amazed at the boy's brazenness. He approached until he stood directly above the young urchin.

"What are you doing here, boy?"

The boy did not speak, he simply put his finger to his lips for the grown-up to be quiet, then looked up to the second-story window, from which music escaped. The adult obeyed. Peter sat down next to the boy and listened. The two had no way of knowing that the words, "Comfort

Ye, My People," were inked on the paper that lay before Handel. They only knew that the music that fell from above may as well have been from heaven. Even though the audience of two came from vastly different backgrounds, music evened them. The longer they listened, the more they had in common. Several minutes passed before Peter LeBlonde spoke again.

"What is your name?"

"Packrat."

"Your given name?"

"Peter."

"Mine also."

The boy appeared quite taken back by the adult's answer. He looked over at the man with a curious stare. The youth was not too sure he wanted the same name as a grown-up, but this one seemed harmless enough and well this side of dim-witted, so he voiced no objection.

"Why do they call you Packrat?" asked the grown-up.

The boy peered at him as if sizing him up. When he was duly satisfied, he answered. "Habit. I always leave somethin' in place of what I steal."

"So you're a thief."

"A packrat. I merely change owners from one to another."

"What do you steal here?"

The Packrat raised his eye to the open window above them then touched his ear. LeBlonde listened for a few moments to the music coming from the window. "Then thieves we are—all of us."

Old Peter smiled at the young Peter, then arose and returned inside the house. He put some bread into a small handkerchief along with a wedge of cheese, then went back out the door. When he appeared around the corner of the house, he was disappointed to see that the boy was gone. For just a moment, he wondered if the boy had taken something while he was away, but what he saw next dismissed any suspicion. He walked over and picked up a small shoe buckle laid carefully on the stump where the boy had been.

And He Shall Purify

FOR FOUR DAYS, HANDEL DID NOT COME OUT OF HIS STUDY. He worked around the clock, pausing only for brief, rejuvenating naps. He slept deeply and soundly for a few minutes every three to four hours. He never allowed himself to fall into nocturnal hibernation, wherein the mind and body could slow. He slept for only as long as absolutely needed. His internal clock did not reckon from day to night, but from stanza to stanza, staff to staff. He was not certain which day of the week it was, nor did he care. He was writing, that was all that mattered to him. The next calendar day for him would be the day he finished. Until then, he was in process—the part of the creative journey which he enjoyed the most. It had been years since he had felt music flow from him as it did now. He dared not stop for too long for fear of breaking the creative trance.

Peter LeBlonde was amazed at the remarkable change in his master. He did not bother him any more than necessary. At meal times, he would bring Handel some food on a tray, then exit promptly. Peter learned that he could tell his master's level of tenacity by the food left on the tray when he returned to retrieve it. It was never completely eaten and often untouched. He realized in the first few days that it was best to serve items that would keep and could be served again. More often than not, the same foods showed up several times before being consumed.

During these days of writing, Peter heeded a principle that he had developed for times such as this, the principle of non-distraction. He passionately believed that the greatest service he could provide both Handel and the world was to make sure that his master was not distracted from his work. He dared not think that a single note of inspiration might be lost because of a moment's distraction that could have been avoided.

Peter perceived his responsibilities as being two-fold: making sure that Handel had at hand whatever he needed to sustain himself through the long hours of writing, and making sure that nothing from without would cause Handel's mind to venture away from his work. So adamant was Peter about fulfilling those duties that he minimized and leavened his every movement when in the presence of Handel. He never spoke. He never tarried longer than absolutely necessary. He never wore clothing that drew undue attention to himself.

It was not just Handel's study that Peter the servant protected, but the entire apartment. Like a target, with Handel's room the bullseye, each circumjacent area away from the epicenter was handled accordingly. The hall outside the study required silent stepping and careful movement. The stairway was to be ascended and descended in slow rhythmic footfalls. The kitchen, doors, and entry were used for preparation and access, but all comings and goings were done expeditiously and without noisy slams and locks. These were the rules that existed when Handel was writing—Peter made them so.

During this sojourn on which Handel had embarked, Peter felt especially responsible to uphold these things. The entire apartment and all in it seemed to revere the task going on within. It was as though the house, the occupants, and all the articles within the house, had been cleansed in the fires of tribulation. Nothing—not one piece of furniture or finery—had been immune from risk through the past months. The very existence of each and every person and thing within those walls was pushed to the outermost edge of the cliff, only to be rescued by the pouch from Halle. Along with freedom, the greatest commodity that Dorothea purchased with her love was time: time for her son to perform the duty to which he was now engaged. All things within the home seemed to reverence her sacrifice.

Because of what happened during the long night before the pouch arrived, Peter felt even more duty-bound to provide Handel with complete freedom from distraction.

In times past, he had watched Handel work straight through for several days to meet critical deadlines. Merciless time constraints and impossible deadlines were the bread in the stuffing of operas. But this was different. There were no pressing schedules or commitments driving his master onward. Handel was driven by a very personal desire which surpassed any prior motivation. This work was a passion play. There was a sacredness about it that demanded reverence. The house had a holiness within and without—not the heaviness of spirit that accompanies mourning, but a quickening of spirit as if to herald an awakening. It was a time of restoration. There was no doubt that the house and its occupants had come through a dark night, but now it felt as though a new dawn was brightening on the eastern horizon. It seemed that at any moment light would burst through the windows in a complete rebirth.

Peter did not want to break the free flow of inspiration, which distilled upon his master in drops of pure melody. He had no idea how long it would last, but of one thing he was certain: it would not be interrupted because of him or anything else that could be avoided. Peter gave himself the charge to do this; he accepted it as his place.

Peter was a not an artist, but he regarded himself as a facilitator. Long before now, he had resigned himself to the fact that he was not destined to be great or do anything memorable. He did, however, believe that he might have the opportunity to assist in some small way in a great task. In earlier years he had availed himself to God in hopes of fulfilling a prophecy which was given him as a youth, but had finally given up, believing that the vision was somehow compromised.

When he was a young boy, Peter had had a dream. He did not hear words, nor did he see himself; he simply awoke with a feeling that he would have the opportunity to see God's hand manifest. He assumed it was a miracle that he would witness—a healing, perhaps, like the miracles performed by Christ himself when he tarried upon the earth. So powerful was the impression that Peter sought to fulfill the prophecy by enjoining himself to the priesthood. Through the most industrious and productive years of his life he sought to walk in holy places, hoping to put himself in the best position to fulfill the destiny embedded in him. And yet, Peter had a flaw that kept him at odds with those in authority over him: he was never allowed in the inner circle, as there was a certain point of doctrine or principle that held him back. He openly confessed his weakness to those above him in search of understanding and peace, but none came. He fasted and prayed fervently for the comfort of clarity. He confided often with those in his fraternity of brethren.

Finally, after years of soul-searching vexation, he laid aside his ecclesiastical robes for servitude. It was a decision to follow his heart rather than attempt to self-fulfill his personal revelation. Peace came, but not without the burden of regret. Only then did he realize that he had acted like the affection-starved child who stands so close to his mother that she cannot move her hands without hitting him. He had positioned himself in such a way that God would have stumbled over him in order to step forward. It was a pitiful day when Peter realized that he had probably lost his endowment because of his impetuousness in trying to bring it to pass. He lived out his later and longer years believing that the simple two words of his chastisement were: "What if?"

It was then that he promised himself not to let anyone he could influence make the same error. He could not stand by and watch anyone else sell a birthright for a simple meal of pottage—least of all Handel. He determined to do everything in his power to aid in whatever task his master was about. For even though Peter was not exactly certain what the subject of the text was that preoccupied his master, he did know that it was conceived the night Handel was driven to his knees.

Peter's ponderings were interrupted by a knock at the door. He hurried as quickly as he could to answer it. The first knock was not loud, but he was certain the second would be. He spoke in nervous whispers as he approached the door.

"Oh, knock softly. We mustn't disturb him. Be patient please."

He swung open the door. Standing on the porchstep in the rain was Mrs. Delaney.

"I stand in the rain and you have me be patient."

She handed him her umbrella, then walked past him into the entryway. Peter closed the door and waited while she unspun her shawl from around her neck and shoulders.

"Now, where is Handel? He has not been making his usual visits."

"He could not, m'lady."

"He's ill again? Poor man."

"He has been ill, but the last few days he seems to have found renewed strength."

"Not enough strength to keep an appointment."

"Would you like some tea?"

"Yes, and fetch me Handel. I wish to scold him."

She sat down as if planning on staying for some time.

"I can't do that, m'lady, he's on an errand. He works even now."

"What is so pressing that he'll not take time for me? And on whose errand—surely not the King!"

"I believe it's a personal errand. I haven't asked. He works in solitude."

"Then he doesn't know I'm here. You must tell him."

Peter made no effort to leave. Mrs. Delaney looked at him with a hint of impatience.

"You protect him from me?"

"I respect the fervor—the passion—with which he attends to this effort."

Peter paused in deep reflection, then spoke in a reverent tone. "He's compelled to pursue it regardless of sleep and comfort. It's like a dream, which I dare not invade for fear of breaking the spell being worked on him."

Peter did not look at her. Mrs. Delaney watched him with great absorption. The room was silent. LeBlonde was immersed in thought and she engrossed with him. Then, as if in answer to their combined wills, music resounded off the walls, down the stairs, and into their ears. Mrs. Delaney closed her eyes. She listened to each note in the progression. Through the past several days, Peter had heard other music played. He knew how the music had reached into his soul, but he watched the visitor with great attentiveness to see how she would respond to what she heard. At first her brow was furrowed with the stern curiosity of critical analysis. With each passing measure, the furrows smoothed. Curiosity melted into wonder—then rapture. Her eyes no longer flitted beneath her lids. Her face became a vision of contriteness.

Peter watched the transformation with humble gratitude, certain now that he was not alone in his esteem of the songs.

When the music ceased, her eyes opened. She stood from her chair. Peter hastened to hand her the shawl and umbrella.

"You will tell him I came?" Mrs. Delaney said at length. "When you deem it appropriate to do so."

"Thank you, m'lady. I'll tell him when he comes out."

She took a step, then turned back to Handel's manservant.

"You serve him well; thus, you serve all of us."

Peter followed her out the door and looked up at the late afternoon sky. The rain had eased into a light misting. Above him the ashen gray clouds were beginning to thin into white and gold. He walked to the corner of the house to see how full the rain barrel was. Water lapped over the lip of the barrel and ran toward the back of the house. His eyes followed the streams of water to the stump, on which laid a small bent spoon. He retrieved the silver piece, then returned inside, knowing that the music had been heard by another.

Handel muttered to himself as he picked a sheet of music off the desk and walked toward the window streaked with drops of rain.

"Sotto voce in the allegro single part passages—keep it veiled. Full severity and power when the parts come together—fortissimo. Sopranos attack the entrance in bar fifteen; take the chorus with you."

He took the music in one hand and lifted the other. He read the words while keeping time with his free hand.

"'And He shall purify. And He shall purify the sons of Levi, that they may offer unto the Lord an offering in righteousness.'"

Illuminated by the glow from the window, his mind filled in the orchestration. On his desk, spread out under the open Bible, was the libretto. The edges of the Bible's pages were stained blue from the ink on his fingers. Handel was grateful Jennens put each scriptural reference on the libretto so he could look up each section as needed. He flipped to each reference to make sure he understood the text of each verse. As never before, he began to understand the meaning of verses he had passed over before. Some verses were committed to memory as he rehearsed the words in his mind, trying to find the music he believed God would desire for each.

Isaiah 40:1-3—"Comfort ye, comfort ye my people, saith your God. Speak ye comfortably to Jerusalem, and cry unto her, that her warfare is accomplished, that her iniquity is pardoned. The voice of him that crieth in the wilderness, prepare ye the way of the Lord, make straight in the desert a highway for our God."

Isaiah 40:5—"And the glory of the Lord shall be revealed, and all flesh shall see it together: for the mouth of the Lord hath spoken it."

Malachi 3:1—"The Lord whom ye seek shall suddenly come to His temple, even the messenger of the covenant, whom ye delight in; Behold he shall come, saith the Lord of hosts."

Isaiah 40:9—"O Zion, that bringest good tidings, get thee up into the high mountain; O Jerusalem, that bringest good tidings, lift up thy voice with strength; lift it up, be not afraid; say unto the cities of Judah, Behold your God!"

Line by line the music came. There were times when the Scripture and the music he penned seemed to meld into resplendent songs of praise. These were moments of creation when the veil between him and the heavens felt particularly thin. Such was the case with Isaiah 9:6—"For unto us a Child is born, unto us a Son is given: and the government shall be upon His shoulder: and his name shall be called Wonderful, Counselor, The Mighty God, The Everlasting Father, The Prince of Peace."

The music was written to be sung pianissimo, starting with a lightness on the part of the sopranos, continuing slightly louder with the other sections, then gradually crescendoing in grand unison in the choruses—as if in affirmation that truly a Son had indeed been given. His names were to be sung with full octave jumps as if to boldly testify to the living reality of each title given the Lord. The words and music came together in a perfect marriage of aural beauty. Like the husband who rises far beyond what he normally would because of the undying devotion of his beloved wife, the words were elevated by song and the two were enjoined in adulation to the Holy One of whom they prophesied. Together they were far more than they would ever be alone. Even Handel recognized the union with reverent gratitude. Upon completing it, he paused to kneel and offer a prayer of hope that his efforts were in accordance to God's will.

While he knelt, Peter LeBlonde opened the glass china cabinet downstairs and laid a broken doll's arm alongside the bent spoon. On the same shelf were a broken belt buckle, a length of string, a thimble, a piece of broken porcelain, and a glass bead. Peter closed the door of the china cabinet and stared through the glass at the growing shrine. He put the tokens in the most conspicuous place he could find so he could see them every time he traversed the house. It gladdened his heart to look upon it. It humbled his soul to ponder it. He knew very little of the urchin boy who bore his same name, but he hoped and prayed that they may be of the same heart—it was not the boy he doubted, but himself.

He seldom saw the youth and even less often heard him. He knew he was there only by the gifts left behind. Peter knew only the name of the boy who was creating the relic, but he loved him regardless.

While Handel was engrossed in songs of the Prince of Peace, the Prince of Wales was also amid song at the theatre. Both were engaged by music, both of their heads were full of strains, but beyond that there was little else in common.

Handel was alone.

An entourage of guests, particularly women, flitted about the Prince.

Handel's hands were busy with his work.

The Prince's hands were busy with the ladies, who feigned respect to the degree of being nauseating.

Handel's room was silent.

The theatre was riotous. Some played cards. Others talked openly while performers were on stage. Rubbish was thrown on the floor in disrespect. At one point, two of the less notable women in the audience tore into each other. No one was of a mind to try and stop the fight.

Handel, on the other hand, was at peace. He determined to rest his eyes and mind for some time before beginning the next phase of writing: the angelic prophecy given the shepherds at the birth of the Savior. He laid down on an area rug in his study, his arms outstretched, his face up. He slept well for three full hours. Nothing haunted his sleep, nor did he chastise himself for requiring it. A childlike smile of contentedness rested on his lips while he slumbered into the night. He awoke with sweet memories of Christmas with Dorothea. He remembered Christmas in Italy and the mountain minstrels who played the song of the shepherds, the *pifferari*, the melody she loved best. His mother had oft told him that the shepherds outside Bethlehem must surely have been playing that same melody on their wood flutes prior to the angelic visitation. The next notes that he penned to paper, the pastoral symphony, were for her.

All They That See Him,
Laugh Him to Scorn

THE LEAVES OF RICHMOND WERE JUST BEGINNING TO DRESS
in the colors of fall. The long, tree-lined path leading up to the large
manorhouse of Edward Holdsworth was still damp from the rain that fell
the preceding evening. Huge maple branches arched over the road, making a great tunnel of green and gold. Large drops of pure water hung like
crystals from the tips of the broad leaves. Morning light streaked through
the steam and branches in brilliant auroral shafts.

The Holdsworth manor had been busy the night before. Edward had
hosted a dinner party for his niece, who was soon to marry a nobleman's
son from Leicester. The party lasted well into the evening and beyond.
Several of the guests who had come from greater distances were invited
to spend the night.

A light breakfast was now being served in the garden for those who had stayed. Edward listened and mused at the varied conversations in the different circles. In one it was politics, in another it was the weather, in another, women. Most of the guests were the impertinent youth of aristocracy; speakers were many, listeners were few.

Holdsworth was quite taken back by their brash outspokenness. They had strong opinions, acquired from limited experience. As he himself was interested in music, he listened with keen fascination to any talk of the goings-on of London's musical world. As he strolled among the guests, eavesdropping, he happened upon the last comments of a discussion of which he wished he had caught more. Several youth stood in a tight group conversing amongst themselves.

"I understand the Prince himself was at the last performance."

"Frederick?"

"And all of his cronies."

"Surely he isn't the sponsor of another revival of the *Beggar's Opera*?"

"A revival of any opera would be too much."

"Oh, I long for anything which makes me think—and which entertains."

While the talk continued on, a lone rider was making his way through the hall of trees. The courier trotted through the silent archway toward the estate and came to the edge of the garden and waited for an invitation to enter.

Upon seeing the messenger, Holdsworth waved him in. The young man was courteous as he approached; he was well versed in the rituals of propriety. He walked straight toward Mr. Holdsworth, pausing only to allow ample room for one of the more animated young guests, who needed the full breadth of the walkway to demonstrate the wedding dance of the *Beggar's Opera*. When the dance was finished, the courier found his way to Holdsworth.

"A letter, Mr. Holdsworth—from Mr. Charles Jennens."

Holdsworth took the envelope from the courier's hand. As he turned it over to affirm the authenticity of the seal, a stray comment slipped from the tongue of one of the more outspoken youth.

"I'm sure that could provide some entertainment."

There were snickers and whispers all around. Another of the guests mused:

"Probably corrected some more of Shakespeare's gross inefficiencies—or the mundane ramblings of a less notable writer. Saint John, perhaps."

There was no effort made to suppress the laughing that ensued. Holdsworth raised his eyes to the group in silent reproach. They quieted as best they could, which was only a little.

Holdsworth opened the letter and read the contents. Finally he looked up from the paper. His guests waited anxiously to see if he would share anything of the letter with the company.

"It seems Mr. Jennens has embarked on another venture. One might construe that he is not content to only criticize."

The snickers subsided. Those most outspoken glanced around sheepishly. Holdsworth's reprimand stung more poignantly than if he had openly rebuked them. Like flies in honey, he had caught them in their own kind of goo: sarcasm. The brassy young men smarted in silence. Holdsworth waited to see if they would formulate coy words to counter him, but none came. Once he was sure that they would hold their tongues, he held up the letter and read aloud.

"'I hope I shall persuade Handel to set to music the Scripture collection I have made for him.'"

"Saint John! I knew it," whispered one of the scorned youth elbowing his companion. Those close enough to hear the comment buried their amusement under throat clearing. Holdsworth continued.

"'I hope he will lay out his whole genius and skill upon it, that the composition may excel all his former compositions, as the subject excels every other subject—the Messiah.'"

There was a brief moment of silence, followed by queries from all around the circle.

"Handel? Working with Jennens?"

"Who else would be so callused as to name a composition *Mess*...what he named it?"

"Doesn't he want it to be performed?"

"Why Handel?"

"He is lost; his music is dead."

Holdsworth had heard enough.

"On the contrary, Handel is neither dead, nor is he lost. No idea, no musical phrase, nothing is ever lost to him. There's no lack of ideas, only lack of time."

The loudest of the group interrupted him.

"Nonetheless, Mr. Jennens's eccentricities have gotten the best of him."

Holdsworth leaned back in his chair. He spoke with quiet dignity.

"Yet, often, craft is elevated to meet the demands of the subject at hand. And who of you will dispute that?"

The group dispersed.

All Ye That Labour

Mr. Wheelock, the baker, didn't understand it. In the early afternoon, when the morning rush was over yet before the presupper parceling to those on their way home, he had a few minutes by himself to think. In the past, this was his time to balance the books. It would take every minute he could spare to check the inventory of supplies, evaluate the needs, add the receipts, and determine the profitability of the day. Now he could do it all and have time to spare. He did not view this time as a gift but a liability.

There was no denying that his business had slackened in the past months. What was worse, there was no apparent reason for the fall-off of customers. One by one, receipts had diminished. Jonathon's absence had reduced productivity, but the few remaining workers were diligent. They ran out of baked goods only a few times, but Wheelock quickly remedied the problem by overcompensating. The result was several nights with excess. But Wheelock preferred this to turning customers away—a hapless circumstance which he utterly despised. He knew there was always someone in need of his extra bread, but there would not always be customers if there were not enough bread. He was stingy with the loyalty of his patrons. He would not tolerate disappointing them and thereby risk losing their business. Thus, giving away bread to the needy was far better than not having enough bread for his clientele.

The day had been unusually slow. He finished his accounting in just a few minutes. This left him a long afternoon to consider his situation. He loathed idle time. He paced back and forth behind the counter, his deep-set eyes staring, his brows furrowed. His business was not yet in jeopardy, nor his household in dire need; he simply could not tolerate losing business which he had worked so hard to obtain.

Wheelock was a pure worker. His hands were large and strong from years of kneading the huge balls of dough and working flour into bread. Work had been his life and living. He was not a prideful man, but a man who prided himself in his work. He learned the art of baking from his father. At a young age, the full responsibility of the bakery had fallen to him when his father suddenly caught smallpox and was gone within the week. Those days were difficult, as he tried to keep the quality of goods at the same level as his father, but it was impossible. He could make bread, but he did not love to make bread. It did not taste or feel or smell the same. It had little to do with the ingredients but much to do with how those ingredients were cared for.

Within a few months, most of the regular customers of his fathers had found other bakeries. He himself could not taste any difference in his wares. He scorned the notion that there was any difference. Then one night, he dreamed he was a boy, sitting at the bakery on a small oak chair, with the huge brick ovens at his back. So real was the dream that he imagined he could feel the heat from the ovens making his shirt hot and his skin itch. In his mind's eye, he could see the kind face of his father as he rolled balls of dough and spoke with him. He could smell the heavy, rich smell of dough and hear the quiet thunder of the fire inside the ovens. It was a dream he had had often, but for some reason, this specific dream was different from those he had in the past. This time, his attention was on his father's hands. The large hands of his father completely filled the dream space in his mind. He watched as those enormous hands picked up a large ball of dough and turned it over and over. The hands did not fight the dough, but caressed it, being very careful not to overwork the mixture until it became tough, or underwork it, which left it damp. When the moisture cooked out, it would leave dry, hard spots in the bread. The timing of the dough was of supreme importance if the bread were to have a crisp, savory crust and a soft, sweet interior. He watched his father's hands skillfully massage the dough into perfect consistency. When he awoke, he understood the difference between his and his father's bread. One made bread, the other cared for it. One provided the staff of life, the other was a steward over it.

It was then that Mr. Wheelock began to put his heart into his work. He became a baker rather than simply working as one. Almost immediately, customers began to return.

Jonathon sensed the care that Mr. Wheelock had for his profession. He too learned the art of caring for one's work and not just the duties of work. Mr. Wheelock invested a great deal of time in Jonathon, tutoring him in the finer points of the profession. When the quality of the apprentice's work began to be comparable to his, Mr. Wheelock was justly pleased. Many of the duties that Wheelock had always done himself were turned over to Jonathon.

Now that Jonathon was gone, Wheelock had to take on additional baking responsibilities, as the other paid workers were simply that: paid workers. It was not that they were not helpful, they just could not add the intangible ingredients. There was much they could do, but also much they couldn't. The increased burden placed on the owner was not back breaking or impossible to bear; it was, however, back bending and very tiring.

For the first several weeks, Wheelock barely noticed it at all. He came in a few minutes earlier and stayed a few minutes later every day. Then it was a full hour at either end of the day. This did not increase productivity, but it was necessary to maintain things as they had been. His sleep was not so sound, as he both fell asleep and awoke with his mind on business. Little by little his strength and vitality began to erode. At first he began to feel tired at those times of the day when he was usually most alert. It became more difficult to wake up at the early hour. Pulling himself from bed required all the will power he could muster. Occasionally he would give in and lie there for an extra few minutes of sleep, but rest would not come. He would close his eyes and lie there, feeling too guilty and weak to sleep and yet too tired to get up. Finally after several minutes of internal bickering, he would get up feeling even fouler than he did before.

Over time, the drain on him began to take its toll. His words were quick and impatient. The smile that had frequented his face became the exception rather than the rule. His steps were heavy and measured. What was most disconcerting was that the more fatigued he felt, the harder he was on himself. There was no specific event to look back on as the culprit. His condition was the result of an innocuous grind over a long and indiscriminate amount of time and series of stresses. It was not the exhaustion brought on by exerting tremendous effort for a short amount of time such as lifting a great weight. This was the fatigue of running a long and difficult race, which slowly burns away every cell of energy the body has stored. Recovery from such a race is often as long as the race itself.

He was not yet treading on the relentless path of depression, but he was aimed toward it. Of the many roads leading to despair, fatigue—the slow grind—is one of the most common. It comes when the mind and body reach to find footholds and branches to cling to as one slides down the cleft, but the farther one falls, the slicker the wall becomes. Finally one's eyes no longer look up to safety, but only downward to the dark abyss below.

As he paced behind the counter, Wheelock was feeling his way for a handhold in the rock. He had not even heard the slight ring of the bell on the door, when another in need entered his store. Here was a soul much farther down the cliff than he—one whose fingers and toes were raw and bloody from groping futilely for even the slightest of rocky holds to grab.

The intruder stood just inside the door, watching him pace between the walls of the bakery. Still he did not notice. Had Wheelock been watching, it would have been difficult to believe anyone could pass through a crack as narrow as the opening through which the stranger entered.

The gray cape and hood the visitor wore were so motionless that they blended into the dark, oiled wood of the bakery wall. Wheelock made several full trips back and forth behind the counter before the visitor finally stepped forward. Her voice, timid as it was, startled him out of his reverie.

"Sir...."

Wheelock spun toward the sound. He sucked in a shocked breath when his eyes found her. She cowered ever so slightly as his full attention swung upon her. He looked at her in amazement, wondering how she could have entered without his knowing. She could feel his eyes upon her, even though hers were lowered.

Momentarily, she lifted her face. The confused look on Wheelock turned to a smile as he stepped briskly to the counter. She stepped back as the sturdy baker leaned over the counter and addressed her:

"Madame, how may I help you today?"

The woman could not speak. She glanced left and right, not certain to whom the baker was talking.

"Madame, may I help you?" he said again, his eyes directly upon her.

She stood frozen. Her heart pounded within her chest. She was not certain why, but tears began to form in her eyes. She could not accept nor comprehend that someone was actually offering to help her. Through the past many months while her sewing jobs were diminishing to nothing, she had been asking, even pleading for help, but none came. Now someone had uttered a simple entreaty to aid, and she didn't know how to respond. She knew that his question had precious little to do with her circumstance, but it didn't matter. To her it was as if the voice of God were speaking to her tired and spent soul. It was a small thing, yet to her it was immense. To be regarded was an experience grown foreign to her. She drank it in like cool water over parched lips and altogether forgot why she had come. The baker inquired of her again, this time more specifically.

"Some pastries, perhaps—or fresh baked bread?"

By this time, the two other workers in the bakery sensed something out of the ordinary and had filled in the empty doorway leading to the secondary room where the ovens were.

"I've come to ask for work," she said in a broken rattle.

The two men in the doorway began to laugh. She looked as though she could hardly stand on two feet. What could she possibly do? They pointed at her worn pauper clothing and her wide eyes. The quaking cloth over her knees betrayed her shaking knees. She looked like a forlorn chick that had fallen from its nest. Until now, she appeared not to know exactly where she was or what to do. But their laughter seemed to shock her back to the present. This was a sound all too familiar to her. Even though she heard it often, it still repulsed her. Her head snapped to the side as their mockery finally and clearly registered in her mind. Her dress no longer trembled. Her dark eyes met theirs the same moment that the baker turned to them. At once, the business of their mouths was dammed. They glanced back and forth between the woman and Wheelock; neither flinched. They slunk back into the oven room.

When the baker turned back to her, she continued to stare at the space where the others had been. She did not blink until the room was absolutely silent.

"I'm sorry," said Wheelock. "Is there something I can do for you?"

"I've come to ask for work." Her words issued forth without the slightest hesitation. She stood erect, her feet squarely planted. This was not the timid, shrinking soul who had entered the room but a formidable spirit who now spoke. Her voice reverberated around the room and through the portals leading to the back room. Again, faces filled the open space, but this time they did not laugh.

The baker looked her over carefully. The other workers glanced at each other, but nothing was said. They were as anxious for his answer as she was. Mr. Wheelock did not keep them in suspense for long.

"No. I'm sorry, we have no need. You don't belong here. The ovens are no place for a lady."

Her first thought was to run—to get out as fast as possible—but her feet did not move. She silently prayed for the strength to go on. The woman stepped forward, her face more serious, her eyes upon him.

"My need is great."

Wheelock did not expect this. His heart was sympathetic, but he knew he could not show it.

"Many have need. You have no experience. Go, please!"

"I'll learn. I'll work hard. Please don't turn me away."

"I'm not a generous man. Times are hard. I must take care of my own people," he said, turning back to his work.

"That is what my husband said of you," she said in a clear voice.

Wheelock stopped. Her words pierced him to the center of his heart. He turned around and studied her face. He had only met Rachel a couple of times: once at the wedding and once shortly after the baby was born, when she brought the child to the bakery for Jonathon's friends to see. Wheelock tried in vain to remember, but it was difficult with her face still under the hood. Rachel discerned his inability to recognize her. She reached up, took hold of the thick hem about her hood, and pulled back the wool from her hair. As the shadow of her hood fell back from her face, the light from the window filled her eyes.

"Jonathon's wife? Oh my! Come here, child."

Her feet could not move. Wheelock lifted the section of hinged counter that separated them and put his large arms around her.

"Rachel." He said her name. Again, she heard the voice of God speaking to her.

"You'll not go hungry," he assured her. "But I can only pay a little."

He held her long, until he could feel her breathing calm. She stepped back from him, lifting his hand to her cheek.

"You are kind," she whispered.

"No, I'm not—but your husband is. We are all better for knowing him. Come back in the morning. We begin at 4 o'clock."

She released his hand, smiled, and returned to the door. It was already open, as the other workers had come forward to get it for her. They each nodded a respectful smile to her as she walked past them and out into the street.

Rachel let out a relieved yelp that sounded almost like a laugh. It was difficult for her not to shout. Instead, she ran down the street, skirting around the other pedestrians. For the first time in months, she was not running away from something, she was running toward something: hope.

Acquainted with Grief

THE HOUSE WAS SILENT. THERE WAS NO MUSIC EMANATING from within the study. It was a peculiar silence, not because of the lack of sound, but, rather, because of a subdued presence. It was a heavy presence, as if a damp, permeating hush had absorbed all sound. The presence was not evil but an intangible spirit of solemn reverence.

Peter LeBlonde had not heard music since the time he first began to feel the supernal influence invade the house. The existence of the spirit compelled him to stay close at hand. He stood vigil outside the study door, fervently waiting for the tide to change. Through the day and night hours he was ready to serve, always making sure refreshment was available, even though it was partaken of only sparsely. When he wasn't outside the study door, he tarried within the house, doing what little he could find that needed attention. He did not want to interrupt his master's work, but the lack of any movement caused him concern. He decided that it was time to investigate.

Peter halted outside the door to his master's study. In his hand was a small tray of food and hot tea. He reached for the door handle, but his hand stopped short of the brass knob. He leaned his ear to the walnut door to listen for any sound from which to surmise what Handel was about, but there was no sound to hear.

"Surely he must be sleeping," whispered Peter to himself. He stepped back from the door, thinking it best to let Handel rest. Just as he was about to leave, he reconsidered. He knew better than to think that Handel was asleep mid-morning when he was in the middle of a creative journey.

"Even if he is asleep, there is still one eye open. I can't awaken one who is never fully asleep."

Peter knocked twice very lightly, then grasped the knob and pushed open the door. Just as he had imagined, Handel was sitting at his desk, the quill in his hand. Handel's eyes were closed, but Peter knew he was not asleep.

He laid the tray on a nearby table. As he was about to open his mouth to speak, he saw the tip of the feather quill flick. Peter knew that another note had been committed to paper. His mouth closed without utterance of any kind. He had not been welcomed into the room, nor had he been excused; neither was required for Peter to know his master's pleasure. Handel did not need to voice his needs to have them satisfied.

Over the years of service and observation, one thing had become very apparent, when Handel sojourned along the paths of creation, his mind was wholly and completely preoccupied. Peter had grown not only accustomed to this preoccupation but comfortable with it. During these times, he needed no approval or acknowledgment; he needed but to serve. That was his sole purpose in being there. He did not need commendation to perform his duties.

This morning, however, was different; it was not easy for him to leave. There was a weightiness in the room that caused him to worry for his master. He was not certain what it was that made him tarry longer than normal, but there was no denying that his heart felt a lowliness that his mind could not articulate. Never in his life had he sensed the absolute aloneness that he now felt in Handel. Peter had been alone through many different crossroads in his life, but never had he felt the bleak separateness that he felt in his master's presence. It was not just solitude or exclusion, it was a loss of spirit. Handel was suffering—Peter knew it. It felt to Peter that God had forsaken Handel. It wrenched the servant's heart to look upon his master, but he said nothing. The quill flicked again, then leaned to the side, motionless. Peter knew well the rhythmic circles of the dancing feather quill when Handel's ideas outpaced his pen. Often he had seen the quill spiral and twirl over Handel's hand as notes were inked onto page after page of score. But only recently had he seen these single flicks, and never was the inking so labored.

As much as he wished he could stay with his master, he knew it was not his place. He left the room. The moment the door closed behind him, Peter imagined he could feel the air around him grow thin. Breathing was easier.

Hours later, Peter again twisted the knob and cracked open the door. Handel sat at his desk, just as before. When the door creaked open, the sound, which seemed deafening to Peter, was not even heard by Handel. Peter entered the room and retrieved the tray. It was untouched.

Now the servant was faced with a dilemma. The Peter part of him wanted to leave, simply to get out as quickly and quietly as possible. He knew that Handel was in a wrestle—concerning what, he was not sure. He himself was familiar with these skirmishes of the spirit and knew that his presence would only delay what must certainly play through to its end.

The servant part of him, however, could not leave without caring for the physical welfare of his employer. Providing sustenance was his stewardship, and he could not turn his back on that for which he was principally employed. It was Handel's comfort and well-being that concerned the servant part of him; he could not allow those things to be disregarded, even in times of painful purging on the part of his master. Peter was, after all, not a confidant but a steward; duty must certainly come first. This argument was most persuasive.

With tray in hand, Peter walked halfway across the room toward Handel. While he walked, he rehearsed the words that would most economically inquire as to his master's needs and well-being.

"Master—you must eat."

He waited for Handel's eyes to look up at him, but they didn't. Peter then became intensely aware of his presumptuous resolve. Had he been wanted, he would have been called for. He censured himself for questioning his first impression, which was to leave his master's room quietly. At once, he understood the folly of his impetuous demand on Handel's mind. His motive had been wrong, and he knew it. He was not so concerned with Handel's health as with quenching his own curiosity. Under the guise of duty, he had broken a higher law: obedience. The sound of his own voice had awakened him to his transgression; he had not spoken in meekness, but in a demanding tone.

His pride had betrayed his better judgment. The untouched food on the tray he had prepared seemed to him a symbol of Handel's neglect. His efforts had neither been recognized nor appreciated. For a brief moment of self-pity, Peter had compromised that which mattered most for that which mattered least. He stood before Handel as contrite and broken as any repentant sinner. He wished for mountains to hide him from the eyes of his master. What he would give to have the power to reel back in the words that he had let so carelessly slip from his tongue, but it was too late. The words were irretrievable. A thousand curved utterances of justification couldn't alter the trajectory of even one ill-spoken word.

Peter was ashamed of himself. He waited for his master's derision. None came.

When Handel raised his tired eyes to Peter, there was nothing there but absolute and complete forgiveness. He was not angry, nor was his face full of disappointment. Instead, what Peter saw was humble absolution. His master understood. Peter knew the sin was forgotten. The hole left where shame had been was instantly flooded to the brim with compassion. Peter's heart swelled as he saw in Handel not only forgiveness but regret at his apparent lack of appreciation for his servant's efforts. He said nothing; he simply and graciously nodded his gratitude to Peter for his concern, then went back to the page.

Handel's worn Bible lay open at his elbow. Peter watched as Handel's head bent over it. Handel's lips mouthed the words on the page before him. His eyes closed, but his lips continued repeating the single phrase. Peter could not discern the words, but there was no mistaking the import they seemed to bear upon the reader. Handel's whole soul seemed to be enveloped in the meaning of the verse before him. It was not like his master to ponder for long periods of time. He was an impatient man, sometimes barely able to endure the slowness of the cognitive process.

His creative surges were more often volcanic than not, erupting in expulsions of both new and long held ideas. For Handel to just sit and think for an extended time was rare, if not completely unheard of.

Peter was captivated by Handel's contentedness to ponder. He wanted to know what it was that could motivate this reverie, but he was too far from the desk to see the page, and he dared not invade Handel's space any further. Again he felt compelled to leave; this time he heeded the impression. He walked through the portal of the study and pulled the door closed behind him. The brass hinge squeaked, but Peter did not look back; he already knew that no one had noticed.

Outside, the light of day was nearly gone. When Peter entered the kitchen, his gaze immediately went to the window. The sheer curtains, which hung listlessly over the glass, were now a deep blue. The stillness of them seemed symbolic of the house. He had seen the day pass from morning until evening without hearing a single note from the study. He wondered how long Mr. Handel had been sitting in that selfsame place. For the first time in the ten days since his master had begun this journey, Peter was genuinely concerned about his welfare. He again determined that he was first and foremost a caregiver, and that is exactly what he should do: give care.

He examined the tray he had brought down from the study. He separated out that which was perishable from that which was not. He redressed the plate with some fresh bread and cheese, then covered it with a muslin napkin. He poured out the water, which had cooled hours before, then rekindled the fire in the stove to heat up fresh water for tea. He imagined the restoring tea bringing needed warmth and renewal to Handel's weary soul. The mere thought of it was comforting to the servant.

As he waited for the water to boil, he took the few minutes that he had to close all the drapes on the main floor. As he passed by the glass china cabinet that stood in the entryway at the bottom of the stairs, he stopped. On the plate glass shelf were several items that he had gathered from the stump throughout the prior week. The collection had grown each day since he had first encountered the boy. He saw him occasionally, but the Packrat had an uncanny sense for when adults were about and tried to avoid them. But like a deer inhabiting a rural garden, he had become accustomed to Peter LeBlonde, and, although he was wary, the adult's presence did not frighten him.

The collection on the shelf now included an eclectic assortment of varied treasures. The most recent additions were a child's tooth and a small, smooth ebony stone. Of all the gifts, Peter was most intrigued by the last, not because of any value that it might have had, but because he knew how the boy must have come to possess it. When he had spied it on the stump, he was frankly surprised. He rolled it over in his hand as he walked back in the house. He rubbed the smooth surface between his fingers and against his cheek. He remembered the cool feel of the shiny black stone against his skin. This of all gifts caused him to reflect upon his childhood.

Peter LeBlonde could not remember a day in his youth when he did not have a stone in one of his pockets. Every boy spent some time of each day walking, and the vast majority of that time was spent with eyes to the ground, looking for stones. There were several kinds of stones to look for: round throwing stones, flat skipping stones, showing stones with unique patterns and colors, and protection stones that fit perfectly into the notch of the finger. These last were for the sole purpose of escape; one always had a protector on hand.

But of all the collectibles, no stone was of more value than a "keeper." These were the rare finds which one stumbled upon only a few times during childhood. Thousands of stones were passed over before a keeper was found. Every keeper had to have some characteristic that made it impossible to use for any purpose other than keeping and studying. In all his youth, Peter had never seen a keeper like this one. So polished was the stone that it reflected back the eye that was studying it.

Peter wondered what boy would give up such a find, yet there it was, sitting on the glass shelf with the other trinkets.

The day the black rock appeared was an unusual day. The music that echoed from the study that day had been remarkable. It was the music of pure adulation. He himself sat for long minutes on the stair outside his master's study, listening to the strains. He was not certain what the piece was called, but when he entered the room to leave food, he had heard Handel say aloud the words:

"'Wonderful, Counselor, The Mighty God, The Everlasting Father, The Prince of Peace.'"

He recognized the verse from Isaiah 9, but never had the words been so alive to him. When he went outside that evening to leave some bread on the stump, he found the black stone, reflecting gold sparkles in the last beams of sunset. It was then that Peter LeBlonde realized that there was an added dimension beyond the simple giving and taking of the Packrat. The boy left behind something he esteemed to be of equal value to what he took. This revelation made the growing shrine in the china cabinet that much more captivating to the servant Peter. Without question, the boy had been touched by the music that day in the same way that he had. Peter became even more pleased that the youth of the stump bore the same name as he. A familiar chord seemed to resonate between them.

The sound of the kettle whistling pulled Peter from the china cabinet back to the kitchen. He moved quickly so the shrill whistle would not last any longer than necessary. He took the kettle from the stove, then poured the steaming water into the urn on Handel's tray.

When he reached the landing outside Handel's door, he stopped short of opening it. He laid the tray down on the hall table, then reached down and took off his shoes. He left them against the wall and picked up the tray.

When he opened the door to Handel's study, he saw his master still sitting in the same position. Peter immediately noticed that the temperature of the room was several degrees cooler than the rest of the house. He put down the tray and walked straightway to Handel. This time, there was no question as to his motives; he was there to serve and sustain.

He took the wool blanket off the valet and laid it carefully over Handel's shoulders. From behind the composer, he could now see the words on the open page of the Bible in front of him. Peter read silently the words in the fifty-third chapter of Isaiah.

"He was despised and rejected of men; a man of sorrows, and acquainted with grief."

Peter looked away, feeling that he had somehow intruded upon something that was very personal. He walked back to the tray on the table and poured a cup of hot water. When he turned back to Handel, his master's eyes were no longer down but were staring at something across the room. Peter followed Handel's gaze to the painting of Christ, which hung on the east wall. Peter looked back at Handel. He seemed to Peter to be separated from all else in the room.

"I didn't understand."

At first, the words seemed nothing more than a fleeting thought crossing the stage of Peter's mind. He was certain he had imagined them.

"I didn't understand."

This time he heard the words with his ears. Like the gentle movement of air around the room, they were hushed, but he had heard them. Although nearly indiscernible, they were real. Peter fastened his eyes upon Handel's face.

"I didn't understand." Handel's lips moved. He continued to stare at the picture before him. It was hardly visible in the residual flicker of the candle, but it didn't matter; the image was etched upon his mind as if with a molten pen.

Peter knew that whatever it was that had come to the comprehension of Handel was of such magnitude as to cause him long and difficult contemplation. He knew that somehow it involved some revelation which had come from studying the meaning of the Scripture laid open before him. Handel read aloud the verse: "'He was despised, rejected of men, a man of sorrows and acquainted with grief. Surely He hath borne our griefs and carried our sorrows....'"

From memory, Peter continued the Scripture, "'...the chastisement of our peace was upon Him, and with His stripes we are healed.'"

Peter understood. All at once he comprehended the message and meaning of the task to which his master was welded.

"It is your work which does this."

Their eyes met in the subdued light.

"I didn't understand," said Handel in a quiet voice.

Peter knew that the truth that had been manifest to Handel was an eternal truth that transcended the earthly considerations of money or fame. Handel had been the recipient of a gift of spirit. It was as if a great and wonderful confidence had been revealed to him by the power of the Holy Ghost.

Peter looked upon a changed man—not physically, but changed of heart. In his utter humility, Handel appeared great. His visage appeared translucent, as though his body were thinly veiled glass with light trapped within. His eyes shone with the peace of understanding and perceiving beyond what they could actually see. He seemed the offspring of nobleness and virtue. His expression was that of the earnest young father who looks into the face of his own child and realizes the values he desires for his offspring are the clear resounding echoes of his own mother and father. Like the teacher who humbly watches the cataracts of confusion fall from the student's eyes, Peter watched Handel pass through the refining fires of comprehension toward pure conviction.

In a calm voice, Handel read aloud the verse on the open page before him.

"'He was wounded for our transgressions, He was bruised for our iniquities; the chastisement of our peace was upon Him, and with His stripes we are healed.'"

There was silence in the room for several seconds before Handel spoke in the same reverent voice.

"I have felt despised, rejected of men; a man of sorrows, acquainted with grief. Why? For what divine purpose does God allow a man to follow a terrible trajectory that leads him through the gaping jaws of hell? Because that is what it takes to put a man in heaven."

Handel took a long, deep breath, then continued.

"Many times in my life I have read those words, but never have I believed and accepted in all actuality that they were in fact prophecy—prophecy to be fulfilled in my behalf. I have always considered myself to be the master of my own fate. Only now do I understand that in spite of all that I may ever do, for good or ill, I can never atone for my own faults and frailties."

Handel's eyes closed.

"I have had days, hours, even weeks when I could imagine no earthly refuge from despair. I've pondered my own suffering—every foul word of criticism, every doubt and debt, every dream laid waste—and wondered how I could ever endure it. I have fought for, waited for, and pleaded for help, but none seemed to come. In the very moment that my prayer was answered and deliverance was granted, I rebuked the giver of it. What hope could one so unworthy and unrepentant as I have in salvation? Redemption was so far beyond anything I could do for myself that the mere thought of it was incomprehensible."

He laid his hand on the open Bible.

"But when my mind caught hold on this, I finally and truly understood. These are not good words, not just comforting metaphors to aid the sufferer. These verses are speaking about the atoning One of all mankind: Jesus, the Christ. He is the Lamb of God who taketh away the sins of the world. He is the author of redemption."

Handel looked at the open Bible, then at Peter.

"'Surely He hath borne our griefs and carried our sorrows.... The chastisement of our peace is upon Him.' No matter what I must endure, there is One who has endured far more. I am only a drop in the ocean of mankind, yet I have a share in the immense redemptive reach of Christ's sacrifice. How unjust and yet absolutely necessary that He who was without iniquity would suffer for the sins of us all. Only now do I understand that Christ is not only the Messiah, the Savior of mankind, He is my personal Savior."

Handel was finished. Peter knew that the clumsiness of trying to speak of things eternal with temporal words seemed so inadequate that Handel would no longer try.

Peter suddenly felt compelled to make a request of his master, but dared not utter the words. And yet so strong was the impulse that he could not ignore it.

"Sir, please allow me to stay with you. I won't interfere."

Peter spoke with great love and affection. The words were released from his mouth before he could stop himself. No answer came, but none was needed. He was not asking permission as much as he was stating what he believed was his stewardship. He walked back to the urn of hot water and poured a second cup of steaming water. It was not for him, it was in place of the first, which had lost a portion of its heat. He put it on a small china plate and placed it at the corner of Handel's desk. Peter's actions were smooth and precise now that he felt his duties were clear. He exited the room without a sound and descended the stairs. He again charged the fire with several large lumps of coal. He had no intention of letting the house get too cool, nor did he want to be more than a few moments away from hot tea. He closed the few remaining curtains that were still open. He took from the closet a small wool blanket to protect his legs from the chill before reascending the stairs. He entered quietly, looked about him to make sure all was as it should be, then sat down in a tall arm chair next to the door, where he could watch Handel work.

For several hours he sat upright, watching for any indication of need from his master. If Handel reached for the cup, Peter would instantly refill it with hot water. If Handel stood to stretch his arms, Peter would rise also, and he would wait until his master sat down and resumed his work before he would sit down. He watched for hours while Handel's pen moved back and forth across the pages of score. In his mind he quoted Scripture from memory to stay awake. He studied the room for several minutes, then closed his eyes and tried to remember every item in the room to the slightest detail. He pictured in his mind the exact creases in the curtain, the color of each book spine that faced outward, and the placement of every piece of furniture. He tested himself many times until he could not find anything in the room that he could not recall. Once the room was committed to memory, he worked on Handel, remembering every feature of his face. This took little effort and time, as his master's face was already etched upon his mind in every mood and attitude. All this he did that he might not be unavailably asleep should his master have need of him.

Each time he heard the distant cry of the watchman in the street calling the time, Peter felt renewed strength at having lasted another hour. Grateful was he when the calling of midnight came, as the eleventh hour had been difficult, and he had felt himself doze in and out throughout the hour.

Unbeknownst to Peter, the nightwatchman was as aware of the dimly lit window in the upper room of the apartment on Brook Street as Peter was to his calling. It caught the watchman's attention earlier in the evening as he walked past the house. Had someone been within the sound of his voice following his calling of midnight, they would have heard him sigh aloud:

"I could call all night and not see that candle snuffed."

The rejuvenation that came to Peter with the midnight and final calling lasted only a few minutes. From then on, the chore of staying awake became painful. He was grateful for the chill in the room; the discomfort of it helped chase away sleep. He knew Handel well enough to know that he, too, did not want to be too comfortable when he was working. Peter held his legs aloft, he pinched himself, even held his breath for as long as he could to try to keep himself alert. The hours now stretched on endlessly. Rest became more and more irresistible. Finally, after he had battled the unrelenting foe of fatigue deep into the night, the fight became too much for even the most faithful. Peter fell asleep.

While Peter and the rest of the world slept, Handel wrote. Through the longest and blackest hours of the night, he worked on, pausing only to re-ink the quill. He rose from his chair only one time: to replace the small blanket which had slipped off the legs of his servant, who slumbered as he tarried. He then went back to work. His hand was not tired, though his strength was utterly wasted. He pushed himself on as though he dared not stop for fear of losing the exact same feeling he was experiencing at that very moment. His fingers were black with ink. his eyes, red, his feet, cold. Yet on he went, writing as fast as he could to put music to paper. He was driven, as a weary traveler against the storm, afraid to stop and rest for fear of not being able to get back up. He knew all too well that when the going was difficult, it was far easier to keep moving than to get moving—to stay warm than to get warm.

Handel worked on.

He knew not exactly why he was writing; he wrote because he felt compelled to write. He simply obeyed, not knowing beforehand if there was any specific purpose for the music or if anyone would ever hear the work at all.

The dim light glowing in the upstairs room did not go out. All through the night, with all else about it dark, the small, square window shone faintly like a golden portal against a black palette. All of London was still and shadowed under the shroud of night. The street lamps were out. There were only stars, no moon. It was too late even for thieves, who had given up their hunting hours before and retreated to their holes. No dogs barked. No leaves rustled. All was still and black, except for one hand moving steadily in the flickering light of a single low candle.

At the eastern edge of the earth, a faint line began to appear. The horizon beyond London began to glow with the arrival of a new day. The black sky began to blue. The faintest stars disappeared as the nearest star began to appear. Morning was coming.

The candle on the desk was wholly spent, but miraculously it had continued to find wick. Only now did it finally expire as the last drop of wax closed in around the last visible flame. So little wick remained that as soon as the tiny flame went out, liquid buried it—no smoke escaped. The light scratches of quill on paper continued. Several sheets of score lay open about the desk and on the cherry wood credenza, the ink still drying. The soft blue light of early morning coming in the window gave as little light as the failing candle had. It was enough to continue and no more. From now on, the world would only get brighter.

Peter's head rested awkwardly on the outside spindle of his wooden chair. His feet were tucked under each other, trying to stay warm. The blanket, which had been about his legs, was pulled up over his shoulders and arms. He did not stir when the paper in Handel's hand rustled as he lifted it off the desk. Black fingers put down the quill, then pinched tiny grains of white sand from a open dish. Slowly the large fingers rubbed together as a light shower of grains fell on the wet ink strokes on the page. The paper was then curled and tipped back to the dish, allowing all those grains which had not stuck to the ink to slide off the manuscript and back into the dish. As his hands unfurled the paper, Handel leaned close. It was difficult to see with tired eyes. He rose to his feet and walked to the window, now glowing even brighter blue. His large hands held the page open to the soft light. He whispered, in musical time, the words:

"'Surely He hath borne our griefs and carried our sorrows.'"

His eyes closed. His head began to move as music filled it. The words of Isaiah flowed from his lips as he spoke the words aloud in time to the music in his head. Peter's eyes opened. Before him, at the far side of the room, Handel stood silhouetted against the glow of the window. As Peter watched, rays of light suddenly streamed through the window. The sun had come. Handel stood backlit in a pool of warm light. A halo of gold rimmed his entire body. Peter heard hushed words from across the room.

"'And the Lord hath laid on Him the iniquity of us all. And with his stripes we are healed.'"

He Looked for Some
to Have Pity on Him

JAMES ALWAYS SAT IN THE SAME CONSPICUOUS PLACE AT THE busiest corner of the market. On the ground next to him sat a large tin cup, big enough for a long, full drink on a hot day. In the morning his cup rang often as the fishermen would come into town from the docks and solicit his skill in evaluating their catches. They would wait in line to have James test their wares so they would know which fish were of unusually high quality. Even though he never came out and asked for it, each left an obligatory token of appreciation in his cup. Most were happy to pay him for his skill, but there were some that tried to take advantage of his lack of sight. They would foolishly drop a meager pence into the cup, assuming that the blind man would never know the difference. What they did not consider was how James' ear had compensated for the lack of sight with a keenness and acuity that they could not comprehend. He could readily tell the coin by the pitch and timbre of the ringing cup. James learned which cup rings accompanied whose voices. To those wise fishermen who gladly shared their good fortune with him, he gave his best judgment and care. Simpletons tried to take advantage of him, but he either waved them off or reproved them sharply. He forgave them readily unless they offended a second time—then he was finished with those who wanted so much for so little.

As the diligent fishermen always came into market early, his cup tinked often with coins of thanks. By comparison, the afternoons were generally quiet, as he was then relegated to depend solely on charity, a far less reliable source of income. But in recent days, even the mornings were becoming thin as more and more of the fishermen chose to bypass James and simply sell their entire catch at a premium.

It was mid-afternoon when the Packrat came upon him. James sat in his usual place, waiting for kindness to bless him. The Packrat had begun to take sport in trying to sneak up on James without his knowledge. It was good competition, since James had learned well the sound of his shoe, his cadence, and his prattle. The Packrat tried to alter all of his natural habits to fool the blind man. Once, he had gone so far as to remove his shoes and approach on the heels of a large woman to mask any sound. It was a good trick, and he had won that day.

This day, however, he chose stealth. Usually it didn't work, but he had determined that with some practice he could win with regularity. He approached James very slowly, doing his best to land each foot in silence. What he didn't know was that James had heard his laugh and skip long before, while he was still a good distance away. When the boy was but a few steps from James, the man patted the ground next to him and smiled.

"Sit with me, Packrat. Tell me the goings-on of the day."

Peter looked at him curiously, shook his head, then plopped down on the ground next to him. "How did ya' know?"

"Know what?"

The boy's face crinkled into a loose knot. "Never mind," he said, disgusted. The tone lasted only through that one phrase.

"James, ya' lucky t'day—ya' 'ave the same color shirt as breeches," Peter laughed.

"I have but one shirt and one pair of breeches."

"God is wise to not give ya' more. 'Twould only complicate things."

They both laughed; the Packrat continued.

"How's business? I'll bet ya' cup rings often, the streets are full—more noblemen than rats."

"Is that so?" queried James with a wry smile.

"Lots of bodies; ya' cup must be very busy."

"Sometimes, yes; more times, no."

"How about today?"

"Mostly, no."

"That can't be." The Packrat bent forward and looked in the large cup. "Not enough for a single loaf. What about the fishermen?"

"Fewer and fewer come these days. From what I can hear, it seems every fish with fins is unmatched in quality." James shook his head.

Peter looked up and down the street at the sea of humanity. He looked back at the empty cup and rubbed his forehead in disbelief.

"This won't do at all."

The boy jumped to his feet and ventured out into the street. A loud group of noblemen came down the street toward him. Peter spotted them. History had proven that the loudest of nobles were usually those most concerned with how others regarded them. More often than not, they were good for a coin or two—not because they were generous, but because they wanted to be viewed as such. The Packrat headed them off and jumped in their path.

"Good sirs, could any of ya' spare some small comfort for the blind."

They all stopped at once and stared down their noses at him. The loudest of the group was the first to speak.

"Blind? You are not blind."

"No, sir, but I know a..." the Packrat's voice disappeared under the loud voice of the man.

"If you were blind, you would not know who I am. I could be anyone. I could even be the King!"

The man took great sport in amusing the others with his mocking portrayal of their portly King. He waddled around the Packrat, barking orders, while the others laughed hysterically. Peter did not laugh, nor did he watch. His eyes were fastened on the man who stood in the center of the group. The man was hidden behind the others as they walked, but when the group stopped and spread out, his was the only face that the Packrat really did see. Peter recognized the face.

The would-be king circled Peter several times. Peter paid him little heed, which irritated the nobleman immensely. The more he tried to get the boy's attention, the more evident it was that he didn't have it. The others in the group began to chide the king about the apparent disregard his subjects had for him. This annoyed the actor further, which was manifest in the loudness of his voice, now nearly a yell. The Packrat was oblivious to all of this. He could not keep his eyes off the face of the man in the middle who was becoming agitated by the boy's stare. Peter was certain he knew him; he was just not certain how he knew him. Finally, the king had had more insolence than he could stomach.

"Bow down to your king, boy. Oh, I remember, you cannot see me. Let me help you find your knees."

The nobleman stopped behind the Packrat, then reached out a foot and thrust the boy forward to the ground.

"Bow down, ignorant wretch."

Peter landed face first on the cobbles at the feet of the man he had been watching. Skin tore from his knees and palms. Smarting from the sores, he looked up into the eyes of the man. The tyrant who pushed him down smiled at the man at whose feet the boy knelt.

"I believe he thinks you are king, Antonio. Blind boy, bow down to your king: King Rolli."

Peter felt several large hands grabbing at him. Several of the others in the group picked him up, and in an instant he was back on his feet, facing the leader who had pushed him down.

"Let us help you, blind man. You're kneeling to the wrong king."

The same hands, which had picked him up, pushed him down to his knees in front of the leader. As he fell forward, he reached out to catch himself but instead caught hold of a pocket on the man's coat. The weak pocket tore loose; several coins fell to the ground along with the Packrat. Before the men could deduce what had happened, the boy's hands were at work picking up the last of the coins.

Hands were again upon him and far more harshly than the first time. While one of the men cinched his arm around Peter's neck, another took hold of his clenched fist.

"Stupids," said Peter, but the word was extinguished as the grip around his neck tightened even more. His feet left the ground as the man holding him leaned back, arching the boy's back over his leg. Peter could feel a large hand squeeze his fist until the coins began to cut into the flesh of his palms. He opened his hand. The coins freely fell into the open hand of the man whose pocket he had torn. Once the money was recovered, the man holding him by the neck dropped him again to the ground. He fell flat on his back. The Packrat rolled to the side and scrambled out of their reach. When he was clear of the men, he jumped to his feet and ran. He stopped several steps from them and turned around, his eyes wet with tears of pain. Those who had held him pulled handkerchiefs from their pockets and began wiping the boy's dirt and smell off their hands.

"Filthy little scum," one uttered under his breath, as he smelled his coat. Rolli turned to Peter with a look of contempt. At that moment Peter remembered where he had seen him. He remembered that same face from the theatre where the fight had been.

"Blind! You are a poor excuse even for a beggar. Be gone, thief," said Rolli.

"Spoken as a true nobleman," shouted the boy in a voice loud enough for all those who had witnessed the commotion to hear. Most in the crowd laughed at the boy's boldness. Peter pushed out his fisted hand toward them.

"Hey stupids," Peter blinked away the tears and smiled broadly. "A good thief always uses one hand to keep the attention away from the other."

His fist opened. He held up a shiny crown in the hand that they hadn't checked. He sprinted down the sidewalk in and out of moving pedestrians. Rolli started after him. A young woman, a mop trundler who had watched the entire encounter, flicked her wrist in Rolli's direction. The mop in her hands spun like a top, throwing a spray of dirty brown drops up the front of Rolli. The crowd roared their pleasure while Rolli groaned and looked down his front. He reached out an open hand to slap the young lady, looked about him at the many working-class men watching, then thought better of it. At that moment, out of the crowd appeared the Packrat. He had climbed up the iron base of a nearby street lamp where all could see him. Rolli's face was contorted with rage. He raised an indignant finger and pointed directly at Peter. The boy threw back his head to the sky and laughed for all to hear. "Ya' must like a good joke, Lord. Why else call the wealthy 'noble'?"

Again, laughter erupted throughout the street.

The noisy crowd parted to allow the noblemen to retreat back in the direction from which they had come. Many in the nameless mass echoed the boy's sentiment as the noblemen made their way back down the street. Rolli followed a few steps behind the others. Twice, he looked back over his shoulder at the boy standing on the pedestal, but said nothing. At length, the group disappeared around a far corner.

Within a few moments, everyone went back to business as if nothing had happened. The Packrat circled the block by way of the back alleys and, a few minutes later, appeared again at James's side.

"A nobleman has noticed ya'; he asked that I give ya' this."

He dropped the heavy coin into the tin cup. It rang out with a rich ting unlike any that James had heard before.

"May God bless that nobleman," said James.

"With scurvy!" smiled the Packrat.

He Is Full of Heaviness

THE SILENCE OF THE HOUSE WAS STRETCHING INTO ITS third day. No music had been heard emanating from the study since Peter LeBlonde first felt that the house was beset.

When he wasn't busy about the apartment, creating work for himself to pass the hours, he was in one of two chairs: either the one outside Handel's study door or the one that stood at the stair landing in the entryway. From the one upstairs he could hear any movement from within which might signify that he was needed; from the one downstairs he could look through the small pane of glass by the front door to see anyone who might pass by in the street. Usually the edges of the day found him upstairs, while the long hours of midday were passed in the entry. The goings-on outside the small, square window provided just enough stimulation to keep his mind awake.

Just knowing that people were in the typical ebb and flow of life was comforting to him. It seemed to help the silent hours pass more quickly. He had never really noticed the amount of time he spent caring for his master until now, when Handel's needs were so minimal. Peter longed to be out among those coming and going but knew that he must be at hand if needed. Duty kept him inside.

He wondered at how the glass portal through which he viewed the street could be so small, but the area that he could see was so much larger in scope. The farther the object was from the small square opening, the more he could see of it. It seemed curious to him that in spite of the smallness of the opening, he could see the full figures of those who walked past in the street. The physics of the phenomenon intrigued him. He was in deep meditation on the matter when a loud knock came at the door. So startled was he that his head jerked back involuntarily, banging the wall behind him. He jumped to his feet as adrenaline shot through his body. To his absolute amazement, he had not seen anyone coming. Whoever it was must have come from the opposite direction and stepped up onto the porch without his detecting the sound.

The shock to Peter's body—due to the sudden change from relaxed introspect to startled surprise—was so severe that patterns of black flashed across his eyes as he stood erect. He had hold of the door and flung it open so quickly that the two men standing on the porch jumped back in surprise. Peter stared at them, not out of rudeness, but because of momentary blindness rendered by the combination of light-headedness and the sudden change of exposure to his pupils from the bright day. Although he knew he was being addressed, he could not hear their words at first. He clung to the door handle to steady himself. He could feel his face begin to heat.

As the first of the men came into focus, Peter recognized him. He knew immediately their purpose in coming.

"Where is Handel?" demanded the officer, his voice harsh and loud.

"Did you hear me, man? Are you drunk? Where is Handel?" the officer demanded even more coarsely.

Peter replied calmly, "Do you have business with him?"

"Would we be here if we didn't?"

"Who are you?"

"You know who we are. You can't keep him from us."

"Should I have reason to?"

"You protect him."

"If necessary."

"Impudent man, move aside—now."

Peter did not move.

"We've come for Handel. We have no cause against you. I think it best for you to do as you're told and retrieve the felon before we lose patience," interrupted the other man, standing behind the officer.

When he stepped forward into view, Peter's eyes shifted to him. The first man was loud, the second, formidable. Peter recognized his face the instant he saw him. The short exchange they had had several nights before left a lasting and marked impression upon Peter. When the solicitor stepped from behind his companion, his face literally merged into the dark impression of the evil face indelibly etched in Peter's memory from their first encounter. This man put Peter on edge.

"We've come to take Handel to debtors' prison," the solicitor said.

"I understand it's difficult to pay past notes from within those walls," replied Peter.

The solicitor's head turned to the side, as if measuring his adversary. He looked up and down the servant in the threshold, then smiled.

"He is here." It was not a question, but a statement of fact. There was no doubt as to the man's intentions or of Handel's whereabouts—both were known.

"You are no longer in his employ. Summon him, then you are finished here."

"What is the sum of his obligations?" inquired Peter.

"It makes no difference. We are here for Handel so if you will step aside, the officer can perform the duty of his employ."

The constable began to move toward the door, but Peter shifted to close off the opening.

"What does he owe?"

"That is Handel's business alone—unless servants are now executors," chided the officer in a condescending tone. Peter did not flinch.

"I should think two hundred pounds would take care of any debts which he might have," Peter said calmly.

The solicitor did not acknowledge that he had even heard Peter speak.

"You have stalled us longer than we have time for; move aside," he said, his voice taut. Peter watched as the man slipped something into his mouth and bit down.

"Wait," commanded Peter, backing in and closing the door behind him.

"The back door is being watched. I'll force my way in if need be," the officer said as the door closed. Peter reappeared moments later with two, hundred-pound notes in his hand and held them out to the lawyer.

"I should think this is ample. I wish to see a balance sheet minus this amount within a few days. When I am confident it is accurate, we will determine if there is any balance or credit owed. It shall then be taken care of immediately, whichever the case may be."

No hand reached for the money. Peter walked forward and pushed the money into the hands of the solicitor. Their eyes met. Peter detected intense disappointment. He did not wait for more words, but walked inside and pulled the door closed behind him. Once inside, he found his way back to the chair in the entry and fell into it. Only now, when he and his master were beyond the grasp of debt and despair did he fully understand the desperateness of their plight. As he realized the divine intervention that had so miraculously snatched them from imminent and certain misery, he could not keep from folding under the weight of it. He had not completely comprehended the extent of peril from which they had been plucked. The struggle to stay the hand of justice had clouded the precipice on which they stood. Only after providence blew away the mist, did he truly perceive how deep and dark was the abyss from which they had been rescued. His mind was instantly flooded with the stark realities of what might have happened if the money had not come. What if Dorothea had not saved it? What if they could not have paid the debt?

Only now was the vastness of their terrible circumstance clear to him. It was terrifying. He was like the warrior who fights all day seeing only the foe before him—whose heart is strong until he looks back at day's end at the battlefield littered with corpses and carnage. Peter did not comprehend the danger through which they had passed until the fight was over. Hindsight now showed clearly the dangers that had been obscured by denial. The realization of it all overwhelmed him.

Peter's heart pounded. His palms and forehead were suddenly wet with sweat; his stomach turned. As dizziness and nausea began to set in, he tried to lock his focus on one steady object. He chose the small window portal to the outside world. As he tried to focus his gaze, he saw the two men walk past in the street; the sight sickened him. His breathing became fast and shallow. He sucked at the air around him, gasping for oxygen, but he couldn't get enough. He felt he was drowning. Peter fell forward on his knees to the floor, his face lowered to the ground. A searing stab of pain crackled down his left side and into his arm and hand. His chest seemed ready to explode at any moment. Certain his situation was critical, he tried to cry out for help, but no sound came, only gasps for needed breath. His eyes began to darken, his temples burned. At the exact moment he felt he would slip away into sightless oblivion, music rang out from the room upstairs. Instantly, his thoughts turned to his master.

As he lay folded over his chest, listening, the air coming into his lungs began to feel substantive. There was life-saving oxygen in his breaths. His racing heart began to slow to a purposeful stride. The pain in his arm began to dull.

He lay on the cold tile for several minutes, his mind full to overflowing with expressions of gratitude for his master's rebirth. Like warm water being poured into his chilly veins, life came back to Peter. After several minutes, he stood back on his feet, steadying himself against the back of the chair. In time, he slid the chair back into its proper position and sat down on it upright. While he listened, Peter knew that he had been both warned and wonderfully aided. In that selfsame moment, he resolved that his life could never be as it had been. His steps would need to be slower, the time required to perform a task would be longer. He would listen with more care to the ticking of his internal clock and do all he could to keep the rhythm calm and steady. All this he considered, not for himself, but for him whom he served. He could not imagine ever having his master be inconvenienced or kept from his work because of Peter's inability to care for him. The mere idea of the servant requiring service was unthinkable. Peter decided on a course of prevention.

The sounds from upstairs calmed his troubled mind. He knew that his impressions were correct. In the song he felt a voice speak to his heart the peaceful reassurance that he had been warned for a reason. He too had a purpose in the scheme being worked within the house. He breathed a long slow inhalation of air, then closed his eyes to rest. The music continued at irregular intervals throughout the rest of the day. Peter knew the darkest hour of the journey was behind.

We Shall All Be Changed

THE PACKRAT CONTINUED HIS VISITS TO THE STUMP OUT-
side Handel's house. He would sit cross-legged and wait on the round, flat
seat which had once been a tree. Through the past few days, his waiting
had been long and unanswered. The stints on the stump had become part
of his daily routine, and often he found himself there without any prior
intention of going. He had become quite familiar with the surroundings
during his many visits. He knew that the deep coal cellar behind the apartment was all but empty. He wondered how long it would be before the
dusty, blackened man who delivered coal would push his cart past his
stump to the back of the house to deliver winter warmth. It was a common sight these days to see men shoveling coal into the open coal bins in
preparation for the coming months of cold weather. It was autumn, after

all, and Peter knew that as early as October the nights would begin to get chilly. The Packrat thought it peculiar that this home's needed coal had not been delivered yet.

The Packrat learned every brick in the side of Handel's apartment. It was dark reddish or brownish brick; he wasn't absolutely sure which—it depended on the time of day and the color of the sun in the clouds overhead. He just called it "darkish" so he would always be right. One of the bricks in the wall had a dark hole below it where the mortar had broken away. Wasps would occasionally fly in and out of the hole. There always seemed to be more of the ornery insects when it was hot outside.

Some of the bricks were chipped at the edges, especially the bricks at the corner of the apartment. When the sun was low, the dark line of bricks at the corner of the house was silhouetted against the bright sky. If he looked closely, he could see shapes along the edges of the marred bricks. Several of the patterns were shaped like various noses: some large and protruding, others pointed and sharp. In one spot, quite high up the wall, two bricks together formed one long severely pointed nose. Peter called the formation "the witch." He named it thus because he didn't spot it until late one night when he watched the moon slowly appear from behind the house. There she was, looking down at him, black against the bright white ball of night coming in and out of the passing clouds. She seemed to fly high above him, her pointy nose leading the way. Even though he knew it was nothing, he made it a point not to look at her at night.

Some of the other chips reminded him of arrowheads, some, stairways. Others were rounded out and looked like the crescent moon. One section looked like the tailfin of a mackerel.

His favorite formation was one of the very smallest and most detailed. The entire face of a woman appeared to be cut out of the edge of a single brick. She had a small rounded nose, large eyes, thin lips and a delicate chin. The chin was originally pointed, but he had carefully smoothed the spur off with a flat stone. Her neck was long, her forehead sloped slightly back and up. All of this was within the width of one brick.

He called the brick "me Mums." The formation was about head high, low enough that he made a point to touch it every time he walked past the corner of the flat to his perch on the stump. He occasionally spoke to the formation, asking it meaningless questions—questions of weather, of ants and bugs—questions without answers about the man who played the music upstairs. Somehow, he sensed that even though "me Mums" could not answer, she knew the happenings within the apartment. It didn't seem to bother him that she couldn't speak; she was someone to share things with that he couldn't say elsewhere. She was a good and trustworthy friend with a listening ear.

Peter observed long blades of grass, which grew out from the base of the building. The once green tips were beginning to curl and brown as summer began to wane. He was familiar with each of the smooth, flat, walking stones set approximately a man's step apart from each other and placed in a line leading to the front of the building.

But perhaps best of all, he knew the windows of the wall: two on the lower floor, one on the upper floor. Music came from the upper window, which was taller than it was wide and separated into eight panes by narrow slats of white painted wood. The paint was peeling away in long white slivers, which he could see flutter ever so slightly when the wind blew. When there was no music to keep his attention, he would try to determine how long the slivers would hold on before finally falling. He knew that those that flittered and danced the most were also the most at risk. "Like the rich," he would say to himself with a grin.

He noticed how the upper window would change, depending on the time of day he was there. He thought it peculiar that when it was bright outside, the room behind the glass was very dark. When it was night and dark outside, the room beyond the glass was light.

"Why are people always tryin' to make things different than how Ya' made 'em in the first place?" he would ask God. "Like people bein' afraid of the dark. If the night was suppos'd to be scary, Ya' wouldn't have made so much of it, would Ya'? I think Ya' just wanted us to see things a different way so we'd always be grateful for day."

On rare occasions, Peter saw a large dark form standing close to the window. This only happened at night when the light in the room cast a distinct shadow of a person on the white, sheer curtains. He surmised, through observation, that the person whose shadow he saw was the music man, because at no time did the music and the shadow at the window coincide. In the last few days, Peter had seen the shadow a couple of times but had heard no music.

At first, the Packrat thought perhaps he had just come at the wrong hour, so he idled away the time by going through his checklist of usual observations. But eventually, after he had checked out all his usual sights, he simply waited and wondered.

"What's goin' on up there, Mums?" he asked the brick. "Is everything all right? Things feel pretty odd around here these days."

The Packrat tried to think of every reason that the music might stop, but was satisfied with none. At first, he passed it off as a slow day, like the days when none of his usual tricks produced any food or money. These were the difficult days when he questioned his ability to work the street and his prowess as a thief.

"Surely, adults have off days too," he thought. But as hard as he tried to convince himself that there was nothing more, the more certain he was that there was something. He then observed something even more odd: the lack of activity in the lower windows. Since he had met the servant, the one with his same name, he had watched him closely through the downstairs window. He learned the man, his walk, the way his head always sloped forward, his narrow frame, the sound of his shoe on the hard wood as he passed from rug to floor. Until the past few days, the Packrat saw him often, but now, only scarcely, and not for any great length. The servant man seemed to come and go at far greater intervals for far less time. The Packrat knew that something was different now—not necessarily wrong, but definitely different. The usual trappings of the home were considerably altered. There was sufficient evidence to rule out the notion that sickness or death had come to the house. The boy circled the apartment many times, finding new places to wait and watch, but nothing out of the ordinary happened other than to say things were not ordinary.

The Packrat came and went several times, never staying longer than was his habit, but he did spend a disproportionate amount of time pondering the goings-on of the house between visits. It was difficult for him not to think about it. At times he had to force his thoughts away from the house on Brook Street and concentrate on his responsibilities, otherwise he and several others would not eat. But, to his astonishment, he thought about it often, more certain that something significant was happening. Whether for good or ill, he knew not. What became most intriguing to him was the role he played in the events of the house.

Peter had determined, for no apparent reason, to continue to leave goods of trade, in spite of the fact that there was no music. At first he thought himself foolish for doing so, and questioned "me Mums" vocally concerning the soundness of his own mind. Then something incredible happened, completely unexpected. There was no way he could have ever anticipated the event, but, once it happened, he was stunned that it hadn't happened before.

Until that day, he had never left anything behind that he found still there when he returned. The exchange of goods had become so commonplace that he was utterly amazed when he arrived and found the piece of blue glass on the stump where he had left it the day before. When he saw it, he wasn't sure what to do. Initially, it startled him. Like every other day, he rounded the corner and touched "me Mums." The second he saw the glint of blue as the sun gently tipped the piece of broken bottle, he stopped in his tracks, his hand still resting on the maternal brick.

"What the 'ell!" He said out loud. "Strange. You must have a hand in this somewhere, Lord."

He looked up at the window high above him.

"What is happenin' up there?"

He shook his head in bewilderment. At length he decided not to take back the gift, but to add to it.

"Even if there isn't any music, at least I'm still gettin' something out of it," he reasoned. "If it's only just a place to sit, that counts for somethin'." He sat down on the stump, being very careful not to touch or move the piece of blue glass that he had laid there the day before. He sat, more to justify his obscure rationale than to rest. Momentarily, he shook his head and rolled his eyes. "I'm a dolt. If gettin' me to admit that is the reason for playin' such games, Lord—You win. You are the champion and with good reason—most the time You're a step ahead of me anyway."

He got up and headed back the way he came. He disappeared around the corner of the house, his head still shaking from side to side. A minute later, he reappeared around the house and walked straight to the stump. He pulled a length of red string from his pocket and laid it over the piece of glass. He backed away from it, then turned around and started walking back along the line of stones leading to the front of the apartment.

"I know what You're thinkin'," he said glancing up. Just as he was about to disappear around the building a second time, he heard something. He stopped so suddenly that he had to put out his arm to catch himself. His fingers landed on his favorite brick. While he stood motionless for several minutes, music rang out from the window above. It was music like before, but somehow—unexplainably—it was different. The Packrat had no idea what was different; he had no formal training, nor instruction to tell him so. He knew it was different because he felt different. The music he heard before made him want to throw back his head and stare into the majesty of the heavens. This music made him bow his head. He listened and felt every sweet note of sublime reverence. Minutes later, he continued his path down Brook street. Although he did not know it, he would never again be the same.

Why Do the Nations
So Furiously Rage Together?

I T WAS WARM AND MUSTY IN THE LARGE ROOM OF THE *Spectator* publishing office where the printing press was housed. One window high up the south wall provided most of the light for the room. The window was so high that, for several hours of the day, sunlight— when there was any—streamed in a long square shaft down through the dusty atmosphere of the vaulted room to where the press stood.

Upon entering the room, one was immediately captivated by the almost saintly appearance of the machine. It shone with an omnipotent, ethereal aura. In the winter, when the room was usually cold, the metal of the press glowed warm in the light of the southern sun. The machine took on a peculiar otherworldly persona, as if heaven smiled on the workings of the press. This did little to temper the self-righteous publishers of *The*

Spectator, who viewed their work as the last great bastion for censuring the unbridled hypocrite—or anyone else who might take issue with them. They served up a steady course of derision. They perceived themselves as the caretakers of sarcasm, as the spoilers of pride, as divinely appointed critics. *The Spectator* was the shining sword they wielded against those at odds with their sacred and canonized opinion. The press itself was the supernal tool in their almighty hands.

The iron screw of the immense press was the strong arm of Steele and Addison, the publishers of the daily periodical. They personally oversaw every word that came off the press. Usually the words were theirs; they spouted them freely and prodigiously. Political rhetoric was the usual diet. The King and his family provided more than enough fodder to fill several pages each week. Parliament was a regular topic. The ongoing hostility with Spain required lines and columns, but London society was their outlet, their creative release. Political news was both demanding and vexing; society was the reward. They fed themselves on politics, but their dessert was music, dance, opera, literature, opinion, society, and business. Here they could meddle—play and dance with words and cartoons just for the sheer fun of it. They could make friends and change friends, as needed, simply to exploit a circumstance. They hid under the blanket of journalistic immunity. They stalked the juiciest stories, masked behind the camouflage of correspondence. All things spoken to them were on the record, whether confidentiality was promised or not. They floated in and out of whatever circles promised to be most gainful. They concerned themselves with information rather than the rights of individuals, and they cared not what flotsam might be churned up in the wake of their words. Society provided a vehicle for them to demonstrate their best wit, most biting sarcasm, and most scathing criticism, with little if any chance of recourse or retaliation from anyone.

It was not difficult to find topics. For personal reasons, certain topics and people were particularly appealing. Handel was a favorite. There was so much prattle from which to choose that he alone was a full course dinner any night they were at a loss as to what to feast upon. He was a Kraut, like the King. Both were imports, awkwardly joined at the hip by heritage. Neither man's English was very good—more often, it was very bad.

But Handel had several other tasty characteristics that made him especially appealing: he had a mighty temper, an affinity for offending, and he was doggedly demanding of those around him—especially his singers, who seldom liked him. He was outrageously arrogant, a favorite flaw of both Addison and Steele. He was a musician deeply entrenched in the volatile popularity battles of English nobility. He was loud. He was proud. He was fat. He had all the things that satire feeds on and more.

There were few others who caught the attention of Addison and Steele as intensely as did Handel. Curiously, one of their other favorites was a close friend and admirer of Handel. It was an easy transition from one to the other. As the iron screw pressed down upon the paper that day, the topic of choice was the other.

When the large plate at the base of the screw lifted, a hand reached for the paper. As it lifted off the set letters, the light of the window illuminated the white paper. Steele smirked as he lifted it to his face. He read silently, then laughed, as he handed the paper to his associate, who stood at his side. Addison joined in the laughter.

"Jennens is such an easy—and large—target," Steele remarked.

The paper was distributed that afternoon, and by the following morning Jennens was on his way to *The Spectator* office. His horse-drawn carriage clanged over the cobbles; the driver was given instructions not to dally.

The rattle of the wheels on the cobbles rang down the length of Worcester Street. Mothers along the wayside grabbed their children's arms and held them close to their sides until the carriage passed by. Sellers with carts moved to the edge of the street. The business of the street stopped for the few seconds that it took for the wheeled machine to pass. Store merchants paused in the middle of their pitches to watch the commotion pass by their front windows. Even dogs heeded the clamor and scampered out of the way. A path opened down the middle of the street like a knife through a ripe melon. Pedestrians, as they are wont to do, speculated on the cause for such urgency, but did so a safe distance away. Had they known the reason for the rush, they might have been quite disappointed, as speculators always tend to expect the worst.

Inside Jennens squirmed and shifted like foam on the surface of the sea. He could hardly contain himself. Rolled in his hand was the recent newspaper. He slapped it against the seat facing him at least once a block, sometimes twice. At his side sat his lovely young niece, Margaret, looking calmly out the window. Every time the paper would slap against the leather seat she would glance over at him, until the frequency of it habit-uated her to the sound and she no longer even blinked at the loud pop. For the greater part, the journey had been in silence, other than the ruckus of the carriage and the loud paper slaps, but finally, like the whis-tle of a boiling kettle, sound poured out of Jennens' spout:

"Rubbish! Written by nitwits for the pleasure of fools."

"You rewrote Shakespeare. Save your criticism for someone unknown and Steele will leave you alone," the girl replied.

"Why? Why dabble in the mundane?"

"Because it will go unnoticed."

Jennens stopped shifting.

"Precisely," he said.

He stared at her long, then his eyes drifted past her to the window behind her head. As he watched the buildings pass outside, he spoke introspectively.

"I could use a bit of providence; perhaps Handel will provide."

"Handel? I'm not sure whom they like less, him or you."

As his gaze came back to her, the carriage stopped. The door swung open, and Jennens was gone, out the carriage door and through the office door of *The Spectator*.

Is Risen Upon Thee

THE NIGHTWATCHMAN WAS STILL CALLING THE HOUR OF eleven when the Packrat came around the corner near the Boar's Head Tavern, only a short distance from his night hole. He was headed home with no thought of anything other than sleep. He had numbly heard the boisterous sounds as he approached the orange light spilling out the line of small windows at the front of the tavern. He thought nothing of it, as such was the case almost every night. And even though the uproar from within was decibels louder than normal, he didn't even look up, thinking it was just another party for some bachelor who would be making vows the following day. The Packrat would have been far more likely to notice the oddity of silence than pandemonium.

Just as he was about to cross the perpendicular corridor where the entrance intersected the street, the door of the Boar's Head burst open. There was a harsh clang as the iron-ringed handle of the thick wooden door slammed into the stone wall of the entry. Peter leaped back, his eyes wide open. Voices were coming his way; feet were pounding on the thick wooden slats of the walkway. To his utter astonishment, a body was flung carelessly out the opening of the tavern to the street. The large form skidded over the polished cobbles to a stop. Arms and legs fell limp, blood trickled from his nose. The body did not gasp or groan. It fell prostrate on the ground like a slab of meat on a butcher's board. Before anyone appeared at the door to wave a goodbye, Peter ducked behind a stone pillar at the edge of the walkway. From where he hid, he could hear every curse uttered by the disgusting men who came out the door to appraise their work, but the Packrat could not see them—nor did he want to. He desired nothing more than to be quite invisible through the entire incident. Only when he could hear the dampened sound of voices turning away and walking back into the tavern, did he peek around the post. What he saw turned his blood to ice: still standing in the open doorway was the brigand from the fight outside the theatre. He had waited behind to take one last look at the still body lying face-down in the street.

As if he felt Peter's eyes on him, the ruffian suddenly turned. Peter had not the time to duck, but remained as perfectly still as his pounding heart would let him. The ruffian looked all the way from left to right. When his black eyes came to Peter, he stopped. The boy had been spotted—or so he thought. The weight in Peter's shoe shifted from his heel to his toe as he prepared to bolt away. He knew that, at this close range, the odds were well against him. His only possible chance might rely wholly upon his first step. Every second prolonged here might cost him desperately needed time down the street, around a corner, or under an eave. An instant to find a shadow on a blind turn might be his only salvation. He could feel his eyes begin to itch, though he dared not blink. Fear started to take over judgment. His leg muscles involuntarily began to contract and tighten in preparation to launch from where his feet now stood. Ugly imaginings darkened his mind and eroded his good sense. Still, he did not flinch, nor did he blink. Had he done so, the enemy's focus might have shifted forward from across the street to a spot nearer. For what the Packrat did not know was that the brute's eyes were looking beyond the mark. A simple change of focal length would have revealed the exact spot where the prey was hiding.

Seconds passed. At the precise moment when Peter was certain he had passed the critical time of non-discovery and that the predator was well into the strategy phase of the hunt, the hunter and the hunted simultaneously turned away. As Peter ducked back behind the pillar, his pants brushed against the rough-hewn stone. The man turned back around, but not before looking into the bright fire in the tavern hearth. The flash of light was enough to temporarily blind him to the dark. There was nothing to see, the boy was hidden. Soon, the Packrat heard the door creak on its rusty hinges and boom back into place. The voices within muted behind the thick wooden door. The boy breathed again. His first thought was to be gone quickly and efficiently. He could think of nothing that would bring him more immediate joy than distance between himself and this place. Yet he did not move.

There was something about the incident that he could not ignore. He retraced in his mind everything that each of his senses had encountered to try and pinpoint what it was that bothered him. He couldn't remember. He was certain that it had to do with the ruffian. He thought of all the encounters that he had had with the evil man; nothing unusual came to him. He looked at the drunk lying face down on the cobbles. Nothing.

When he was certain his mind was turning to mush, he shook his head and walked forward, determined to be more cautious than he had been before. Still, there was something about the event that hindered him. As he walked, he considered every detail of what had occurred, trying to discover the aberration for which he strained. Frustrated, he kicked at the loose pebbles in the street. One broke free of the ground and tumbled out in front of him. As he walked, he kicked at it, sending it bouncing over the cobbles. Several times he kicked it, each time rocketing it forward in front of him. He watched it hop and skip over the undulated surface of the street. He forgot his goal to be more careful and quiet. So bothered was he by his lack of attention to detail under the duress that he kicked the stone with no thought of discretion. In disgust, he kicked it one last time as hard as he could. He listened as it bounded away into the shadows of a long alley, clicking and clinking away over black, unseen cobbles. Peter listened as the clicks slowed and the stone finally came to rest. Shortly after, the sound of a window sliding open echoed down the alley.

"Who goes there?" shouted a voice from the darkness. "Go away!"

There was no answer. The boy was gone, running as fast as he could back to the tavern. He was no longer tired, nor sleepy. He was back at the tavern in just a few minutes. Even he was surprised at how fast he made it back, assuming he had wandered much farther than he actually had.

When he came around the corner, he sighed in relief to see the drunk still lying face down in the street. The tavern door was closed and he could hear voices inside.

He cautiously walked out into the street to where the drunken man lay. His first thought was to kick at him to see if he was as soundly incoherent as he appeared, but he thought better of it and left him alone.

"Why wake up what I hope is asleep?" he whispered under his breath.

The boy walked past the man, his head down. His feet inched forward as he searched the ground. He studied the cracks between each cobble.

"Where are ya'? I heard you fall," he muttered. "When the man hit the ground, I heard ya' run away from him."

In the instant of silence between the time the drunk hit the ground and the tavern vomited out its putrid occupants, Peter had heard something bound away over the cobbles. That was precisely the reason his head had been out from behind the pillar when the men came out the door: he was listening. Had he not heard his kicked stone tumble away and down the alley he might never have retrieved the tiny detail. The ruffian had taken him off track, but now he was back on the scent and closing in.

The boy knelt down and lowered his eyes to just above the ground. He scanned the horizon of rounded stones, looking for anything that might give off a tiny glint and reveal its hiding place. His head hardly moved; his keen eyes were alive and bright.

Then, out of the blackness, he saw it. A little fracture of blue light reflected back at him, then extinguished. He moved his head back and forth. A tiny sliver of shine glistened in the stones several feet away. He crawled forward, keeping his head steady and as close to the same plane as possible. As he bobbed back and forth gently, the object sparkled back that his bearing was accurate and on course. Like a ship spotting a lighthouse in a midnight squall, the Packrat used the intermittent specks of light to navigate his way in.

The closer he got, the more frequent the twinkling, until it became almost one continuous shine of bluish white—like the morning star during the vernal equinox. Peter slowly approached the shining object until he knelt over it. Staring up at him, unmarred and unbroken during its journey across the stones, was a lustrous gold-rimmed monocle. The Packrat stared down in disbelief. He blew the tips of his fingers before carefully picking up the piece from the ground. Never had he held in his hand something of such marvelous ingenuity and art as this. The gold was meticulously bent and molded around the clear glass. The last several links of the thin, gold chain, which had broken in the fall, were still clasped onto a tiny ring on the outside edge of the gold rim. Peter was fascinated at how the cobbles beneath the rounded glass appeared large and distorted. He touched each feature of the prize with his fingers, trying his best not to sully it with the dirt on his hands. He held it to his eye as he had seen the noblemen do when they read the newspaper or eyed street vendors when they were told the price. Everything looked more blurred to him the closer he held it to his eye. It was beautiful, and it was his. In all his young life, only once before had he possessed something he considered as extraordinary as this. He thought of the bent gold button that he carried for so long at the bottom of his pocket. Since he gave it back to its rightful owner, he wondered if perhaps this was God's way of evening the score, or maybe God wasn't watching and missed the entire event. It then occurred to Peter that perhaps he was supposed to find it; this piece of good fortune was meant to be.

He pulled a tiny feather from his lapel, walked over, and dropped it above the drunk. He watched it float back and forth until it lit softly on the back of the man's head. He held the monocle close and stared up at God with one huge eye and laughed aloud, "Lookin' elsewhere, perhaps? I think not!" The Packrat reflected for a moment, then grinned. "A gift, You say? I accept. I helped You, and now You helped me. We are even!"

"Not even close," said a voice.

The Packrat looked up to see a man standing on the wooden planks outside the tavern not ten steps from where he stood. The only thing between them other than empty space was the drunk lying in the street. The man had somehow gotten to that place without Peter's knowledge. He was so engrossed with the monocle that he had missed the slight creak of the boards beneath the intruder's feet until it was too late.

Peter took a step back. The space between them did not increase as the man stepped forward also. The man took the initiative on the next step; Peter was quick to answer with his own. The intruder now stood just a stride from the street. One more step and he would be off the board-walk and on the same plane as the Packrat. Peter didn't need to see his face to know who it was. He recognized his shape the moment he saw his shadow against the wall, but that did little to quell the shock of actually seeing the ruffian's face when he finally did step into the moonlight.

The Packrat's feet froze in place. He knew the thug could catch him now. There was no element of surprise or advantage at hand—only time, of which he had precious little. He thought fast.

"I have something for you—money," he said.

"I'll bet you do."

"And this..." The boy held up the gold monocle. "It's gotta be worth somethin'. A lot I'll bet."

Peter held the round glass to his eye and stared at the ruffian. The scoundrel said something, but his words were submerged beneath the clamor of an approaching carriage. Peter's magnified eye flicked toward the noise and then leveled again on the ruffian. The boy lowered the glass and ventured a glance the other direction. The ruffian saw it.

"Don't try it," he shouted loud enough for the boy to hear.

Then Peter did something remarkable: he didn't try it. He stepped toward the brute and lowered his shoulders in an attitude of abdication. There would be no chase. Peter sighed as he looked down on the drunken sot, ashamed that he had let the man or his monocle dull his senses to the point of being caught. He felt stupid. Then he looked again at the monocle in his hand. It was amazing. The beauty of it even made him rationalize that it was worth whatever the consequence of acquiring it. It took the bite out of his being caught. He was so enthralled with his find that he forgot about the carriage until he looked up and could see horses legs nearly upon him. He jumped back to avoid getting trampled. The ruffian mistook his movement as an attempt to escape. Certain the driver would guide his horses around the body to the widest channel of the street, the ruffian leaped forward to seize the Packrat.

The driver of the carriage jerked on the reins when he saw the boy and the hapless body on the ground. The frightened horses shied from Peter. They bolted the opposite direction toward the narrow gap between the lifeless body and the walk just as the ruffian jumped into the street. He couldn't stop himself. The Packrat saw a dark figure disappear under the steel shoes of the horses and bend over backwards as it vanished beneath the carriage. A horrible snapping sound made its way to the Packrat's ears between the claps of the horse's hooves. The large wheel bumped up as it rolled over something. The driver stopped the carriage and looked back at the crumpled black form lying in the road, shaking. Peter saw a tiny fracture of light shine on an eye staring up at him. The shaking stopped, the form relaxed—but the eye did not close. It stayed opened and fixed on him. Peter turned away from it and gazed up at the driver. The man shrugged his shoulders and cried aloud that it was not his fault. The gesture was true, it wasn't his fault—nor was it the Packrat's.

Peter couldn't help himself—he looked back to see if the eye had closed. It stared right back at him. He put the monocle in his pocket and ran. The image of the eye stayed in his mind. He tried to forget it by counting out loud but it continued staring at him all the way to his hole. It didn't matter if he closed his eyes; that one eye was still open and watching him. It scared away sleep. Everywhere he looked, it was there. The more he thought about it, the less he wanted to sleep, afraid that the ruffian would come back to life in his dreams. Finally, when he could think of nothing else to do, he pulled the monocle from his pocket and looked through it. He looked at his hand—it seemed so big. He peered at the dead flies on the floor—and saw their thick black hairs. When he held the glass up to the light shining down from the fireplace through the narrow slats in the floorboards, light sparkled and danced on the floor like fiery rings.

Before he knew it, he had forgotten about the eye. When he tried to remember it, it came back, but the memory was dimmer than before. Each time he thought about the eye looking at him he got out the monocle. Each time he looked through the glass his memory of the eye weakened until it no longer frightened him. To Peter, the glass was clear, the gold, bright. No memory of the ruffian could tarnish the gift; if anything, its power to help him forget made it all the shinier.

They That Dwelleth in Darkness

Voices CAME AND WENT IN A PROCESSION OUTSIDE THE huge, black, tarred door of the prison like entries in a slow-moving parade. The empty stone walls reverberated noise in every direction throughout the prison catacombs like muscles contracting down the tentacles of an octopus. A voice could sound as if it were just outside the door, when in reality it could be coming from many hundred feet away down another corridor.

Specific words were difficult to discern unless the speaker was very close at hand. The narrow halls carried sound like an ear canal, with the exception that the consonant corners and appendages of words were beveled off by the halls of the stone quarry; the vowel abdomens stayed intact. The resulting effect was haunting. The corridors of confinement could transform normal speech into the dreadful haunting of evil specters. Shouts from the guards sounded like demonic taskmasters torturing their helpless victims. Laughing took on the shrill cackle of the Devil himself. The cries of dying prisoners were most unnerving. They had a sickening sound like the last desperate cries of the damned as fiendish hands groped and clawed them down into the hot, black holes of hell.

The wooden door of the prison cell worked like a huge mute to all sound coming in or out. When the flicker of torchlight licked the wet stones under the door, recent arrivals would crowd close to the two small openings in the door for a view. After several attempts, it became obvious that there was nothing to see. One of the openings was about head high. It was a small window, hewn through with an ax. It was narrowest at the center and thickest on the outside. The carved notches and blade nicks from the ax were worn smooth from a hundred years of men's attempts to reach hands through the hole to signal anyone who would endure their stories of injustice.

The other opening was somewhat larger. It was a rectangular notch cut from the bottom of the door, through which things could be passed—usually meager food rations and water. It was just big enough that one could be certain that men had tried to squeeze through the hole and escape. It was, of course, impossible to do so, but the hole had a curious way of appearing deceptively larger than it actually was.

No matter what the time of day outside, the halls of the prison were dark. There were no comings and goings without a torch.

Jonathon sat with his back against the moist, algae-blackened wall, where the sun had never before touched its warm light. He was in his usual place, the spot along the wall that had become his. It was relegated to him as those owners before either passed on in their sleep or were fortunate enough to join the pitifully few who had actually been released. It took many months for him to get there. His tenure had finally earned for him this place against the wall, where there wasn't a constant seep of frigid ground water through the cracks in the stone blocks of the prison walls. New gaolbirds had to wait for a place to lean their backs. The eternal seconds passed even more slowly for those poor wretches who were forced to sit inside the perimeter with nowhere to lean back and rest. They would sit on the floor, hunched forward, their backbones arched like grass bent down by the wind, until the pain and cramping forced them up to their feet or flat onto their backs.

The vast majority of debtors were not so much criminal as they were unfortunate. Most were forced to accept prison convention and waited their turn, as Jonathon had. Some new fish bullied their way to the wall only to find that they had sacrificed one of the only redeeming virtues that still had value in prison: the respect of peers. Bullies were generally heeded but not regarded. Stolen wall space had its consequences.

The ground was damp and putrid. The floor ever shone with various unknown fluids. Drippage accounted for the larger part of the puddles, men the rest. The ghastly stench of urea was ever present. One's nose never acclimated to the overpowering odor of ammonia. Unlike most smells, the pungent bite of the noxious stench never dulled nor diminished. The chemical sourness was so overwhelming in certain corners of the multi-chambered prison room that no one would go near it except to relieve themselves, and then with breath held.

The dampness of the cell made the winter colder, the heat, more humid. There was no pleasant season, no breeze to clear the air. The only windows in the stone quarry were high up the wall, and inexorably small. The deep bowels of debtors' prison knew only two seasons: unmerciful cold and suffocating heat. Of the two, most preferred the stinging cold of January to the stifling stickiness of August. In winter, the firecan produced minimal warmth; in summer there was no altering the sweltering torridness of the prison belly.

There was no fresh air to breathe, only stale, saturated toxins already used countless times by other lungs and tainted by other malevolent molecules. Little of the festered air ever escaped through the tiny windows, and little uncorrupted oxygen ever found its way in. Any subtle change outside produced no change inside. The only atmospheric conditions that had any effect on this inner world were gale-force wind and torrential rain. Both were prayed for, longed for; they were the only cause for any celebration in the dungeon. Hopeless men's eyes moistened to feel air move around their heads and past their cheeks. There were cheers when the wind forced clean drops from the sky through the small portals above and down onto upturned faces.

No one inside was certain of the date or day. Some kept a reckoning from the time they entered, but, at some point, it had all become unclear. None in the stone room knew that September had come.

From his place against the wall, Jonathon could see most of the others who slept, sat, or paced. He didn't need to see their faces to recognize them. The activities of each had become habitual. Some he knew by name, others by sight, and still others, only by their sound. He watched one of the latter, who lay on the floor close to one of the more squalid chambers. Jonathon could discern his tormented breathing apart from the other sounds of the jail. At times, his breaths were interrupted by coughs and liquid wheezing. When night came, Jonathon could pick out the unfortunate sufferer's feeble sounds from all the others.

Recently, the coughing had dampened into his chest. Choking, which had before sounded like one struggling to stay above water now sounded submerged. Coughs seemed to rise and splash forth with the grotesque resemblance of bubbles rising from the deep.

For the many months that Jonathon was incarcerated, the man was more an object than human. Men walked past him without a look or nod. Others would step over him like they would a sleeping dog. He was never fully upright. When he did walk, he stayed close to the wall, always in the shadows. Jonathon saw that he went out of his way to avoid any contact with others. No one spoke to him; no one homesteaded next to him. He was a loner in a lonely place. Each day, Jonathon had watched him descend closer and closer to the ground. He observed him more and more, measuring his collapsing against the mortar lines between the bricks in the wall behind him. The man had shrunk the width of a full brick in the past three days alone. In the dim gray light of the room, Jonathon could see deep open sores on the arms of the infirm man. The more painful the sores appeared, the farther the other inmates would stay from him, not wanting to contract the same malady from which he suffered. It was just a matter of time before his place would become available, undesirable as it was.

"Who is he?" asked Jonathon in a hushed voice.

"Who cares," replied a younger man at his right. "Look at 'im, he's cursed, vile wretch. He probably deserves to be here."

Another inmate spoke from Jonathon's left.

"No one goes near him. He's diseased."

"He'll die soon," said Jonathon.

"Not soon enough," said the first. "I don't like bein' too close to the likes of 'im."

"Why is he here?"

"No one knows for sure—he's been here longest," answered the man at Jonathon's left. "No one's gotten close enough to find out."

"Probably robbed the crown right from the head of the King," smirked the first with a contemptible laugh.

"He's in pain," said Jonathon, his gaze fixed on the sick man.

"Who isn't in this wretched hole?"

Several minutes of silence passed. The men on either side of Jonathon could tell he was in deep thought. At length, he rose to his feet. His companion's stares of disbelief rose with him.

He made his way through the main company. The sick man saw him coming and turned his face away from him. Jonathon knelt down on the wet floor near him. He reached forward and took hold of the man's arm near the wrist. The man recoiled, trying to pull the weak arm away, but the hand that had carried countless hot trays from the oven held firm. Jonathon could feel surrender in the man's arm. Momentarily, the struggle was over; the arm fell limp in Jonathon's hand. He studied the open sores. He tore a small piece from the sleeve of his shirt, then reached high above the man's head where a tiny trickle of water dripped between the cracks in the wall. When the cloth was damp with water, he gently cleaned the open wounds. He picked up the man in his arms and moved him to a dry spot against the wall. Men scurried out of the way when he approached carrying the living corpse. He laid him down near the wall.

"He's a fool! He'll die of the same disease and probably infect us," said the first man, still watching from his place at the wall. "Death would likely be a welcome relief from this place."

"He gives hope where there is none," whispered the other, getting up and going to Jonathon's aid.

Unbeknownst to those inside, there was the slightest movement outside the prison chamber. Only those closest to the entry heard a slight shuffling of boots beyond the black hole at the bottom of the door. Since there was no light accompanying it, they passed it off as the scratching of rats. What they did not realize was that hidden eyes had watched everything that had transpired within the prison cavern. Ears had heard the voices speak from the dark. The jailer moved away from the door slowly, undetected by anyone within. What he had witnessed was unexplainable. He spoke of it to no one; he dared not try. Only he would ever know of the small act of selflessness in this belly of misery. He recognized the man who went to the aid of the other. He excused the act away as the offspring of a demented mind, but he never forgot it.

This Day Have I Begotten Thee

Those in prison were not the only ones who knew not that September had come. Handel, too, was unaware of the change of month. He was now in his third week since starting the work to which he so diligently committed himself. The days and nights ran together like oils on an artist's palette. He lived from stanza to stanza. There was no clear end to one day or beginning of the next.

From the time that Peter LeBlonde again heard music, following the painful interval of silence, Handel had worked steadily. He soon reestablished the same urgent pattern of work that he had employed through the first many days of his sojourn. He slept little, ate little, and worked feverishly. Yet he did not appear exhausted. His short naps were renewing. His brief meals restoring. To his servant, his health appeared to be improving, rather than diminishing. This pleased Peter greatly, as he knew that his master was at his best in process, not in completion.

Peter also was most fulfilled when he was busy. In spite of his slowing down and self-monitoring, he was rejuvenated by the opportunity to be of service. The quiet witness he had received of his own purpose gave him a deep sense of humble gratitude. He performed his duties with gladness, never viewing them as menial, but as meaningful.

When Peter entered the study in the late hours of the September evening, Handel sat quietly at the instrument, manuscript in hand, reading the notes he had inked just minutes earlier. Peter watched him lay each of the sheets, one by one, across the top of the clavichord before him, making sure they were all in proper order. With an air of quiet calmness, Handel's hands rested on the keys. He began to play. Unbeknownst to Handel, Peter had opened the door behind him. Upon seeing Handel at the instrument, he stopped in the threshold.

As Handel played, Peter could hear him sing in half voice.

"Hallelujah, Hallelujah—for the Lord God Omnipotent reigneth. The kingdom of this world is become the kingdom of our Lord and of His Christ. And He shall reign forever and ever."

Outside, alone in the dark, another listened. Moonlight shined off his eyes. He looked up at the window above him. The Packrat could only imagine what Handel looked like sitting at the instrument, playing. He had never actually seen him play at all. He could picture in his mind the candlelight shining on the narrow keys as Handel's fingers pushed down on them. He could see the shadow of his hands moving on the wall. All of this he could only imagine, but of one thing he was absolutely certain: the same feeling that filled his heart filled the heart of the man in the room above. In the Packrat's view, he and Handel were connected—not by situation or circumstance, but by strong unseen cords of spirit.

The Packrat revered the man who made the music for him. He had heard other music before; the boy's lusty voice rang out with song regularly. But this music reached him in a place far deeper than anything had reached before. This was his music, and he knew that the author of it must surely be a kindred spirit. How else could the man touch his soul so completely?

The boy's eyes ventured away from the window and upward. The glories of the night sky opened before him. Millions of stars stared down at the world from a brilliantly black sky. Peter could easily discern the wide milky ribbon that stretched all the way across the wide expanse above him. As the music continued, his view seemed to reach beyond what his eyes could see. He began to see things differently than he ever had before. Behind the black blanket of night, there must certainly be light, he thought. What else could the myriad of pinholes in the fabric of night bespeak? In his mind's eye, the night sky was suddenly reversed; the broad expanse of black became white and the stars were black. It was as if he were seeing the stars from the other side of the wall of night. He was no longer looking through a thick curtain of darkness, but could see an immense source of light that shined through tiny holes in the darkness. He stood on the other side of eternity looking back at the fabric that separated the earth from heaven.

While he pondered, the music from the window became more clear in his ears, as if it were being played right within the walls of his mind. Like the rushing sound of water, he thought he heard a voice.

"What you see is the music."

The Packrat did not understand at first. Again the thought came to him. The second time he felt it more than he heard it, but the words were the same.

"What you see is the music."

There was nothing more, only the sound from upstairs. His vision of the bright sky overhead closed and darkened back into night. The stars again shone bright against the black palette. The Packrat's head tipped sideways. He thought it a curious dream. He spent much of his idle time imagining, but he had not concocted this. The dream had come from somewhere else.

"I think I know—but certainly God is not so high that He's above raisin' questions and not givin' the answers."

His words were not spoken to the heavens, but were uttered as if to keep them from being heard by deity. It was not meant to be a prayer; it was a musing of mortality prompted by a feeling from beyond. If the vision did actually come from God, it seemed only natural that God would have to be aware of him. The assumption seemed presumptuous, and yet he could not deny that it felt entirely possible.

In reality, the Packrat was not sure if it meant anything at all, but in his heart he knew that it was more than just a fleeting fancy. He perceived that his dream was symbolic of the music that he had heard. Perhaps there was something glorious behind the music—light, perhaps. He wondered if the sounds he heard coming from the window were, as the stars of the sky, only hints and clues of something far greater shining through. If the beautiful noise was evidence of something greater, what could it be? He did not know the answer, but, like the wise men from the East, he would follow this star of song to wherever it might lead him.

When the music ceased, Handel's face was streaked with paths of tears. He turned and saw his servant watching him.

"I believe I did see all heaven before me, and the great God Himself sitting upon His throne."

Outside Handel's house, a shadow silently passed by the wall, then was gone. In the deep blue glow of the clear, moonlit night, a gleam of light shined from the old, gray stump. On it lay a gold-rimmed monocle.

Speak Peace

THE SERVANT DID NOT TARRY WITH THE MASTER THROUGH the remainder of the night. Peter knew well that there were times for blessed companionship, as well as times for needed solitude. Handel needed the latter. After hearing the brief testimony, which Handel witnessed to Peter so simply and powerfully, he retreated through the door and closed it behind him. He did not, as had been the case for over two weeks, busy himself with chores or remain close at hand to see if perchance his services were needed. Instead, he retired to his room. He undressed and changed into his nightclothes. He knelt silently at the side of his bed before pulling back the down comforter and climbing under it.

Peter fell asleep quickly. He did not fret about his master, nor did he run down the checklist of chores in his mind. He closed his eyes and fell away into slumber. He peacefully slept through the night. He did not awaken until light shone through the sheer curtains of his window.

The moment his eyes opened, he arose from bed. Again he knelt at his bedside before dressing for the day. His movements did not betray a sense of urgency, but of purpose. Since the frightening incident in the entry, he had been more careful about keeping his walk and actions steady.

Upon entering the kitchen, he fanned the coals in the stove to an orange glow and added new fuel. Within a few minutes, water was warming. While waiting for the tea temperature to arrive, he climbed the stairs to ascertain the needs of his master. When he opened the door, the room was full of light. Sunlight streamed in the open window in a spillway of radiant gold.

Peter spotted Handel asleep on the couch. His breathing was deep and clear. Peter softly walked to his master's side. Handel's fingers were black with dried ink. His arms were folded tightly about his chest, and his knees were tucked up close. Peter smiled at how in sleep the man appeared so much the child. He pulled the blanket over his master's arms, then blew out the candle still burning on the desk. As he did, his eyes fell on the last page of score. On top were these words: "I know that my Redeemer liveth."

Sunlight from the east streamed low and flat down the streets of London, backlighting the wisps of steam rising off the wet cobbles. Bells from the wharves could still be heard above the rising din of the street, but each passing minute, as the activity increased, the bells grew more faint. House and apartment doors opened and closed as people exited one life and entered another. Brooms swept away the dust gathered around storefronts. Carts rattled on the bumpy stones towards Covent Garden to park for the day. Commerce was awakening.

It was still very early when James felt a presence sit down next to him against the granite wall. He was quite surprised that he had not heard any sign of anyone approaching. He did not speak, even though he could feel the person at his side within arm's reach. It was not long before he recognized the Packrat from his sounds and his smell. James had grown both accustomed to and fond of both. On this morning, he was curious about the unusual behavior of the boy but waited for the Packrat to speak first.

Slowly the sun rose up above the low horizon of the street and landed full upon the wall against which they leaned. The radiant light bathed them in a pool of amber warmth.

The smell of baking bread penetrated the early air. Blindness rendered the nose more sensitive than James had ever imagined. Between the light, the bread, and the boy, James was a contented man. Several more minutes passed before the boy spoke.

"Is it...?" Peter's words trailed off. There was a short pause before he finished the question.

"Is it possible to change?" he asked.

"All things change," answered James.

"All things?"

"All things. There is change in every new day."

"Is it a good thing?"

"It can be."

"What about people?"

"Even people change."

James heard the boy's lungs fill with a deep breath, then exhale slowly. It was a long time before the Packrat spoke again.

"Can a heart change?"

"A change of heart? It's not practical, but possible, yes. Why?"

"I've felt somethin', somethin' good perhaps, or maybe to do somethin' good."

"Your heart hasn't changed. You simply found the heart that you have always had."

James could not hear it, but he knew the boy smiled. By now the street was approaching full occupancy. The vendors were not yet calling, but the voices of hooves and wheels and feet filled the air with rich, low sounds like the deep rhythm of an enormous pulsing machine. The next to be added would be the middle-pitched sounds of voices speaking and small wheels on cobbles. The penetrating, high-pitched calling of vendors, children, and cranky women would be the last to join the cacophony of the street. Peter seemed quite oblivious to all of it.

"Do ya' think I could learn to sing?" piped up Peter, with a laugh. James could tell that the boy was back to himself.

"You already sing. You just need to learn the notes."

The Packrat was on his feet in a moment. He leaned over and kissed the blind man on the top of the head, then laughed at the sky.

"Lord, choose me to sing Your praise, then the Devil is outsmarted. He will not even notice, he is too busy with the rich."

"Try the cathedral; they have a boys choir," shouted James as he heard the Packrat's feet patter off down the street. Peter noticed a nobleman coming toward him. In his pocket was a leather wallet with a small protruding talon. When the Packrat spotted it, he turned to follow the man.

"You should thank me, Lord. I'm only fixin' Your error."

Lift Up Your Heads

ANY PAINT LEFT ON THE OVEN DOOR HAD BURNED OFF years before. Radiant heat emanated from the great iron door for the better part of the day. Only large chunks of coal were used in the oven, because they burned hotter and more consistently. The temperature within the chamber changed only a few degrees from early morning to midday when the baking was finished. One of the duties of the employee responsible for maintenance was to arrive an hour earlier than the others to fire the ovens and shovel the coal bins.

Rachel's call time was 4 A.M. on week days, an hour earlier on Saturdays. Her responsibilities included the general cleanliness of the bakery and assisting the other few employees with their duties as needed, but mainly the fires were hers. It was dirty and difficult work. Starting the coals took time and patience to make sure that each chunk burned equally and evenly. By the time she was ready to spark the stack, her hands were completely black, whether she wore the provided gloves or not. After the day's baking, expired coal dust had to be shoveled out and disposed of.

The ovens were the beating heart of the bakery. Her duty was to make absolutely certain that the pulse of that heart was never interrupted by so much as a murmur. Firing the ovens required her constant attention. Only once did she get so preoccupied (she was helping drip icing on the cinnamon buns) that the temperature of the oven dropped ten degrees without her being aware. The next batch of bread was substandard due to the extra baking time needed. She did not need scolding, because her employer's disappointed face was more than enough reprobation to make her resolve never to allow it to happen again. She watched the oven religiously, anticipating any change in temperature beforehand. She studied the color and pattern of flames when the coals were optimum. By looking through the small window in the fire door at the front of the oven, she memorized the exact nature, color, and feel of the perfect fire. She emblazoned in her mind the deep reds and oranges of the flames and coals when the mixture of oxygen, heat, and fuel were best. Even with her eyes closed, she could tell the oven temperature within a few degrees just from the heat on her face. Little by little, the compassion by which she had been employed was turned to trust and reliance upon her great work. She made herself a necessary element in the success of the bakery. What made her even more essential was her unfailing cheerfulness. She helped wherever she could, bringing a smile to the dullest of duties. Her face shone under a mask of coal dust like the morning sun on the Thames. She greeted customers as though they were dear friends. She hummed as she stoked the fires. She was a light in an otherwise dim room. Not only was she responsible for the heart of the bakery, but, in large measure, she became the heart of the bakery. She worked with joyful purpose as though each minute of labor brought her closer to a cherished goal.

"Watch yourselves—it's hot! Hot tray, fit for royalty," she would call out as she excused herself through employees and customers with a pan of bread fresh from the oven.

"You forget, this is work." Wheelock reminded her.

"Work? Not if it buys freedom."

But in spite of her cheerfulness, deep beneath her bright countenance were dark clouds of sadness. Only those who knew her best could see the edges of gray through which she smiled.

Everyone at the bakery understood Rachel. They loved and pitied her, but none more than Wheelock. He wished he could help beyond providing employment, but for now, that was the best he could do. But each day, he determined to put aside a small part of the day's take to help Rachel. He believed that if the money helped buy Jonathon's freedom, it was a good investment, since he had been his most productive worker. But he would have done it, regardless. He stopped Rachel on her way out the door one evening with a small loaf under her arm.

"Good night. Until tomorrow," Rachel said, opening the door.

"Wait. You forget," said Wheelock from behind the counter. "You're forgetting your pay—well-earned pay."

She stopped mid-step. She turned back as he came around the counter toward her. Wheelock took hold of her hand and laid several coins in it. Rachel stared at the pounds in her palm in disbelief. Her head began to shake from side to side. She looked up at Wheelock, her eyes filled with uncertainty. In her hand there was unquestionably more than she had earned or expected. Wheelock squeezed her hand closed around the money and smiled. She could not speak. She reached one arm around his neck and held him tight for several seconds. She kissed him on the cheek, then left through the open door. It was the only time she ever forgot to pull it shut behind her.

The hour was late when the bell above the door of Cooke's shop signaled that someone had entered. The store was empty. A musty-smelling haze filled the room. Upon seeing the store empty, the customer did not leave, but closed the door behind with a loud clap. A voice shouted from the back room.

"We're closed."

There was no audible answer, neither voice nor door. Cooke glanced up from his work. When he saw the pauper's attire through the semi-transparent curtain, he was even less inspired to be of assistance.

"If you don't have any money, go away!"

"I have money," the customer said with a voice as strong and loud as his. Now Cooke did look up. There was a brief exchange of whispers in the back room, then a long silence. The customer did not move, but stared at the curtain, knowing full well that eyes were staring back through the curtain at her. Her face was hidden under the shadow of the hood that covered her head, but her eyes could not be hid. Like distant flames in the night, her eyes sparkled in the shade. She did not blink until the fabric parted and the shopkeep appeared from behind. A trailing wisp of foul-smelling smoke followed him through the slit in the curtain. His hands were spotted with dirt and specks of blood. There was a groan from the room behind, which caused a faint smirk to cross Cooke's lips.

This time when he spoke, his voice was amicable.

"Do you have need of my help?" he asked, "Does something here interest you?"

There was no answer beyond a disgusted flick of the eyes toward a wooden cradle that sat in the corner of the room. Cooke followed the glance to the cradle.

"Nothing here interests me," she said. Cooke's brow furrowed in thought. He tried his best to put the loosely bound clues together. "How do I know you?" he whispered, more to himself than to her.

"You sent my husband to debtors' prison," she said. Black-streaked hands appeared from out of the dark cape she wore and pulled back the hood. Cooke stepped back.

At that same moment, the syphilitic solicitor stepped through the curtain from the back room, still tucking in the long folds of his shirt.

"So, have you had your way with that pauper wench? The one whose husband..."

He saw her and stopped mid-sentence. Rachel's unyielding eyes shifted to him, then back at Cooke; her face was unchanged. She stepped toward Cooke with her hand out. He stupidly reached forward a cupped hand out of pure habit of receiving money. She dropped several coins into his hand, being very careful not to touch him. His hand automatically closed around the money.

"This is partial payment. I'll continue until the only debt remaining is your own."

His mouth opened to speak, but when her penetrating stare at him sharpened, his mouth closed.

The bell rang a second time as she pulled the door open and disappeared through it. For the second time that night, she did not pull the door closed behind her.

We Shall All Be Changed

The quill rested on the desk. Handel took a deep breath as he stared at the manuscript before him. He had gathered the many papers into a stack and laid them neatly on his desk. Only the last page was loose from the others. He took another deep breath before picking up the quill between his stained fingertips.

"Amen," he said, then dipped his pen into the bottle of ink. His fingers were black; his clothes, hard-worn and wrinkled, his face, serene. The feather danced as he wrote at the bottom of the page:

"September 14, 1741. S D G."

He laid down the pen slowly. "*Solo Deo Gloria*, to God alone the glory," he whispered. Handel added the last sheet to the manuscript and straightened the stack of papers into one uniform pile. He then pulled open the lower drawer of his oak desk, laid the manuscript inside, and closed the drawer.

He stood from his chair and walked to the window. He stood for several minutes in deep contemplation, looking outside on the world. Like the turns in a mighty river, his thoughts flowed back and forth between the immense satisfaction of finishing the task and the sadness of ending the journey. The exhilaration of accomplishment was shadowed by a solemn sense of loss. As much as he wished and wanted to cling to the process, it had ended. He knew this time would come. He had prayed it would come. Now that it was here he prayed that it might not end. His path had been both desperate and divine, his spirit had been both poor and enriched, his heart, both broken and bound.

Of the many emotions that engulfed him, there was one that enveloped them all: profound gratitude. He was the recipient of a great, ennobling gift. He had not earned it but was somehow granted it through the eternal goodness of God. His head bowed in humble prayer, yet no words were uttered, nor were any conceived in his mind. His voice of prayer was no more than the simple sweet yearnings of his heart, yet never had prayer been more eloquent. His whole soul was drawn out in thanks, not for anything he had done, but for what the journey had done to him. Even the agonies through which he had passed felt so necessary, when he comprehended where the journey had started compared to where it had ended.

Handel had no idea how long he had been standing at the window, when the door opened on the other side of the room and Peter entered. Handel turned from the window to his faithful servant.

"It is finished," he said.

Peter bowed, then left the room.

Lowly of Heart

THE SUN HAD LONG SINCE SET, BUT RACHEL HAD NOT retired, nor had she thought of sleep. For the first time in as many months as she could remember, Rachel had hope. From the moment she had left Cooke's store, excitement at the prospect of freeing Jonathon began to build up within her to the point that she could not contain it. The greater part of the debt was paid. Now she had only to continue on the course that she had put in motion, and she and her love could possibly see spring arrive together.

With Jonathon at her side, she was hopeful they could fetch Christina from the Foundling Hospital and ably prove that they could care for her. Any effort that moved her closer to that goal was regarded as blessed. She was even more excited now that she had seen her plan work. She did not fear the early morning work hour and the pain of waking a fatigued body not ready for waking; she looked forward to it like a child waiting for Christmas to come.

The evening hours were spent in scheming the things she would do to welcome home her beloved. The night hours were spent dreaming of her Christina. The mere thought of being together was overwhelming to her. So close were her affections to the surface that it took little to uncover them. Often, and in the middle of various attitudes and activities, tears would stream freely down the length of her cheek. Any who knew her, especially those with whom she worked, accepted the tears as a part of her day.

She viewed the days ahead not as an enemy but as her salvation. She knew that each day brought work, work brought money, money brought Jonathon home. It was a simple enough plan that there was no part of it which she did not understand. It didn't rely on providence or mediation. It simply required hard work and frugality, two things she knew well. The equation was simple: there was a debt, the debt would be paid, Jonathon would be freed. The plan was fail-safe. She laughed out loud at the mere thought of how well it seemed to be working.

The act of putting coins in the hand of Cooke had been therapeutic. At the time, she was terrified, but with each step away from his store, the hideous chains that held her in bondage seemed to lighten. It had seemed, to her, a miracle. Now, as never before, she wondered if the all-seeing eye of God had somehow found her from out of the darkness. In the deepest recess of her battered soul, she had a feeling that God knew her plight. She heard a knock at the door.

A chill ran up Rachel's back. So seldom did such knocks bring good tidings that all joy left her. She searched her mind for a clue as to who it could be. Trembling, she moved to the door. She leaned her ear close to the wood; no sound. She pushed her ear tighter to it, but still, nothing. The pressure of her body was enough to stir the door on its hinges. It creaked ever so slightly. The noise did not go unheard by the caller. There was another loud knock. With her ear pressed against the door, the pounding sounded as thunder. She jerked back from the door.

"It's me. Open up."

Rachel could not get her hand on the latch fast enough. She was so relieved to hear the boy's voice that she forgot her fear. The door swung open, Peter stepped through.

"Packrat. Come in, warm yourself."

The boy stopped as soon as he was past the swing of the door. He didn't know to take off his hat, but he was careful not to go where not invited. Out of habit, Rachel looked out to make sure the street was clear before pulling the door shut. When she turned back, she was surprised to see that the boy had gone no farther into her house. He obviously did not want to impose. She wondered where he had learned such a thing, as she urged him forward.

"Go to the fire; you must be cold."

"I don't really notice it, usually, but tonight..."

"Where is your home?"

"I live in a cellar under the inn. It's somewhat warmer than the street."

"Do you have a family? A mother and father?"

"They left me when I was little.

"They abandoned you?"

"Aye—both dead a' the fever."

The boy smiled. Rachel thought it a curious reaction but did not ask. The boy continued.

"But family, aye—others like me that nobody wants."

Rachel stared into the fire for several long seconds. She purposely did not look at Peter when she asked her next question.

"Would you like to stay here?"

The boy looked at her somewhat bewildered. When she felt his eyes, she turned to him.

"Oh no, I can't. There are others who count on me for bread. I can't leave 'em alone. I promised I'd never do that. Anyway, ya' have your baby to care for. Ya' don't need another."

Rachel turned back to the orange flames. Peter watched a backlit drop of water slide from Rachel's eye to her chin. Against the fire, it sparkled like a diamond against the curved horizon of her smooth skin. Peter wasn't sure what to say. Perhaps he had said something bad; he didn't know. His face twisted into an expression of confused hurt. As with all children, the boy had not yet learned to curtain the window of his heart. His face and eyes told all: he didn't understand. Rachel saw it.

"No, no, it's not you," she reassured him, then continued with difficulty, "Christina's not here. I've given her away—to the Foundling Hospital."

"Ya' left her? Ya' left her—alone?" The boy unconsciously retreated backward. It was not a question he had asked so much as an appalled gasp of disbelief. His eyes revealed a growing storm of dread that was undeni-able. Now Rachel didn't understand. She tried to remember what she had said. Whatever her words, the boy appeared tortured, as if they had slashed like ravenous teeth at the very core of his heart. What had she said or done so despicable as to make this boy hate her?

Then, as if the thought were blown into her mind like a bitter wind, she understood. She had done to Christina the same thing that Peter hated his parents for doing: she had abandoned her. Seeing Peter's face brought all the miserable feelings of shame back to her full remembrance. As heart-wrenching as giving up her Christina had been, she now faced the added prospect of enduring the agony of having others despise her for doing the only thing she thought would save the child. Did she do the right thing? Rachel had asked herself that question a million times, but a true answer of peace had never come. Was the boy's reaction simply a type and shadow of what Jonathon would say and feel? The mere thought of it made her shudder. Damnation beyond this life would be nothing com-pared to the endless torment of living with the knowledge that she had lost her husband's love and confidence. Would he ever forgive her? The joy she had experienced before the knock at the door was gulped under and drowned by the oppressive guilt which now engulfed her.

Distraught, Peter stood up and walked to the door, rubbing his head all the while. When his hand touched the latch, a pitiful stream of sobs spilled out of Rachel

"We were starving. I couldn't bear to watch it. She would cry into the night, and there was nothing I could give her. No milk! I had no milk to give her. No money to buy food. Her fingers were getting thin—and her cheeks. I'd nuzzle her cheek, but there was no fat to kiss. I couldn't stand it any more. God forgive me. "

The Packrat looked back at her. She stood with head bent, sobbing, her trembling frame a thin black outline against the glow from the fire. Rachel's sorrow was unlike any he had ever seen before. He began to feel something inside that he wanted no part of. He fought back the swell of pity he could feel rising within him. He tried to suppress it, not give way to it. He retreated behind the emotion that sustained him through all his own pain-filled days, months, and years after his parents left him: anger. That was what gave him the strength to endure the days of starvation on the street. Never had he even considered forgiving his parents for leaving him alone. How could he now look away and forgive another grown-up guilty of the same sin that his parents had committed against him. To forgive her was to forgive them.

But then he had a different thought: perhaps things were not as he thought they were. Perhaps this woman did the right thing to save her baby. Perhaps his parents had no choice. The thought of it made him wince. Peter felt that he had come to a crossroads unlike any he had ever faced before. All his life he had sustained himself by not getting into circumstances requiring decisions of right and wrong—he did what was necessary. Peter was a man of options, always seeing a hundred ways to slice the bread. But this predicament had come out of nowhere; it was completely unexpected. He was certain he had been steered into it. He couldn't help sneering upward in dismay at the God who would thrust him into this quandary.

"You've got the nerve," he hissed.

Peter knew what he must do—he just didn't want to do it. His heart bade him to love and forgive; his mind bade him to leave. Whatever the choice, he sensed the decision would change his life. There was no doubt in Peter's mind that God was finding great amusement in wreaking havoc with his world. Why else the music under the window? Why else the talk with James? Why else this?

Peter might have remained in this state of introspective argument endlessly, had Rachel's hushed voice not interrupted him.

"Dear God, please forgive me for what I've done. Please, help me," she pleaded. "Only two things have I ever wanted in this life; both are gone. What manner of God answers prayers in this way?"

"Amen," agreed Peter.

Rachel's head dropped onto her arm on the table. Peter's decision was made. He walked back to Rachel. Next to her arm, he laid down a wallet with a leather talon. Several of the coins slid out of the opening onto the table. The clinking of coins against each other roused Rachel. Her tear-swollen eyes opened. At first, she didn't appear to see the money. Then, all at once, she saw the wallet and money before her. Stunned, she looked at the coins, then up at the Packrat. He could not help smiling, knowing that the look on his face must have been just as bewildered as the look on her own. Peter walked to the door.

"Happy?" he asked glancing upward. The door opened and closed. Rachel's head fell back on her arm.

"Twice. Twice I call for God, and I'm sent a boy."

Seconds later, the room was empty.

Despised and Rejected

THE DOOR WAS LOCKED WHEN SHE TRIED THE HANDLE. IF she had taken even a moment to think about it, she would have realized that there was no chance the door would be open. The shop was closed; it had been for hours. The night was well into the second watch.

But a simple locked door would not stop her. Rachel pounded on Cooke's door. At first, she waited a few seconds before pounding again, but soon the loud knocking was a continuous stream of staccato beats. Lighted lamps and candles began to glow in nearby windows. She didn't care. Her reason for being here far superseded any discomfort or annoyance she might cause at this late hour. She was not to be denied. The loud banging continued. In spite of voices yelling down obscenities from bedroom windows, she persisted. Finally, a lighted lamp appeared from the back of the store and moved across the main floor of the shop. The brighter the light, the harder she pounded.

"Wait a minute—just wait. Stop that knocking," a gruff voice demanded from within.

"Who is it? What do you want?" Cooke bellowed. "Go away."

Rachel could tell he was right on the other side of the door; she started pounding with both hands. The door swung open.

"What is going on here?" Cooke barked. Rachel strode past him and into the store. Upon seeing her, he made no effort to intervene but closed the door as soon as she was through it.

He watched out the side of his eye as she walked directly up to the cradle in the dark corner and stared down at it.

"You've finally come," he said. "You've finally come to see things my way. I knew it would come to this, one way or another. I wonder how I shall have you pay off the debt?" His voice softened.

"I'm sorry, but we're closed for the night, but you didn't come to buy anything did you? No, you are not buying, you are paying. Oh, I'm sorry, you'll have to excuse my appearance. I was just getting ready for bed."

Rachel did not move. She stood with her back to him, running her index finger along the smooth wood of the cradle.

"How much for this piece?"

"What's that?"

"How much for this piece?" Rachel asked calmly.

"What are you willing to give for it?" He smiled.

Rachel turned around. Taking a deep breath, she walked straight up to him. She stopped one step short and pulled back her hood. Her hair fell in rapturous folds about her neck and shoulders. Her eyes did not leave his. She held out her hand to him; in it was the leather wallet with the talon.

"I've brought the balance. You will now have Jonathon released— NOW."

The smile on Cooke's face collapsed into a flat line. Cataracts seemed to drop over his pupils like gray curtains. Even though his eyes were still on her, Rachel knew he was no longer looking at her. He had departed to where evil men go to conspire. Suddenly his eyes focused again on her. His eyes rolled to white as he threw his head back in hideous laughter.

"Oh, have I forgotten? Did I not mention interest? I'm afraid your pittance has barely managed to pay the interest. You haven't even begun to pay off the principle."

Rachel did not blink. "Have him released."

Cooke's face became contorted. He thrust a finger in Rachel's face.

"Do you take me for a fool, Rachel? Do you think you can order me about? You are nothing. Nothing! How dare you talk to me like this."

Rachel stood steady. Cooke's voice softened into a sympathetic tone.

"If you wish your husband to be free, you need me. I could perhaps forget the interest if you'd show me some...interest"

A stupid smile crossed Cooke's face. He reached out to touch her hair. His hand stopped short at the sound of her voice.

"I would do almost anything to free Jonathon."

Cooke's smile curled even steeper.

"But to do what you desire would cost me his respect, which I cherish even above his love."

Her eyes sharpened.

"You disgust me. Your vile fingers will never touch me. Should all hell come between us, I would rather starve to death trying to free Jonathon than endure one sickening moment with you."

She dropped the wallet on the floor. Coins spilled out and spread around Cooke's feet.

"The debt is paid. Free him."

Rachel strode past him and out the door.

Once out in the street, she fell back against a dark wall, barely able to stand. Her knees, which were so steady seconds before, began to tremble.

Inside, Cooke stood dumbfounded. He looked at the coins strewn about the floor. His fingers tightened into angry fists. He dropped to his knees, groveling for loose coins. His angry voice roared out the door to where Rachel stood in the shadows.

"Never! He'll never be free. Die in prison. Starve, wretched girl. Starve and die—both of you. He'll never be free. Never!"

Rachel stumbled out from the shadows near Cooke's store and into the street.

All night long the firecan burned. The guards of the third and fourth watch came and went from the heater between walks, but none tarried too long. Each time one would come into the light of the fire, a frail form would appear out of the darkness and accost the guard. The warmth of the fire was not worth the grief of dealing with the loiterer. The usual gathering and gossip arena for the guards was vacant. The pleas from the woman were so pitiable that the guards stayed away.

Through much of the night, the iron gate of debtors' prison was literally left unguarded. The usual walks were made, but breaks were taken in the dark, tea taken in the cold. In the frigid, predawn hours when no one stirred, she was still there, pleading her cause. What she didn't know was that the guards had no authority to acquit or condemn. Her pleas were utterly wasted until one of the guards finally listened to her. She was told to wait until morning when the barristers came to review the disposition of each prisoner. She was lucky, since this procedure only took place once a month. If she had indeed paid the debt, certainly someone would hear her case and free her husband.

Again, Rachel had hope. She rested the last few hours of night against the wall closest to the firecan. It was not warm but it was not unbearably cold, either. The wall provided just enough shelter from exposure to allow her to nod in and out of sleep.

When she awoke after the last nap she was uncertain of the time. She didn't recognize any of the guards; the sky was full of light. She jumped to her feet and ran to the gate which spanned the long, narrow stone ramp leading down to the debtors' prison. There she waited. Solicitors began to come and go. She approached each one, but most pushed by her without a word. What she didn't know was that these were the few decent solicitors who came early to avoid the despicable melee which would develop later in the morning.

Over the next few hours, many more women gathered to plead for their men. She was not the first and only one to beg a cause on the morning of petition. With the exception of a few small boys, the group was made up entirely of wives, mothers, and daughters of those incarcerated. Once the solicitors began to arrive, the women queued into two lines on either side of the path to the prison gate. The drill seemed entirely rehearsed as though all knew their role and what was expected. It looked much like a troupe of prostitutes soliciting men on a street corner. The sad truth was that the appearance of virtue being offered and accepted was more often reality than illusion. What made the situation even more loathsome was the obvious sport the solicitors made with those who had come to invoke their aid. The criminal irony of the situation was that the more service a woman gave, the less chance of having her loved one released. Illicit performance became the ransom by which the lawyers held the desperate women hostage. They were no more free than those whose freedom they sought to purchase. It was the vilest of prostitution, not because of the unchastity of the women, but the absolute, unconscionable exploitation of them by lying men, who had no intention of helping them. More often than not, solicitors who accepted the propositions most freely didn't know the convict that the received gratuity represented. It required appallingly little deception to instill enough trust in a hopeless and starving wife or daughter to make her believe that a solicitor's promise to help was sincere. Tragically, few appeals were ever made. Of those solicitors who chose not to participate, the reason for abstaining was more often infection than honor. Those already infected were also the most predatory. The spread of venereal disease to the women of the prisoners was both rampant and thoughtless.

If a new beggar appeared at the gate, especially a comely one, it was not uncommon for several solicitors to offer help for a small price. Debtors were the refuse of the judicial system; the abandoned women were esteemed as even less. Whatever indiscretions the solicitors accepted were considered nothing more than a career amenity.

Rachel watched the procession from behind the others. She called for help from a distance, but no one even heard her voice. She did not get so much as a glance. When she saw certain solicitors who did not seem at all interested in the prostitution, she would press forward and beseech them for aid, but they refused to notice her. She leaned forward twice, grabbing at the arms of those passing, and praying in her heart that they would find pity on her. Instead, they pulled away as though she had sullied them with a mere touch of her hand.

Rachel was about to withdraw when she saw someone who both terrified and thrilled her. Coming through the gauntlet was a face that she did recognize. It was the man she saw come through the curtain from the back of Cooke's store. She could not remember his words, only the disgust that his words invoked in her. Only for a moment did she lay her full sight on him, but so detestable was he that his face was eternally imprinted on her mind. The empty, black void she had always imagined in the fiery hood of the devil was immediately filled with his face the first time she saw it. It was a face she would never forget. This same man was coming through the crowd toward her carrying an ebony cane.

As much as he frightened her, she knew that he was somehow involved with Cooke and the cradle. She did her best to filter back through her memory to the brief encounter at the store. For some reason, she had the faint recollection that he had made a reference to her. She did her best to assemble in her mind the puzzle of events from the fortnight. When she remembered, her stomach turned.

"Did you ever have your way with that pauper wench—the one whose husband…" The rest of the sentence was cut short because of her presence. She was the pauper wench to whom he referred. He did know about her, and he knew about Jonathon. Like a dousing of ice water on her back, the realization that he was party to Jonathon's incarceration made her gasp. If he could have Jonathon imprisoned, certainly he could have him released.

She pushed through the crowd with reckless abandon. When she came to the front of the line she groped forward and caught him by the shirt just as he was passing. He spun around toward her and slashed at her hand with his arm. Angered at her rudeness, several of the other women reached out at the same time and yanked her back. When the solicitor's hand severed her grip from his garment, she was no longer braced between the opposing forces. Her hood pulled off as she stumbled back into the line and tumbled down to the ground. Her joints took the brunt of the fall. She scraped the skin off her elbows and knees. Shoes kicked at her as she struggled to get up. She somehow rolled onto her bloodied knees just as one of the prison guards took hold of her hair and pulled her head back over his knee. Her face was laid open to all, including the offended solicitor. All eyes were suddenly upon her. The beauty of her face stood out from the scene like a gem trapped in the grip of gray sediment.

The solicitor's first reaction was to wave her away, but the gesture was never finished. He stared down at the face of the woman held captive before him. Other solicitors came close to see the commotion. Once they saw Rachel, several feigned to offer aid.

"Stand back!" demanded the man standing above her. The area cleared immediately. The solicitor studied Rachel's face, then he studied what he could see of the rest of her. The awkward position of being pinned over the guard's knee with head pulled back, thrust her chest and hips forward. The solicitor liked what he saw. With a nod, he dismissed the guard. Rachel fell on her back when the leg beneath her was removed. A hand was pushed in her direction. She looked up the arm, directly into the face of horror. She did not take the hand, but spun up onto her knees before him. She watched the man take from his pocket what appeared to be a nut and put it in his mouth. The muscles of his cheeks tightened as he gently bit down.

"Madame, may I be of service to you?"

"You know who I am."

"Yes."

Rachel expected more, but no more came. Her response was met, received, and responded to, but not at all as she had anticipated. Her bluntness did not provoke him in the least. Instead of reacting, his answer was disarmingly quick and candid. He gave no explanation, good or bad. The ensuing silence increased Rachel's anxiety. She began to question her recollection of what she had heard in Cooke's store. Then when she heard a woman behind her pleading for her husband, Rachel remembered why she was there.

"Help me, sir," she said, lifting her eyes to the man. "I have paid the debt, paid in full."

The solicitor looked down on her with a look of scrutiny.

"Paid in full," she reassured him. "I work at a bakery to earn money. I have given all of it to Cooke to pay the debt. I was given a gift, a wonderful gift—more than enough to pay the balance. I returned to the store last night, late last night, long after the door was locked..."

The man's eyes widened. His head tipped to the side as he waited for her to elaborate further. Rachel misconstrued his increased interest to be in response to her fulfilling the obligation.

"I gave him everything, everything I had. The cradle truly is paid for every whit, I have made sure of it. The debt is paid. What more can I give?"

Upon hearing this, the man lifted a handkerchief over his mouth and cleared his throat. He did so through a hidden smile. By the time the handkerchief was put back in his pocket, the grin was wiped from his face.

"My husband's name is Jonathon Liddle, sir. Jonathon Liddle. Please remember it."

The solicitor stepped closer and leaned down towards her. Rachel noticed a small sore on his lip that she had not seen before. He spoke softly, so that only she could hear.

"Cooke is a fool. He is a loathsome man who profits from people's misery. It is not your husband he wants. He can have your husband imprisoned, but he cannot keep him there. Only I can do that."

"You can have him freed?" she gasped.

"Today if I wish."

Rachel's breathing quickened into short panted breaths. Her face undulated between looks of utter disbelief and ecstatic joy. She covered her mouth with her hands. On the one hand, it was impossible to believe, and yet she knew he had spoken the truth. She saw how the others cowered back when he demanded it. Even the guard had obeyed him without any hint of resistance. In all she had observed, his word was the word.

Suddenly, she felt a weight on her shoulder. Her thoughts hid the feeling initially. She turned her head to see the solicitor's hand resting on her shoulder. Horrified, Rachel looked up into his eyes. She watched him roll something across his tongue and into the other side of his mouth. Wincing from an unseen sting of pain, he bent down close to her face. His eyes reached over every part of her with the exception of her eyes.

"I will have your man freed," he whispered. "But there is a price. There is something you must do for me."

His hand slid forward from her shoulder and down her collarbone. Before it could drop further, she had hold of it. The strength gained working the ovens held his descending hand in check. The pressure exerted against her eased and pulled back; she released it from her grip. Now he did look her in the eye. For several seconds they measured each other in a locked stare. The solicitor was well rehearsed in the stages of surrender. He had been refused many times on first pass, but if he waited for his victim to reconsider, the second pass was always accepted on behalf of the prisoner.

He allowed Rachel ample time to evaluate her intentions before his second advance. When he thought he saw submission pass across her face, he reached his hand forward again, certain this time that no barrier would stop him.

What he could not see, as he looked in Rachel's eyes, was the hand on which she was leaning. Her fingers curled tightly forward into her palm. Before his detestable hand could find its way to touch her, Rachel's clenched fist ripped into the side of his jaw. The precious nut that he teethed so tenderly hurled from his battered jaw to the ground. Her bony knuckle tore open a small slit at the corner of his mouth. He reeled back to his feet, towering over her. It all happened so quickly that few in the group actually witnessed it, but when they saw the solicitor's face and the small cut, it was easy to surmise what had happened. All waited in shock for his retaliation. He composed himself, wiped the blood from his mouth, then picked up the cane, which had fallen from his grasp. He then leaned down close to Rachel and whispered so that only she could hear.

"My mouth shall sting for a moment, but you will be in agony for a lifetime. When you watch me go through those gates, know without any shred of doubt that you will never see your husband again. He is dead to you. He is worse than dead. He is reliving death over and over again every day, and there is no escape. You have sentenced him to a lifetime of misery, with no chance of pardon. I will personally make sure of it."

He paused for a moment, then smiled.

"Jonathon Liddle—isn't that what you said?"

Without warning he brutally rapped his black cane on her hand. The sharp edge of the tip caught the fold of skin on the knuckle of her small finger, shearing away the skin. Rachel yanked back her hand with a cry of pain.

"Excuse me, madame," he said aloud. He laughed as he whirled around and walked briskly down the remainder of the line. Rachel listened to the rusty hinges scrape and moan as the huge iron gate swung open. The solicitor glanced back at her one last time before passing behind it and disappearing down the long ramp to the prison.

Messenger of the Covenant

Lord, make 'em blind to all rodents," the Packrat breathed out loud, his eyes darting back and forth in the darkness. He worked his way down the inside wall of the spiral stairs, cringing every time his foot touched the icy water of an ancient puddle. He went slowly, inching downward until his forward foot could not find another stair. It had taken what seemed an eternity, but, finally, he had reached the bottom.

"It's about time," he sighed. "Hell was several stairs back."

He sat motionless, hoping his eyes would adjust to the dark. He could barely discern the walls of a long, curving corridor leading off in either direction. The stair he had come down was not the main entrance, but a side stair used only by those most familiar with the tunnels and halls. Down one direction he could make out the faint, yellow flicker of a torch glowing on the wall in another side tunnel. The other direction had slightly more light—blue light—spilling from exterior exhaust holes cut in the eaves high above him. He chose the blue light over the yellow.

He worked his way along the wall, stopping to listen every few steps. His feet didn't make a sound as he carefully rolled from heel to toe. Stealth was an art that he had practiced religiously; this was a chance to exercise his best skill.

He came to an intersection with a smaller hall. It might have passed unnoticed had the wall at his back not given way. He nearly fell backwards into it. The air around the orifice was cold and sticky. So lightless was the hole that he was certain, at any moment, that a dreadful goblin hand would reach out its ghastly fingers and pull him into the hideous black bowel to devour him. He looked back the other way, reconsidering the direction he had chosen. As always, he had followed his instincts. But this time, maybe he was wrong. Perhaps some demon had willed him to come this way to drag him into his den for dinner. Even the smell emanating from the hole made his stomach turn. He could imagine rotting bones piled in discarded heaps. He tried to convince himself that he was concocting the horrific images and that the hole was nothing more than an alternate tunnel, but it felt too evil. He wanted to walk past and just look away, but he couldn't. As much as he wished to go back and forget this place, he had given his word; his course was already determined. He had no choice but to go forward.

Sneaking past the dozing guards at the prison gate seemed like a child's game compared to this. At least he could see when the guards were looking away. Now he felt like a bug trying to tiptoe across the arachnid's web without being noticed. Peter imagined demonic green eyes hidden behind the veil of darkness, waiting for him to venture across.

He dug his toe into a narrow crack in the floor for leverage while mustering all the courage he possibly could. With one great effort, he leapt forward with all the spring his nimble legs could deliver. For the moment, he chose speed over silence. The initial bound landed him halfway across the opening. His shoes slapped the wet stone beneath him as he touched down, and his legs were already in motion. Like the paws of a drowning dog clawing through water for the shore, Peter's arms and feet churned through the fluid of darkness. He was certain that malevolent hands were sliding under each step, just missing his leg by inches. He dared not leave his feet grounded any longer than necessary. He knew he had finally made it when the patter of his shoes was no longer swallowed into the black orifice but echoed back from the wall.

As soon as he was clear of the hole he stopped and leaned against the wall to regain equilibrium. His ears rang with the loud beating of his heart. He took several deep breaths, waiting for his vitals to calm before going on. With each long breath, his heart slowed until he could hear a clean space between beats. At once, terror struck him.

Voices!

Voices were near, but he hadn't even heard them coming.

Torchlight!

The wall in front of him glowed with yellow light. Foolishly, he had closed his eyes when he was trying to calm himself and never even saw it coming. He leaned against the wall, hoping he might somehow be absorbed into it and disappear from view. In the few seconds he had, he weighed his choices; none were good. He would either have to flee or be caught. The second wasn't an option. He turned to run, then realized the voices weren't getting closer. He waited briefly to hear if the sound would increase, but it didn't. That changed everything. He was no longer on the defense. The boy who hated being chased from behind had no problem going into any situation facing forward. Besides, knowing where his enemies were gave him an advantage.

He proceeded forward. The light grew brighter as he worked around the curving tunnel toward the voices. He could hear the talk as clearly as if he had been part of the discussion. Two distraught jailers were sharing their discontent regarding their jobs. In spite of fear, the Packrat couldn't help shaking his head in disgust at the grown-ups whining. Peter listened for several minutes until suddenly, without warning, the conversation was over. Peter could hear feet shuffling toward him. The light on the wall opposite him brightened with each passing second. By his reckoning, the guard could not be more than ten steps from him and closing fast.

The Packrat searched the lightened hall for any notch where he could duck until the jailer passed. Nothing. Back he went in the direction from which he had come. On his right, ahead of him, he could see the gaping mouth of the black throat. The thought of hiding within the dark tunnel never crossed his mind. The fear of what waited within was more terrifying than being caught. He came to the edge of the opening, where he stopped to look back. Fragments of firelight kicked off the wet seeps on the wall. The light was still moving. He took a deep breath, then vaulted toward the far side. His feet were already running when they touched the hard floor. He hurdled himself forward in a frenzied dash for safety.

Then, as if he had run into an unseen and impenetrable wall, he abruptly stopped. The hole was his only chance of escape. Another step and he might have lost the one and only chance he might possibly have for freedom. The prospect of going in made his eyes water. He rationalized every possible reason to not enter, but none were strong enough to supersede the one reason most pressing: escape.

Peter closed his eyes—knowing they would be of no use anyway—and ran blindly into the cave, fully expecting never to return.

The ground beneath him sloped downward. The stones beneath his feet were no longer smooth but rough-hewn. With each descending step, the temperature seemed to drop several degrees. Cold exhaust from the deep, black throat blew in his face like a headwind. Even though he could not see them, he was certain the walls were closing in. His left arm scraped the slimy wet wall. What he hoped was water trickled down his arm and dripped off his fingers. Only after he had gone farther than he was certain any guard would ever go did he stop.

Moist, subterraneous strands hanging from an unseen ceiling licked his face. He opened his eyes; it was darker than before. He was in absolute blackness. Strangely, there was a tiny part of him that was grateful not to see where he was or into what creature's lair he had blindly strayed.

He began to walk slowly backward, as if some inexplicable horror lay just ahead of him. His feet quickened as terror of the unknown began to quash his spirit. In the palpable darkness, fear became loathing. He felt that he was in peril as never before. He didn't let his feet linger in any one place too long, perchance a vile tentacle or vine might subdue him. His head bumped against a protruding cleft in the ceiling; it lanced through the skin on the top of his head. A sharp, searing pain shot through his head. Tears filled his eyes, but he dared not cry out. His head swirled in momentary agony. A long string of profanity flashed across his mind, then dissipated, like the tail of a falling star. The cursing made him feel both better and worse.

"Get used to it," he silently said to God. "No doubt I'll probably die here, and that'll be the last thing I say before Ya' see me again. Besides," he murmured, "don't try to tell me that Ya' 'aven't thought the same thing when *You* bumped *Your* head."

Even though Peter would admit that what he had said wasn't a real prayer, he had said it sincerely and with real intent, so it had to count for something. And, to his surprise, he was not so afraid as he was before. Either the jolt or God or both had calmed him. It didn't matter which—he felt better.

"Call Your ways mysterious if Ya' want, Lord. I call 'em strange. But right now, it don't matter. I'm not complainin'."

He started back up the tunnel. After several steps, he began to see a faint glow from the torch in the far distance ahead of him. He had been heard. The mouth of the cave was being watched, of that he was certain. The only thing more certain was that he would not be followed into the abyss. No one with any choice in the matter would enter this pit, least of all a disgruntled jailer. By and by, he would be passed off as just a rat and the guard would leave. The irony of being passed off as a rat in this foul place made him smile.

The boy walked toward the firelight near the entrance. If he had to wait, being close to the top was a far better alternative to staying where he was. There was now enough amber glow from the torch to see the walls of the cave. They were organic—moving. He adjusted himself toward the center of the hole, away from the walls. He felt something crawl down his forehead. He slapped it away, then looked at his hand; it was blood.

The trepidation he had felt about going down the hole was coming back. How long would he have to wait? He still could not see more than a few feet down the hole behind him. Some foul denizen could be pursuing him up the tunnel right now. Fortunately, the guard's patience was running out. Peter watched as the torchlight moved back and forth across the opening, then down the main hall. He hurried up the sloped tunnel before the light was completely gone. He leapt free of the mouth as if vomited out.

The dim blue light of the main tunnel seemed bright compared to the vacuous dark of the hole. He moved forward, getting back to his business before another guard forced him into the putrid throat again. He had been lucky. Whatever monster had missed the first opportunity to snatch him for supper would not let another chance go unrewarded.

He proceeded forward, past where he had first heard the voices. Several yards farther it became obvious why they had been there. A huge black door appeared ahead of him on the right wall. If Peter's deducing was correct, that door was right where the men had stopped to talk. He could see a small opening in the door, well above where he could reach. He looked around for anything to stand on but the halls were bare. He studied the loose mortar between the massive blocks of stone around the door for foot- and fingerholds. Maybe he could climb the wall high enough to lean in. He studied each chip in the mortar from top to bottom to find his line.

When he sat down on his haunches to check the lower stone blocks, he saw it. The outline of the hole cut in the bottom of the door had merged with the black floor. If he hadn't leaned down close, he might never have detected it. He knelt down on his callused knees and leaned low, peering through the open hole. An acidic stench from within blew in his face. Through the hole he could faintly see the far walls of a vast room. There was little light, but he could discern people walking back and forth in the large open space.

"Is anyone there?"

A face appeared in the opening.

"Who's there?"

"Where is Jonathon—Jonathon Liddle?"

The face stared back at him.

"Go find him—please."

The face disappeared. A few seconds later, a bearded face appeared in the opening. The Packrat recoiled at the sight of it.

"Who is it? Who's there?" asked a voice from within.

"Do you remember me?" asked Peter, leaning his face down close to the opening.

"Boy! What are doing here?"

"A question I've asked myself. I bring ya' food...and a letter."

"Rachel? Is she all right?"

The Packrat pushed a folded knapsack through the slot. It was instantly gone, but Jonathan was still there.

"I hear voices; someone's comin'," whispered Peter, glancing down the long hall. As he started to rise back to his feet, an open hand appeared through the opening, reaching for him. The Packrat took hold of the hand with both of his. The large, dirty hand folded around Peter's. The hand held tight, as if clinging to a lifeline hanging above a bottomless pit.

"They're close," Peter urged.

The powerful hand released him. Eyes watched through the hole as Peter's feet disappeared without a sound. Bread was passed among the prisoners. Jonathon handed it over without a second thought. He turned the letter over and back in his hand. He walked to the corner of the room where the overhead windows shed the most light. He opened the envelope, giving great care to not tearing it. He recognized Rachel's writing. He smelled the paper; but there was nothing of her on it. He read silently, hearing Rachel's voice in his mind.

"My beloved Jonathon,

What do I say? It is now the second winter that you are gone—Christina also. She is no longer in my care. She is now in God's care at the Foundling Hospital. Do not mourn too greatly; if prayers are answered, she is in the cradling arms of Christ Jesus, though it breaks my heart that the arms that hold her are not mine. Please do not hate me for what I have done. I could not work for your freedom and care for her also. I pray that one might bring the other. Perhaps it is possible for God to move upon hearts that are stone in behalf of those who have hope beyond reason. If so, we shall again walk in the gardens of Covent, hand in hand. Oh, my dear Jonathon, how my heart lingers on your smile. How I miss the small talk. Little words of love spoken seem so much larger now. Often, I hear your voice in the still night air or feel your warm breath against my cheek. You are ever with me—every word, every deed, every squeeze of my hand. You are my hope and my longing—you and our little Christina. For if God's eye can see devotion—devotion that reaches through walls, through iron bars, even beyond death—then surely His hand can gather together those whose spirits are so tightly bound. And whether here or beyond the grave, we shall again be one."

Jonathon finished the letter. He laid his head on his knees. Two of the other prisoners laid some bread next to him but it was stolen before his eyes opened.

Lift Up Thy Voice

MASTER, YOUR INVITATION IS A TIMELY ONE, AND FROM the Lord Lieutenant himself," Peter LeBlonde said, pulling a large trunk from the closet.

"We shall see what mood is in Dublin," Handel answered, taking a stack of folded clothes from the dresser drawer and laying it on the bed. He paused, looking around the bedroom as if searching for something. It felt peculiar for Peter not to be going with his master, but Handel was very specific about wanting him to stay and finish the work of cleaning up all past obligations.

"Who are you taking?" asked Peter.

"Singers?" queried Handel.

"Yes."

"Signora Avolio. And Mrs. Cibber. She is already in Dublin, await-ing our arrival."

"That is good."

"That is very good," reiterated Handel.

Peter could see the relief that Handel had in knowing Mrs. Cibber would be included. Peter felt a great kinship for Handel's faithful—espe-cially those artists who remained faithful, as their loyalty had been most tested in the past two years. Mrs. Cibber was one of them.

"She is a great admirer and a friend," Peter said.

"I'm pleased she's decided to join us."

"You are partial to her."

Handel stopped what he was doing.

"She sings from her heart. There are better singers, stronger, voices; but none more pure."

The servant looked at Handel with a peculiar look. Handel's com-ment was another example of the transformation that had somehow been wrought upon his master. It was not a wholesale change but a very subtle divergence, almost imperceptible. Peter began to notice it in the few months since Handel finished the work of writing the piece given him by Mr. Jennens. While the season had changed from fall to winter outside, Handel had changed inside. Weeks passed before Peter even took thought of it, but the accumulative sum of all he had witnessed was undeniable. There was no doubt in Peter's mind that the director had changed direc-tion; even if only by the slightest degree, the course had been altered. Peter knew not where the deviation would lead, but he was certain it would not be where it had been before. If questioned, it would have been difficult for Peter to explain the modification. It was very likely that he was the only one close enough to Handel to even entertain the notion. There was nothing outwardly different, nothing really apparent in his speech or tone. He was different—that was all.

"How could he not be changed to some degree?" Peter justified to himself, thinking of all his master had experienced in the past year.

Others noticed the disappearance of Handel, but not much else. To any who inquired, Peter cited the loss of Dorothea as the reason for Handel's reclusion. He felt no need to tell more and, in fact, felt a need not to disclose more. He was protective of Handel. He did not look for-ward to the day that Handel would reenter London's musical foray. He was afraid that the abrasiveness of it would callous the places in Handel's character that had softened. Given the choice, Peter preferred the new animal to the old, even though it would be difficult to say why. Therefore, he was genuinely pleased at the Lord Lieutenant's invitation for Handel to come and perform in Dublin—all the more gratifying when he considered that the disposition of the audience would be benevolent, since the majority of the concerts would be for charity. His master had spent little time in Dublin, but the time he did spend there was rejuvenating. The Irish loved his music and were not careful about letting him know it. In Dublin, he had a true and loyal following of sincere appreciates. Londoners looked down their noses at the people of Dublin, but Peter much preferred the commoners of there to the high-minded of here. This seemed the perfect reentry place for the retooled Handel.

"You must be very pleased," Peter reinforced.

"Dublin has been kind. I hope they remember me."

Peter chuckled.

"I believe they will."

"You, too, are kind."

"What will you perform?" Peter asked, looking at the music scores set out on the bed next to the trunk.

"*L'Allegro* first, *Alexander's Feast*...possibly *Imeneo*."

"And the oratorio?"

"*Samson*? It's not finished. It would be a mistake to try it before it's fully ready."

"I speak of the other."

Handel stopped what he was doing. At length he spoke in subdued reflection.

"I did not write it with the intention of performance."

"All the more reason to perform it."

"It was an act of devotion."

"As are all great deeds."

"I'm not ready."

Peter knew he had already passed over the borders of propriety. Yet he felt compelled to say one last thing.

"You will have a Lenten performance."

Handel thought long before answering.

"There will be a time—possibly for charity."

"Such is your call to Dublin, sir."

Peter bowed low before leaving the room. Handel gazed down at the music scores lying on the bed, but his eyes did not focus on the notes; he was looking through the paper.

"Mrs. Cibber," he said to himself.

The door to the study swung open. Handel entered and walked to the desk. He sat down in his writing chair and opened the drawer wherein the manuscript lay. His hand stopped when he read the title on the cover sheet.

"*Messiah.*"

He gazed at the manuscript. He did not pick up the stack of paper but gently put his open hand, palm down, on the pile of music. He did not move from that position for several minutes as if waiting for the paper to speak to him. At length, he reached his hand around the stack and pulled the paper from the drawer. He looked around the room as if searching for something else.

His eye finally fell on what he was looking for. He reached and took the olive wood heirloom box from the shelf behind him and dumped the contents into a pile in a floor basket. He laid the *Messiah* score in the box; he was impressed by the perfect fit. He slid back the beautiful lid on which were carved his initials and left the room.

Good Will Towards Men

Four days by carriage found Handel in the western coastal city of Chester at the mouth of the Dee River. The trip was long and cold, yet therapeutic. The thin country air was a welcome relief from the thick, smoke-blackened air of London. Handel watched the country go by out of the small window of the carriage. It reminded him of the late-winter days growing up in Saxony.

When he arrived in Chester, the weather was worsening. Crossing the Irish Sea to Dublin was impossible for the time being because of high winds and changing tides. An unexpected layover was necessary. How long? No one knew for sure, but the seamen and fishermen who had followed the skies for the past week anchored their boats for what they called "a good one." In all probability, it would take just about as long for the storm to move out as it took to move in. The ferry captain said to plan on about three day's layover.

Handel might have spent the delay languishing in an old inn, but he enjoyed the change from London—of both scenery and spirit. He walked about the town, remarkably anonymous. Chester was a shipping town, not a musical town. The people of Chester were of the working-class sort, more concerned with daily life than social life. Some had heard of Handel, but few, if any, had actually heard him. Thus, it was of no particular consequence that Chester had a visitor. The complete lack of notoriety gave Handel unexpected pleasure. He had forgotten the simple joy of living unburdened and unknown. The long-carried weight of expectation, debt, and despair had emasculated him to the point of numbness.

From inside his home on Brook Street, his evolution from vitality to vulnerability was gradual and invisible. Little by little, his love of life had eroded away. Vigor degenerated into vexation, gusto into grief. Even in recent days, after the debts had been paid, laughter and lightheartedness were rare guests. Like the winds that now beset Chester, misery had been long in coming. Handel prayed it would not be long in going. In Chester, his prayers were answered.

The stormy sea brought in the boats; the boats brought in the men; the men brought their thirst and money to the pubs. When he wasn't walking about, smiling through the wind and rain, Handel also found the pubs. He mingled and drank like a local, contributing freely to any conversation or song he could find. He did not even introduce himself as Handel, but as George. He told old jokes—jokes he was surprised he could remember—none of which had found their way to Chester. Laughter boomed out of his rotund frame as if it had come from a huge, empty whiskey barrel. The rich, deep sound of it was absolutely contagious. Men laughed out loud when they heard him laugh. Handel's face shone with the innocent happiness of a child. He laughed for the pure joy of laughing.

The fishermen mimicked his German-spiced English with great delight. He mimicked their salt-and-vinegar-spiced English with even more zest.

When the pub-keeper revealed the sparse details he could recall of Handel's musical prowess, the crowd insisted that he play. There was no instrument in the pub except an old squeezebox accordion. Never having played one did not slow him down. The instrument had ivory pads which resembled keys, and that was all he needed. He had seen them played in fairs and by traveling minstrels, so he was aware of how the mechanism worked. Pumping the accordion took some practice, but the hand on the keys made up for any shortfall in squeezing. He played every request thrown his way. If a melody was asked for which he didn't know, he asked that a few bars be sung or hummed. Without missing a beat, he would join in and continue. Men raised their voices all around him in lusty song. For the first time that he could readily remember, George had fun.

When he laid down the box and reached for a drink, cheers went up all around. He sat down at a large table with several swarthy men. One spoke up:

"I must say, Dublin is not the typical vacation destination for London nobility."

"Which makes it all the more attractive," laughed Handel.

"Why Dublin?" asked another.

"To perform for three charitable objects."

"So you're staying with us in Chester before crossing. Waiting for more favorable winds?" a local inquired.

"Not entirely," Handel said in a serious tone. The thought that a man such as this might have other business in Chester piqued their interest. Ears perked up all around him.

"I've heard the people of Chester are unmatched in their appreciation of fine music."

"As long as you can drink to it!" yelled a voice from the back.

The group erupted with spontaneous approval. As the clapping diminished, Handel spoke again.

"If one wanted to try out a new aria in Chester, whom would he employ?"

"A new what?" asked one of the younger sailors.

"Song!" answered several voices in the same sarcastic tone. Handel laughed and patted the boy on the shoulder.

"The best singers are in the Cathedral Choir," volunteered a voice from the bar.

Heads turned in the direction from where the answer had come. A slender man sat on a tall wooden stool. The man nearest Handel called to him.

"Nathanael—you're in the choir. What do you say?"

"Janson. Janson is the one you want," Nathanael answered emphatically.

"Where do I find him?"

"You don't. I will find him. We will meet you at the Chester Cathedral this evening at seven."

A broad smile crossed the entire width of Handel's face. Every face watching did likewise.

It was dark when Handel arrived at the cathedral with the olive wood box under his arm. Nathanael and Janson were already inside waiting for him. When he saw them, he shuffled the wooden box he carried to his left hand and thrust out his right to Nathanael.

"Good evening, sir."

"Mr. Handel—nice to see you again, sir. May I introduce Mr. Janson.

"Good evening, sir. I'm told you can sing."

"I sing in the choir."

"He is the finest we have," interjected Nathanael. "He won't tell you, so I will."

"Can you sing at sight?"

"I've had some sight training," nodded Janson. "But I've no..."

"Would you be willing to try a piece I've been working on?" interrupted Handel, while handing him several sheets of music. Before Janson could answer, Handel was headed toward the organ. He sat down on the bench, laid several pages of score on the stand and began pushing and pulling dampers on the organ console. Janson looked over at Nathanael, who just shrugged his shoulders. Organ music preempted any further discussion. Janson scanned the page, trying his best to find his place while making his way to the organ. With a nod, Handel cued Janson's entrance. He missed it.

"Pick it up there. Again, please." Handel said, segueing right back through the introduction. Janson waited for his cue. Handel gave the nod; Janson sang:

"'Every valley...'"

"Late," said Handel, raising his head, then cueing the next entrance with his head.

"'Every valley, shall be exalted.'"

"Rest," said Handel, cutting him off. "Ready on the 'B.'"

"'Shall be-e-e exalted.'" Janson did not anticipate the long breath needed for the sustained three-bar scale. He ran out of air well before it was finished. Handel impatiently filled in the missing notes. Janson picked up the next entrance, somewhat flustered.

"'Shall be exalted.'"

"Rest, 'shall be-e-e-exalted.'"

Janson blew the timing. Handel stopped abruptly, his face flushed.

"Count, man! Eighth notes into sixteenths. Again, bar 21." Handel played bars 19 and 20 to lead him in. Janson was lost, which flustered him even more.

"'Shall be exal-a-a-a-alted,'" spoke Handel, in time. Janson caught up and took over the line, while Handel counted underneath:

"One and two and one and rest—'shall be exalted,'" Handel kept on playing, even though Janson only hit about every third note.

"Rest—'shall be exalted,'" sang Handel, trying in vain to bring Janson to the count. The poor man did his best to catch up, but there was no waiting. Handel forged onward, his face reddening with each missed note.

"Rest—'shall be exalted.' Sixteenths—pick up the tempo."

Again, Janson totally blew the line. Handel rose out of his seat, his face purple.

"You scoundrel. Did you not tell me that you could sing at sight?"

"Yes, sir!" said Janson indignantly. "But not at first sight."

Handel stared at the confused face staring back at him. His visage changed from anger to regret. "I am so sorry! God must think me a slow learner, or he would not make my faults so painfully obvious. Sirs, please forgive me."

Janson and Nathanael enthusiastically nodded their acceptance. Handel bowed, then looked back at the score.

"Would you care to try another piece?"

"No."

Deep laughter bellowed out from Handel's huge chest.

"I did not think so," he guffawed. "Well then—enough for tonight."

Every One to His Own Way

WHEN THE LETTER ARRIVED FROM DUBLIN, JENNENS WAS sitting at tea with Holdsworth. The letter was not unprecedented, as Handel made it a point to keep Jennens informed as to his whereabouts and whatabouts. There had been some correspondence with regard to the oratorio, but not without some disagreement. Before the butler entered the room with the tea service, he put the envelope on the tray for Jennens to see. It was the first thing that he picked up off the tray.

"A letter from Dublin," he said, opening the envelope.

"You have friends in Dublin—or others you've offended?"

"It's from Handel."

"He's in Dublin, then."

"For the past month."

Jennens took the letter out and began to read aloud.

"I give you an account of the success that I have met here. The nobility did me the honor of making amongst themselves a subscription for six nights, which did fill a room of six hundred persons, so that I needed not sell a single ticket at the door. Signora Avolio, whom I brought with me from London, pleases extraordinarily. I have found another tenor who gives great satisfaction, the basses and countertenors are very good, and the rest of the chorus singers, by my directions, do exceedingly well. As for the instruments, they are excellent, Mr. Dubourg being at the head of them."

Jennens stopped reading.

"So he performs in Dublin," inquired Holdsworth.

Jennens read on: "Without vanity the performance was received with general approbation; and the music sounds delightful in this charming room, which puts me in such spirits, and my health being so good that I exert myself on the organ with more than usual success. So, I let you judge of the satisfaction I enjoy, passing my time with honor, profit, and pleasure."

"It seems he has Dublin under his spell," remarked Holdsworth.

"It would seem so," Jennens answered.

"What does he perform?"

"*L'Allegro, il Pensieroso ed il Moderato*; then *Acis* and *Galatea* together with Dryden's *St. Cecilia Ode*."

"He's been very busy," observed Holdsworth.

"He also did two representations of *Esther*," said Jennens. He continued reading.

"The audience included the Lord Lieutenant, the Chancellor, the Auditor General, many bishops, deans, and heads of the colleges. And the Flower of Ladies of Distinction and other people of the greatest quality."

A puzzled look appeared on Jennens's face.

"He's announced a second subscription," Jennens rubbed his chin. "I wonder if the oratorio is in his plans."

"The libretto you gave him. It's finished then?"

"He thinks it is."

"And you?"

Jennens stood from his chair and began pacing back and forth across the room.

"He won't risk it; he'll wait for a London debut," Jennens said, more to himself than to Holdsworth. Jennens folded the letter and slipped it back into the envelope.

"He'll wait. He must wait."

God With Us

THE NEWLY BUILT MUSIC HALL IN FISHAMBLE STREET WAS employed for Handel's performances in Dublin. It was a fine room, with seating for six hundred. Every seat was occupied for the several performances during the first series of concerts. Handel and company were now well into their second run with no less success. Audiences were enthusiastic and orderly. Musicians reveled in the adoration poured upon them by each and every gracious patron.

Handel was a new man, buoyed up and energized by each new night's success. He played with fervor; he conducted with flair. He was witty with both spectators and participants. He showed praise upon his cast as never before. In short, Handel was revitalized. The good will of Dublin called back to his memory the ambition and enthusiasm of his early exploits. He employed directorial strategies to extract the very best from his performers—strategies that he had long forgotten. He recalled the subtleties of rehearsal which do so much to instill confidence in his artists. He praised them, supported them, and readily picked them up when they fell. His suggestions were inspiring; his motives, incontrovertibly clear.

He was no less demanding of his performers, but his style of leadership was changed. He was no longer the tyrant manager, but the servant leader, aiding and assisting his players to new heights. Those who had worked with him before recognized well his expectation of perfection, but they hardly recognized his means for reaching it. Instead of railing on mistakes, he reinforced the strengths, corrected errors, and inspired his performers to rise. To be sure, Handel's stage and pit were safe for his artists.

In return, his cast gave him their unmitigated trust and loyalty, a thing grown foreign to him. Their work exceeded Handel's highest expectations. Many delivered performances that reached beyond where they had ever been before. They esteemed him as both director and friend. He accepted their confidence humbly and graciously.

Even the audience could discern the single-heartedness of the performers. Patrons became active participants, contributing greatly to the overall spirit of the performance. The Dublin concerts were more to be experienced than simply heard.

Of all the doings on stage that pleased the audience, one thing stood alone as the crowd favorite: when Handel accompanied the orchestra, his wig bobbed in time to the music. This acted as a catalyst to the audience who responded with ardent applause. Truly, Dublin was won.

In the second series of concerts, Handel included two new selections; *Alexander's Feast* and *Hymen*. Both were energetically received and critically acclaimed. There were additional performances of *L'Allegro* which also played to full houses. Not since the London premiere of *Rinaldo* and *Radamisto*, had Handel enjoyed the consummate success and notoriety that Dublin now afforded him. He dined with royalty, mixed with nobility, and drank with commoners.

When early success had come in London, it was expected. The sweetness of it had no contrary standard against which to compare. Thus, it was enjoyed but not wholly appreciated. But in absolute contrast to the desolate inferno of the past year from which Handel had miraculously emerged, Dublin was like a walk through a cool glade of spring flowers.

Signora Avolio, Mrs. Cibber, Mr. Maclaine the organist, who accompanied him from Chester, and Mrs. Maclaine, whom he had employed as soprano soloist, were all astounded at the new creature. Although no one dared inquire of Handel directly as to the reason for the change, the fact that he was indeed different was undeniable. Success was blamed for most of the change in Handel. There was no doubt that circumstances in Dublin were indeed agreeable, but those who knew him best, Mrs. Cibber especially, believed the fountainhead of change had sprung forth from a deeper source. Handel was reborn.

As Handel's group entered the final weeks of the second series, all was in line for a strong finish to a brilliant run. The remaining concerts were announced, ticket sales were brisk and the performers were prepared. Rehearsals went as expected. Nothing out of the ordinary took place—no glaring mishaps or miscues.

After one such rehearsal, while the group disassembled, Handel sat at the organ, deep in thought. Mrs. Cibber—"Susanna" as Handel called her—curiously watched him as she stood on the stage speaking with Mr. Dubourg. She had noticed Handel's odd preoccupation earlier in the evening during practice. Several times, tiny mistakes were made without correction as if he hadn't heard them at all. That alone removed any question in her mind that Handel's thoughts were elsewhere.

"You've made the Irish believe," Mr. Dubourg said, interrupting her reverie.

"They seem to have accepted our little invasion, haven't they," she replied with a wink.

"Mrs. Cibber, you've not merely invaded, you've captured." Dubourg excused himself and left by the back stage door. She picked up her cape, and turned one last time to Handel, the only other remaining person in the hall.

"Goodnight, sir," she said warmly. "Until tomorrow."

"Madame? Could I impose on you to stay a few minutes longer?"

"Sir, you cannot impose on time which is already yours," she assured him. Handel paused, as if weighing out one last time the consequences of his request. In time, his eyes focused back on her. She could tell that his mind was made up.

"I know it is late, but would you indulge me by trying an aria I've been working on?"

"An aria? You have a new oratorio?"

"Please."

He stood from his chair and offered her a piece of music. She studied the music, singing the words in her mind. So engrossed was she that she did not see Handel walk to the harpsichord and sit down. He waited until she looked up from the sheet in her hand.

"*Dolce*," was Handel's only word of direction.

Mrs. Cibber's face was radiant. She walked to a place on the stage nearest the harpsichord, poised herself to sing, then gave the maestro a nod. He played the introduction simply, without any embellishment. As he approached her entrance, he looked up at her.

"'He was despised.'"

As hoped for, her voice was as pure as a child's prayer.

"'Despised and rejected.'"

The clear tone of her voice rang through the hall, resounding back on itself like a chorus of many voices singing in immaculate unison. Handel accompanied her flawless melody with restrained mastery, gently leading her to each new refrain.

"'A man of sorrows and acquainted with grief—and acquainted with grief.'"

The more she sang, the more enraptured she was with the music. She laid her whole soul upon each new phrase, tenderly caring for each note and word. She sang as though her song reached the very ear of the Savior Himself. It was the song of forgiveness, the song of prophecy fulfilled. With deep feeling, she sang the sweet redemptive melody of the brokenhearted, the poor in spirit, the meek, and the mournful.

"'He was despised; despised and rejected. Rejected of men. A man of sorrows and acquainted with grief.'"

Handel continued, eyes closed, totally engaged by the song. He did not realize that Mrs. Cibber had stopped until her next entrance, which she did not sing. His fingers did not move to the next notes on the page. The music resonated in the hall momentarily, then silenced.

"It's masterful," she said.

"You're the only one to ever hear it."

"Perform it. It is sublime."

"I can't risk failure with this."

She considered his words with great import, then smiled at him.

"Not to give it to the world—that would be failure."

"I must think about it."

"What better time or better audience than you now have? Dublin will understand."

Handel looked out across the empty seats of the theatre. Susanna followed his gaze to the open hall.

"I will consider it."

Susanna's eyes came back to him.

"You're careful with this piece," she said.

"I am different because of it—changed. It is the child of my heart."

Susanna's eyes went back to the empty seats. They were no longer empty to her. Faces filled with hope stared up at the stage from the vacant hall.

"Then let the child grow. If it is not shared, you render it stillborn."

Handel stood up. He took the score from the stand and walked to her. She reached out her music to him. When his hand touched the paper, she held on. She did not let go until his eyes met hers.

"It is as beautiful as anything I've ever sung."

She walked off the stage to her dressing room. Minutes later, when she walked past the open door at the back of the hall, Handel was still standing where she had left him.

Glory to God

HANDEL STARED INTO THE FIRE OF THE SINGLE CANDLE sitting on the desk. It seemed peculiar to be again in the selfsame attitude as when he had written the score laid before him. It didn't matter that months had passed since the time he had finished; the memory of his musical journey was still fresh in his mind. Even the rich smell of the ink and paper seemed to conjure back emotions familiar to those he had experienced while writing in the solitude of his study. As he peered into the flame, he recalled the many times he had stared into his own flickering candle in quiet reverie, pondering, praying.

Now his thoughts were absorbed in the oratorio a second time. This time he was not writing but laboring over the destiny of the writing. Although he was hesitant to commit to it, he knew in his heart that performance of the piece was inevitable. To say otherwise was less than the truth. There was no denying that he had already heard the full length and breadth of the score performed in his mind. He had imagined brave choirs singing grand choruses, soloists singing rich recitatives.

When the voice of Susanna Cibber graced his ears earlier that day, it was the fulfillment of what he had already heard with his mind's ear. Indeed, she had moved him. She gave perfect voice to the testimony of music that he had borne. Handel wondered if the harvest time had come. The thought of taking the grapes to press to test the sweetness frightened him. His entire life was devoted to trying to second-guess what audiences wanted; this work was devoted to trying to determine what God wanted. The notes were manifestations of what his heart felt.

For Handel, performing it was not a question of willingness, but of worthiness. It was a question that had haunted him every time he had put a stroke of ink on the page; a question with which he had wrestled night and day during the three-week sojourn in his study; a question which oppressed him more now than the moment he first started: Was it worthy of Him whose name it bore?

Often, he had felt compelled to look up at the shadowed picture of Christ on his wall and wonder if his music was equal to the prophetic verse to which he had put it. At no time in the ordeal had his doubts been more poignant than during the very last day of writing, when he scored music to the prophecy of John as recorded in Revelation:

"Worthy is the Lamb that was slain, and hath redeemed us to God by His blood."

The message to Handel was clear: Was his Messiah worthy of the *Messiah*? The very assumption that he could put music to divine, canonized prophecy humbled him to the ground. During moments of solemn reflection, he wished the task had not come to him. He was forced to ask himself if it was by chance or divinely ordered providence that he was so compelled to take up this cross. The mere thought of the latter was incomprehensible. There were many other gifted artists whose lives of service made them better prepared for such a task.

At earlier times in his life, he would have expected to be the artist chosen to sing God's praise. Pride would have deceived him into believing that he was the most qualified to accompany the words of the prophets. His heart had been beyond feeling. That was before his chastening.

Preparation came through walking the paths of despair. Only after his heart was broken could the Spirit finally reach inside. Repentance rendered him reachable. The work of writing began when Handel felt wholly and totally insufficient for the task. Guilt robbed him of the valor to start when Jennens first approached him; brokenness gave him the strength to begin when he did.

Like an obsession, he was compelled to continue to the end. When it was at last finished, it was Handel's feelings of inadequacy that forced the work into the drawer. He viewed the effort as a personal atonement more than a public petition.

Beyond even this, there were elements in the score with which critics and zealots alike would take issue and think that he regarded himself as the authority on not only the subject matter but also on style and structure. There were places in the score where he had broken with tradition, not followed the conventional paradigm. He simply followed what he felt inspired to do with each element. He knew he would offend the beat counters, whose sole purpose was to make sure that he had not technically ventured outside the gated yard. He also knew he would offend the musical pharisees, whose sole purpose was to make sure he piously and religiously stayed within the gated yard. There was also the problem of the title. To presume to call an oratorio after the name Messiah without being commissioned would cause no small stir. He could think of no one other than Jennens who would be so bold as to try such a move.

All of these things concerned Handel, but they didn't stop him. He had obediently proceeded with the hope that the spirit of music and word would transcend both convention and orthodoxy and be weighed upon the greater scale of ennobling the soul. In truth, he wasn't sure what to do.

The flickering flame of the candle on his desk caught his eye. As he stared at the burning candle, he noticed a small breach in the outer rim of the burning candle. He watched a clear drop of liquid wax spill over the breach and slide down the length of the stem. It continued over a small crest of hardened wax built up at the base of the candelabra. The heavy drop then fell to the desk where other drops had fallen before. A small mound of wax was building up from the bottom, reaching higher and higher with each new drop that escaped the candle. As the candle diminished, the spire grew. He watched several more drops cascade down the candle to the rising peak. A thought suddenly occurred to him: the journey of the drop was a similitude of his own desperate journey. The falling of one made possible the rise of the other. When he considered the significance of the growing steeple of wax, he knew what he must do.

He picked up the quill lying on the desk and dipped it in the inkwell.

"Faulkner's *Dublin Journal*," he wrote in large script.

"For the relief of the prisoners in the several gaols and for the support of Mercer's Hospital in Stephen's-Street, and of the Charitable Infirmary on the Inns Quay, on Monday, the 12th of April, will be performed at the Musick Hall in Fishamble Street, Mr. Handel's new Grand Oratorio, called *MESSIAH*, in which the Gentlemen of the Choirs of both Cathedrals will assist, with some Concertos on the Organ, by Mr. Handel. Gentlemen are asked not to bring swords, and Ladies are requested to not wear hoops. The performance will be preceded by a Public Rehearsal at which all could be present who buy tickets for the actual concert."

He finished by signing his name. As he laid down the pen, he spoke aloud, "May it do for them what it has done for me."

He blew out the candle.

And Be Ye Lifted Up

THE ANNOUNCEMENT REGARDING HANDEL'S NEW GRAND
oratorio was met with tremendous excitement and approval. This would
be the premiere of a work not yet performed in any other venue. It came
as quite a surprise to all, since Handel was well into the second series of
concerts before there was any written mention of it.

The tickets to the new oratorio sold at once in spite of the fact that
it was difficult to get any advance information about the piece.
Rehearsals were closed door; musicians and vocalists alike were tight-
lipped about the nature of the work. Even the chatty chorus members,
whose tongues were double-jointed for just such times as this, treated
the information with extreme confidentiality. As if by design, there was
little if anything to be known about the upcoming concert. And yet,

instead of the secrecy breeding skepticism, as is usually the case, the highly anticipated oratorio became even more anticipated. Handel had earned Dublin's respect and confidence; patrons did not question his motives but waited anxiously.

At last, when the day came for them to hear, their highest hopes and expectations were exceeded.

As asked, attendees came without swords or hoops, which made it possible to fit an additional one hundred people into the hall for the public rehearsal on April the 8th. The concert was an unprecedented success. The oratorio was hailed by Dublin critics as "the finest composition of Musick that was ever heard."

The first actual performance of *Messiah* was postponed one day to April 13, 1742.

The day was resplendent. Spring had arrived in Ireland with tulips and blue sky. Those who attended the rehearsal were even more excited the second time. For the few ticket holders who were unable to attend the rehearsal, the reports had been sublime. At the least, the music had been hailed as exquisite; at the most, people spoke of having been elevated with the angels. No one was disappointed.

One adoring patron was so transported by Mrs. Cibber's appassionato singing of "He was despised," that he rose to his feet and exclaimed openly, "Woman, for this, be all thy sins forgiven."

The sentiment was well intended, yet in poor taste, as rumors regarding infidelity had plagued Mrs. Cibber for the past few years.

Handel conducted his small orchestra of thirty from his place at the harpsichord. Maclaine was employed on the small organ with its dozen or so light stops, which Handel brought with him from London. His remaining instruments consisted of strings, oboes, bassoons, trumpets, and drums. The choir was quite nearly the same strength, consisting of men only.

There was great variety in the soloists, a total of nine in all. Signora Avolio provided grand bravura in "Rejoice greatly." It was Mrs. Maclaine who with a voice of absolute clarity and diction, sang the words of Luke, "There were shepherds abiding in the field."

John Mason was employed on most of the bass solos, including the revelatory air "But who may abide the day of His coming." James Bailey was the principal tenor. It was he who foreshadowed the majesty of the performance with "Comfort Ye" and "Every valley shall be exalted." William Lamb and Joseph Ward traded off between alto solos, the former singing "O thou that tellest good tidings to Zion" and the latter joining with Bailey for "O death, where is thy sting."

The resources were meager as compared to the casts and divas with which Handel had worked in London, yet never had a sound been so stirring.

There were some in the admiring audience who wept, but most sat motionless, their eyes forward. When the choir rose to sing the first chorus, "And the glory of the Lord," the sound filled the hall like a great gust of wind, permeating every soul to the very core. For over three hours the music went on ceaselessly, and yet every new piece was as fresh as the first.

One unexpected and joyful event of the night involved Mr. Dubourg, who contributed by singing the bass recitative "Unto which of the angels said he at any time." As Mr. Dubourg sang the last bars of the solo, he ended the number *ad libitum*: After wandering about in different keys for quite some time, he finally came to the shake. As he did, Handel cried aloud, to the delight of the audience:

"You are welcome home, Mr. Dubourg."

The following day, the Dublin press could scarcely find words to declare the triumph of the great occasion. During a brief break in the rehearsal, Susanna Cibber rose to her feet, newspaper in hand, and read aloud to the full cast and orchestra.

"Words are wanting to express the exquisite delight it afforded to the admiring audience; the sublime, the grand, and the tender adapted to the most elevated, majestic, and moving words conspired to transport and charm the ravished heart and ear. Such is Handel's *Messiah*."

Susanna approached Handel, took one of his hands in hers, and presented to the group their conductor and maestro. In one great wave, the entire cast simultaneously rose to their feet in a roar of spontaneous applause and cheering.

So passed the days of Dublin. While there, Handel made countless friends. He was treated with such kindness and consideration that he promised to return the following season. The promise was not kept.

London was his home; he could leave it, but he could not leave it alone. Although London had scorned him, he knew he must return and face the conflict from which he had narrowly escaped. He convinced himself that he was ready for whatever good or ill may await him there. In the midst of his recent accomplishment abroad, his memory became short and his will strong.

Handel's success in Ireland had proved the viability of oratorio as a medium. Including his now-finished *Samson*, he was confident that he had a portfolio of scores strong enough to contend with any and all who remained entrenched in opera. He had no plans to perform *Messiah* in London; on the contrary, he specifically made plans not to perform it. It was an unnecessary risk, which he dared not take.

As the summer began to wane, so did Handel's desire to stay in Ireland. Finally, in August he boldly embarked for the city from which he had retreated just months before, armed with his new weapon with which to fight.

And Received Gifts for Men

THE CLOSER HANDEL'S CARRIAGE CAME TO LONDON, THE more his confidence waned. He was strong and tall when he left Dublin; by the time he could see the outskirts of London, it was all he could do to look out the window. He contended with shades of doubt, which clouded his vision. Old wounds, which had gone unnoticed for months, suddenly began to smart. For the traveler returning home after an extended vacation, the stress of daily life had been forgotten until home was again in sight. Handel's remembrance of hardship was dulled by his heroics in Ireland. He had severely underestimated the heavy toll that London had extracted from him. The sight of distant buildings against the southern horizon pricked his memory.

Handel was uncertain of what awaited him at home. It had been well over a year since his last public performance in London. He was hopeful that the head winds of adversity, which had buffeted him so incessantly through the recent past, might have calmed in his absence. It was not that he was afraid of a fight; on the contrary, he understood that opposition kept him awake and alert. Resistance forced him to keep his skills sharp; his craft was enlarged through difficulty. Handel learned well the principle that adversity was never a welcome breeze, but it filled the sails none the less. In the past, he had followed his instincts to turn into the wind and fight face to face. His natural action was reaction. But as the city grew in size outside the carriage window, Handel knew that his very survival relied upon learning to tack into whatever gales might cross him. He must learn to find silver edges rimming the dark clouds of adversity. Never was he in a better position to do so.

Handel was virtually starting over. He was no longer working under the oppressive bondage of debt. For years he had been a slave to his obligations. Debt was a relentless taskmaster from which there was no rest nor reprieve. The freedom his mother purchased with her self-sacrifice gave him a second chance. From the grave, she paid the heavy price for her son's peace of mind and spirit. Handel felt as though he had been dragged from a burning house, only to awaken and find that his life had cost the life of his rescuer. In honor of her, he was determined to make of his life a legacy of which she would be proud.

Traffic increased the closer they came to the city. Cottages became flats; the skyline rose in height; the number of buildings multiplied. The sudden loud rattle in the coach let Handel know that the road had changed from dirt to cobbles. The smells of the city greeted him, familiar as an old friend. The noise of the street amplified as the coach drew near the center of town. From inside, Handel could hear vendors calling out their wares. As the carriage wended its way toward his home, Handel felt a sudden impulse to do something extraordinary: he leaned out the window for a better view.

As soon as he felt the wind in his face he remembered how much he had loved doing the same thing when he was a child. It was curious to him that he had never again thought of it until that very moment. He instantly recalled the many rides from the Handel cottage into Halle, when he would hang half out of the carriage to get a better view. Father Handel scolded him on several occasions for his dangerous habit of being more out of the carriage than in, but it did little to curb young George's actions. Even the severe tongue lashing he had received for falling out of the back of a wagon while standing up for a better look didn't discourage him. He loved the wind in his face, the fragrant smells of the passing fields, the chance to wave "Hello!" to anyone else on the road. It infuriated the elder Georg, but he knew any discipline imparted to his young son would come back to him two-fold from Dorothea. Handel's father endured the annoyance to avoid a double dose of derision from the boy's mother. In spite of the reality that the Handel home was patriarchal, the patriarch understood that there were times when the woman of the house was considerably more mother than wife.

Handel leaned out the window as far as his corpulence would allow. He no longer hid in the cave of the carriage but filled the window with his round face. After a few minutes of simply letting the wind lap at his cheeks, he opened his eyes to see the people on the street. It was a view he had not taken in for a long time. He saw children playing in the muddy gutters, mop-trundlers cleaning their walks. He could see the shadows of men leaning against the tinted windows inside taverns. He could see in those faces on the street a vision of the people he had met in Chester and Dublin. All around him were commoners like those with whom he had passed the days waiting for better winds. When the carriage passed by the entrance of a small pub, he heard deep, resounding laughter echoing from within the small room. Into his mind came the words of a joke, one that he had heard from a foul-mouthed fisherman on the Chester dock, who was digging oysters from the shell. He laughed out loud at the mere thought of it. When he passed a mother and child sitting on the steps of a worn-down flat, he ventured a wave. The smiling mother pointed out the round-faced man to the child. They waved back.

This was a view of London that had gone completely unnoticed by Handel before. The city was full of people exactly like the gracious souls of Dublin and the unpretentious folk of Chester. These were his people—this was his audience. He made a promise to himself never to let them go unregarded again. He was no longer afraid.

When the carriage turned the corner onto Brook Street, he could see his home only a few apartments away. A huge smile crested his face. Peter LeBlonde saw him from the window of the flat; the front door swung

open. On Peter's face was a look of bright anticipation. Before the carriage could stop, the compartment door of the carriage flung open. Handel was out of it before the driver could get down from his perch on top. Peter came down the step toward him. Handel met him half way, his huge hand outstretched. He took Peter's hand in both of his and greeted him warmly. For the first time since leaving the poppy-covered fields of Saxony, Handel was home.

Their Sound Is Gone Out
into All Lands

THE MAN OF THE HOUSE HAD JUST ASCENDED THE STAIRS
of his home for the day's last time. He proceeded down the hall and into
the bedroom entirely from memory. So tired was he that he would have
been unable to remember anything of the walk up the stairs. His eyes were
open for little of the trip.

From the street, only one lamp could be seen burning in the house:
the one closest to his bed. The man sat down on the mattress, hardly able
to sit up long enough to push the slippers from his feet before falling
over, asleep. He could hear the restful breathing of his wife next to him
as she slumbered peacefully. He rolled his bare feet under the down comforter, then leaned out of bed, cupped the flame of the oil lamp, and blew
it out. A moment later, his head was on the pillow. It didn't take long for

his body to warm the down comforter spread over him. His wife had already warmed much of the bed. Within seconds, he began to doze off into quiet and restful sleep.

At that moment, there was a loud pounding on the door downstairs. The man shot upright in bed, startled out of sleep by the thunderous banging. His wife also awoke, clutching his arm with an iron grip. The man peeled away her fingers and leaped to his feet.

Downstairs, the door slammed open. Heavy footsteps entered and passed over the tile of the entry. With his heart racing, the man of the house started down the stair to contend with the intruder. Any thought of sleep was instantly quelled. He stopped mid-step at the next sound.

Music rang out from the dark entrance to the parlour. It was not a frantic sound, but a gentle sound of sweet longing. The music rose up the stairs, climbed past the man and through the open door of the bedroom to where his wife waited, wide-eyed. To her astonishment, her husband soon reappeared through the door.

Without a word, he returned to bed while the music continued downstairs.

"He's back," he said.

His wife lay back down next to him. Together, in the soft glow of the moon through the open window, they listened to the gentle strains reaching up to them from below. At long last, just before nodding off a second time, the man leaned up on his elbows briefly to call downstairs.

"Lock the door when you leave."

Indeed, Handel was back. Word of his success in Dublin spread quickly through London's high society. The news was generally treated with scrutiny, but there were some who rejoiced in what they heard. Handel still had a small but strong contingency of friends who remained ever faithful. One of the most loyal, Mrs. Delaney, delighted in the reports from Dublin. When she received a letter from Handel informing her of his plans to return, she began to solicit support to secure a venue wherein he could perform. She was surprised at the reception she received. Apparently, Handel had been missed in London, even though it was unpopular to admit it. In truth, most Londoners didn't know he had even departed for Dublin until he was well into his first series of performances. Once they did know, the reality of his absence caused many to rethink Handel's contribution. Few would contend that some of the grandest moments in the city's musical history had been provided by Handel. Only after he was out of the picture were people forced to stop and consider his role in painting the picture. Even his enemies missed the battles he had provided. He was a worthy foe, passionate and unyielding. It had taken some doing to bring him down, and the prospect of a renewed conflict was intriguing, especially in view of the mixed sentiment of society. If nothing else, Handel provided variety, a commodity in dire need among those who appreciated the arts. The *Beggar's Opera* was growing stale. The Italians were continually discontent. Their bickering and hair-splitting had become tiresome if not outright boring. Opera was dwindling. Even politics were less than titillating as King and Prince had miraculously found a means to coexist. London needed something to talk about, and even though the news of Handel seizing Dublin was not catastrophic, it was something.

Those who tended toward snobbery would not so much as acknowledge his accomplishments across the water. Many of London's nobility had to look so far down their noses to see Dublin that any acceptance on that front was treated as dross. They completely dismissed his success:

"Dublin would heartily toast a change of its own underwear—little wonder that the Irish are taken with London's dirty laundry."

But, in spite of the relatively small factions who were adamantly against any Handelian revival, there was a larger segment who, at the least, were willing to give him another listen. The ground, however, was unstable.

What made his return even more interesting were reports of the medium that Handel had employed so effectively while in Ireland. The oratorio was still relatively new in London. It was tried but not necessarily true. Handel had tested it to some extent, but the oratorio had still not fully caught on with the vast majority of people. By nature, it required more of the listener. Hence, it did not enjoy immediate acclaim but progressed slowly. This created an additional element of consternation among the most stubborn of critics. Though no one voiced the dismay outright, the use of the oratorio in the Dublin foray deeply annoyed the stiff-necked of London. Dublin had taken a tremendous shine to a style of performance relatively obscure in England. The fact was indisputable:

the Irish had led in their acceptance and appreciation of the oratorio. This infuriated a small faction of Londoners, who determined to make sure that it would not succeed as a medium on the homefront.

But most people simply wanted the opportunity to judge the concept for themselves. Still others, who were weary of the persnickety opera environment, were just grateful to have an alternative that didn't require the fanfare and ostentatiousness that opera thrived on. Something simpler suited them fine.

There was another element about Handel's return which conjured up considerable fascination with many people: the story of redemption unfolding before them, Handel's illustrious rise to fame, his desperate fall into obscurity, and now the beginning of what could gestate into a courageous comeback. His unintentional underdog status aided his chance for some unanticipated support.

So mixed and muddied was the overall sentiment that the entire Handel issue was ultimately reduced to two platforms: "Wait and see" and "Impress me." One side cautiously hoped for an impressive new emergence for the artist, whereas the other wished for fizzling failure. Regardless of the outcome, he would give them something other than the worn-out whispers of illicit affairs to gossip about.

One man, however, resented the very mention of Handel's name. Handel's success in Dublin or any other town repulsed him. There was nothing curious or amusing in his view of Handel, only consummate hatred. Even a humble reception for the Saxon was more than he could tolerate. He read the Dublin papers the entire time Handel was abroad, already conniving ways to vanquish any semblance of what might be considered a regeneration of his career. Long before Handel's return, the dark strategy was formulated. Handel had been wounded, his ego pierced, his music maligned; but his will was never fully broken. That feat would require breaking his heart. Rolli knew that to destroy the man, he must destroy the very thing that he held most dear. The plan was simple, quite obvious in fact. Simply turn Handel's new weapon back on himself. To take aim at the oratorio was to take aim at Handel. The final stroke would need to be debilitating. It would be a blow from which Handel could never recover; Rolli would make sure of it.

The sayings of success in Dublin also found their way to the ear of the King. George privately pleasured in the news of Handel's exploits in Ireland. He still considered himself principally responsible for bringing the composer to England. When politics and Handel himself made it impossible for George to continue financial and moral support of the Saxon, the King's desires for Handel had to be closeted. Nevertheless, he hoped that his countryman would have a reversal. If so, Handel would do it alone. If he were to have a second time around, King George was determined not to assist or intercede in any way, regardless of the outcome. Nothing could be better than if Handel could make a strong reentrance into the music scene. The King will have bested his critics. It would prove, once and for all, that the common heritage of King and composer had little to do with Handel's success. If anything, King George should be congratulated for recognizing genius, in spite of the sharp criticism he was forced to endure at the hands of those who had accused him of nepotism. The last laugh was a commodity that George valued as much as any man—possibly more. He cautiously waited to see if his German cream would rise back to the top of London's milky music world.

Politically, the environment for a Handelian revival was cleaner than ever before. The King and son had experienced a restoration. After years of petty dispute, common ground was finally found in royal heritage. It seems that both were singed with regret for actions and words that were far beneath their birthright and blood. The father's attitude toward his son was far less than kingly. He had vocalized hostile emotions that he, of all men, should have kept in check. Of commoners such behavior might be expected, but not of kings. His disgust of Frederick was made public, a gross folly, for which he was ashamed. The most-guarded man in all of England had let down his guard in the one place where he was most vulnerable: his mouth. Once he realized his transgression, he prudently committed to prevent a similar offense. He could not alter the course of that which had already escaped his lips, but he could certainly dam off any future indiscretions. His regard for Frederick began to change immediately. Silence beget thought, thought beget understanding, and understanding beget mercy. He resolved simply to forgive and forget. It was then that George the King began to find power and influence from a source that he had allowed to grow dormant—from within.

His Highness had relaxed into the common view that his kingship was measured by borders and subjects. Quiet reflection endowed him with wisdom, and with it came far more kingdom than he knew he had. Even with his own son, he began to see the fruits of a calm word of caution as opposed to a shouted rebuff. Pure and simply, the King determined to act like a king.

The new monarch remembered the intimidating pressure he had experienced when the full comprehension of royal responsibility began to settle on him. Heirship was not without its challenges. Where much was given, much was expected. When the memory of his own insecurities came back to him, so did tolerance. Even if he did not approve of Freddy's doings, at least he could reprove his frailties privately. It was the one consideration for which he had futilely wished from his father.

The Prince's path home was far more complicated. He was so immersed in his derision of the King that his preoccupation superseded his occupation. His entire world seemed to revolve around finding fault with his father. It was only after the true intentions of Rolli and Hervey were disrobed that he began to comprehend how malignant the effort had been. Its infecting fingers had spread through every aspect of his life, strangling off any chance for restitution. He had surrounded himself with people of like mind. They were hunters, and he was their guide to the prey. All of his doings and goings were motivated by malevolence. The realization that he had no life beyond destroying his father's life was astounding. He tried in vain to pinpoint the exact event that had altered his course onto the wide road of spite, but he could not remember. He had simply followed along with his pithy peers. He had warnings of danger ahead, but they were ignored. Miles of malice were behind him before he ever looked up for a road sign to see where he was. The sign given him was in the words of Rolli. When he overheard the Italian's conversation with the Madame, it was as if he could see their true character. All comeliness seemed to peel away from his comrades, leaving nothing but ugliness underneath. Every one of his senses was suddenly attuned to the wretchedness of his surroundings; the air stunk, his taste bittered, even their voices sounded shrill and high-pitched. He utterly loathed what he had become and those who had helped him get there.

It was as if he had been awakened from a deep sleep and found himself far away from where he wanted to be. Like his father, he had followed the path of men, not of princes. He was feeding with swine on dry husks of corn when he could have been dining at the table of his father. The only way back was literally to turn away from his group and head cross-country alone, uncertain of what obstacles he might encounter on the way.

The terrain was rocky, the trail unclear, but slowly he inched forward towards the man he thought he should be. What caused him most remorse were the many periphery lives ruined in the effort to get back at his father—Handel not being the least. He had no cause to embrace the Saxon, nor did he approve of his tactless ways. Handel's style was wholly disagreeable to the Prince, but that was not cause to destroy him in order to vicariously injure the King. As stubborn as Frederick might be, his faults were nothing compared to the loathsome Rolli, with whom he had aligned himself. At the very least, Handel had some redeeming qualities, not to mention his incontestable talent. Rolli had nothing. It was devastating to think that he had ever degenerated so far as to enjoin himself with the likes of Rolli. The Prince was the dupe of a crippling plan to mutilate the reputation of the composer under the guise of infuriating the King. It was the kind of perversion that would make moral men squirm. The reality that he had played a key role in the treachery was detestable. The only thing he believed could salve his conscience was for Handel to somehow dig himself out of the quagmire into which Frederick had helped push him.

Thus, even the Prince was pleased to hear of Handel's good fortune in Ireland. He hoped that the tide of good fortune might even land Handel back on safe footing in London.

September 21, 1742
To his most gracious sir:
Mr. Charles Jennens

Dear Charles,

I am arrived back in London one week ago today. I trust that you are well and that my letters arrived safely from Dublin. As mentioned therein, I intend to be found again in that country forthwith, for a kinder audience I have never found. They are a gracious and pleasurable people.

Concerning my plans here, I am uncertain. I shall likely do something of an oratorio here, I cannot determine as yet. Certain it is that this time twelvemonth, I shall continue my oratorios in Ireland. The Lord Lieutenant is planning to make a large subscription for that purpose.

Your most humble servant,
George Frederic Handel

Let Him Deliver Him

Before the letter made its way to Jennens, his mind was made up. Covent Garden was to be the first venue of performance for the returned Handel. Mrs. Delaney's efforts to warm theatres to the idea of Handel's performing were rewarded quickly. He finalized negotiations with the theatre for a series of Lenten performances, and, as expected, the performances were to be oratorios.

Yet, long before Handel made any appearance in the theatre, he made many appearances in the street and local churches. He would often, without any prior announcement, go to the local taverns and play for the occupants. He played what they wanted to hear, not what he wanted them to hear. He played love songs. He played sad songs. He accompanied drinking men in rowdy choruses. He would open the doors of the church and play for any who might venture in for some solace and sacred prelude. Never did he expect anything in return for his time or talent. He played for the love of the people and his love of music.

But what he enjoyed most of all was playing for the children. Mrs. Delaney opened her home to the children of the street, who would come each week to hear Handel's musical stories. The children would stare up at him with round eyes from their seats on the floor. The number of children grew each week until the floors of several rooms were filled. Mrs. Delaney had the instrument moved to the most central part of her home. It was inconvenient for the house help, but it accommodated far more children than the conservatory. The only hour of the week that Mrs. Delaney enjoyed more than the children's hour was her own personal hour with Handel.

Handel availed himself to the people of the street. They likewise availed themselves to him. He was their friend. Occasionally, he would even invite Susanna Cibber to join him for his children's concerts. She obliged him graciously.

He began his theatre season on February 18, 1743, with his newly finished *Samson*. The move, although risky, proved to be prosperous. Eight successive concerts were announced, each entirely subscribed. Night after night, carriages lined the streets in front of Covent Garden. The medley cast Handel had assembled was a far cry from the preeminently accomplished singers of the Italian opera; nonetheless, seats were occupied, and occupants were pleased. In appreciation of her unfaltering faith and friendship, Handel gave Mrs. Cibber the part of Micah. He rewrote the lines to suit her voice. For Signora Avolio he composed the beautiful and stirring "Let the Bright Seraphim." The tenor John Beard was given the title role. It was an unusual cast by London standards, but it was a loyal cast by Handelian standards. As the series progressed, additional disgruntled opera singers migrated to his company. London accepted the return. The witticist Horace Walpole wrote of Handel's endeavor:

"Handel has set up an oratorio against the opera, and succeeds. He has hired all the goddesses from the farces and the singers of roast-beef from between the acts at both theatres, with a man with one note in his voice, and a girl without even one; and so they sing and make brave hallelujahs, and the good company encore the recitative if it happens to have any cadence like what they call a tune."

Of the many talents that might have been employed, Handel opted to work with those in whom he had trust. The decision proved profitable—the run of eight concerts was a solid success. Handel carefully evaluated whether his reception was genuine or inflated. He believed it to be real. It was only then, on the heels of victory, that he decided that the time had come to unmask himself to the audiences of London. It was the decision for which others with not so noble intent had been waiting.

Glad Tidings of Good Things

THAT IS FAMILIAR TO ME," SAID PETER FROM THE THRESHOLD of the study after Handel finished playing.

"An aria, from the oratorio," said Handel, his hands rising from the keys. "'Comfort ye.'"

"It's a good name," Peter said while putting down a tray of chocolates and tea on the table. He had been standing in the doorway for several minutes, not wanting to interrupt Handel or his playing. Peter had missed Handel. He had missed the music of the house, the voice of the clavichord. The spirit of the home had become so closely knit with the spirit of the music that when it was absent, the house felt empty.

"Sir, I've brought something to take your mind off your work for a moment," said Peter while pouring tea.

"Ahh—what would work be without diversions?" sighed Handel while getting to his feet and reaching his arms high over his head. He spoke while he stretched.

"'Twould just be work, nothing more. No wonder God created the seventh day. He not only created heaven and Earth, but also the first diversion."

Handel picked up from the tray the darkest and largest chocolate and plopped it into his mouth. Peter chuckled at how the chewing made Handel's round face appear even rounder.

"London missed you, sir."

"Aye—I am England's knick-knack," said Handel through the mouthful.

"Sir?"

"It seems I am hard to keep—and yet harder to throw away."

"You're playing to packed houses."

"We've done that before."

"Yes, but..."

Handel interrupted him.

"I am an odd dog, and the Master—the Master, an odd trainer."

"Indeed," nodded Peter, his face growing solemn.

Peter went on with his duties, but his thoughts were faraway. Handel watched Peter's change of attitude with great interest. It was not the first time he had observed a marked change of disposition in Peter's visage at the mention of God's dealings with men. Of all the men that Handel knew, few had a better understanding of the ways of God than his servant; yet, Handel could discern a blemish in his blanket of faith. Peter still carried beneath his skin a deep sliver from his own cross, of that Handel was sure. On many occasions he had considered asking a question of Peter which to this day remained unasked, it was a personal question regarding a past issue that Handel knew little about. Yet Handel sensed that, for Peter, it had been life altering. Handel ascertained that a single decision in Peter's past had changed the course of his entire life. Handel knew the result of that decision, but he knew nothing of the emotions and circumstances surrounding the event. Until now, he had always erred on the side of propriety, but tonight he ventured into a place he had never invaded before.

"Please excuse my intrusion, sir. If there is nothing else then?" asked Peter.

"Please, Peter. May I now intrude?"

Peter nodded.

"You studied for the ministry, then left. I've never asked why."

Peter took a deep breath. He sat down in the chair near him, his head bent forward as if in deep thought. He stayed in that position for a long time. Afraid he had trespassed far deeper than he had previously supposed, Handel asserted, "You aided me through the darkest hours of my life. If I can somehow repay that trust in the smallest way, I would consider it a blessing."

Peter looked up into Handel's eyes.

"It seems I was backwards. It was easier for me to put the second great commandment first—'Love thy neighbor as thyself'—then let God judge my heart on the first and greatest commandment."

"Love the Lord with all thy heart, all thy soul, mind, and strength," finished Handel.

Peter thought for a moment before continuing.

"One is not without the other—but each must decide from which path to pursue obedience. While in the ministry, it seemed to me that the person who benefited most from my study and efforts was myself. I was learning to pray for the people, but all I could see was their hunger; they needed bread to eat. I chose to try and find them bread, then pray that they would know and recognize from whence it came.

"So you started the kitchen to feed the poor?"

"I would never presume to say one path is better than another, I simply did what my heart compelled me to do."

"But you could have taught, preached, prayed for the people. What better way to serve than by speaking the word of God?"

Peter leaned back. His eyes turned toward the window. "The more I found out about God, the more of God I found within myself. 'For God so loved the world that He gave His only begotten Son.' Prayer is eternal, learning is essential. But charity—pure love—that is where God's own heart is. Paul said, 'And though I speak with the tongue of angels, and have not charity, I am nothing.' If God's love was manifest by giving that which was most precious above all, His Son, then what better way to show my love for God than by giving also. 'Lovest thou me?' Christ asked of Peter. 'Feed my sheep; feed my lambs.'"

Peter looked back from the window to Handel, "Words are good, but what if God had done nothing more than just talked about giving His only begotten Son? Eventually, after all the prayers and good words are spoken, there comes a time for taking up crosses. I can only hope that I chose the right one to take up."

"Charity never faileth," said Handel, with a reassuring smile. He looked into Peter's eyes, not as master to servant, but as kindred spirits.

"You do understand?" Peter asked apologetically.

Handel took a deep breath.

"While I was writing, there came a time when I was constrained from writing. Perhaps you remember. It seemed I was damned by my unwillingness to let go of the past. The thought came that if I was to become worthy of Christ's sweet forgiveness and mercy, I must be willing to forgive too. It felt to me that the price of His mercy was more than I was able to pay. How could I let go of it all—all the bitterness, all the anger? Then, after an endless day and night of helpless flailing to find forgiveness in my hardened heart, I uttered a sincere and earnest prayer, 'Please, Lord—help me forgive.' In that moment, it was gone. The hole left behind was filled with peace. I couldn't take away the burden—but He could."

Handel smiled, then reached for another chocolate. He offered the tray to Peter.

"If the creator had been so well diverted," he said, taking a bite, "there would have been two days of rest."

Handel put the remainder of the confection in his mouth, then rose and walked to the clavichord, "If I am to have another of your diversions, I must earn it. An unearned diversion would be an indulgence—nothing more."

Music filled the room.

Their Rulers Take Counsel
Together Against the Lord

HE'S BACK. PLAYING TO PACKED HOUSES," SNAPPED ROLLI, the sourness of his voice in complete contrast to the beautiful morning.

"My dear Italian, your malevolence offends the day. Speak your hostility, but do so more peaceably," crooned Hervey from her garden chair.

"My apologies. Forgive my stridence," Rolli begged, with feigned sincerity.

"Better. Much better. Now enjoy yourself," Hervey said waving her arm. "You must learn to take more pleasure in the hunt, not just the kill."

Butlers appeared through the manor doors carrying trays of fruit and bread. After their wares were placed, the Madame excused them.

It was an unusually warm day for March. A gentle wind blew from the west. The warm trades reached far more northerly than usual, bringing tropical air and pleasant weather. Feathery cirrus clouds wisped in the highest layers of atmosphere. Madame Hervey anticipated the weather perfectly when she invited the small circle of perpetrators to her garden retreat in celebration of Handel's return to London. Included were Rolli, Addison, Steele, and two other young nobles eager to learn the ways of mischief.

The Prince no longer took company with the antagonists. They each in turn expressed their dismay at his decision to leave their companionship, except Hervey. She expressed no remorse with regard to Frederick's absence other than to lament the loss of his information and agenda. Her communication succeeded, but it was only words. To compensate, she did her best to make it apparent that she valued the inside information far more than the bearer of it.

Steele and Addison followed suit. They appreciated Hervey's specious attachment to the Prince in order to exploit him since they were of the same predatory breed as she. They understood perfectly her intentions. They followed her every lead as though they knew in advance what her next step would be in the milking of Frederick. The opportunity to suck royal blood was so mutually understood by the three that no rehearsal of lines or roles was ever needed. They simply improvised on the befriending of Frederick as if their cat's-paw play of the Prince had been coauthored. All three were so expertly polished in the art of deception that the falsified friendship was earnest.

Rolli, on the other hand, was so obsessed with Handel that he did not recognize that the manipulation of Prince Frederick was nothing more than a type and shadow of himself. Rolli had no way of knowing that when Frederick separated himself from the other antagonists there was serious talk of severing ties with him, too—since the biggest fish had torn free of the hook. But in the pernicious plot to deface the King, a subplot had emerged which was almost as engrossing as the main theme. Even though Handel was not nearly the catch as was the King, the battle with him was stimulating. He was a fine foe, with formidable strength and persistence. He had become almost as interesting as the politics of the original plan. They did not need the Prince to continue waging war with Handel. Most of what they needed was still in place. Rolli sufficed as antagonist. He was capable of villainy with which the others wouldn't dirty their hands. He was so possessed by hatred that his vision was severely amblyopic. Other assets of Handel's enemies included *The*

Spectator, the instability of public sentiment, the Italians, opera, the divas, history, and Handel himself. His eccentricities were so well documented that if all other lines of offense disintegrated, personal character attacks were always viable.

Hervey hummed as she took from the tray a large, drooping stem laden with fat grapes.

"It is a day for celebration. Like the prodigal, our boy has come home."

"Too soon for my liking," said Rolli.

"He is our answer for boredom," replied Hervey. "He is a challenge; a worthy opponent. Don't begrudge his determination—exploit it."

"As long as we're quick about it," said Rolli, pacing.

"What do you suggest?" asked Steele between sips of juice.

"Kidnapping, perhaps—that is if we could find a place big enough to hide him," mused Addison.

"We could snatch him right from his own home. No one would ever recognize him with a bag over his head."

Steele laughed out loud at the mere thought of it.

"Wrap him up in old newspapers and roll him out in a wheelbarrow; better still, just thrash him with a roll of yesterday's news."

While the editors laughed, Rolli schemed.

"Write something," he said, unveiling his plan.

"Use the paper. You've done it before. Jennens is one of your favorite targets."

"Jennens? We were talking about Handel?" Addison said.

"Get one, you get the other. Jennens wrote a libretto for Handel. He performed it in Dublin."

"You think he'll perform it here?" queried Steele.

"To be certain. He is too strong-willed to take small bites for very long. Pretty soon he'll try to swallow the whole cake."

"Why is this opera different from any other?" asked Addison.

"Who said it was an opera?"

"Not an oratorio!" Steele rolled his eyes. "There's so little to spurn."

"You will see," said Rolli. "You will have no shortage of soft spots to put to advantage. This one is more ripe for reproach than any yet."

"Why so vulnerable?"

Rolli leaned forward. He spoke in a hushed voice, "This piece is different. He cares about it. Failure with this won't just break his back—it will break his heart."

"What does he call it?" asked Steele.

"*Messiah.*"

When the announcement appeared in *The Daily Advertiser*, some were surprised, but not all. It was a curious announcement in that the performance being advertised had no specific name. The listing was more a description than it was a title. Few recognized Handel's aim. Only those people at the extreme ends of the Handelian scale, those who either adored him or despised him, pieced together what Handel was up to. He was rightfully cautious, knowing that even the disposition of London would be far more critical than Dublin. It was entirely possible that the Bishop of London might declare a work titled *Messiah* to be unfit for the playhouse.

Despite Handel's reticence to introduce the new oratorio so soon, the reception it had received in Ireland was enough to persuade him to proceed regardless of his trepidation. But still, he was cautious. In not calling the piece by its title, he hoped to avoid undue attention to the subject matter without the transcendent support of the music. Hopefully, any zealots who might be offended solely by the name would be so elevated by the cumulative experience that their pious minds might be put at ease. Thus was it announced:

Covent Garden.
By Subscription. The Ninth Night.
At the Theatre-Royal in Covent-Garden,
Wednesday next, will be perform'd
A New Sacred Oratorio.
A Concerto on the Organ,
And a Solo on the Violin by Mr. Dubourg.
Tickets will be sold on Tuesday next, at Mr. Handel's
house on Brook Street. The Galleries will be open'd
at Four o'clock. Pit and Boxes at Five.

For the Benefit and Increase of a Fund establish'd
for the Support of Decay'd Musicians, or their
Families.

As in Dublin, the majority of the proceeds were for charity. The day
was set for the London debut: March 23, 1743. To Handel's surprise and
delight, both King and Prince secured boxes for the performance. With
the coming of Easter, many attributed the Royal interest to be more
political than musical; regardless of the reason, they came. No one was
more surprised to see both George and son in the same room as was
Handel. Since his return, he had heard rumor of a reconciliation between
the two but had not fully believed it until now. He hoped that neither
would be disappointed. The balance of the audience was an eclectic and
unusual group, which included the full range from friend to foe. Mrs.
Delaney sat only a few rows ahead of Steele and Addison. Baron
Kilmanseck's box was directly across the hall from Madame Hervey's box.

Handel led from his place at the front of the orchestra. He nervously watched for feedback from the audience, but it was difficult to discern whether the general attitude was one of solemnity or apathy. He took
heart in the reactions offered up by the King, who appeared genuinely
pleased. The King watched with great interest as the performance moved
through soloists and chorus numbers. He sat forward in his chair as the
chorus answered the solo "But Thou didst not leave His soul in hell" with
"Lift up your heads."

Throughout the performance, whenever the King seemed particularly charmed, glances flashed back and forth between Addison and Steele,
who sat in prominent seats in the middle section on the floor. Prince
Frederick saw them but did not acknowledge them.

Rolli was intensely interested in the reaction of the audience. He sat
next to Madame Hervey in the box that she had specifically picked for the
view that it offered. The full audience and stage could be seen from their
perch. She and Rolli could watch both the performance and patrons
simultaneously. While she busied herself watching the audience, Rolli fastened his eyes on Handel. His gaze would shift briefly to those seated
below, isolating faces in the crowd for their reaction to the sound, but
always, and with increasingly sustained looks, he would come back to
Handel.

As the music of the oratorio unfolded, one bar at a time, Rolli seemed at times oppressed, then moments later, calm and serene. His countenance undulated between awe and anguish so rapidly that the violent inner struggle that waged in his heart was visible through the window of his face. The more respect and reverence that the music seemed to exude from him, the more horrific the resulting rancor, which deepened the red in his cheeks each time the cycle turned. It was painfully obvious that Rolli was both venerating and vile in his thoughts. The King's expanding approbation acted as a catalyst in propelling Rolli's hatred past the point of rational thought. He became wretched to view, his entire face contorted and menacing; then slowly, like a healing balm, the music would draw the infection out of him, gently swabbing away the pus of pride. This was the music that he knew Handel had in him. This was the music he had hoped Handel would have created with his librettos but didn't. The injustice of it tortured him. To have music such as this publicly pushed in his face was the last and greatest humiliation. He could hardly endure it; he boiled in his seat like a steaming cauldron. Each note of sweet melody pricked at his soft ego like hot pins. Hervey gave up her sport of audience-watching once she became aware of Rolli's anger. She teased him with little comments designed to fuel his rising bile.

"The King appears pleased," she purred in his ear.

Rolli could sit no longer. He marched to the back of the box and paced in the doorway, wringing his hands in the black curtain at the box entrance. The shadow of the threshold darkened everything but the whites of his eyes. They darted around the theatre, always coming back to the conductor. Every minute seemed an hour to him. He wanted to leave but could not advance his thoughts into action. He had business to take care of after the concert to assure that there would not be a second performance.

The Glory of the Lord Shone
Round About Them

THE STREETS WERE THINNING OF PEOPLE AS THE PACKRAT made his way toward home for the night. It had been a good day by his standards. Noblemen were mocked, bread was procured, even the weather was tolerable. He walked with his usual bounce, happy to see another day end profitably. As he walked, a few coins jingled in his deep pocket, giving him added reason to keep his step vibrant. He loved that sound like few others. It was not that there was anything he needed so desperately as to require money, he just liked knowing he had it perchance an emergency should arise. Peter knew the purchasing power of it would probably never benefit him directly, so why not enjoy the sound and pleasure of having it for what little time he could.

"A good day, Lord. A very good day," he said to heaven. "But don't go thinkin' Ya' get all the credit. I did me part."

Peter walked a few more steps, then stopped.

"All right! So it was easy—and I'm certain Ya' had a hand in that, so I say, 'Thanks.'"

He smiled.

"I'd be willin' to give Ya' all the credit if Ya' just show me a sign that it was You. One more—a good one."

"Hey," a deep voice bellowed. "You best get out of the way."

The Packrat turned around to see a street vendor closing up his cart for the night. Peter didn't get out of the way. He stood right in the man's path staring wantonly at the last unsold peaches still remaining in the cart. The man saw the boy look back and forth at the remaining fruit.

"The answer is no," he said gruffly. "Move along."

"No?" quizzed Peter.

"That's right, the answer is no!"

"Ya' say no?"

"Yes."

"Right!" shot back Peter.

"What's right?" asked the vendor.

"Your answer."

"What answer?"

"Yes!" declared Peter.

"Yes, what?"

"Your answer, it's yes!"

The vendor shook his head, half in confusion and half amusement. The boy smiled with a face full of fun. The vendor couldn't help himself; a smile crept over his lips. When Peter saw it, he smiled even bigger.

"I've been outwitted by a—a rodent."

"I'm a cheap and easy blessin'; all I want is what won't last 'til tomorrow anyway."

"It'll all last."

"You'll sell a lot more tomorrow if ya' do," reassured Peter.

"You think so?"

"I'm certain of it."

"How so?"

"I will ask the Lord to move upon all who pass Ya' by to stop and buy peaches."

"And if I don't?"

"Ya' have no promise."

"And he listens to you—God, I mean?"

"So far." The boy reached in his pocket and jingled the coins for the vendor to hear. The man's eyebrows raised.

"Why don't you just buy the peaches?"

"Then it won't work. If I have to pay for 'em, God won't have any reason for helpin' ya'."

The vendor's deep laugh rebounded off the narrow walls of the street. The hearty exuberance of the man's rich voice made the boy smile again.

"I'll need to bring extra tomorrow," the man said, putting some peaches in a brown bag. "I'll be selling every peach I can fit on the cart, right?"

"You'll be packin' up early and headin' home."

The boy watched each of four peaches go into the bag. The man held them out. Just as Peter reached to take them, the vendor pulled them away.

"You won't forget our deal?"

"By tomorrow, He'll know your name by heart," Peter said with a nod heavenward.

The man handed the bag to him. The boy took them and skipped off down the street. The vendor called out from behind.

"Do you know my name? How will God know who to bless?"

There was no hesitation in the boy's answer.

"I'll tell Him, 'Mister Peach Man—the good one.'"

"You think He'll know which one?"

"How many can there be?" The boy shouted. He could hear the man's fifty-gallon-barrel laugh ring through the street. The rich, unrestrained sound of it made the Packrat laugh too.

Now, it was better than a good day, it was one of the best. Peter thought of the smiles that he would put on the faces of the little urchins when he would pull the sweet fruit from behind his back. Except possibly for bread, he couldn't think of a time that he had brought home such a fine prize. In fact, he was certain that neither of the rodents he cared for had ever tasted anything as delicious as what he had in the bag. The thought of their eyes widening as the juice dripped from their lips was pure delight. The new acquisition made the Packrat completely forget the coins tumbling in his pocket. The fruit was an even better prize to take to his hole. What made this take especially appealing was the pure size of it. On a typical day, he would rummage up for himself what he could as he went and save the bulk of the winnings for those who awaited his arrival home. Tonight, he had enough to share liberally and still have a peach left for himself. As far as Peter was concerned, even though money could buy food, having food far exceeded having money. One was a means to an end, the other was the end. There was so little beyond sustenance that the boy cared about or needed that the thought of doing anything else with money completely eluded him. Like all those with whom he associated, he had but one need and each day was spent in the pursuit of it.

Peter walked briskly; he was already on to his next step before the full weight of his foot could hit the ground. He had no reason to dally since his hands were full of everything he wanted. The day was growing bluer with each passing minute. It was the cool hour of change from day to night. There were still a few in the street, but the vast majority of those who tread the cobbles by day were already gone. Those who remained were putting the finishing touches on shutting down for the evening.

"Open" signs in storefronts were flipped to "Closed." The unmistakable clicking of door locks and windows were all around like crickets in an abandoned hay barn. As the night came on, the dark sky seemed to suck the sound from the streets, revealing the subtle tones of life which go unheard throughout the day. This hour and the hour of sunrise were the times of day that Peter loved best. He could not only see, but he could hear too. There were still loud distractions from those who were tardy in their day-ending drills, but for the most part, things were quieting.

It took time for his ears to adjust to the lack of noise. On especially noisy days, his ears never fully cleared, but rang well into the night. But usually, within a few minutes his ears would acclimate to the quiet. He could then hear through closed doors. He chuckled at the talk and singing from pubs and taverns. Occasionally, if he caught wind of something newsworthy, he would stand outside the pub doors and listen. This was usually how he kept informed on current events. Of course, the information came thickly coated with editorial opinion, but he still had that amazing quality of youth: the innate ability to chip away the unwanted shell of nonsense and expose the nut of common sense. But he didn't pause at any doors this day, as he was certain there could be no bigger news than the kind of day that he had already had. The Packrat had absolutely no intention of veering away from his course home for any reason, until he heard a different sound—the distant sound of music.

He stopped the moment his ears first caught the sound of it. At first, he was not even certain he had heard anything at all. He strained his ears in the direction from which it had come, but it was gone.

He started on his way home again, then heard it a second time.

He stopped.

He held his breath, hoping to eliminate any distraction from what he thought he had heard.

He waited.

There it was—music. The strains reverberated back and forth down the walls of the street and finally into his ears. It was unmistakable. And what was even more remarkable, it was strangely familiar to him. In his mind he hummed the melody as though he somehow knew or felt it—he was not sure which. Either way, he seemed to know where the melody was leading. Had the music stopped, he could have finished the line. When the sound would diminish, his mind would continue the melody until it once again swelled loud enough for him to hear; the two would meet in the same place. He knew this music, and he knew he must find it.

He hurried through the streets, trying his best to follow the sound, but it was difficult. He would advance in one direction, listening carefully as he went. If the sound grew softer, he would retrace his steps and try a different direction until it began to get louder. He proceeded in this manner for some time, trying desperately to find the source of the music. The echo of it in the streets was confusing. Several times he would come around a corner fully expecting to be close enough to behold the source, only to find that he had entered a long, narrow street with high walls wherein the echo was unusually bright.

He kept going. Little by little he began to hear the clear sound of voices singing. He stopped and listened, trying to get his bearings. As he listened, he reviewed in his mind his location and what possible concert venues might be close. Then, all at once it hit him. His eyes lit up; he was only a few blocks from Covent. On numerous prior occasions, he had witnessed large gatherings of carriages and people at Covent. He remembered music coming from within the building while he robbed freely without. It was easy pickings, since those who attended the concerts were not only more deeply-pocketed but also more careless. He couldn't believe he had not thought of it sooner.

His steps were now certain. He knew the area well and knew the quickest way to Covent Garden. He passed down two long alleys, taking minutes off his walk, as opposed to staying on the street. He climbed a short wall between apartments, then dropped off the backside. He appeared out from a small courtyard into full view of the scene.

Carriages were lined down the street in front of him. Footmen and drivers alike milled about the carriages, waiting to take home their employers. Beyond them rose the steps to the theatre. The huge lobby area leading into the theatre shone brightly. Doormen were positioned at the entrance; other than that, the doors were empty. Peter could hear much from his place across the street, but still he wanted to be closer. As he surveyed the area, he tried to imagine the looks of the man he could hear singing from within.

"Large," he whispered through his teeth, "round-faced and large."

Peter proceeded forward. The words that the man sang were understandable. Peter thought them curious.

"'Thou shalt dash them in pieces like a potter's vessel,'" he said aloud. "Dash who in pieces?"

Still, it was not the words that had drawn him this far—it was the music. The song ended. Peter paused.

What he heard next sent shivers up his spine. The full orchestra began to play something that pierced his soul with absolute certainty. He stood erect, his heart pounding within him. With one clear word from the chorus, he understood.

"'Hallelujah.'"

The sound reached the very center of his heart. His mind was immediately taken back to a certain night, over a year before, when this same sound had seized hold of his soul, never to let it go. In his mind's eye he could see a lone stump sitting in the dark, the faintly lit window, the perfect moon. The music of that night changed him forever; he knew not exactly how or why, but it had changed him. That same music now echoed out of the hall before him.

Like nothing he had ever wanted before, he wanted to be inside. He walked straightway to the door. As he passed a playbill hanging on a post in front of the theatre, he pulled it from the nail and stared at it. Even though he could hardly read, it had tremendous meaning to him. He did not drop it, but carefully folded the paper announcing the sacred oratorio and slid it into the pocket with the coins.

He climbed the stairs, completely absorbed in the music. Just as he was about to pass through the open door, someone caught him by the shoulder.

"Where do you think you're goin'?"

The Packrat looked up into the stern face of the head usher.

"Inside," Peter said.

"Have a ticket?"

Peter thought briefly.

"I have a peach," he said, reaching a hand in the bag.

"A peach is not a ticket."

"It can be for a hungry doorman."

"Out! Stay out," the usher snapped, pushing the Packrat away. He stood between the boy and the door.

"But I must see. I must go in, just for a moment."

"Go away! You'll offend the patrons."

With his head drooping, the Packrat plodded away and around the corner of the building. Just beyond the corner he noticed a dark window with a cement eave over it. He moved into the shadows, only to appear several seconds later with something in his hand.

"You should have taken it when I offered it the first time," shouted the Packrat, his mouth dripping and full. Suddenly, out of nowhere, a mostly eaten peach slammed into the side of the usher's head. Wet peach flesh covered his face; the pit left a red welt on his cheek. Peter burst into laughter, then leaped around the dark corner of the building. He watched from his dark hiding place by the window as the legs of the doorman ran by. Once his footsteps died away, Peter was back out and moving along the outer wall. He peered around the area one last time before disappearing through the open front door, unseen.

He quickly moved across the lobby area and down the hall to the back of the theatre. The music crescendoed with each step. Exultant "hallelujahs" resonated through the hall—and through him. Never had sound so permeated his very being. It felt to Peter that unseen hands were all about him, pulling him toward the source. He yielded himself entirely to the enticment, feeling as though his chest could not contain his soul. The simple majesty of the melody had touched him as he sat outside the upper window on Brook Street, but he was incapable of imagining that the full fleshing of it would sound like this.

He came through the back arched doorway of the theatre. The entire audience, orchestra, and chorus opened to him as a mountain of music and song. He stood reverently, his face shining.

Suddenly, without any warning, he witnessed that which he could never have dreamed. The King, a man the Packrat would never have imagined he would ever see, stood from his seat in an unprecedented display of sanction. Respectfully, the entire crowd rose to their feet in unison. Even Prince Frederick rose from his chair. As the grand chorus continued, the Packrat, a lowly urchin destined to live out his days on the street, stood tall among kings and princes.

From his perch, Rolli looked on in desperation, his spirit torn between the bitterness of what might have been and the splendor of what he was now beholding. When he seemed but a breath away from standing himself, he pushed through the box curtains and left the auditorium.

When the chorus ceased, the King sat. All the audience did likewise. Only then did the Packrat become aware of where he was. He moved against the wall to not draw attention to himself. He determined it best to leave. When he was about to step back out to the hall, he could hear someone coming. Peter slid back against the wall to let the intruder pass. He watched the shadow of a body pass by. The moment he saw him, he recognized the man from the window at Lincoln's Inn and the incident in the street near James. The man seemed none-the-more happy now than he did then. Peter saw a gleam of light shine on something in the man's hand. Peter did not emerge from his hiding place until he was certain that the man had left the theatre.

When the music started again, Peter was glad. The song would not only hide any noise he might make, but it would also take people's attention forward to the stage. As soon as the way was clear, he slid down the hall and out the door. No one saw him leave.

Where Is Thy Sting

THE THEATRE EMPTIED SLOWLY AND ORDERLY. WELL OVER an hour had passed since the last sustained note was ended with a flip of the conductor's hand. Only Handel remained. He walked back and forth across the stage in quiet contemplation. Like an anxious father waiting for the sound of a crying child to know that the miracle of birth had taken place, Handel paced, unclear of what exactly it was he was waiting for.

He rolled over in his mind the decision he had just executed. Was it right? He knew not. What he did know was that the decision was irretrievable. He had let the child go, and, whether he liked it or not, it was now in the public domain. Before, it had belonged solely to him, but that would never be the case again. He had slowly eased his fingers from around it, note by note, until he had lost grip and it was out into the world.

The first to hear it was Mrs. Cibber, then the cast in Dublin, then audiences in Dublin, more audiences, and now, London. The longer he paced, the more he felt like a mother waiting for the child to return from the first day of school, simultaneously wanting and not wanting to know the outcome. Doubt crept into his mind as he considered the potential consequences of the concert. He wished he could stop the spiderlegs of sound that he had sent off in every direction. He was certain that, even now while he paced, conversations in quiet corners were discussing the Sacred Oratorio.

The thought of this composition being talked about by false tongues and grappled by foul hands made him sick. The entire experience of writing it had been a holy one. It had been a creative explosion by any standards, but more importantly, a spiritual reformation. How he wished he had been content to keep it in the drawer where it belonged. In truth, he didn't need to perform it. The other oratorios he had tried were enthusiastically accepted. He wasn't forced under duress to try the piece. The decision was clearly personal; he himself had determined to give it to the world. He chastised himself for his impatience and shortsightedness. The most sacred of utterances are prayers of the heart, spoken in silence during one's darkest hour. Such was *Messiah*.

"It is a prayer which never should have been uttered aloud," he said in a quiet voice. "I have prayed as the pharisees, out in the open, on the street corner, for all to see.

"But then, why would God allow me to hear it alone? Is it not meant for others to hear also?"

Another thought came into his mind. Perhaps he had acted just as had been expected of him. Indeed, he had been cautious. His actions had not been rash in any way. The decisions to proceed in both Dublin and London were scrutinized carefully. He could not deny the whisperings in his heart that beckoned him to share the gift. Was it probable that God would grant it unto him and then not want it to be heard? Could it be that it was just for him and not for the benefit of anyone else? He was unsure if things were happening the way they were for a reason. Uncertainty was the only thing he could count on with certainty.

Two more performances were scheduled for the next night and three nights hence. He wondered if he should cancel them now and not proliferate the mistake. Perhaps there was still time to stem the tide if he acted with haste, but that would be an open admission of failure. He wondered if the harshest of criticism would be curbed by the fact that he would not personally profit from it, but the moment the thought entered his mind he dismissed it. His motivation for performing the concert for charity had nothing to do with stemming aspersion. The choice simply to give, as it had been given to him, was made long before the time came to perform it. He did not believe it was his to profit from. The decision was one from which he never strayed.

As he contemplated, Handel walked past the curtain to the harpsichord. He did not hear a man come out of the darkness behind the curtain and follow him. Handel sat down at the instrument and stared at the score before him. The shadow approached slowly until it stood only a few steps behind him.

From behind a dark cloak, an arm began to rise, revealing a long silver letter opener in a clenched hand. When Handel stirred, the hand dropped behind the cloak. Momentarily, the dark shadow eased closer to the prey. When Handel's back was within reach, the hand began to rise a second time. Before the blade began to appear, Handel spun around. The man froze. Handel looked directly into the eyes of Rolli. He studied him, trying his best to ascertain his intent. Rolli did not move. At long length, in spite of Rolli's menacing and taut face, Handel's penetrating stare softened.

"Antonio—"

"No!" screamed Rolli. "You cheated me. You had music like this still in you. Why not let me share in it?"

"I gave what I had at the time," Handel said.

"You gave nothing. You made a mockery of me and my words."

"I had nothing else to give."

"You had this." Rolli slashed at the music in Handel's hand and ran the blade through the pages. "Don't mock me again by saying you had nothing left in you."

Handel looked at the silver opener and the torn pages. He was trapped between feelings of vindication and pity. Before him was the man that he had had the hardest time forgiving in his hour of atonement. He had learned to despise Rolli like few others. Of all his enemies, Rolli was most pernicious. He had hurt Handel in places that only an insider could. Others had harmed him from without, but, of all his enemies, Rolli was the lone betrayer. He was the one who had destroyed the set of *Deidamia*. He was the owner of the third key to Lincoln's Inn theatre. Handel intrinsically knew that this was the great and most difficult test of his resolve to leave bitterness behind. He knew himself well enough to know that he needed to confirm his decision with action before he had time to reacquaint himself with the details of Rolli's treachery. He stepped forward.

"Write another libretto," he petitioned Rolli.

"It's too late!"

"Antonio."

Rolli pulled the letter opener from the score and fingered the hard steel edge. His hand tightened around the handle. He began to raise the blade over his head. Handel could see the sharp tip quiver above him. At the moment Handel was certain the blade would fall, Rolli turned and ran across the stage and out the door.

Learn of Him

THE KNOCK ON THE DOOR WAS LOUD AND LONG.

"Who is it?" asked Rachel, holding a small baby's blanket in her white hands.

"Peter."

Rachel folded the blanket and laid it carefully on the straw bed at her side. The moment she unlocked the door, the Packrat was through it.

"Come with me."

"You haven't been around for a few days," said Rachel, not really hearing what he had said.

"Come with me," Peter urged with uncharacteristic firmness. He did not sit, but stood, staring her in the face.

"Where?"

"To the theatre—Covent Garden."

"Why?"

"The music I heard below the window on Brook Street—I heard it again tonight."

"At the theatre?"

"Tomorrow night it's to be performed again."

The Packrat took a peach from his bag and laid it on the table.

"I can't. I must be up very early for work. I can't go to the theatre," Rachel said, shaking her head and turning away from him.

"Come with me—listen outside."

"I can't."

"It will give you hope."

Rachel's head fell forward to her chest. The Packrat's voice softened into pleading. He walked to her, taking her hand and turning her back around.

"Your heart will change, come with me."

Rachel picked up the folded blanket and wrapped her hands in it.

"I can't—I can't go," Rachel's voice was broken and empty. There was nothing more Peter could say, nothing more he could do. He slowly walked to the door, then paused and looked back before leaving.

"Come with me."

Rachel stared at the blanket. She continued long after the boy was gone.

Cast Away Their Yokes

————————

Handel sat at his desk, the score of *Messiah* spread before him. Charles Jennens was bent over him, scanning the music with his finger. Jennens was up before dawn and on the road to make sure that his arrival at Handel's home was early. He too had been at the previous night's concert. What he had heard kept him awake most of the night. When he finally made up his mind to do something about it, he woke his servants, had the horses hitched to the carriage, and was off at dawn. Both Handel and Peter LeBlonde were quite taken aback at his early, unannounced arrival. He was greeted, offered tea—which he refused—and within a matter of minutes was about his business with Handel.

Handel submitted to Jennens' request to show him the score. He laid out the manuscript on the desk where it was written. Jennens stood over him, frantically flipping back and forth between pages. At length he shook his head, flipped back to the first page and pointed a sharp finger at the overture.

"Start here," Jennens said sternly. Handel did not move. He sat looking at the music before him. Jennens reached forward, putting his finger on the register.

"E minor? Have you lost your mind completely? This isn't Samson, not David. It is the Christ, Jesus. The overture must be triumphant— majestic. You've made a dirge of it. Are we heathens? Pick up the pen!"

Handel's hand slid across the paper, but that was all. Jennens's voice loudened.

"Pick up the pen. You can't perform it again as it is. What of the transformation from the E minor of the overture to E major for the recitative? Where is the minuet?"

Handel's eyes moved around the room. He looked at the window and then the instrument on the other side of the room. His eyes shifted to the chair by the door. He glanced at the small painting that hung on the wall opposite him. His gaze went back to the page. Jennens reached over him, picked up the quill, and placed it in Handel's fingers.

"Change it," he said.

Handel's fingers tightened around the quill. The tip of the feather snapped forward. Jennens leaned back in anticipation. Handel dipped the quill in the inkwell, then positioned it over the first bar of music. The point touched the paper, but that was all. He pulled back his hand, then laid the quill down on the desk. Jennens was aghast. His head rolled to the side as he audibly moaned his disbelief. He walked around to the front of the desk, where he could look into the face of Handel.

"This is an outrage. Not only do you scorn me, you scorn that which is most sacred. I demand that you correct your error."

"I can't," whispered Handel.

"You what? You can't? Yes, you can and you will. Pick up the pen."

"It is as it should be," said Handel.

"Have you gone mad? It must be changed. I demand you change it."

"No! No, I say. I will not change a note," Handel shouted. "It is exactly as it should be. Exactly as it came to me."

The sheer force of Handel's words sent Jennens back a step. He stood mouth open, stunned at Handel's obstinacy. He had expected some resistance, possibly even an argument, but nothing like what he had just witnessed. Handel took several deep breaths, each longer than the previous. When he spoke again, his voice was again steady and calm.

"'He was a man of sorrows, acquainted with grief; He was bruised for our iniquities, wounded for our transgressions. Thy rebuke hath broken His heart. He is full of heaviness. He looked for some to have pity on Him, but there was no man, neither found He any to comfort Him.' You, better than anyone, should understand; you compiled the Scripture. Are they just words, or are they prophecy? You tell me." Handel rose to his feet, holding the first page of the score in his hand.

"The overture, the beginning—the very first notes any ear will hear—shouldn't they, more than any that follow, be true? This, Charles...this is a story of sacrifice, divine sacrifice. Sacrifice that cost the best blood this world has ever known."

Handel's voice broke. He reached out a steadying hand to the desk. Carefully, he settled back down in his chair. It was a long time before he spoke again. Jennens watched as Handel closed his eyes in reflective contemplation. The muscles in his face and forehead relaxed. When he again spoke, his voice was solemn.

"It was painful to write. It was a blessed sacrifice. Any sacrifice of any real worth breaks your heart."

Handel opened his eyes.

"*Messiah* is the story of the greatest of all sacrifices. It is a celebration of hope. I'm sorry, it isn't mine to change."

Jennens looked at Handel, then at the music. He nodded silently. He turned and walked to the door, pausing in the open threshold.

"Will you consider some of the other things we discussed. I do believe they are good suggestions."

When Jennens was safely seen to his carriage, Peter LeBlonde entered the study. Handel looked at him with a face full of anticipation. Peter simply shook his head.

"Nothing," he said.

"No handbills, no critiques?" asked Handel.

"No."

"And nothing in any of the papers?"

Peter shook his head.

Handel pondered. He glanced at the music, then up at Peter.

"It is as though it never happened."

"Perhaps they are waiting for another performance before making analysis," said Peter.

It was true. There was nothing in *The Daily Advertiser* regarding the first performance. No handbills were printed denouncing or upholding the concert. No editorials. No revues. Even Addison and Steele at *The Spectator* were curiously silent. It was literally as if the performance had never happened. The response was in direct contrast to what he had expected. Not that he expected the kind of glorious reception he had received in Dublin, but he did expect something. Handel assumed there would be some talk about the oratorio; whether good or ill was the only question. But silence was peculiar. He had prepared himself for just about anything—except nothing. The complete lack of response was the one scenario for which he was totally unprepared.

He picked up the quill and began flipping through pages, making small notes here and there. In some sections, though only a few, he made minor revisions relative to his discussion with Jennens.

Behold, I Tell You a Mystery

WIND BUFFETED LONDON THROUGHOUT THE EVENING.
Any music that escaped the hall at Covent Garden was quickly whisked away
by the fervent breeze. The March gale had more of winter in it than spring.
It lashed the streets of London, driving back indoors any who might have
ventured outside. The cold in the wind felt more than a month late. There
was a dampness in the chill, which penetrated the deepest of wools. Even
the theatre manager stoked the furnace fires equal to a January night for the
concert. It was not the strength of the wind which created the discomfort,
but the teeth of it, which bit through any protection. Even the theatre walls
seemed porous on this night; they held out the bluster, but not the cold.

Drivers broke with social convention and waited inside carriages.
Doormen tended to their duties from inside the lobby. There were even

a few empty seats in the hall from elderly patrons who could not muster the will to go out on such a dismal night. The entire day had been overcast. The wind began in the early afternoon; by evening, it was at gale force. All boats came in off the water and were safely moored by mid-afternoon. It was not a question of whether rain would follow, but when.

The concert was well underway when the rain did finally arrive in one great torrential wave, drenching all in its path. Thunder announced the arrival with earth-shaking explosions. Horses whinnied in fright at the first bursts. A few minutes after the rain started, the wind subsided some, and the rain fell in steep angles from the sky. There was little if any protection from the elements.

Water poured down rain gutters, almost instantly filling rain barrels to overflowing. The large roof gullies atop the theatre funneled water down the corner gutters of the hall in streams. It cascaded down stairs and along sidewalks. While music played from within, chaos reigned without. Unlike the night before, when strains echoed out the open doors and down the streets of London, any sound that might have escaped on this night was swallowed by the storm. No one who didn't have a seat inside the great hall could have heard a single note—except one.

Hidden under the crude shelter of a low window eave sat a boy. He could not fully fit under the narrow overhang. Water dripped down his legs from the knee down. He sat quietly, huddled close to the window, which was propped halfway open for venting. Rain pooled on the pavement around his sopping wet shoes. A fall of water cascaded off the roof to an overflowing barrel not fifteen feet from where he sat. Frequent drops slid down the front of the eave and fell on his face and neck. And yet, there was not one person sitting comfortably within the theatre who heard more.

August 30, 1743

Mr. Edward Holdsworth—Richmond.
Dear Edward,

I shall shew you a collection I gave Handel, called Messiah, which I value highly, and he has made a fine entertainment of it, though not near so good as he might and ought to have done. I have with great difficulty made him correct some of the grossest faults in the composition, but he has retained his overture obstinately, in which there are some passages far unworthy of Handel, but much more unworthy of the Messiah.

I also thought the conclusion of the oratorio not grand enough; though if that were the case 'twas his own fault, for the words would have bore as grand musick as he could have set them to: but this "Hallelujah," grand as it is, comes in very nonsensically, having no manner of relation to what goes before. And this is the more extraordinary, because he refused to set a hallelujah at the end of the first chorus in the oratorio, where I had placed one and where it was to be introduced with the utmost propriety, upon a pretense that it would make the entertainment too long.

I could tell you more of his maggots; but it grows late and I must defer the rest till I write next, by which time, I doubt not, more new ones will breed in his brain.

Your most humble friend,
Charles Jennens
Gopsal

All We Like Sheep

"IT WAS SIMPLY NOT TO MY LIKING," SAID ONE.

"The King was obviously moved to his feet—and the Prince; they were together in the same room!" said another.

"The last time that happened was when the King and Caroline conceived."

It was common knowledge that the joke was more true than false, which made it all the more amusing. Even Madame Hervey chuckled as she listened to the central conversation of the party that she hosted. As if in direct contrast to the silence following the first performance, the floodgates of criticism burst open after the subsequent concerts. In turn, each of her guests offered up their assessment of Handel's oratorio.

"It lacked direction. The soloists just stood there."

"So little to look at."

"An oratorio is to be heard."

"But so many choruses?"

"And what of the libretto?"

"Jennens!"

"Of course."

"It was entirely scriptural. Jennens took every word straight from the Bible."

This was the cue Hervey was waiting for.

"Was it entertainment or a sermon?"

"So speaks the devil's advocate," an older guest said with a smile.

"I am his handmaiden," Hervey said, then asked the question a second time. "Was it entertainment or a sermon?"

"What's the difference?" commented one young man, hoping to draw some needed attention, but all dismissed it without so much as a nod. While most contemplated the inquiry, one guest took the opportunity to pick up *The Daily Advertiser* from the tray at her side, and read aloud.

"'Cease, zealots, cease to blame those heavenly lays,

For seraphs fit to sing Messiah's praise,

Nor for your trivial argument assign

The theatre not fit for praise divine!

These hallow'd lays to music give new grace,

To virtue awe, and sanctify the place,

To harmony like His celestial power is given

To exalt the soul from Earth, and make of hell a heaven.'"

"'An oratorio is either an act of religion or it is not. If it is an act of religion, I ask if the playhouse is a fit temple to perform it, or a company of players fit ministers of God's word,'" read Rolli from *The Spectator*, standing atop a chair in the center of the tavern. He looked around at the large group assembled, pausing between lines for impact. He continued in an even louder voice.

"'If it is not an act of religion, why call it 'A Sacred Oratorio?' It is either one or the other.'" Rolli dropped the paper from his hand. When it hit the floor, the din in the room swelled. He shouted over the top of the noise.

"And who determines for us what is sacred and what isn't—Handel? Do players now speak for God?"

"Some players think they are God," came a shout from the back.

"That is the difference between God and Handel. God does not think He is Handel."

Uproarious laughter ensued.

"'A Sacred Oratorio?'" chided Rolli. "He doesn't even call it by name for fear of stirring up the zealots."

"So will ministers now sing their sermons?" asked a bullish man.

"Who will receive confessions?" asked another.

"The actors," came a shout from the corner.

"Perhaps we'll now see comedies in the chapels," called out another voice.

"Even I would go to church," smiled one drunken sot, leaning over the bar. The entire group bellylaughed. As the laughter subsided, a stout man at the bar turned to Rolli.

"You say he doesn't dare call it by name. What is the name?"

The room quieted. Rolli did not answer immediately, but looked around from face to face, as if he were about to share some great secret. He spoke in a hushed voice, but all heard him.

"*Messiah.*"

"He blasphemes," gasped a voice. No one was exactly sure who had said it, but it was clear that almost all agreed.

"Who has seen it besides you?" the stout man asked Rolli. Before he could answer, an elderly man who had been silently sitting on a chair in the corner stood to his feet.

"I have," he said boldly. All eyes left Rolli and moved in the direction from which the sound had come.

"I've seen it. I was at Covent Garden for the first performance."

"Tell us. Tell us," said several voices.

Silence fell on the room.

"I have heard great music—even sublime music. I've heard music fit for princes, for kings. I have heard music fit for any monarch. But that night, for the first time in my life, I heard music fit for God."

Rolli climbed down from his chair.

Thou Art My Son

HANDEL COULD FEEL THE FLESH OF HIS CHEEKS AND FOREhead become thermal. His neck tightened inside the collar of his alreadytight shirt. Waves of heat emanated from his skin like the hot summer sun on black cobbles. He had endured criticism before, but never did it feel as deep or painful as it did now. His skin stung; his bones seemed to ache. His head pounded with the beat of his heart.

During the days of opera, when critics had openly lashed out at him, pride had dulled his pain like a stiff shot of rum. He hardened his heart against the cutting words of the critics by fighting off their attacks with counterattacks. When London apostatized from Handel, he reacted by spurning their comprehension of music. When they snubbed him as artist, he scorned them as listeners. Contempt bred contempt.

But concerning *Messiah*, he felt as if his very soul was under siege. The criticism he now received seemed to be aimed directly at the place he was most vulnerable: his intent. He felt violated—as if the enemy had sent spies to ascertain where the defenses of his heart could be most easily breached. Words of criticism felt like wounds inflicted from within. There was no protection from the hurt nor numbing of the pain that he felt with regard to his sacred oratorio. The tools of retaliation that he had employed earlier in his career were no longer in his toolbox. Not only did the criticism feel different, Handel himself was different.

Peter LeBlonde wasn't sure of the nature of the problem, but that didn't matter. He needed only to hear the door slam and Handel's feet on the stairs to know that things were not as they should be. He listened to the heavy steps ascend the last few stairs. Peter followed the sound up the stairs.

The door of the study slammed open, jostling everything on the walls around it. In walked Handel, carrying the olive wood box under his arm. Several feet behind was Peter, quickly closing the distance between them. Even though Handel had not seen his servant, he knew he was closing in fast. Handel began talking the moment he entered the room.

"What the Devil was I up to? I know better. They want entertainment only, nothing more. I should not have performed it. It was foolish!"

He pulled out the drawer of his desk, nearly jerking it off the guides. He dropped the box in the drawer, then slammed it shut. He spun around, his face flushed, and collapsed into his chair. Peter was now in the middle of the room, bent over, wheezing, his hands on his knees. Handel did not see him. His head was down also, buried in his hands. He rubbed his forehead in frustration.

"It was a mistake to try it here. I should have just let it be. I've done more damage than good."

"Some heard, sir. Dublin heard," Peter rattled out between breaths.

"I should have left it at that. I'm a fool."

"Some here also. Someone heard it here," Peter coughed. He balanced himself by leaning heavily against the back of a chair. He finally fell into it, his face white, beads of sweat standing out from his brow. Peter lowered his head between his legs to allow the blood to come back in. Handel still had not seen him. He pulled back open the drawer and stared at the box.

"It's not meant to be performed. It's not meant to be heard. Its purpose for being written was accomplished the moment it was finished." Handel looked up. Peter was arched low over his knees. His face was pale as death, his eyes dilated and distant. Handel jumped to his feet and ran to Peter's side. He knelt ground alongside him, then took Peter's hand in his. It was clammy and cold.

"Peter—are you all right? Are you ill?"

"It will soon pass," choked Peter, but Handel knew the seriousness of the bout was being underestimated on his account. Peter took several deep breaths before lifting his head and looking at Handel. A slight hint of pink was coming back to his temples and upper cheeks.

"I must have come up the stairs too fast," he said, trying his best to smile.

"You need rest. Let me help you to your room," beckoned Handel.

"No. I'm well past the worst of it. I'll be fine if I can take just a moment longer. I'm sorry for the inconvenience."

Handel started back to his feet. Peter gripped his hand before he could stand fully.

"It's not the voices of critics that matter. They look for clay feet on any who dare greatness. They have their reward." His words were interrupted by a short burst of coughing. Peter released Handel's hand as his body convulsed. When the coughs ceased, he continued, "I alone witnessed the devotion, the anguish, the effort. For twenty-three days you were consumed by a fire that burned from within. If you truly believe it worthy of Him whose name it bears, it is a victory."

By the time he had finished, most of the color had returned to his face. Peter stood up slowly, allowing time for his feet to become securely planted before putting his full weight on them. He bowed, then left the room.

Handel rose and walked back to his chair. Several minutes passed in quiet contemplation. In time, he reached down and pushed the drawer shut, then pulled it right back open. On the lid of the box he read the inscribed letters: G.F.H. He slid the top back and looked at the top page of the overture.

"Perhaps Thou hast a different purpose in mind. I shall listen more closely."

He watched the word, *Messiah*, darken and disappear as he slid the lid back on the box and closed the drawer. He pressed his eyelids down and took a deep breath. He held his breath long before exhaling. Handel stood from his desk and walked to the door of the study. Before leaving the room, he glanced to the side and saw the wooden side chair sitting by the door. He pictured Peter there, nodding restlessly through a long night, a blanket over his shoulder and knees. How terribly uncomfortable the chair looked, with its straight back, flat seat, and no arms. He sat down in the chair, shifting back and forth, trying to find the most tolerable and comfortable position. There was none. Finally, after several futile adjustments, he gave up trying. He noticed the desk across the room. He tried to picture himself as Peter had seen him, sitting hour after hour, sheets of music spread across the desk. He noticed the stalagmite below the candlestick where wax dripped down night after night. He saw the quill lying motionless alongside the open inkwell. In his mind he could see the tip spin in small circles as notes were inked on the page.

His eyes moved to the window, growing dark in the lessening day. He again imagined what he must have looked like to Peter, standing in silhouette against the bright background, his hand moving ever so slightly in time with the music in his head.

His eyes moved farther—to the harpsichord. Echoes of the notes he played during the long hours of writing reverberated across his memory. Handel scanned the walls, the books on the shelves, the wooden floor.

Finally, he gazed at the painting, which he had silently studied so many times and in every condition of the day. He envisioned himself standing in front of the depiction of Christ, struggling to understand better the things of which he wrote. Often he had stood there contemplating the one question that still haunted him the most: Was the music worthy of Him whose name it bore? The harsh answer to that question was now painfully clear.

"No," he said, putting his face in his hands. He had failed. There was no denying the fact that he had tried and faltered with the one thing that was most meaningful to him. In the depths of his heart he had hoped that it would be the key to his emancipation. As much as he might have tried to conceal his wish for validation, the latent desire was irresistible. In light of the recent events, his most personal and guarded intentions were glaringly obvious.

In his impatience he had succumbed to his desire for restitution. The success of Dublin had jaundiced his judgment. He was careful, thoughtful—even prayerful—about his decision to perform the oratorio. The decision was confirmed with a feeling of peace and calmness. London was different.

He desired for his return to London to be triumphant. He subconsciously hoped to vanquish those who sought his ruin. Both Handel and the music he most cherished were felled by pride. Arrogance had dulled his ability to see things as they truly were. He had acted out of self-interest; he tried to use *Messiah* for personal gain. It was not money that he had desired, but the last word. He alone knew that he had selfishly sinned against the sacred endowment he had been given. Now he could only live with the terrible regret of the rash and irrevocable decision he had made without fully considering the outcome. When he thought of the closed box in the shut drawer, he realized that he had compromised *Messiah*'s chance to be a cause for good. He was certain he had cast his bread on the water prematurely, possibly robbing it of the potential he knew it had. In his anguish, he desperately hoped that at some future day he might be granted a second chance. He had learned much, but he was now more aware than ever that he had not learned all.

Brokenhearted and contrite, his mind caught hold on Christ. He remembered the merciful atonement that he had come to understand better through his own suffering. Suddenly, words began to take shape in his mind, words to which he had put song:

"'For unto us a Child is born.'"

"'Come unto me all ye that labour and are heavy laden, and I will give you rest.'"

"'And with His stripes we are healed.'"

"'The Lord hath laid on Him the iniquity of us all.'"

"'In Christ shall all be made alive.'"

"'Who is the King of glory.'"

"'Worthy is the Lamb that was slain, and hath redeemed us by His blood.'"

Handel dropped to his knees in front of the chair. He began to understand what he had not fully comprehended before. Through the experience of writing *Messiah*, he had come to know of Christ! But until this moment he had never fully grasped the eternal truth that he needed Christ each and every day of his life. He was a debtor in need of redemption. At long last, Handel finally understood that Christ was more than the Savior of mankind, He was his personal, living Savior. A spark of hope suddenly flashed bright in Handel's dark world of despair.

Humbly, he prayed for forgiveness. In a small and still voice, words came into his mind, they spoke comfort to his heart and sweet peace to his soul.

"Be still, and know that I am God."

At that moment, as surely as he knew he was alive, Handel knew that the time for *Messiah* was not yet; in God's due time the lid would be removed, and light would again fill the box and its contents. The joy of hope swept over him. The sudden and overwhelming sense of freedom that accompanied the feeling was remarkable. Handel no longer felt guilt. He no longer felt pain. Fear dissipated into the air as if blown away by a cleansing wind.

Finally, he truly understood the verse:

"'The chastisement of our peace was upon Him.'"

Handel then remembered the words of his servant Peter.

"Someone heard it here."

No truth spoken could have struck with more impact to Handel's soul. The moment he thought it, he knew it was true. It was performed so that someone could hear it, of that he was sure. It was not important for him to know whom—it didn't matter, but it did matter to God. Even in his frailty, his actions had been according to omniscient design. Handel knew there had been divine purpose in his performing the oratorio in London, not for Handel's purpose, but for God's.

Since by Man Came Death

THE PACKRAT VISITED RACHEL OFTEN, ALWAYS BRINGING with him a smile and a story. A typical visit was short—fifteen minutes at the most. His knock was instantly identifiable. The very sound of it made Rachel's heart leap within her. The second she swung open the door, he was through it and headed to the fire. At first, he held back until invited to the hearth, but Rachel had insisted on so many occasions that he finally heeded her admonition without waiting.

Most days, his voice chattered from the moment the door cracked open until it closed again upon his leaving. Rachel was grateful for the sound of his voice in the house. The noise of youth seemed to chase away the loneliness that beset the home. Even if it was only temporary, it was a welcome relief from the overwhelming silence that prevailed.

The Packrat's stories were most often about something funny he had witnessed in the street. Nobles were a favorite topic, as they were always doing something he deemed ridiculous. Vendors provided good material. Hardly a day went by that there wasn't an argument or more between two shouting vendors. But recently, his stories seemed to be centered on one theme. For weeks following the performance of the sacred oratorio, the Packrat talked about little else. He routinely talked about each of his favorite songs, doing his best to recount both the melody and words. What usually came out was skewed heavily on the side of music. At the behest of his friend James, Peter had joined the Cathedral Boys Choir. The Packrat loved what he learned. Using his newly found knowledge of song and score, he did his best to give Rachel a small taste of what he had seen and heard at Covent.

Rachel mostly listened. She said little, other than to answer his special questions, which were posed to her at some point during every visit. Even though the queries put to her were rote, she knew they were always sincere. Never did the Packrat put the questions to her halfhearted. His inquiries were repetitive, but they never lost their shine.

"Are ya' all right?" he always asked. Rachel could not remember a single time when the boy had moved on to the next question before he was satisfied with her answer. He truly wanted to know. If she avoided the question, he would not give her amnesty from answering, no matter how long the wait. Even if her reply was no more than a nod, there had to be affirmation before continuation. Once he was satisfied, the next query was posed.

"Is there anything I can do?" This query was most humbling to Rachel because of the absolute true-heartedness of it. No matter how many times it was asked, his desire to be of service was ever genuine. Occasionally Rachel would make a request, but most of the time her answer was simply to shake her head from side to side. Peter understood well that the vast majority of shakes meant "no," but there were some shakes that meant "yes." If he surmised that a shake meant "yes," he would press the issue further until she would confess her need. Such was the case with the letter that he had delivered to Jonathon. Rachel wrote it believing that her beloved would never read it. She had really never considered the idea of the Packrat stealing into the prison to deliver the letter. But one night when Peter asked his usual questions, the thought crossed her mind, and the Packrat sensed it. He insisted that Rachel confide in him the notion she had had. Once he got it out of her, he was supremely sorry he had been so insistent.

At first, Peter had agreed with her that going into the prison was a bad idea and completely out of the question. But like most moral imperatives he faced, it was impossible to forget. He finally took the letter just so he could rid himself of the thought of it.

It had been a feat of which he was justly proud, and he congratulated himself on his prowess as a sneak. At no time, however, did he mention to her the black tunnel in which he had hidden. It was a memory he deliberately tried not to remember. Whenever the thought of it came into his mind, he would hum one of the hymns he had been practicing in the choir. Replacing thoughts of the insipid hole with inspiring song was a strategy he often employed, and with much appreciated success. He was frightened enough when he was there, but to think back on it was terrifying. Like the sailor who escapes the Devil's squall without fully comprehending his miraculous deliverance until the storm has passed, Peter was more afraid of what might have happened in the diabolical hole after he was safely out. At the time he had entered, much of his wit was engrossed in hiding from the guards. Once outside, his brain was able to recall, with precision, every detail of the abyss. He did his best not to think of it. He avoided the slightest mention of the prison, as it always caused his mind to go straight to the black tunnel.

Because of this fear, when Peter asked Rachel if there was anything he could do, and she didn't shake her head "no," he expected the worst. He did not press her, as he usually did, but began to hum in his mind the first melody he could think of. Momentarily, Rachel did answer.

"There is something. Please—please go with me to the prison."

The boy's spirit cowered within him. The song he had been humming was gone. Before he knew the reason for the request, he assumed the worst.

"I can't go in there again," he said, backing toward the door.

"I would never ask it," said Rachel. "I just need someone with me when I go to ask forgiveness from the solicitor. I can't…I can't be alone."

"Why do ya' need me?"

Rachel did not answer. Peter was not certain what he could see behind Rachel's eyes, but it most resembled fear. At length, she spoke just one word:

"Please."

Early the following morning, Peter met Rachel at the designated place. They walked the last few blocks to the prison together. A simple greeting was all that was said between them. Normally, Peter would have talked incessantly, but he could see on Rachel's face that her thoughts were far away. He determined not to say or do anything that would require her mind to leave that distant place. The Packrat walked a half step behind Rachel. He had no mind to lead out in an undertaking he knew so little about.

When they came near the prison, Peter could see many other women queued into two lines near the gate. Rachel approached the group but did not encroach upon it. She stood away from the others, a satellite to the larger body. Peter stood faithfully at her side. They watched in silence as several solicitors passed among the women on their way to the gate. It was difficult for the Packrat to watch the proceeding. The sad faces of the sisters, wives, and mothers pained him. All he could think about was the men below, who knew nothing of the pathetic play unfolding above their heads. Peter had seen enough through the small hole in the bottom of the prison door to know that the only place more miserable than where he now stood was the underground cavern that held the men for whom these pitiful creatures petitioned.

After beholding several minutes of the disheartening scene, Peter looked up at the face of Rachel, fully expecting to see more of the same. Instead, what he saw was complete dispassion. She appeared to be neither seeing nor hearing the horror of the drama before her. Her eyes were fixed, her jaw set. Peter knew her too well to be misled into thinking what he saw was apathy; on the contrary, it was fierce self-control. Rachel was schooled in the desolate tutelage of injustice. Many times she had fallen prey by displaying her emotions prematurely. The mistake had cost her dearly on several occasions. Her naiveté was a severe disadvantage when it came to the ways of the world. Through the months of loneliness and being taken advantage of, Rachel learned the ropes of wretchedness. She became skilled at shielding her feelings from those who might search for a soft spot in her defense.

Rachel and Peter stood side by side for more than an hour. They watched from a distance as the steady stream of solicitors walking between the lines of women slowed to a trickle. Spaces began to appear in the lines as wives and daughters gave up hope and left. By the time the second hour passed, there were less than a dozen women remaining. Only then did Rachel step forward to the line, where she then continued to wait. Peter followed. Two more solicitors came to the gate, but neither was the man for whom she waited. The last of the women finally departed, leaving just Rachel and Peter at the gate of the prison with the guards. Another hour passed. Peter was pleased the crowd had dispersed and equally displeased that whatever Rachel had come for was still undone. Still he remained at her side. He could not think of a single time in his life when he had stood in one place so long, but he did not question her. Leaving was not an option. Because of his own situation, he had determined—long before he ever found himself here—that he would never be guilty of abandoning someone who was in need, no matter how difficult it might be for him.

When the guards could see that the two remaining petitioners had no intention of leaving, the guard with the least amount of tenure was sent to shoo them away. The inexperienced young prison employee walked up and stood before Rachel. She did not flinch.

"You need to leave now," he demanded.

"I've not completed my business here," replied Rachel with comparable firmness.

"What business?"

"Business with a certain solicitor."

"Which one?"

"I don't know his name."

"Was he not here?"

"No."

"Is there any feature you recall which would separate him from the others?"

"His face is evil."

"Many faces are evil."

"His is more evil than the others."

"Can you remember anything else?"

Rachel pictured in her mind the hideous face of the lawyer. She searched every repulsive feature in her mind, trying to find some characteristic that might distinguish him from the others. A sickening vision came to her. "He had ugly sores around his mouth."

The guard began to laugh, "If he's the one you're waiting for, I'm surprised you don't have sores around your mouth."

Rachel's face did not alter in the least. Upon seeing her steadiness, the young guard evened himself.

"He's dead. He went mad. They found him drowned in his own vomit."

Rachel flinched. Her equanimity finally faltered as she heard the news. Her next words were much thinner than the previous.

"He prosecuted my husband."

"Whatever that man did is done. There's no changing that."

"There must be some recourse."

"Possibly. What was his sentence?"

"It was never determined, but he..." Rachel paused, "He recently issued new orders."

"What was the sentence?"

"Life."

The guard looked at Rachel, then at the boy with her. He took a deep breath as if in prequel to speaking, but words never escaped his lips. He turned away and walked back to his post at the gate without saying a word to the other guards. Rachel watched his head lower and his eyes go to the ground. She stared at him for several long minutes—he never looked up. Rachel started toward the guard, but stopped short when she saw him turn away. The other guards followed suit and turned away from her. Peter walked to her side.

The Packrat and Rachel did not move for many minutes. Eventually, the two walked back to Rachel's flat in the same manner in which they had come; with only one exception: the boy walked a half step in front of the woman.

The Last Trumpet

HANDEL MOVED ON. HE REMEMBERED THE WOUNDS inflicted as a result of his shortsightedness, but he would not let them paralyze him. He had received the comforting assurance that he had been forgiven. Now it was his duty to press forward. He knew not the Lord's mind regarding *Messiah*, but he did not let it vex him. He was patient to wait until moved upon to pursue it again.

He busied himself with other writing and performing. He put on *Samson* twice again that year, enjoying success with each performance. Other oratorios were penned and performed with equal success: *Belshazzar*, *Judas Maccabaeus*, and *Solomon* were among the greatest. In spite of the criticism unearthed by performing *Messiah*, the medium had proved itself to be both fulfilling and acceptable to London. Audiences became benevolent in their praise and support of Handel's efforts. Not only had he lost the desire to venture into the fray of opera again, there was no need. Out of the defeat of opera had sprung the victory of oratorio.

The dynamics of the new medium were not nearly as volatile as opera. The simplicity of oratorio smoothed the peaks and valleys normally encountered in production. The vanities pervading opera were all but avoided. Handel did not miss them. He had had his fill of wardrobes and sets, of hours lost to makeup artists, and of silly quibbling over inches farther upstage or down. He lost no sleep trying to make sure there were equal matching bars for contentious divas. He actually found great humor in it all. There was nothing that tickled him more than a good joke bolstering the absurdity of beehive brassieres or gargantuan girdles. The very things that once seemed so vitally imperative were now the pasture of puns. The foppery to which he had given servitude was laughable. In his older years, the memory of having battled in the conflict was good enough. He had an endless supply of stories—more than enough to sustain him through as many mugs of ale the most prolific drinker could hold. That was sufficient.

The calm and profitable existence he now enjoyed was the retirement he wanted. What made his life even more tolerable was the ceasefire that apparently existed between him and his enemies. Handel did not know how the truce had come to be, only that the shots in his direction were not nearly so accurate or frequent.

In the aftermath of the *Messiah* debacle, Handel's enemies—with the exception of Rolli—lost interest in him. Prince Frederick had been the real draw. Once he was gone, the stakes were not nearly so high or rewarding. Handel's return from Dublin and the opportunity to prick the ire of the religionists concerning the sacred oratorio, were amusing for a time, but they did not have the sustaining power of the battle of King versus son. For Addison and Steele, Handel was not the prey but the lure for angling a much larger trophy. When the opportunity to land the "big one" was lost, cutting bait was no longer fulfilling.

Besides, Handel was getting old. The public was not so tolerant of attacks on the elderly. Addison and Steele found more fertile ground in military politics and the zoning wars of London's East Side.

Without Frederick, even Hervey eventually lost interest in Handel. She had thoroughly enjoyed the romp with the Prince, and, even though she was careful not to openly admit it, she was disappointed to have it end. When he first departed their company, the Madame feigned apathy; however, she missed her frolic with Frederick. The opera skirmishes were a pleasure. The competition of opposing operas, always under the umbrella of the more engaging competition between father and son, was nothing short of pure, unadulterated fun.

Her Italian boy, Rolli, provided no societal titillation compared to Freddy. In fact, Rolli was irritatingly dour. Hervey held Rolli personally responsible for driving the Prince away. The Madame hated him for it. The more she was subjected to Rolli's obsessive hatred for Handel— without the savory spice of royal entanglement—the more she despised him. Rolli was a meaningless pawn whom she had foolishly allowed to put her side of the board in check. Handel was not the only means for creating melee in the royal menage, other avenues could have kept young Frederick preoccupied far longer. Rolli's anathema had soured the Prince prematurely. The fact that she had Frederick in hand long before Rolli entered the scene ripened her venom even more.

In the months following the silencing of *Messiah*, Madame Hervey eliminated Rolli from her guest list. She would have nothing to do with him or his librettos. Several times he tried to gain an audience with her, but she would not so much as acknowledge his existence. Her house help were told to dismiss him in any and every circumstance. She literally erased him from her life. Rolli was left to embark alone on the quest to bring down Handel.

With the restored support that Handel enjoyed, the feat was more than Rolli could accomplish without the help of more influential players than himself. Without the option of writing for Handel, work became more and more difficult to find. Necessity forced Rolli back into employment that he believed to be far beneath him. He rejoined the Academy, not as director of Italian affairs, but as liaison. He was reduced to negotiating the egotistical whims of the Italian divas. He hated them. The enmity he felt for the warbling wenches was only a hint of the contempt he had for Handel, but he was alone. None would hear him. Those who were forced to hear his ranting categorized them as the petty quibbling of a jealous subordinate. Rolli disappeared from the forefront of the music arena. He was obliged to wallow in his own vile slime of deprecation. He found bitter solace in but one last chance for final and rightful retribution. His last hope for revenge was contained in a beautiful olive wood box.

Though Worms Destroy this Body

IN THE MIDST OF HANDEL'S GREAT RESURGENCE, ADVERSITY once again came as an uninvited guest. Opposition did not come in the form of enemies or bitter failure as before, it came more quietly and gradually. Little by little, Handel began to lose the use of his eyes. It became difficult for him to see the notes on the page. Bars of music started to run together with no clear break in stanzas. Faces in the audience blurred and softened until he could not tell them apart. He adjusted the music stand closer and closer to him until it could adjust no more. His servant Peter was the first to notice the change. Handel would call for him at times when Peter was in the same room. Handel asked Peter to read letters more frequently. Often, letters would sit unopened until Peter could read them. His master winced from headaches brought on by squinting and straining.

Handel's musicians were next to perceive the change. During rehearsals an individual within a group might ask a question; Handel would often direct his answers to some other person in the vicinity of where the query originated. Close acquaintances observed that he did not seem to recognize them until they were very close. Often it would take the sound of their voice before he could identify them by name. Handel's world was dimming. He visited several different physicians to see if the debilitating malady could be treated and remedied, but there was no altering the inevitable. The best he could do was pray that the blindness would not be complete. The process of degeneration finally stopped before his vision went completely dark. As it left him, he could not distinguish features but he could still see general shapes. The light of his eyes was not fully extinguished but it remained severely impaired. The balance of his elderly life would be lived in large part by memory and by ear.

Years came and went from the time of Handel's return from Dublin. Through the many changes of season, one clear thought had remained in the back of his mind. He was determined not to act upon the thought until prompted but it was ever present.

The music he had put away for another time frequently filled his soul with sound. He could hear the voice of Susanna singing in his dreams. He remembered well his experience in Dublin, the beauty of the soloists, the power of the choir. But there was no venue which suited the piece, no theatre where he would be comfortable performing it. He determined once again to leave the oratorio alone. Only then was he truly prepared to listen to the quiet whisperings of the spirit. In time, the purpose for and a place to perform *Messiah* were revealed to him. The place was a small chapel; the purpose, as always, was charity.

Behold Your God

SPRING OF 1749 CAME IN GLORIOUS FASHION. THE FROST-
filled days of winter passed as they should, tapering off little by little
through the long days of the short month of February. The temperature
was a degree or two warmer each day as the sun worked its way northward.

By the first of March, the deep penetrating chill of winter was past;
the earth-warming weather of early spring had fully begun. Rain fell almost
daily but not all day. Few storms lasted much more than an hour.
Mornings were usually moist and gray, but within an hour or so, golden
sunlight would dissipate the fog into long ribbons of mist, which hung low
against the rolling green hills and along the river. By mid-morning even
those were burned away, revealing bright, beautiful sunlight and azure blue
sky. Just past noon, high clouds would begin to form, reaching upward and

outward in tall plumes. The tops would spread like petals of a flower opening to the sun. By mid-afternoon, rain was typically announced by a deep resounding boom of thunder and a sweeping burst of wind. Layers of dead, stifling coal smoke that had thickened over the long months of winter were blown away to sea in a single afternoon. Leafless tree branches shivered in the gusts of wind as if in anticipation of the inevitable rain.

At the onset, huge drops would fall in steep slanted sheets from the blackened sky. Shortly, the wind would stop, and the rain would ease to a gentle sprinkle, which would last nearly half an hour. Before the call of the next hour, streaks of sunlight were already starting to erode through the thin layers of the cloud blanket. At sunset, the sky was a burst of oranges and pinks as the low sun filled the clouds with amber light, illuminating them as if the source of light were coming from within.

As the days advanced further into March, the storms lessened in both intensity and length. As if divinely ordained, each day preceding the equinox was circumspectly more temperate than the prior. There was little alteration in the pattern. Mother Earth responded cautiously at first, as if guarding her tender offspring from a rebellious and errant frost. But the blades and buds of foliage were irrepressible. Shoots of green rose unrestrained from the ground, awakened from the soil by the deep-reaching warmth of the sun.

Even men's spirits began to uncurl and stretch from their winter hibernation. Faces that steadily looked down through long gray months of cold were lifted up to greet the new days. Lungs were gladly filled with the clean, invigorating air. So consistent and constant was the change of season that even the most wary and distrusting weather watchers were converted by the enticings of spring.

Nowhere was change more anticipated and welcomed than by the children. The new world beckoned them out to play. Laughter and frolic filled the air with happy sound. Their joy was contagious, infecting all who heard it with gaiety. The noise from schoolyards grew louder and happier each day. Children with umbrellas danced in the afternoon rain, seemingly oblivious to the dampness of their feet or its coldness. Mothers walked their babies in the late morning for no other reason than to be outside. Young boys splashed in the puddles; girls smelled the lilies. Indeed, all of London welcomed the change—but none more than one particular young girl who embraced the coming of spring like no other.

To her, the time of year held special meaning beyond even the rebirth of nature. The glories of the earth provided the perfect setting for the glory of song. The change of season, with all its newness and beauty, not only heralded the coming of spring but also a long-awaited event.

Months before, when London was wrapped in the heavy shroud of winter, plans were made for a concert. Not just any concert, but a musical celebration of Easter and the glorious resurrection of the Christ, Jesus. Word of the musical celebration spread through halls and walls, infecting every child with joyful anticipation.

Apparently, by God's good grace, the Foundling Hospital was to be the beneficiary of a charitable concert. What was even more splendid was that the concert was to be held in the hospital chapel.

Everyone heard the news, from the youngest child to the oldest. But of all who heard the glad tidings, it touched the heart of no one as it did Christina. She loved music. She loved the songs that the children were taught. She loved to hear the sweet voices of the sisters singing hymns at Mass, praising God with pure melody. Her soul was ever drawn out in song. She hummed wherever she went, rehearsing in her mind the melodies she learned from the sisters. Her excitement at the prospect of possibly attending the concert was boundless. It was all Christina could do to keep her voice low until the girls were out of the large main building door leading out into the open courtyard.

The children approached the large doors at the south end of the large central hall in an orderly fashion, all the children dressed alike in simple but clean uniforms. The girls' blouses were white, their skirts blue. The boys' pants and shirts were of like color and fabric. Christina was near the back of the procession, walking side by side and holding hands with another young girl, Ellen, about her same age. Ahead of them were the younger children, starting with the very smallest at the front of the line.

At age ten, Christina and Ellen were two of the oldest children in the line. One sister walked just behind them at the end of the line. Light streamed through the tree branches and into the hospital hall through the square-paned windows high above the east entrance.

The moment the doors were flung open, Christina's mouth did likewise. Her voice increased in volume as she passed through the doorway from inside to out.

"Today is a day for romance—a perfect day," she said through a smile, her face radiant.

"What would you know of romance?" laughed Ellen.

"Look at it," said Christina, stopping to look up through the trees.

"The sky, the sunshine, the grass and flowers—smell the air." The sister at the rear of the line passed by her as she stood looking up. Christina noticed her black nun's frock out of the corner of her eye as she passed by.

"Sister Anne, is today romantic?" The sister stopped and looked up, revealing her aging face. Her lips turned up as she looked on the elegance of the dew-fresh garden around her.

"Yes, indeed. It has all the makings."

"I knew it. I had a feeling."

This was the time of day Christina loved best, when the children were let out into the yard for recreation. The lilies were in full bloom of yellows and reds. Other perennials bloomed and budded in the beds around the perimeter of the grassed yard. Leaves were just beginning to break open from sprigs in the overhanging trees.

While the other children broke from the line to run on the grass, the two girls followed the sister down the stone path leading through the trees. Christina spoke again.

"Spring is my favorite of all seasons. So much new life."

"Mine too—for the same reason," observed the sister, coming to a stop in a pool of warm sunlight. "It is the time of our Lord's resurrection. We are already making preparations for Lent."

"The chapel is never so full of people!" Said Ellen.

"Many turn to the Lord this time of year. There are some who don't turn their eyes upward any other time of the year."

"And the concert?" asked Christina, sitting down on a long wooden bench in the warm sunshine. The sister sat down next to her, well aware of what her next question would be. "Will we be allowed inside this year?"

"Perhaps; yes, I believe you are old enough."

The two girls looked at one another. The sparkle in their eyes told far more than words could ever express.

They watched the other children playing in the courtyard. Ellen moved behind Christina and began pulling back her long, brown locks of hair. Christina's round eyes shone with the same rich color of brown. As

Ellen caressed the long rich folds of hair, she saw something through the shining strands. She carefully pulled the hair off of Christina's neck, revealing a small brown mark behind her ear.

"I've never noticed that before. Have you had it long?"

"As long as I've known her," Sister Anne said, looking over with a reassuring smile.

"Tell me again," pleaded Christina, letting her head fall back with Ellen's gentle tugs. Christina closed her eyes. Sister Anne spoke with a gentle voice.

"I only saw your mother's hands and heard her voice—she called you by name. That is how we learned your name."

The sister reflected before going on:

"It broke her heart to leave you."

"Then why? Why leave her?" asked Ellen.

"Because they thought we could care for you better here." The sister could see by the curious look on Ellen's face that she did not understand.

"Some children are left because the parents do not want the burden. Others because they cannot care for them. Christina was simply left out of love. She thought it was best for the child."

"I think my mother loved me," Christina said, her eyes still closed to the sun.

"You will understand all the better when you have a child of your own," answered the sister. Christina's eyes opened. She reached over and took the sister's hand in hers and squeezed it. The nun pulled the little girl's hand to her cheek and pressed it against her warm skin.

"I'll never forget your mother's hand, her voice, the way she said your name," said Sister Anne.

Christina's smile was brighter than the morning sun.

The third-story window of the hospital governor's office overlooked the courtyard. As the children played, a tall gentleman, Principal Lewis, stood near the large window, watching the activity below. His assistant paced back and forth near the door. Mr. Chadwick, the Governor of the Foundling Hospital, sat at his desk busily reading over the announcement that he held in his hand. Their attitude was one of expectation.

"This will be the third year," observed Principal Lewis from the window, his back to the others.

"It has become our greatest fund-raiser," said Chadwick, laying the announcement of the concert down on his desk. "As grateful as I am for the gift, I must confess that if the opportunity arises, there is something I should like to ask him."

He said no more, but the looks on the faces of the others in the room affirmed that they entertained the same desire. There was something very odd in the circumstance by which the benefit concert had come to be. After years of asking for aid from every charitable foundation they could think of, the most generous contribution the hospital had ever received was proffered freely by an unsolicited benefactor. The idea of the annual fund-raising concert was not theirs, but a gracious volunteer.

Three years ago, they were approached with the idea of holding a concert during Lent in the chapel of the Foundling Hospital. The orchestra and singers were to be entirely donated or compensated by the organizer. Tickets would be sold, the proceeds of which would be given to the hospital for the maintenance of the children. All of this was done at the behest of one man.

The governor and the principal of the Foundling Hospital were both quite taken aback by the selfless offer. But regardless of the apparent demonstration of good will, their initial reaction was skepticism. Never had anyone come to them to request their permission and cooperation in raising money for the institution. It was not until the first concert was over and the money collected that they comprehended the grandeur of the gift. The receipts were astounding when compared to the other meager donations made in behalf of the abandoned and lost children. What was even more amazing to the hospital administration was the increase in positive public awareness that the concert provided. General sentiment, which had forever been a stumbling block for the hospital, was suddenly transformed as if overnight. Whereas the hospital had been perceived as the embodiment of society's ills, it now became known as a safe haven for the unfortunate. The same buildings that were once considered blight to the neighborhood were transformed into a community monument. The Foundling Hospital was now viewed as the most noble of philanthropies. Residual endowments of both goods and money were inspired by virtue of the concert. From the inception of the concerts, donations were received year round.

It was not the event itself that changed the hearts of so many, but the content of the concert. The music and words together instilled in the listener convictions to do more—to be more. Often, the hospital was the fortuitous receptacle of the covert expressions of those elevated convictions. The people who attended considered themselves very fortunate, as the piece was seldom performed in other venues. The oratorio, which became the hallmark of the Easter season, was rarely heard elsewhere. Those not familiar with the history of the oratorio assumed it had been written specifically for the Foundling Hospital. The supposition was entirely rational, since the piece was never performed for any reason other than charity.

While the three men were considering the blessing so freely given them, there was a loud knock. The assistant principal remarked before opening the door, "'Ask, and ye shall receive. Knock, and it shall be…'"

He grasped the brass knob and opened the door. In walked Handel, cane in hand.

"Gentlemen, I greet you—a day older than yesterday."

"A day younger than tomorrow," the principal replied, knowing by heart Handel's greeting.

"Thank goodness!" laughed Handel, "lest we all grow old with nothing to look forward to."

He shook hands with each of them.

"It is wonderful to see you in such fine spirits," said the governor. "You look in excellent health."

"Tolerable health would be more accurate, sir. But I shall take what the good Lord grants and be grateful for it."

"We've heard rumors that you are having trouble with your sight," said the man nearest the door.

"No trouble," said Handel, "it just seems that I keep losing it. I must try to remember where I left it."

The men were uncertain how to respond. Handel's fervent laugh put them at ease.

"We are now making plans for your upcoming performance, as part of Lent," said the governor.

"It's with great charity that you give this concert," added Principal Lewis. "Your performance has become a tradition here."

"It is well-suited for your needs—and your chapel," said Handel with a wink.

"We're in your debt."

"Gentlemen, you are in debt to no one. It is for a purpose such as this that *Messiah* came forth."

Children's voices rose up from the courtyard and through the open window to Handel's ears. He turned in the direction of the window, listening to the laughter from outside.

"We are planning on the evening of the 9th of April," said the governor, picking up the announcement from off his desk.

"Exactly ten years," sighed Handel under his breath.

"Sir?"

"I'm sorry, it is a terrible habit I have. You see, the first public rehearsal of *Messiah* in Dublin was on April 9th, exactly ten years ago to the day."

"If you would excuse my intrusion, there is something I've been wanting to ask."

"Yes?"

"To my knowledge, you've only performed it a handful of times; and now you perform it only in our chapel."

"It is safe here," Handel said. He chose his words carefully. "It seems I've been forgotten. I must have grown old, toothless, and sightless. I am a poor foe. There is no longer any pleasure in the chase, so I am left alone."

"I'm sorry. I don't understand?" queried the governor.

"This is where *Messiah* belongs," answered Handel.

"But why? Why wait 'til now?"

Handel turned in the direction of the children's voices rising up from the courtyard. He listened for some time before continuing.

"From simple and small means is God's greatest work accomplished."

The governor glanced at the others, then stepped toward Handel.

"We have imposed on you enough. If there isn't anything else?"

"There is actually one thing—regarding the proceeds. I feel compelled to redirect a portion elsewhere."

"What ever you wish, sir. We would be unprofitable stewards to be selfish with a gift."

Handel handed him a slip of paper, then shook each man's hand again before leaving.

Any Sorrow Like Unto His Sorrow

A LOUD SCREECH RANG THROUGH THE STONE ROOM. THE prison door opened. The jailer stood in the opening with torch in hand. By the time the eyes of those inside adjusted to the bright light, he had reached back, grabbed a young man by the collar of his shirt, and pushed him into the room. The youth stumbled forward onto his hands and knees. His palms slipped out from under him on the slime-ridden floor. He fell face down into a foul-smelling puddle. He crawled up to his elbows, his face dripping. Wide-eyed, he stared into the abyss.

"There's more the likes of you!" the jailer shouted to the shadows of the dark prison.

"Hey, you in there—take good care of this one, he's just a boy!" The jailer laughed while slamming the door shut. The violent crack of the heavy wood against metal rebounded down the long empty halls. The jailer's laugh was sustained long after the sound of his footsteps on the stone faded.

"The jailer would have you believe we are worse than we are," a voice said from the shadows.

The boy jumped to his feet. He impulsively backed up to the door, wiping the filth from his eyes.

"Give us news of the outside," another voice pleaded from the shadows.

"Stay away. There's been a mistake; I'm not supposed to be here. I won't be here long. There's been a mistake. I don't deserve to be here. There's been a mistake."

"No one deserves to be here, but we are," said a lifeless voice. "Get used to it."

"No," the boy repeated over and over again, pushing harder and harder against the door with his back. The heavy door began to shake on its hinges with each convulsion of the new incarcerate.

"No, no! It was a mistake." The boy's voice tightened in his throat. "I shouldn't be here. I'm not a criminal. There's been a mistake. God help me; I'm not like you. I'm not one of you. I only need more time, I can pay. I just need more time."

"Wasn't it fair, boy?" The voice loudened. "Were you dealt with unjustly?"

"Stay away from me," the boy warned, his eyes darting about wildly. "Don't come near me. You will see. I will be free again soon. They are probably coming right now to correct the error. Just stay away."

"Free?"

"You will see. It is only a misunderstanding. Justice will win. I will go free—soon I'll be free."

"Eleven years," shouted the voice. "Eleven years. Does that seem soon to you? That is how long you may spend here. Is that just? Those who betrayed me…liars—they are free, is that just?"

"Eleven years—God have mercy!"

"No! Mercy is for sinners, not for you or me. We are debtors. We receive neither justice nor mercy. God will save the sinner, but no one pays your debt!"

The room fell silent. In the midst of the darkness, the boy saw movement against the wall. There was a rustle of old paper unfolding.

Now that his pupils had dilated, the boy could see a light-colored square against the dark background. Even though it was browned and torn, he recognized the sound and shape of paper. He deduced by the folds and frayed corners that it was a letter. At length the paper was lowered. Slowly, that which was invisible before began to take shape. He could see the dark outline of a man sitting against a black wall holding the paper with shadowed hands. The boy watched as the lowered head rose and leaned back against the wall. A stream of soft blue from an opening above shined in the man's eyes.

Through the small hole in the door, the jailer saw the same sight. He had circled back when he heard the loud voices from within. He said nothing but heard much.

Shall All Be Made Alive

Behold the Lamb of God,'" sang the altos on the
second beat of bar four, followed by the sopranos on the last half of beat
four. The basses then reprised the line in bar five, followed lastly by the
tenors on the second half of beat four of the same bar. The Packrat
watched from his designated chair in the midst of the tenor section of
the choir for the conductor's nod to enter. He stood tall, now a full-
statured young man. The nod came. He, along with the other tenors,
joined the chorus in one great swell, their voices in eloquent unison,
echoing the line already sung by the other sections. This chorus was
among his favorites, not because it was easier to sing than many of the
other choir numbers, but because of its humble yet affirming invocation:
"Behold."

The Packrat, who was now more commonly known as Peter, kept his eyes on the maestro. Long had he waited to sing this music, but never had he dreamed of singing it under the direction of the man who had penned it. To Peter, Handel radiated a celestial aura. His countenance seemed to illuminate the immediate area around him with a holy spectral of light. Peter did not know if others could see it, but to him the vision of light was as real as the man himself.

Through prior rehearsals, Peter had thought many times to reveal himself to Handel. From the time he was fourteen and departed his prior profession to work full-time buying and selling fish with James, he had taxed his poor, blind partner with the idea of someday approaching Handel. There was no question that Peter was tethered to the artist in a peculiar way, but over time he had surrendered himself to the belief that Handel would have no recollection of any of their brief encounters. For Peter, the events were monumental, even life-altering. This man who he doubted would have any memory of ever having crossed paths with him changed the trajectory of his life. Peter felt drawn to Handel as if God himself had led his footsteps to intersect with the man standing at the front of the orchestra. In the deeply honest parts of his soul, he knew he had been guided throughout the course of his life. But to what end, he was not certain.

The chorus sang through the final bars. With one great wave of the conductor's hand, the choir rested while the orchestra played out the remaining three bars, then silence. Handel stood before the large group, his head down. At long length he looked up, his face stretched tight into perplexed dismay.

"What the Devil is this?" he said scowling. "Have I been given angels to sing?" His face relaxed into a grand smile.

"My eyes don't allow me to see whether you have wings, so I assume you must." The entire group expelled a sigh of thankful relief in one happy chord. Handel laughed through his words:

"No more tonight. You must remember—I am old. Though I had hold of your coat tails, still I could not keep up." The chorus of song became a chorus of laughter.

"Tomorrow night we perform. Please, be early!"

With a thankful wave he said goodbye, then returned to his podium to write some notes on the score. The group began to disperse. Peter rose to his feet. For several minutes he stared at Handel, watching his every move. Finally, another of the tenors walked over and waved his hand in front of Peter's face.

"Good morning," he said. "And how was your nap?"

"I must talk to him," said Peter, his gaze still focused on Handel. The friend followed Peter's line of view to Handel.

"You want to talk to him?" he asked, pointing to Handel.

"But why? He is to be heard, not spoken to."

"We have met before."

"You and..." the friend's voice trailed off as he looked back at the composer.

"I have followed after his music for years. Finally, it has brought me here."

Peter walked down the aisle toward Handel, who was in the middle of a discussion with one of the soloists. Peter waited for the conversation to conclude. When the encounter ended, Handel turned back to his podium, away from Peter. He was still unaware of the young man's presence.

"Sir?" Peter said.

Handel jumped forward, almost knocking over the music stand.

"The Devil," he spun around to Peter. "Good that you do not bite before you speak."

Peter was embarrassed at his inadvertent breach of etiquette.

"I'm sorry."

"We're all sorry, I'm afraid. But, truly, if the Lord is nothing else, He is patient."

Handel took a deep breath, then leaned close for a good look at Peter.

"You're in the chorus—from the Cathedral Choir?"

The Packrat nodded his head, but no words came out.

"Are you a student of music?"

"I have wanted to sing this since I first heard it,"

"Then you've seen it performed? You're familiar with it?"

"I've heard it on two occasions: once outside the theatre and once outside the window of...outside the window of Covent Garden."

"That was long ago," said Handel. He looked at Peter as if trying to imagine what a young boy might be doing at Covent. The elderly man leaned close again, looking carefully at Peter's face. His scrutinizing eyes made Peter uncomfortable.

"I must go. I'm sorry for the intrusion," said Peter, bowing low.

Handel's face warmed.

"You need not be sorry. Intrusion, no—diversion, yes."

"I'm looking forward to the performance," Peter said.

"As am I..." Handel paused. "Your name would be here if I knew it!"

"Peter."

"Peter."

"Good night, sir," said Peter.

"Peter—do I know you?"

"No, sir. But I have known you. Thank you. Until tomorrow."

The Packrat did not wait for further discussion. He was gone from Handel's failing view almost instantly. Handel rubbed his chin with his hand before picking up his music and making his way to the door. Just before exiting, he looked back one last time in the direction in which Peter had left. He smiled.

And We Shall Be Changed

IT WAS NOT UNUSUAL FOR A CARRIAGE TO BE PARKED IN front of *The Spectator* office door. What was unusual was the time of day that the carriage was there. Most often, if *The Spectator* had visitors, it was late in the day after the paper was printed and distributed. A carriage bearing an angry recipient of the editor's sarcasm or prickly criticisms was a fairly regular sight in the late afternoon; often there could be more than one at the same time. When politics preempted other topics in the newspaper, there could be a line of discontented readers waiting at the door late into the evening to voice their indignation.

But it was quite out of the ordinary for *The Spectator* to have visitors prior to the paper's distribution. The shopkeepers adjacent to the office kept an eye open to see who would come out of *The Spectator* office door. They were especially interested because the carriage belonged to someone of influence and wealth. Most of the carriages on the street at any given time were for hire, but this carriage had the trappings of being personal. The woodwork of the cabin was handsomely crafted. The brass handles and intricate detail work were elegant and artistic. Clearly the hands of the finishing craftsmen were skilled. Even the wheels reflected wealth. They were somewhat bigger than most carriage wheels, making the ride considerably smoother, with less jostling. The metal work was forged in hotter fires. The steel rims were more silver than the dark iron that was mounted on most wheels. The spokes were meticulously lathed, sanded, and stained in perfect style and symmetry. The spokes were cut from the heart of the same tree, the grain identical. Only trained eyes would ever see any difference in the hand-carved spindles.

The artistry of the carriage was not the only evidence that the carriage belonged to someone of import—there was an additional feature, which removed all doubt. It was a large J, beautifully carved into the side panels of the coach doors on both sides. The same style letter was etched into the steel hubs at the center of each wheel. The rear of the cabin also had a gold-leafed J in the middle of an elegant frame painted with golden flowers. At first glance, one would tend to describe the carriage as grand and garish.

When the door of *The Spectator* finally opened, all eyes watched to see who would appear. Most didn't recognize the two men who emerged; the few who did slapped their foreheads for being so stupid that they did not realize immediately upon seeing the J who the owner was.

Charles Jennens strode out *The Spectator* door, with a smile so broad that his ears lay back against his head to make room for it. A step behind him followed William Holdsworth, his smile nearly as big. The footmen of the carriage barely had time to get the door open before Jennens had his foot on the step. He took hold of the handles on either side of the door and stopped just short of entering. Jennens looked up to find all eyes on him. Those who had paused to watch him hurried back to their chores like children caught raiding the pantry. Jennens appreciated the attention.

"What do you have to say for yourself, Charles?" asked Holdsworth from behind.

"I need not speak for myself; others do me the good pleasure."

Jennens pulled from his coat a copy of the paper about to be published and held it aloft.

"You're pleased then?" asked Holdsworth.

"Reluctantly, mind you!" Jennens said, climbing into the carriage. "I did not expect Steele to be quite so complimentary. There's nothing like benevolence to take the bite out of the dog," said Jennens.

"Your music man finally has it right, and not a moment too soon," replied Holdsworth, getting in.

"Fools that they are, not even Addison and Steele would dare take issue with a charitable cause as moral as the Foundling Hospital. 'Twould be suicide."

"Then this was your idea?"

"Nay—'Tis Handel's. His intentions are true."

"But we are not so veracious as to refuse the unintended benefits of his good will—such as notoriety..."

"Or retribution." Jennens tapped his finger on the newspaper sitting on the seat next to him.

The driver leaned to the window and addressed Jennens.

"Which way shall we go, My Lord? Have you a preference?"

"We're in no hurry. Take us home by way of the open market."

"As you wish," said the driver before climbing to his seat on top.

"It's crowded this time of day. Perhaps we shall see—and be seen by many. After all there is a performance tonight," Jennens said.

"You are shrewd, my dear Charles," chuckled Holdsworth as the carriage rolled over cobbles toward the busiest part of London.

How Beautiful Are the Feet of Them That Bringeth Good Tidings

---

Y OU MUST COME. IT CAN'T BE DESCRIBED IN WORDS. YOU must hear it." Peter said, his voice urgent, as he paced around the dimly lit room. Rachel sat motionless, her body arched forward, her hands folded between her knees. Peter could see her hunched, dark shape in the waning light of the room, but he could not see her face through the dark tresses of hair that fell from her head around her face and down her long, thin arms.

"Please! Please come with me." Peter stopped in the middle of the room, staring at Rachel as if demanding an answer.

She lifted her face, but she did not look at him. Her hollow eyes were fixed on nothing. She stared forward, without so much as a blink of reaction. Peter moved to a place in front of her where he was certain she could not avoid seeing him.

"When we sing, I feel that my heart will swell to bursting."

Even though he stood directly in her vision, her numb, tired eyes seemed to look through him.

"The music—you will feel it too."

"I am past feeling," she said, her voice monotone.

"You'll feel hope."

"What is to hope for?"

Rachel's expression still did not change. Now that he was close, Peter could see wrinkles along her cheeks. Dark circles hung around and under her eyes. Peter had seen Rachel often through the past several years, but, now, for the first time, she seemed old. He hadn't really noticed the change because it had happened so gradually, but now he was looking at her as if for the first time in many years. His eyes suddenly beheld what time had done. Age had taken its toll, but not so much as her broken heart. She was and ever would be beautiful, but the light which had shone from within—the same light which had made her beauty radiant—was extinguished. If any fire still burned inside her, it was no more than the embers of a dying flame. Innocence and hope had kept her beautiful. Once that was gone, years of loneliness had had their way with her. Her body lived, but her spirit was spent. There was little to give her life meaning, little to look forward to. The lake of love that had given her the stamina to meet each day anew had no restorative spring—the water flowed out only. Her faith evaporated away under the drying sun of prolonged despair. To Peter, Rachel appeared utterly and wholly used up. He could now plainly see what the dreadful years of sorrow had exacted from her.

Sadly, he turned to the door; there was nothing left to say. It was best for him to leave. His good intentions had only added to her grief. In an effort to help, he had inadvertently scraped the scab off an old festering sore. His thoughts went to his experience with James and how his desire to assist him had resulted in the man's loss of sight. Peter had learned, through personal experience, that there were intrinsic liabilities in trying to go outside oneself. Even Christ was crucified for trying to raise men's eyes. Perhaps it was better to mind one's business and leave things well enough alone. He decided it was best for him just to leave, and to do so quietly. His prudence would probably be saving Rachel's eyes from beholding a vision that might render her forever blind to all things bright and beautiful. He knew her view of life was dimming. An ill-fated attempt to help might darken it completely.

Peter moved toward the door. His lowered eyes watched his hand reach for the door handle. His saw his hand fade to black against the bright orange line of sunlight seeping in from under the door. The last, low rays of the sun reached under the loose-fitting door, making his feet and everything close by glow with warm light. He forgot what he had been thinking the moment before. The preeminent splendor of the blazing streak took complete dominion over his thoughts. The light was glorious to behold. It bathed the immediate area around him in a wash of golden luminance. A voice suddenly came into his mind—it was the voice of his friend James.

"When is hope used up? Even the blind can see light."

Peter looked back at Rachel. Light bounced up from the floor and spilled over her, creating the effect of lifting her body away from the sullen background. She seemed suspended above the darkness in the room. Sparks of light danced on the clear surface of her fully open eyes, but she could not see them. Peter ran back into the room, took hold of the heavy curtains and threw them back from the window. Bright penetrating beams poured into the room, illuminating every dark place within. The room was transformed into a receptacle of life-giving light, resplendent and clear as noonday. Rays of sunlight pierced Rachel's wide, dilated pupils, making her eyes sting and water. She blinked again and again to ease the smarting burn. She turned away from the light, covering her eyes with her hands. Peter heard her whimper in pain, but he didn't care.

"When is hope used up? Even the blind see light. Look at it!" he demanded in a loud voice. "Look at it!"

Slowly, Rachel turned her face back to the window. She lifted up her fingers one by one and opened her eyes to the light. Her skin was lustrous in the brilliant shine of the sun. At once, years seemed to shed like molted skin from her translucent face. Caressed by the warm, remedial glow from the celestial lamp, Rachel was as beautiful as she had ever been. Peter watched her for the many minutes that she stared out the window until the bright ball dropped to just above the black line of the horizon.

"Where?" she asked in a whisper.

"I'll take you there."

They walked down the street together in the soft light of dusk. Far off in the western sky, the sun glowed below the edge of the earth. The heaven above them was a vibrant blue with patches of luminous pink and orange clouds. It was a perfect spring sunset; droplets of water from the afternoon cloudburst hung like lavender crystals on leaves and branches. The still air smelled of rich, wet earth.

Rachel saw little of it. She walked slowly, her head sloping forward, her face down. Her eyes were hidden behind the worn wool of her dark hood, shielded from those they passed on the street. She could see nothing but the ground directly ahead of her. Peter had his arm around her, supporting a good part of her weight through each step. Rachel was subject to Peter's will, not knowing beforehand their direction or destination. For blocks they went, pausing only briefly for respite. At no time did Rachel look up long enough to determine their whereabouts. She put her full trust in Peter. She went willingly, supported by both his arm and his resolve. Rachel did not look up until a small bench came into her limited view. She stopped abruptly. Peter thought she was resting, but her eyes were fixed on the wooden bench. His gaze lifted to the wall before them. She pulled from Peter's arm, recoiling from the open gate of the Foundling Hospital. Tears filled her eyes.

"I can't go here," she cried. Peter took hold of her, securing his arm around her in a tight grip.

"Please," she stammered through sobs. "Please, don't take me here."

She tried in vain to pull away from his grasp, but Peter held her firmly at his side.

"If you'd have known, you wouldn't have come."

Peter moved forward, dragging the forlorn burden along with him. Anxiety seized Rachel; she fell limp in his arms, her legs, nearly useless. Peter swung one of her lifeless arms around his neck and held it tightly with one hand while keeping the opposite arm around her waist. He could feel her shuddering body against him as she choked through mournful cries.

"Please, no. Peter, have mercy on me—please, not here. You are cruel to bring me here. Why torment me so?"

Peter lifted her trembling body up with his shoulder. Though her voice broke his heart, on he walked.

"Please no. God help me, please. It is more than I can stand."

Peter did not stop to rest again. When his arms went numb, he somehow summoned up the needed strength to shoulder and support the full weight of his listless and desperate friend. Rachel's cries were no longer audible to anyone but him. With each step he could hear her murmuring sobs and feel her trembling body. Every several steps she would shake violently as if her feeble frame were about to give out completely; then she would fall limp again.

Her feet dragged over the threshold of the open door. He carried her forward through the chapel foyer. Down the center aisle of the chapel they went, Rachel's face hidden deep within the shadows of her hood. When the two were near the front of the nave, Peter slid into an empty pew and sat down with Rachel near the center of the row. He leaned her gently back into her seat and took her arm from around his shoulder. When she was thus seated he took her hand in his. She grasped Peter's hand so tightly that it startled him. She looked up into his face as if beckoning him one last time to rescue her. He put his other hand over hers and smiled, she relaxed her grip, and he released her. Peter then reached over her and pulled back her hood. He laid the cloak behind her on the back of the bench, then slid out the row to the aisle and began to make his way to his seat in the choir.

Through tear filled eyes, Rachel watched him leave. Once his back was turned and he was well enough away, she rose to her feet. Rachel slid down along the pew toward the side aisle. But before she could get there, a large group of girls and boys entered the chapel through the side doors and began to file in and slide down the empty bench in front of her. Forced back into the pew, she slid along the bench toward the center aisle, but she was too late. A long line of children had come through the back door and was swiftly making their way down the center aisle. Before she could get out, children were filing into the pew from the other direction. They came from both sides, trapping her in the middle of the bench. She had neither the gumption nor the will to try to escape past either group. In her disconsolate condition, the distance between her and freedom seemed insurmountable. She cowered on the bench—her eyes cast down. The two young girls seated on either side of her watched her curiously, trying their best to not be impolite. As difficult as it was, they withstood the impulse to stare. Rachel would never have noticed either way; she closed her eyes, praying that God would take her now rather than force her to endure any more torture.

The choir members finished taking their seats. While the orchestra tuned, the young girls beside her sat up in anticipation of the arrival of the maestro.

When Peter was in his choir seat, he searched the long benches for Rachel. She sat so low that she was difficult to see, but he finally spotted the top of her head in the place where he had left her. The tuning ceased; the conductor entered. A respectful hush fell over the audience as Handel made his way through the orchestra toward the harpsichord.

When the room fell quiet, Rachel began to weep silently; her head bent forward to her chest. Unconsciously, she began to rub her quivering hands together on her lap.

Suddenly, without warning, something touched her hand. Rachel opened her eyes. A hand half the size of hers had reached over and gently taken hold of her hand. Rachel looked up into the dark brown eyes of the beautiful young girl sitting at her side. The soothing warmth of the child's hand and her reassuring smile was overwhelming.

"Are you all right?" the little girl whispered.

Rachel could not speak. She could not nod or shake her head no. She simply stared back into the girl's eyes.

"I cry sometimes, too," the girl whispered, her hand tightening around Rachel's.

The child smiled again; her innocence was sweet and comforting. Rachel's breathing slowed and deepened.

"Have you been here before?" asked the little girl.

Rachel shook her head, "No."

"I have—a lot. It's a good place to come if you are sad." The girl smiled at Rachel, then looked over to where Handel was sitting down at the harpsichord. Rachel could feel the excitement of the small girl through her hand. It pulsed as only a child's can when the anticipation is more than a small body can hold. Rachel remembered feeling that sensation in anticipation of Christmas. It fascinated her to think that what was about to happen could elicit such an emotion from her young friend. She followed the girl's eyes to the man sitting before the orchestra. His hand rose. When it came down, music filled the chapel. The girl sat straight up and erect upon hearing it. Rachel's eyes turned back from the orchestra to the face of her small companion. As she watched the infinite wonder in the child's face, she forgot herself. Rachel's sadness was consumed in absolute amazement. She stared in awe, looking back and forth between the musicians and the girl. She located Peter in the choir, and his face reflected the same wondrous countenance as her young friend. Though she was not conscious of the change, Rachel was no longer afraid.

And the Glory of the Lord Shall Be Revealed

———

THE FIRST HOUR PASSED AS THOUGH IT WERE BUT A MINUTE. From the moment the music started, Rachel lost all track of the passing time. With each new phrase of resplendent melody, Rachel was miraculously transported from misery to solacement. In spite of her vehement attempts to dissuade him, how grateful she was for Peter's insistence that she accompany him. Now that she was here, and could personally witness what Peter had told her, she realized that what he had said was true: the music did somehow have the power to stir her very soul.

The words "Comfort ye" had comforted her. The voice of song was as the voice of God crying to her in her own wilderness. Truly, just as had been sung, the glory of the Lord had been revealed to her as if the Lord himself had spoken it.

———

But equal in influence to the music in awakening her tired heart was the simple and innocent touch of the one at her side. The young girl, with a tender caress of her hand, had brought comfort to Rachel in a way she had not experienced in years bereaved of affection. To Rachel, the warmth of the child's small hand, together with the healing strains of perfect harmony, was a sign from God as real as any angelic visitation. Her heart burned within in her, not from an imaginary source, but from an undeniable testament of spirit that God actually knew her and that He loved her. For the first time in as long as she could remember, hope began to inch its way back into the void where it once had been. Strength seeped back into her failing limbs. Color pressed back into her pale cheeks, forced there by the swelling of her spirit within her. In the very moment she began to believe that all of the events of the night were divinely orchestrated and executed for her behalf, the floor dropped out from beneath her.

"'He shall feed his flock like a shepherd; and He shall gather the lambs with His arm, and carry them to His bosom, and gently lead those that are with young.'"

No words the alto soloist could have sung would have stabbed at her more deeply. These were the same words the priest had told her years before, and they came back into her mind with frightful force. The despair of that dreadful day flooded back in a torrent of abominable shame. Rachel suddenly found it difficult to breathe; suffocating walls of inadequacy closed in all around her. A dark urgency and fear of impending doom encircled her. She suffered as only a mother can when faced with the most basic and difficult of maternal questions: Did she do all that she could? Did she put her child's needs ahead of her own? The question of negligence was like a terrible maze which she had to negotiate her way through every day. Every doubt she had ever confronted herself with over years of self-analysis seemed to combine into one great load of perilous guilt. The atrocity of abandoning her child suddenly seemed more repulsive than any act of which a mother could be capable. She had shunned and forsaken her divine nature. She became intensely aware of where she was: in the very place that haunted her most.

For the first months after giving up Christina, she remembered going to the Foundling Hospital often, pressing her ear to the outer wall in hopes of hearing an infant's coo or soft cry. She heard nothing. In subsequent years, when she realized there was little hope that her daughter was still there, she stopped going back. Surely, the baby would have been placed in a home where she would never learn of her true mother and father; they were simple paupers, there was nothing to tell.

The more time passed, the more careful she was not to get within sight of the building. The large gate menaced her dreams. The shadowed walls of the hospital towered over any chance of happiness. Now she found herself in the middle of it again, hearing the same words spoken to her on that irretrievable day. The same words that had once brought peace now brought only pain.

"Why am I here?" she asked herself, searching the chapel for a way out. "Why would God let this happen? Haven't I suffered enough?"

Rachel had unwittingly allowed herself to be lulled into believing that God had somehow devised this night as a sign of absolution; instead, she now felt utterly forsaken. Tears of self-reproach streamed down her face, falling in drops from her chin to her chest. Her fragile body began to tremble with the regret of her awful decision of so many years ago. She felt the warm hand of the child at her side take her hand and hold it tight; but Rachel was beyond comfort. There was nothing that could convince her that she had done the right thing. Rachel wished she could hide—dissolve away into nothingness. But that was impossible. There was no place to run where she could escape the judgment of the two she feared most, God and her own.

At the moment that she was about to abandon any hope of forgiveness in this life or in the life to come, a last pitiful prayer fell in a whisper from her lips.

"Dear God. Please forgive me."

At that moment, the words of the soloist changed.

"'Come unto Him, all ye that labour. Come unto Him, all ye that are heavy laden, and He shall give you rest.'"

As if raised by the omnipotent hand of God Himself, Rachel was compelled to lift her head. When her tear-filled eyes opened, they were met by a smile. Her young companion held her hand and gazed at her with a smile of flawless purity. Rachel felt small fingers press tightly around hers; then the child turned back to the front, but not before gently pulling her hair back from her face and neck.

What Rachel beheld sent a flush of emotion through her entire frame. Her eyes gleamed with childlike wonder.

There, on the girl's neck, just below her ear, was a small birthmark, an unmistakable birthmark. The tiny brown mark was indelibly imprinted in Rachel's heart and mind. She had kissed it a thousand times with grateful lips, rained drops of gratitude on it from thankful eyes, caressed it countless times with loving fingers. There was the mark before her, in the exact place where Rachel once loved to nuzzle her little baby the most. She knew unequivocally that the beautiful child at her side was her own dear Christina.

Never could she have expected this. In her time of deepest despair, at the very moment that she felt she would be consumed both body and spirit, she had been snatched from the jaws of hell. To her, it was as real as emerging from her own personal Gethsemane after a long night of excruciating agony. Her prayer was answered. In God's tender and infinite mercy, she was redeemed. Nothing could have proved His forgiveness more than the realization that she was looking on the face of her own beloved Christina. Truly, a blessing beyond any she had dared hope for sat at her side.

She cradled Christina's hand in both of hers. She lifted it to her cheek, wetting it with grateful tears. Christina did not offer the slightest objection, but tenderly smiled her approval at Rachel. The child looked long into Rachel's moist eyes, but did not speak.

"'Take His yoke upon you, and learn of Him; for He is meek and lowly of heart; and ye shall find rest unto your souls.'" Again the alto was singing the sweet melody. The words found their way into Rachel's heart. Her gaze moved to the silver-wigged man at the harpsichord, who was accompanying the singer with the beautiful voice. In the quiet of her heart she thanked the Lord for the man who had restored her life. Her eyes then went to a handsome young face in the choir. For Rachel, those two people had been the means by which God had granted her a miracle. Each had done his part to bring to pass the glorious gift now bestowed upon her. She would never forget them.

Yet still, along with the unimaginable joy in Rachel's heart, there was also one quiet corner of sadness.

Surely He Hath Borne Our Griefs

THE ABSENCE OF LIGHT WAS PROFOUNDLY COMPLETE IN THE large stone room. The chamber was silent; nothing stirred, nothing moved. The moon was still very low in the sky, not nearly high enough to reflect any light through the high windows. Only those who inhabited the room had sight sufficient to penetrate the darkness—not because their vision had grown keener, but from years of seeing so little for so long. In the black of night, they could visualize from memory unseen objects as clearly as they could see them during the dim hours of daylight. They learned to identify the source of even the tiniest movement without the help of sight. For those in debtors' prison, there was little difference between day and night; their brains were conditioned to see and hear what their eyes and ears couldn't.

Thus, it was nothing short of miraculous that no one heard or saw anything to warn of an intruder prior to the beam of light shining through the small opening in the prison door. Whoever it was had come as if out of nowhere.

The lock clicked. The door opened, but not with its usual clang from smashing against the interior wall. Instead, it opened slowly, until the narrow doorway was fully vacant. Into the empty portal stepped the jailer, his large body filling much of the opening. He reached forward with the torch until the light filled the interior of the room. Several of those crouched closest to him winced at the bright light. Many shielded their eyes with their arms. Whispered curses slipped from the lips of some of the prisoners far enough into the shadows to not be detected. The jailer did not speak. He stood solemnly, peering at the filthy faces of the men within the glowing influence of the torch.

Jonathon watched from his place against the wall. He knew nothing of what it meant, but something had happened, of that he was sure. He immediately assumed the worst. Over the many years that he had been condemned to the foul chamber, he had seen the jailer enter the room on only a handful of occasions. Never had the news been good. Twice before it was to announce the death of a prisoner's closest kin; twice to announce new prison policies designed to make the unpleasant more unbearable.

But this event was especially peculiar because of the time of day. If the jailer were nothing else, he was both prompt and punctual about leaving when quitting time came. His work efforts were strictly perfunctory. A visit from him at night was unprecedented. The absolute oddity of the event was the only plausible explanation for why no one had heard his approach.

In time the jailer spoke, his voice serene and clear, "You are free to go—all of you."

The young convict, the most recent incarcerate, jumped to his feet. "Is it true? Are we free?"

"Your debt has been paid, come on now—hurry along." The jailer stood to the side as the boy leapt past him and disappeared out the door. The others in the room reacted as if they had not understood. There was a long, nerve-racking interval before another inmate cautiously slipped through the door. Once the second man disappeared, other men jumped to their feet in disbelief. More prisoners poured out the opening, some unconsciously wincing when passing the guard as if anticipating a blow, but none came. A bottleneck started to form at the door, since only one could fit through at a time, but once in the hall, men ran wildly for the stairway leading out, both laughing and crying.

Jonathon had not moved from his place. Instead of watching the evacuation of the cell, he stared at the jailer. Jonathon incredulously studied his face throughout the cleansing of the prison, trying his best to determine what mischief he was about. But the jailer's eyes and jaw were fixed; Jonathon could find no deceit in him. Still, he did not believe they were truly free.

When the last of those at the door disappeared through the opening, the jailer took a step toward Jonathon.

"Did you hear me? You're free," the jailer said. "Go."

Jonathon did not stand, nor did he move. The sudden turn of events was incomprehensible to him. The jailer saw the confusion on his face.

"Go," he assured him a second time. "I speak the truth. Go home, you are free."

The moment he heard the word "home," Jonathon felt warm blood flood to the surface of his cold skin. A tremor of excitement shot through his entire body. Still, a part of him dared not believe. He rose to his feet and walked toward the door; then stopped and turned back. Without a word, he moved back to a dark corner where the stone ceiling reached closest to the ground. He knelt down and reached deep into the darkness of the cave. When he stood back on his feet and turned around he had in his arms the frail body of an old man, ragged and feeble. The old man's face was as pale as death. Jonathon carried the man to where the jailer stood. He started through the door then stopped short. He turned back to the jailer and asked in a whisper, "How is it done?"

"The *Messiah* has freed you. Your debt is paid."

Jonathon looked at him astonished. He slid past the jailer through the doorway and started up the stone stairs. He paused one last time when he heard the jailer's voice echo from below:

"Handel performs it even now at the Foundling Hospital.

Jonathon did not fully comprehend the circumstance of his emancipation, but he accepted it with humble gratitude. He took a deep breath, then continued upward.

The air grew lighter and fresher with each step. Instead of his legs growing tired from the climb, they became stronger. He still feared the gate might be closed at the top of the stairs, but, to his amazement, it was open wide. He walked up the long ascending ramp to the outer gate; now only a sky full of stars was above him. The impenetrable walls that had long surrounded him gradually lowered as he walked, until they finally dipped below his head, his chest, then his feet. For the first time in eleven years, Jonathon stepped out onto the street, a free man.

Far from the abominable hole dug for debtors, the music of hope rang out into the streets from the open doors of the Foundling Hospital chapel. With the exception of the governor, none who heard the joyful noise had any knowledge of what was transpiring in the distant prison cell beneath the earth. A generous portion of the concert proceeds was directed by Handel to go to those imprisoned for insolvency. Handel requested it, the governor made sure of it.

"'Surely, surely, He hath borne our griefs and carried our sorrows.'"

The words struck with great power at Peter's very center of being. All around were others like him, their voices raised in song. Music engulfed him.

"'He was wounded for our transgressions; He was bruised for our iniquities.'"

The words of Isaiah prophesied of Christ's suffering. Handel's music was the fulfilled ennoblement of those verses into song. Peter reached his voice to heaven, fully believing that it would be heard. He had spoken to God innumerable times in years past, but now he sang to Him. He had long followed this *Messiah* which he now sang. It changed him—changed his heart forever. It had bound him with cords so strong that he could not escape.

In one great crescendo, the chorus and orchestra bore witness musically of the great truth that Peter had come to know beyond any shadow of doubt.

"'The chastisement of our peace was upon Him.'"

Peter could hardly sing the words. Emotions he had known only at a distance were suddenly as familiar as a long-forgotten friend. He sensed that he was meant to feel as he did—that a path had been prepared for him as real as if someone had gone before. In that very moment he realized that this was the exact place to which he had been led. His words became a prayer, his song, a petition. Peter's spirit was filled with deep and abiding gratitude. As he looked on the man whose conducting hand he followed, Peter thanked God for landing Handel's bent gold button within reach of his small hand so many years before.

Rachel stared without ceasing at Christina, who did not shrink from the gaze. It was not that she enjoyed the attention, but she innocently sensed that it somehow brought peace to her new friend. She endured it graciously.

Now that Rachel knew for certain the identity of Christina, she thought herself a fool for not recognizing her sooner. Every detail of her face was exactly as Rachel remembered. Each day in the years since she had given up her child, she had imagined her growing and the maturation of her perfect features. She passed the hours at the bakery picturing Christina in her mind. In her meager and humble way, she celebrated each birthday—humming and singing to the child she could not hold. In her dreams, Rachel had witnessed her daughter's first step. She had wiped away countless tears from little falls, and rocked her little girl to sleep in the soft crick of her arm. In her mind, Rachel had studied her sleeping child's face, silently praying that, according to God's grace, she might sometime see her again and recognize her.

Rachel's prayer was answered: her daughter was here, now, at her side. Now that the truth of her daughter's existence was revealed to her, blessed memories vividly returned. The child's chestnut-brown eyes were exactly like Rachel's. Like clear round crystal windows to her heart, they beamed sweet purity. Christina's hair, although slightly lighter in hue than Rachel's, fell in long thick curls about her shoulders. Even though age separated them by many years, the one mirrored the other as summer does spring.

Christina's gentle, comforting smile was Jonathon's. In it was security, enduring loyalty. It was an assuring smile of safety in an unsafe world. When the daughter smiled, the mother was calmed. Rachel could innately sense so much of Jonathon in Christina—the touch of her hand, the unspoken confidence she felt in her presence. There was not a whit of falseness in the embrace of her hand and smile. Somehow, incomprehensible though it may have seemed, Rachel felt a comforting peace that things were as God wanted them.

Hallelujah

JONATHON PLODDED THROUGH THE STREETS OF LONDON,
trying his best to find a section of town more familiar to him. He looked
for signs, landmarks, anything that might steer him in the direction of
home. The night was not far enough along to dispel the faint glow on the
western horizon; once he spotted it, he headed towards it. He had no idea
where the man whom he carried belonged or if he belonged to anyone. For
now, he belonged to Jonathon.

The failing elder slipped back and forth between delusion and sleep.
Jonathon believed with some care, the man could retrieve enough strength
to tell him of his people and their whereabouts. Regardless of the difficulty, he was determined to deliver the man to his home.

But there was another matter which preoccupied Jonathon's thoughts far more than any other. It was something he had been able to suppress while in prison, but freedom, especially his unexpected and unannounced freedom, had brought the harrowing feelings to the forefront of his mind. He could not disregard the long repressed fear that after long years of separation, he had been replaced. Jonathon could not imagine how Rachel could have endured or lived alone. It was difficult enough for them to make ends meet before he was imprisoned, likely impossible without him. It was an undeniable reality that it was Rachel who gave him the stamina and will to live within those terrible walls, but now his liberation demanded that he confront the awful possibility of what he had daily denied. Perhaps Rachel had either found another to support her or died of starvation and exposure trying to sustain life alone.

Jonathon trudged toward home very uncertain of whether he had a home. How painfully uncomfortable it would be for him to show up without any warning. The thought came to him to go elsewhere, but he had nowhere else to go. The prospect of arriving in the night, without giving Rachel time to prepare her mind and circumstances, seemed especially cruel. It had been years since the letter was delivered to him by the Packrat, so much could have happened in the interim. He tried to mentally prepare himself for any possible scenario he might happen upon and the subsequent response that would be most appropriate. As he considered the possibilities, he experienced every emotion he might be forced to endure. He shuddered at the thought of Rachel's being dead. His soul groaned within him at the thought of silently enduring the pain of seeing her with someone else, but, if such were the case, he would not interfere. His heart skipped at the impossible thought that she and Christina would be alive and daily watching and waiting for her father's return. It was then that a truth he had long denied swept into his mind like a bitter wind: Christina was already gone. During the endless days of incarceration, he had imagined a perfect world to which he would return. The hope of it was the only joy he could muster in that dismal place. However, the burden of sudden freedom forced him to face the inevitable reality that his daughter would not be home. The thought of not seeing her again cut into his already wounded heart. It was more than his body could sustain. His strength gave out; he fell forward to his knees, cradling the man in his arms from the fall. There, in the twilight, out of the sight of all, Jonathon wept.

Long before he was close to home, Jonathon resolved that it would be in Rachel's best interest if he did not interfere if she had taken another husband. It was likely that she would not even recognize him in his emaciated state and fully bearded face. He could pretend himself a beggar, make a brief assessment of the situation, then act according to what he saw. He already assured himself that regardless of what awaited him, he would not think any the less of her. He could only imagine the terrible hurt and desolation that she must have suffered over the past ten years. Whatever she had done to stay alive was justified a hundred times over.

The faint glow on the horizon faded away into night. Building fronts and street corners began to be familiar to him. He recognized street signs and lamps as he entered the neighborhood of his home. Much had changed, but more had not. He stopped at the bakery to look in the window. He could smell the faint aroma of bread even outside the door. Instantly, the smell stimulated volumes of memories, but there were other remembrances more pressing.

He moved on, certain now of every step from here to his destination. When he came around the final corner, the flat on the corner was dark. No light shone from within; there was no firelight, no candle. His first thought was the worst of thoughts, but it was only brief. He forced it out of his mind, refusing to assume anything without undeniable evidence of it.

His walk slowed as he crossed the street to the small door he had pictured in his mind through the past years of incarceration. He had imagined this moment many times. He paused at the door, not certain what to do. It was then that he noticed something he considered both strange and an answer to prayer: the curtain of the window was wide open. He laid the man in his arms on the ground near the door, then peered through the grayed glass. It was difficult to see in at first, but in time his eyes, which had grown accustomed to seeing in the darkness, adjusted to the shade of the room and he could make out the interior. What he saw sent a chill down his spine, but not a chill of fear; it was joy, for nothing had changed. The room was exactly as he remembered, with the exception of considerable wear and aging. Nothing was added that would indicate another had joined her, nothing was taken away, to indicate a move. Anyone who might have taken over the place would have thrown away most of the furnishings. The bed was bowed, the blankets threadbare. He could not spot one thing that was new or different from his memory. But still he was not fully certain until his gaze settled on a bittersweet and undeniable sign that Rachel was indeed alive.

On the corner of the bed, folded perfectly with the corners tucked under, was a tiny baby blanket. It bore no wear—no holes, no spots. Whoever put it there had done so with great care, for there was not one wrinkle, nor a corner out of place. Jonathon recognized the tiny blanket of his infant daughter. By some miracle, Rachel was alive and living there. To anyone else, the small blanket would have been only a rag, to her it meant the world. Another chill went down his back when he considered the countless nights she must have suffered with only the small blanket to remind her of her baby. Only Jonathon knew the vast extent of Rachel's love for Christina. He shuddered to think of the agony she must have suffered in losing both her husband and her infant daughter. He could only imagine the heart-wrenching pain she must have gone through in the miserable years of being alone. While he looked in, a ribbon of smoke curled up from the fireplace. The gray wisp removed any last shred of doubt. He did not know where she was, only that she lived. Once he was certain of Rachel's existence, his mind suddenly caught hold on what the jailer had told him:

"Handel performs it even now at the Foundling Hospital."

Jonathon did not know anything of Handel, but he knew he must find him and thank him. He could not remember the location of the hospital, but he recalled hearing talk of it. He hastened to the door—perchance it would be unsecured. When he turned the lock, the door swung open. He carefully picked up his sick companion and entered the small flat. He stopped just inside the threshold long enough to take a deep breath of home, then gently laid the old man on the bed and covered him with a thin blanket. As he pulled his hand from under the old man, the man grasped hold of Jonathon's arm.

"You're going there. Take me, please!"

Jonathon understood. He did not question the man's intent or his physical ability to carry on, he picked him up and hurried out the door, pulling it closed behind him. He followed his feelings, not knowing beforehand where he should go. He prayed silently that God would lead his steps. He simply walked forward, putting one foot ahead of the other in the hope that by some miracle he might find his way to him to whom he owed his freedom. In spite of fatigue, he continued on, trusting himself to the voice of his heart. When he rounded a corner, expecting that maybe he was close, he recognized a storefront he had passed minutes before; he had circled back to the same place. Frustrated, he sat down on the steps of a large building to rest. He determined to rest well before trying to find his way back home.

Disappointed, he waited for his heart to slow and his panting to cease. When he felt rested enough to get up, he heard a sound. The distant sound of music echoed down the length of the street. He could barely discern it, but it was there. Had he not stopped in the place that he did and rested long enough for his internal noises to silence, he was certain he never would have heard it. He needed but to follow the sound to the source. He started to pick up the old man.

"I can do part," his companion stammered while struggling to his feet. Jonathon pulled the man's arm over his shoulder and together they walked in the direction from which the music came. For the first few blocks they lost the sound several times. Each time, they would stop and listen quietly until it again revealed itself, then on they would go. When the sound became constant, they moved faster, certain they were close.

Within a short time, the lighted chapel came into view through the opened gates of the Foundling Hospital. They could clearly hear the voice of a bass soloist as they passed through the gate.

Jonathon could hear the words as he helped his companion along a narrow walk leading to the short stairway up to the chapel doors. The soloist sang no more, the orchestra finished, there was a pause. Jonathon walked on, though he did not breathe until the orchestra started up again with the introduction of the next piece. He climbed the stairs one by one; it was all he could do to wait for his companion to get his feet up the next stair.

"Go," the old man said, out of breath, but Jonathon's hold on the man did not waver in the least. He would go only as fast as the man's feeble legs would allow. As they reached the top of the stair, the doorman turned to see them. It was the first time that Jonathon considered how they must have looked. Torn, tattered—filthy in every way. The stench of their clothes must have seemed hideous to the doorman. Long locks of matted hair covered most of their faces. Jonathon was certain that he and his friend had the sure appearance of the vomited offscourings of hell. He knew they would not be allowed to enter; but to his astonishment, the man stepped to the side and pulled back the door to allow them entrance. As he did, a grand chorus of voices burst forth from within.

"'Hallelujah.'"

Peter felt the word swell within him, then gush forth as a spring of triumphant praise.

"'Hallelujah.'"

Just as he had witnessed in Covent Garden, Peter watched the entire congregation rise to its feet in one great wave. He looked for Rachel among the throng. Peter spotted her in the center section exactly where he had left her, surrounded by children on every side. She stood erect and tall, her face upward. A heavenly glow seemed to radiate from her. Their eyes met across the expanse of the chapel. Nothing Rachel could have spoken in words could have exclaimed her gratitude any more powerfully or completely. As thankful as she was for him, Peter was just as grateful for her. The boy had come to know and love her as his own mother. Her suffering was the crucible in which their friendship was forged. She helped him and influenced him in ways that only a mother could. If there was anything he could do to ease the suffering of this woman he esteemed above all others, he would do it happily. How many times would Peter have gladly given himself up to prison in trade for her beloved Jonathon, but he could not. If he could have somehow reached over the wall of the hospital and rescued the baby back into Rachel's arms, he would have. To see her now and know that in some small way he had brought even a glimmer of hope in her otherwise lonely world meant the world to him. Joy and delight at the goodness of God filled him to the point that he could not contain himself. He praised his God in song for allowing him to be an instrument of peace to one so entirely deserving. As he sang the verses, a silent voice spoke to his soul of the absolute reality of that which he sang.

"'For the Lord God omnipotent reigneth. For the Lord God omnipotent reigneth.'"

Handel stood tall and large before them. When he felt the audience rise to their feet behind him, he abandoned his seat at the harpsichord, preferring to stand with them. For Handel, the entire night had been one of holy solemnity. To this point, the performance had been flawless. Had his choir been the same that sang on the plains of Judea, they could not have sounded more perfect than at that moment. His soloists sang as seraphs, granted mortality in this world for the very purpose for which he had employed them.

What Handel had lost in sight was compensated for with his already perfected ear, but even he could find no blemish in the heavenly strains.

At bar twenty-two, upon the entrance of the basses, in a spontaneous display of unbridled ecstasy, Handel began to rock from side to side, his upward-raised arms swinging back and forth in joyful time. His wig bounced atop his head in marked cadence with his arms.

Finally, Handel understood: This was indeed the purpose that the Lord had in mind for *Messiah*. It was not to be profited from, it was to be profited by. *Messiah* was written that men might look to God and be raised in both spirit and body as truly and completely as Christ was raised from the tomb. Handel sang aloud with the choir, "'The kingdom of this world is become the kingdom of our Lord, and of His Christ; and of His Christ.'"

Rachel leaned forward with anticipation when the choir and orchestra subdued to little more than a whisper. Suddenly, as if the roof had opened and choirs of angels had joined in, the anthem amplified into magnificent exultation. Rachel stood in awe, holding Christina's hand in her own. She did not think it possible for the awkward speech of humans to express the gratitude and adoration of her soul at being again united with her dear Christina—but music could. As if a shining conduit connected her heart to the choir and orchestra, she was hearing the grateful hymn of her own soul. The anthem was a celebration of spirit. Rachel's soul rose up to sing praise with all the others.

She watched the face of her beloved Christina. The child marveled at it all, her eyes wide, her lips mouthing the words as she heard them. The music held her spellbound, permeating the innermost reach of her being. She was thankful for a hand to hold. She trusted the woman at her side. Though she did not know why, she felt at home with the sad visitor. She leaned her head on the woman's side, then felt a gentle hand on her shoulder.

"'And He shall reign forever and ever.'"

"Who is the man who buys men's freedom with song," wondered Jonathon. He stood in the back door of the chapel, trying desperately to see the face of the man he believed to be Handel. Jonathon stepped forward to the area immediately adjacent to those seated at the rear of the chapel. Many near him glanced briefly, but no one spoke, nor did their eyes tarry long.

Seated near the rear door was the hospital governor. The moment he saw them, he knew from whence they had come. His thoughts were quickened to recall the one leper of the ten. He didn't question them; he knew why they had come. He silently signaled those at the door not to impede the intrusion. Jonathon was unaware of all of this. His eyes were forward, fastened on the man he believed to be the instrument of God's pure love. Without considering his own appearance, he touched the shoulder of a finely dressed man at the end of the bench nearest the aisle.

"Handel?" he queried.

Without a second glance, the man pointed to the large man leading the music near the front of the chapel. His identity was as Jonathon had thought. Through the standing crowd, he could only catch glimpses of the conductor. He could see his flailing arms and the prodigious bounce of his body, but it was difficult to see his face. He believed it odd that a man such as this, a man of culture and art, should have any interest in the lowly men of debtors' prison; yet he was grateful he did.

"What manner of man is this?" wondered Jonathon aloud. He watched Handel with indelible interest, riveting his entire mind upon him to whom he owed his freedom. After spending many years in prison for the crime of debt, he had never truly considered himself a debtor until this moment. The man Handel had restored everything that he held sacred: his life, his freedom, and, hopefully, his Rachel.

As he watched from a distance, he committed himself to a life of doing as had been done for him. Then, as if shaken out of sleep, Jonathon's head jerked back as the words of the choir gripped his mind.

"'King of kings.'"

Until that moment, he had been so preoccupied with Handel that he had not fully considered the music. The sopranos and altos followed those words in unison.

"'Forever and ever, Hallelujah, Hallelujah.'"

The truth of which they sang pealed in his ears, clear as the moon, fair as the sun. In his haste to praise the instrument by which the song of redemption was played, he had forgotten the author of it. He was so captivated by the healing water that he had unwittingly overlooked the precious spring from which it came. All at once, the everlasting truth of the salvation of all mankind was made manifest to him in the jubilant hallelujahs.

"'King of kings.'"

"'Forever and ever, Hallelujah, Hallelujah.'"

"'And Lord of lords.'"

"'Forever and ever, Hallelujah, Hallelujah.'"

"'King of kings.'"

"'Forever and ever, Hallelujah, Hallelujah.'"

"'And Lord of lords.'"

"'King of kings and Lord of lords; and He shall reign forever and ever.'"

Brown-stained tears coursed down Jonathon's soiled face then disappeared into the long hairs of his beard. The choir's hallelujahs became his own personal prayer of rejoicing, for he that was dead was alive again, he that was lost was found. In one last triumphant shout, the choir raised to heaven their anthem of praise.

"'Hallelujah! Hallelujah! Hallelujah! Hallelujah!'"

With one last great chord, Handel raised his arms high above his head. When they came down, the room fell silent.

I Know That My Redeemer Liveth

WHEN THE CONCERT CAME TO A CLOSE, NO ONE WAS prepared for it to finish. So enraptured were the occupants of the chapel that the end arrived before anyone was ready to leave. At first, everyone stayed in his and her seats, but in time, people began to look for the exits. In order to minimize any confusion, the children of the hospital were the first to be escorted out. Rachel did not want to see Christina leave, yet she remained calm. Her first thought was to reveal her identity to her daughter and petition the sisters to let her take the child, but her motherly instincts forbade her. To uncloak herself now would surely be unsettling to the child. If she were ever to reveal her secret to Christina, it must only be after she was certain that the life she could give her was more desirable than the life her daughter now enjoyed. Rachel knew she must again do what was best for Christina. At that moment, her decision was made.

"Good-bye," said Christina.

"Wait," beckoned Rachel, as Christina began to slide down the narrow space toward the aisle. Christina spun around.

"May I visit you?" Rachel asked in a whisper. Christina heard her perfectly well.

"Ask for Christina," she said smiling. "The sisters will find me. Goodbye."

The little girl raised her hand with an excited wave. Rachel waved back, her arm never feeling so young. She watched Christina move out into the aisle and take her place in the row of other children. A sister led the line toward the back of the chapel and the rear door. Before Christina disappeared through the door, she turned back smiling and waved one last time; Rachel was waiting with her open palm held high. Christina saw the upraised hand through the moving crowd just before being escorted past those standing near the back exit of the dark hall.

No sooner had Rachel's waving arm fallen to rest at her side than Peter appeared next to her. When she saw him, tears filled her eyes. She collapsed on the bench with her hand held over her mouth in disbelief.

"I have seen her," she said through the cracks between her fingers. Peter sat down on the bench next to her.

"I have seen her," Rachel said again, taking her hands from her face. "We spoke—she held my hand. Oh, blessed night, wonderful night! She was here at my side the entire time. She was here." Rachel put her hand down on the bench.

"She is beautiful, Peter. My dear Christina was here at my side—my Christina. She is just as I imagined. She was so kind to me. Of course, she doesn't know that I am her mother, but I know who she is."

Peter was uncertain what to say. Although it was difficult to believe, he dared not injure the delicate petals of Rachel's hope with doubt. As much as he wished for it to be true, it would have required nothing less than a miracle.

"Are you certain?" he asked, more introspectively than to her. He did not realize he had even spoken until she looked at him, her face translucent.

"I saw the birthmark behind her ear. I would never have known otherwise, but it was there. I saw it." Rachel could see by his bewildered face that Peter did not comprehend what she had said.

"Remember—remember the night she was born, I showed you. 'She will always have it. It is a mark placed by God to remind us that her life is a gift to us. Christina, our Christmas gift from God.' Do you remember?'"

All at once, the events of the night long ago surged back into his mind. He remembered the baby, especially the mark on the side of her neck. He himself had touched the little brown spot of skin behind the infant's ear. Peter put a finger on his chest and rubbed gently. Rachel could not see it, but beneath his shirt, next to his skin was a small locket hanging from a gold chain. The moment his fingers found the precious token he had saved through the years, he knew she had spoken the truth. Christina had been there; Rachel did see her. Of that he was absolutely certain.

"My prayer is answered," she sighed peacefully. Her words struck with great force in Peter's mind. He looked in her eyes. Profound gratitude flowed like morning light from her bright eyes to his. At that moment he understood why it was so important for Rachel to attend— why he was so compelled to bring her to the chapel, regardless of her refusals. Her presence in that exact spot on that exact night was divinely arranged. When he realized his role in the sacred scheme, an eternal truth that had vexed Peter his entire life was wholly affirmed. The one question that had beset his mind from the time he was a child was finally answered. The miracle of this night was as much for him as for Rachel. He knew that it was not by chance that he had brought her to the concert. It was not by chance that he had gone to her home, seen the light under the door, thrown open the curtains, and carried her most of the way here. It was not by chance that he was in the choir, not by chance that throughout his life the music of *Messiah* had so resonated within him that he could not let go of it. At long last, he knew why he had been led to the stump beneath the window, heard the music, and followed it to this very place. Most of all, he finally understood why the sword found its way to Handel's gold button, which then found its way to him. All of it was designed to answer the deserved and faithful prayers of Rachel—Earth's most humble inhabitant. God needed Rachel to be at this place at this very moment. And God needed Peter to help Him.

As the thought came to his mind, with it came also the burning witness to his heart that her prayer was not the only petition that had been answered. The Holy Spirit testified to Peter of the one thing that he desired to know above all others: that God personally knew him. God knew the Packrat. He could not use Peter if He did not know him. Of a surety, God knew his name, and what was even more significant, He knew he could count on him. Peter had found his answer. The tiny seed that was planted in his soul while he was sitting below the window on Brook Street had flowered into a harvest so wonderful that his soul could hardly contain it.

Upon concluding, Handel took occasion to thank his musicians before they began to disperse. He then graciously thanked those in the audience who took occasion to speak to him directly.

Handel was spent. Between his tenacious efforts on the harpsichord as well as conducting the choir and orchestra, it was all he could do to lift his arms. The majesty of the performance sustained him easily through the three and some hours of the concert, but, once finished, fatigue was quick to come. He leaned heavily on the harpsichord to catch his breath while he spoke to those who approached him personally. Once the front rows were emptied, he made quick business of putting his things together to get on his way. He was just finishing the task when a man of influence, Lord Kinnoul, stepped to his side.

"Excellent work, Mr. Handel. You have provided our town with a fine entertainment."

Handel turned to him, his face somber.

"My Lord, I should be sorry if I only entertained them. I wished to make them better."

He picked up his score, slid it under his arm, and began to make his way to the stage door.

Jonathon did not notice the people walking by him and out the rear exit. Surprisingly few uttered any disdain at his unkempt attire and the putrid smell as they passed by, but Jonathon did not hear them. His eye and mind were firmly fixed on Handel. He hoped that the benevolent composer might find his way to the back of the chapel where Jonathon might approach and thank him. It was certain that Jonathon would not be allowed to go to Handel; already there were ushers making their way up the aisles, escorting patrons out and clearing the chapel. Jonathon wondered if he would ever get the chance again, when his appearance and words might be better prepared. He anxiously waited while people surrounding Handel thinned and eventually left. He still held out hope that Handel's exit might be through the door next to him; he prayed that it would be. As he waited, a sudden feeling of gladness came over him. A surge of unexplainable elation filled his soul. So real was the emotion that he assumed his prayer had been heard and would be granted. His companion rested at the end of the last bench. Jonathon could hear his rattled breathing under the noise of people's voices and moving feet. He glanced at the sick, old man, considering whether to wake him so he too might meet their liberator, but he determined to wait and let the man dream of sweet freedom. However, because of what Handel had done for him, Jonathon determined to not let the sun set again before he would find and deliver his companion to loved ones.

Jonathon fully readied himself to express his profound gratitude to Handel. He had not words commensurate with his appreciation, but prayed that Handel would feel his profound thanks. Jonathon watched the conductor pick up his things, fully expecting him to turn his way—but he didn't. Handel walked toward the side door. Before he disappeared into the dark hall and out of sight, Jonathon whispered solemnly.

"Thank you."

While the words were still on his lips, a woman, aided by a young man, silently walked up the aisle inches behind him and out the open door.

But Thanks Be to God

PLEASE, MAY WE SIT A SPELL," RACHEL ASKED IN A TONE OF apology.

"Of course, I'm sorry; I should have suggested it before. You must be tired," Peter said, spotting a bench in the courtyard near the large front gate. He helped Rachel take a seat, then sat down at her side. The walks were full of people finding their way to waiting carriages and dispersing in every direction. The general atmosphere was one of reverence. There was little talk; what needed to be said was done so with prudence and quietude. The concert had been a collective catharsis for many of those in attendance, evidenced by their subsequent actions. Even the night was calm and serene. The temperature of the air was gentle and comfortable, the night black and starlit.

Neither Rachel nor Peter felt the need to speak. Each reflected on the events of the night with humble gratitude. The rest stop was not needed so much to renew limbs and body as for quiet reflection, for pondering the significance of the preceding events. It was a time to process internally the greatness of God. It was a time to savor the deep abiding goodness and love, through which they had journeyed in the preceding hours. They knew that the exact feeling of that night would never be theirs again. Tomorrow they would remember the events, but seldom would they feel the pure charity and unconditional love that filled their hearts at that very moment. They each basked in the absolute joy of now, drenching themselves in the cool, clean waters of tranquillity.

Rachel thought of Christina. In her mind she visualized every soft feature of Christina's perfect face over and over again. The sweet song of her voice reverberated with spotless clarity in Rachel's ears. The stark contrast between her despair when entering the chapel and her current state of happiness was staggering. All pain, all fear, all hopelessness were swallowed up and forgotten the moment she recognized her daughter. So exquisite was her joy and so marvelous the miracle given her that she felt as if years of agony were washed away and forgotten that very hour.

Peter thought of *Messiah*. The grand music of redemption filled his mind and soul with thanksgiving. Throughout his life, he had spoken to God; tonight, God spoke to him. His voice was not a voice of thunder, but a still voice, which bore witness to Peter's whole soul of the absolute truth of the words that he had sung. Peter had felt the voice more than he had heard it, and yet the reality of it was preeminent. He felt as sure of this witness as if the words had come directly to his ears from the mouth of God Himself. Surely, God knew him, and, as never before, Peter knew God.

It was a long time before the two rose from the bench to make their way home. Whether minutes or hours had passed, they did not know, nor did they care. They walked home in silence, arm in arm. When they arrived in front of Rachel's small dwelling, she paused before going in.

"Again you've given my daughter to me."

"Are you all right?"

"I'm well. This is a blessed night."

"Is there anything I can do?"

Rachel kissed him on the cheek, then entered the door. Peter watched the door close behind her before leaving.

The room was dark. Rachel couldn't remember if she had left the candle burning or not, but it was most certainly out now. From flawless memory, she walked across the room and put her hand down on the candle sitting at the corner of the table. She took a deep breath through her nose and smelled something that had befouled the room and needed disposing. As she knelt down in front of the gray coals in the fireplace and blew steadily on them, she wondered what it might be. "Bad fruit," she thought, passing it off.

Soon, a fleck of orange appeared in the gray. Slowly, the orange glow spread out from the center until it was the size of a coin. She took from the woodbin a splinter of kindling and held it against the glowing coal. She blew a long steady stream of air on the burning ember until smoke curled up from the wooden match. Seconds later, the tip flamed. She lit the wick of the candle, blew out the match, then rubbed the charred tip of it between her fingers before returning the match to the kindling box.

She stood back on her feet and put the candle on the table. When she turned from the flame, she was startled to see a body lying on the bed. Her first reflex was to withdraw. She stepped back in horror. The body did not move. She thought how foolish she was to leave the door and window open. Surely, some vagrant from off the street had seen the opportunity and seized it. Unsure of what to do, she backed toward the door to secure her escape while she weighed her alternatives. A sudden shiver went up her back. She could sense the presence of someone else in the room. What was more terrifying was that the person was behind her, blocking her escape to the door. She turned around, dreading what or who might be there. Her fears were confirmed. She could perceive the tall image of someone standing in the shadows by the door. He had hidden himself behind the door when she entered. She stepped close to the candle.

"Who is it? Who is there? I have nothing!"

The man stepped forward into the outer edge of the candle's influence. Rachel recoiled at the sight of him. Thick black hair covered his face; his clothes were ragged and torn. Now she knew the source of the foul smell. The man took another step toward her. She backed away from the intruder. His mouth opened; one word came out.

"Rachel."

She looked at him in astonishment. The harrowing feeling of dread she had felt seconds before departed. She picked up the candle and began to inch toward him. The closer she came, the less fear she felt. Clearly, the intruder was not of malicious intent.

"Rachel," he said a second time. The voice was familiar. She stared in disbelief.

"It's Jonathon," he said in a whisper, his voice breaking with emotion. She held up the light to his dark and dirty face. All she could clearly discern through the growth were his wet, blue eyes. It was enough.

"Jonathon," she mouthed the name, but no sound escaped. Tears filled the paths worn down her cheeks from earlier that night. She touched his filthy cheek with her fingers. She saw no beard, but looked through it to the face she adored. He reached out and caressed her cheek with his dirt-stained hand; it was as soft as the breast of a dove. Finally, the well of her soul could no longer be constrained.

"Jonathon," she cried. "My Jonathon. Dear God, Jonathon has come home."

She laughed through tears of joy. He could no longer stand. He dropped to his knees, Rachel with him. He buried his face in her chest and wept. His body shook in her loving arms. She tenderly lifted his face to hers and smiled. To him, she was more beautiful than he could ever remember. She covered every inch of his tarnished face with kisses; no lips had ever touched skin more pure. She loved him wholly and he loved her completely. The candle fell and the flame went out, yet the room was never more full of light.

If God Be for Us

_____

IT WAS MID-MORNING WHEN THE DOOR OF THE MAIN
building of the Foundling Hospital opened and two people emerged.
Christina walked alongside Sister Anne down the exterior stairs of the
hall and across the courtyard.

The grass of the inner court never seemed greener to Christina. She
purposely altered each step of her walk to make sure that her foot did not
fall on the new spring blades which were trying to grow in the narrow
cracks of earth between the placed stones of the walk.

"They have it hard enough without my making things even more difficult," she said aloud.

"Are you making things difficult?" the nun asked.

"On the contrary, I want to make things easy."

"You do make everything easy."

Christina skipped from stone to stone while Sister Anne walked steady and straight. Sister Anne's mind was preoccupied with their destination, Christina's was absorbed in the journey. She looked at the leaves above her, the flowers below—every beauty with which she could fill her eyes. The morning mist was almost completely burned off, but there was still enough vapor in the air to make the dappled sunshine through the trees look like the shafts of heavenly light.

"There are lots of saints about doing good works this morning," Christina said, her head back and looking up at the light through the limbs. Anne smiled. Christina often referred to the spectral phenomenon as "saints doing good works," since all the paintings and stain glass art of God's anointed in the chapel had similar shafts of light coming from heaven to the heads of the blessed saints. She was certain that good works were rewarded with beams of thankful light from the heavens.

When Sister Anne reached the stairs leading up to the chapel door, she stopped. She kneeled down in front of her young companion so she might talk to her face to face.

"Trust your heart, Christina. If God will reveal truth to you, He will do it through your heart. You have a good heart, a pure heart. If there is truth to be found, He will not refuse it to one whose heart is so like His own."

Christina did not understand. She knew that she had visitors—nothing more. In all her days at the Foundling Hospital, she had never had a visitor. But there was something in the words of Sister Anne that gave the event significance beyond a simple visit from a new friend. There was no doubt in her mind that it was the woman from the concert. She was the only person from the outside who had ever even expressed a desire to call upon her. She did not, however, know why the plural form of the word visitor was used. Surely the woman must have brought an additional acquaintance, possibly even her child, perhaps a daughter; the thought of it gave her a thrill.

Sister Anne continued up the stone steps and pushed open the chapel door; the two entered. The light within was subdued. The stained glass panels around the perimeter of the chapel were the chief source of light. They glowed brighter on the eastern wall than the west. Christina learned at a young age to tell the time of day from which windows glowed brightest. She smiled to herself when she saw the bright yellow shafts of glass leading from heaven to the heads of the saints portrayed in the glass art. She was so focused upon the windows that she didn't really notice the couple seated near the front of the chapel until she and Sister Anne were partway down the aisle.

Christina spotted the couple at the same time they turned to see her and Sister Anne coming toward them. Upon seeing them, the two stood to greet them. It was a handsome couple; simply clad but clean and well groomed. Neither looked familiar to her. Certainly this could not be the same lowly woman she had met only a few nights before. The face of the woman she remembered was sad, despairing; she hardly had the strength to sit upright. The woman who stood before her now was beautiful, strong, completely vitalized. It was difficult to imagine that this was the same woman whose hand she had held throughout the concert. But then again, who else could it be. Christina was positively certain she did not know the man. She assumed him to be either a husband or brother. Although there was not an accompanying child, she was not disappointed. Seldom had she been in the immediate presence of an adult man. Her interaction with such a person was infrequent and usually quite formal, almost frightening. Yet, even at first glance, there was something in the face of this man that was reassuring.

Christina glanced back and forth at the two people standing side by side. Her head tipped curiously to the side. When she was close enough for their eyes to meet, Christina recognized the woman. A thrill of excitement swept over her; she had made a friend, and her new friend had come to visit. Nothing like this had ever happened to her before. Her steps quickened; the woman kneeled down to greet her. Christina wrapped her arms around the woman's neck and hugged her. She looked up at the man standing a few steps behind; water filled his eyes. She stood back from the woman kneeling before her; a smiled filled her face.

"You never told me your name," she said.

"Rachel," the woman answered, smiling no less than Christina.

"That's a pretty name."

Sister Anne stepped forward.

"Christina has told me about you. She tells me you joined us for the concert."

"Yes. What a blessed night, sitting with Christina—dear Christina," said Rachel tenderly.

"She told me that you…"

Sister Anne's words trailed off. She watched as Rachel took the girl's hands in hers.

"She told you her name?" the sister asked..

"Yes, Christina. Dear Christina," Rachel answered.

"Christina…dear Christina," Sister Anne echoed softly. She leaned forward and took Rachel's hand from the girl's. The Sister studied it carefully, rolling it over and back in her wrinkled hand. Finally, she lifted Rachel's hand and held it to her cheek in remembrance; Rachel, too, remembered.

"Christina. My dear Christina," Rachel whispered, her voice trembling. A drop of water streaked from Sister Anne's eye across the back of Rachel's hand. Sister Anne smiled at the woman kneeling before her. She took Rachel's hand to her lips and kissed it, then put it back into the hand of Christina, who had been watching. Sister Anne cupped Rachel's face in her hands. She leaned forward and whispered in her ear.

"Your prayer has been heard. I knew you would come."

Sister Anne stepped back from Rachel. Christina's eyes moved back and forth between the sister and Rachel. She looked down at the woman's hand in hers. The sister looked at Jonathon, then held the other child's hand out to him. He quickly stepped from behind Rachel and knelt down in front of Christina. Sister Anne laid Christina's little hand in his. Jonathon's rough, callused hand folded completely over the child's small hand. Christina looked at the man kneeling before her, then at the woman. She glanced back at Sister Anne standing behind her; the sister smiled. Christina looked back at the man. The words that Sister Anne had spoken earlier resonated within her.

"If God will reveal truth to you, He will do it through your heart."

She took a long deep breath, letting her mind quiet so she could listen to the silent voice of her heart. She looked again at the man kneeling before her. She took another deep breath, then leaned forward and put her arms around Jonathon and laid her head on her papa's shoulder.

His Glory Shall Be Seen Upon Thee

THE ANNUAL LENTEN CONCERTS AT THE FOUNDLING Hospital continued through several subsequent years. Handel kept at it until he finally could no more carry on the duty. As Handel's health lessened, he relied more and more on his able friend and contemporary, John Smith. When he no longer had the strength to hold the baton, he handed it off to Smith. The new conductor was diligent about conforming his direction to the standards and expectations that Handel had established.

The proceeds from the yearly concerts protected the interests of the Foundling Hospital, but always there was an additional charity that was aided with the proceeds. Unless there was a need that dictated otherwise, freedom was annually purchased for many debtors by *Messiah*. The hospital governor and Smith acted as agents of the funds, allocating the money where it was most needed. *Messiah* became a great charitable institution, the proceeds of which accomplished much to quell the misery of many, in accordance with the author's wishes.

Through the winter of 1758-59, Handel's health seemed to improve. Many of the faculties that he had lost seemed miraculously to return. He was able to get up on his feet with the use of his cane and go outside for short walks. He rejoiced in the return of some strength in his fingers, allowing him to play pieces he had not been able to in the recent past. And although his sight never came back in any degree, his memory did. Long evenings were spent with Peter LeBlonde, reminiscing about past ventures, both wins and losses, neither of which were taken very seriously any more. Handel's spirits were light while spring began to warm London. As the Foundling concert scheduled for May 5, 1759, approached, there was talk that Handel might make a guest appearance to conduct; but it was not to be. Through late March and early April, each day showed some loss in his health. He managed to conduct *Messiah* at Covent Garden on April 6th, but collapsed from fatigue while making his way out of the theatre following the concert. The experience entirely drained him. Inexorable exhaustion forced him to stay in bed throughout Holy Week. He had not the strength to rise from the mattress, yet he had full possession of his wits. He knew the end was near and wanted to make any last arrangements in this world before departing for the next.

Peter LeBlonde cared for Handel's every need throughout the long week, making sure that linens were clean and the tea was hot. He sat faithfully at Handel's side while the solicitor responsible for executing Handel's will and trust finished his final business. Peter watched the executor make several notes on the papers laid before him on the desk. Next to the papers laid the beautiful olive wood box containing the original manuscript of *Messiah*. Peter remembered watching his master pen the music, the notes urgently sloping forward, his hand hardly keeping up with his head. He thought it strangely peculiar to watch the man now penning notes concerning the destiny of that same music.

At length, the solicitor finished his writing. He took the several papers before him and folded them into a leather folder. He pushed back the chair on which he had been seated and stood with the folder in his hands.

"I've amended the codicil. I will take care of the matter according to your instructions."

"That is what I wish," answered Handel, his eyes opening.

"Is there anything else, sir?"

Handel shook his head slowly from side to side.

"Nothing more," he said. "Thank you."

The solicitor bowed low. He picked up the wooden heirloom from off the desk, put it under his arm, then left the room. Peter watched Handel's eyes close again.

Where Is Thy Victory?

<hr>

MY LORDS, I STAND BEFORE YOU IN PROXY OF HIM WHO sent me." The words of the solicitor resounded through the near empty halls of the Royal Academy of Music. Even though there was no jury meeting planned, the generous gift rumored to be coming from Handel inspired proper audience. The assembly gathered on short notice late in the evening to receive the bestowal. Several large wooden boxes full of manuscripts were delivered earlier in the evening. The boxes were neatly lined against the wall awaiting proper filing and care. The solicitor often referred to them as he outlined Handel's endowment to the academy.

Other than those in the room, the building was empty, with the exception of one other who had surreptitiously obtained news regarding the dying man's grant. Quietly, he stole into the great hall outside the chamber and eavesdropped from outside the door.

"Mr. Handel has asked that I extend to you his profound gratitude for past confidences and commissions. In appreciation, he grants you leave and license to those musics that you have desired from the various scores and manuscripts which he has authored and which I now present you. With the specific and noted exception of that which I have already explained in writing, these are the works he believed to be most worthy of your consideration. If there are other omissions you wish to peruse which are not included herein, once he is deceased, you are granted leave to glean from his portfolio whatever else you may deem to be of worth. That which he greatly values has all been accounted for."

There was a shuffling of papers as the solicitor handed each man seated at the table a written list of the operas and oratorios presented to the academy. The members of the jury each reviewed the list. There were a few simple questions, followed by simple answers. After a brief pause of silence, there was the dull scraping of several chair legs sliding on the hard wood floor. The jury rose as the solicitor bowed to them, put on his cape, then straightway left the room and walked down the center of the long corridor leading to the front of the academy building.

As he traversed the long great hall, the eavesdropping intruder suddenly appeared out of the shadows in front of him. Rolli did his best not to seem overly anxious.

"Am I too late?" he inquired. The solicitor imagined him one of the jury.

"Yes, I am just leaving. You will learn all upon joining your colleagues."

"What of the list? Have you the list?" Rolli asked, looking at the papers in the solicitor's hand. When he saw what looked like the list to which he had heard the man refer, he snatched it from the solicitor's hand and read it carefully—and then a second time.

"They are not here," he muttered under his breath. "Where are they? Is this all?"

"Indeed—with one exception. Handel made the last amendment to his will earlier today; he must put great value on it."

The solicitor's hand touched something held in his arm beneath his cape. He walked away, but, as he did, the sudden movement peeled back the fabric of his coat, revealing the olive wood box. Rolli instantly recognized it between the folds of his coat. He chased down the hall after him.

"Wait, hold on there."

Rolli quickly caught up to him. He pulled back the man's coat to reveal the box. The initials G.F.H. on the lid stared him in the face.

"He amended his will for this?"

"He didn't seem to care about anything else. It was all that really mattered to him."

Rolli could not contain himself. He became giddy; he became delirious at the prospect of what Handel had in mind for the box. Rolli tried to think of the most glorious venue in which his operas might be performed. Theatres and audiences even greater than those the Academy could procure. Only one came to his mind; surely Handel must have saved these operas to be a dying gift to the King himself. This was better than the Academy; this was better than anything he could have hoped for. His plan had worked, it would make him immortal. The greatest composer that London had ever known, with his last dying breath, singled out these works to be of such import and value that he endowed them upon the crown.

"If not the Academy, then the King," Rolli declared in a jubilant voice. "He has amended his will to bestow these to the crown?"

The solicitor shook his head. Rolli did not understand.

"Who then?"

"Who are you?"

"I am the librettist," Rolli snapped back. "Who receives this?"

"The Foundling Hospital," the solicitor said. "Now, if you will excuse me."

"What will the hospital do with the librettos?"

"I don't know about any librettos."

"They are here—in the box. My opera librettos!"

The man looked at the box, then back at Rolli.

"No operas here," replied the solicitor.

Rolli ripped the box from his arm and slid off the lid. The top sheet read *Messiah*. Rolli's face lapsed into disbelief.

"Where are the librettos? There were several librettos in this box. There's been a mistake!"

"Handel doesn't care about any opera librettos, never said a word about them."

"This can't be. My librettos!"

Rolli's own voice betrayed his guise. The solicitor snatched the box from his hands with a look of disdain. He slid the box under his arm and covered it from Rolli's eyes with his overcoat. He whirled away from Rolli and hastened away without another word. His echoing steps had the mocking sound of one person clapping as he made his way down the wide corridor toward the exit. Rolli stood motionless in the shadowed hall. His teeth began to grind together; his jawbones clicked under the intense pressure. He heard a far-off squeak as a distant door opened, then slammed shut with the roll of distant thunder. His eyes closed into rolls of skin. Loud hisses escaped his mouth as air squeezed through the tight cracks of his teeth. Rolli put his face in his hands and pressed his fingers into his forehead. The pressure of his fingers forced the blood from his skin, leaving white circles where he pushed. His movements became violent. His head jerked to the left then right as he began to pace back and forth across the stone floor of the empty hall. Seeming altogether lost, he slunk off into the shadows and disappeared.

Not long after, a haunting sound echoed down the hall. It was the dull clap of a body hitting the stone floor at the base of the great Academy staircase. The black shape did not move, nor was it found until the following morning. The body was identified and handed over to the Italian consulate. A notice was posted, but no one stepped forward to claim the body. When stench became a problem, it was determined that rather than spend the necessary money to transport the body to Italian soil, a common grave would suffice. No marker was placed.

Worthy Is the Lamb

HANDEL SLEPT THROUGH THE GREATER PART OF THE DAY-
light hours. He rested calmly, with few interruptions of pained movement
or altered breathing. The apartment was still and quiet. Many visitors had
come to offer expressions of gratitude and "get well" wishes throughout
the early part of the week, but by Friday the front door was not disturbed.

Peter LeBlonde stayed close by through the long hours. He left the
room only a few times and then for only a few minutes. The sheets and
spread were perfectly white; Peter made sure of that. He kept water hot
through the entire day perchance Handel should awake and want a sip of
tea. Again, as when Handel had written *Messiah*, Peter had two chairs
which he used approximately the same amount of time. One was directly
at Handel's side next to the bed; the other was just outside the open door

in the hallway. He used the first when his concerns for the master were immediate and pressing; he used the second when his concerns were more at rest and his spirit calm. When Peter sat in the chair near the bed, his mind was filled with the present—sadness about the inevitable, making his master as comfortable as possible, the awkwardness of death and endings.

When he occupied the chair in the hall, his mind was filled with the past—memories of music resonating through the corridors and walls of the house, diversions, failures and triumphs. Peter required a good mix of both to keep a good balance of spirit as he awaited the end, the final enemy which he knew must certainly come.

When Handel's strength began to falter, Peter had rehearsed in his mind the things he wanted most to say when the end came; however, the closer that death came, the less consideration he gave his words. He had no fear of saying any less or more than he wanted, for it was not what he said in the end that mattered most, but what his deeds had articulated long before the end was near. As uncharacteristic as it was for Peter to regard himself, he was at peace with what he had done. In the honest hours of personal introspect, he did not find himself wanting. He loved his master and had served him in the best way that he knew how. He had no regrets but that the time had passed so quickly. For Peter, quiet reflection was not painful reflection.

Through the afternoon and evening of Good Friday, he watched the sunlight through the window make a long arc from the floor, across the bed, then back to the far floor and up the wall. There was no part of the sun's journey that he did not witness. While the last golden shafts of light began to dissipate, Peter had a premonition that Handel would soon awake.

Through Holy Week, Handel's pattern of rest had been fairly constant. Sunset and early evening were the times that he had usually been awake. Peter rose and went to the kitchen to stoke the fire so that water would be hot if the same schedule prevailed. When he came back into the room with a steaming tray, Handel's eyes were open.

"It is being performed at this very moment," said Handel with some effort. Peter smiled as he put the tray down on the small table at the foot of the bed. That which had slipped his mind all the day, Handel had remembered even in slumber. A second concert of *Messiah* was scheduled at Covent for the 13th of April, Good Friday. The performance was, in fact, proceeding at that very moment.

"Yes, sir," replied Peter.

"And I am not there," Handel said.

"Do you regret it, sir?" Peter queried as he poured tea.

Handel took a long breath and pondered some time before answering with a tone of resignation.

"It's in God's hands. He can do with it as He wishes."

"But it will always be yours," reassured Peter.

"No. It never was."

Peter held the cup while Handel took several sips of hot tea. Peter was glad he had kept the water hot—the sips seemed to warm and comfort his master. In time, Handel nodded that he had had enough and thanked Peter for his assistance. The servant put the cup back on the tray and then sat down in the chair near the bed.

"Is there anything else you would like?"

Handel turned his head from side to side thoughtfully. It was evident to Peter that Handel's mind was elsewhere. He determined not to interrupt the reverie. Peter waited to be spoken to before speaking again.

"Peter? Is it...?" Handel did not finish the question. His words fell off into deep contemplation.

"Yes, sir. It is a victory—a triumph," answered Peter from his chair. Handel's head turned to the side. When their eyes met, Peter continued with conviction.

"Your *Messiah* is worthy."

Handel took another long, deep breath. When he exhaled, his countenance changed. Years of impairing doubt seemed to exhale from him with the air in his lungs. A holy peace filled his eyes. He no longer appeared the dying man, but the living spirit. Peter knew that the time was drawing ever more near.

"Though I shan't deserve it, I would that God will grant me one last wish," said Handel with a twinkle in his eye.

"You wish for your sight again, sir?"

"Blindness? I have memory to serve me. I have found the longer I live without sight the better some things look."

"What then, sir?"

"I wish to breathe my last word on Good Friday—in hopes of meeting mine good God and sweet Lord and Savior on the day of His resurrection."

"Today is Good Friday m'lord."

"Then it would not inconvenience Him. I do not want to be a burden."

"You are no burden, sir," replied Peter. He watched Handel's eyes slowly shut. Minutes later they opened again. Peter remained as he was before they closed.

"Is there anything else, sir?"

"My dear Peter, you are forever my good friend."

Peter watched his master's eyes close again. He listened to Handel's breathing ease into sleep. He stood from the chair and carefully straightened the spread. Gently, he touched his master's hand. Handel's eyes opened.

"All is well. 'Tis Good Friday. Please allow no more visitors. I am now done with the world."

Peter smiled, then stood back from the bed. He pulled the door and walked down the hall to the study. He stopped outside and peered through the narrow opening of the almost-closed door. He reached down and carefully took off his shoes. Very slowly, not making a sound, he opened the door and entered. He sat down on the wooden side chair next to the door. He folded his arms tightly across his chest.

Although he could not actually hear the distant strains from Covent, he began to hear anthems of praise as if they had been carried on the wind over the expanse of London and into his heart. Sweet music began to distill in his mind as dew from heaven. In the music were the words:

"'Worthy is the Lamb that was slain, and hath redeemed us to God by His blood, to receive power, and riches, and wisdom, and strength, and honor, and glory, and blessing.'"

Unseen to all but God, below the high window of the study sat a dark figure on an old weathered stump. He too heard music. In the music was but one word. He reverently whispered it as it came to him.

"Amen."

And All Flesh Shall See It Together

MORNING CAME IN SPLENDOR. THE HEAVENS ABOVE SHONE a perfect blue. Night breezes carried away any foulness from the air so that when the sun beamed from the east, it was absolutely pure and untainted. When dawn reached over the horizon, it appeared as though the earth had been cleansed and purified.

Peter LeBlonde entered Handel's room just as light filled the sheer curtains of the east window. He walked straight to the window and pulled back any fabric that might prevent the light from entering. Clear beams of sun streamed in the east window, brightening the room into glowing amber.

"'Tis a beautiful day, sir. Truly a day worthy of celebrating the resurrection of our good Lord."

Handel did not stir. Peter walked to the bed. He stared into the pallid, still face of his master. He touched his hand just as he had the night before, but his master's eyes did not open. Peter stood over the body for several minutes, his eyes closed, his hands folded. When he opened them, he leaned down and tenderly pressed his lips against the forehead of his master. "God be with you til we meet again." Peter quietly left the room.

Outside, the pure light of the morning sun slowly worked down the side of the building. Long shadows shortened as the celestial sphere rose upward on its new day's journey. As the light reached deeper and deeper into the shaded places of the earth, an object suddenly sparkled in the morning sun. A tiny shaft of golden light pierced unimpeded through the bricked buildings of London until it landed at last on a rotting stump at the side of Handel's apartment. There, shining bright against the aged wood was a tiny gold locket on a thin gold chain, laid over a single rose of pure whiteness. The rose was left behind in trade for that which was taken. It was not left for those in the house, but for God. The tiny locket had a different purpose. It was left as a mark, a mark to remind us all that his life was a gift—a gift from God.

At the same time Peter LeBlonde was opening the curtains in Handel's room to let in the morning light, two men spoke in hushed voices near the back of the Foundling Hospital chapel. Handel's solicitor arrived early to carry out the last and most important item of business his employer had entrusted to him. The governor of the hospital felt it most appropriate that he meet with him in the chapel itself. The two men talked in hushed voices. Their words were indiscernible above the whispered supplication of the many children kneeling for morning prayer in the first rows of the chapel. Sister Anne knelt with them. Ellen occupied the place at her side. Few of the children were aware of the men until the solicitor's voice rose above their hushed murmurs.

"He appended his will to include you. I quote, 'I give a fair copy of the score and all the parts of my oratorio called the *Messiah* to the Foundling Hospital.' It was his final request."

Handel's representative laid in the governor's hands a beautiful, hand-crafted, olive wood box. Inscribed in the sliding lid were the initials

G.F.H. The governor slid back the lid to reveal a full, hand-written copy of *Messiah*. With a shake of hands, the solicitor exited out the back of the chapel.

The governor walked down the center aisle of the chapel past the praying children and into a small organ loft in the front of the chapel. He laid the elegant box on a shelf with other folders of music, then left, closing tight the door of the small room behind him.

At the foot of the Duke of Argyle's Monument in Poets' Corner of Westminster Abbey is a marble stone. In the morning when the sun is new, light streams through the high windows to the Abbey floor. If there is haze in the air, the sunbeams reach in shafts to the ground and shine on the saints buried below. In spring and fall, when the sun is centered in the sky, one narrow shaft lights the gray, marble stone. On the stone is etched these words:

"Beneath this place are reposited the remains of George Frederic Handel. The most excellent musician any age ever produced. Whose compositions were a sentimental language. Rather than mere sounds; and surpassed the power of words in expressing the various passions of the human heart."

For the next several years, the *Messiah* concerts continued as an annual fund-raising event. Countless children were blessed and provided for by the proceeds of the concerts. Literally thousands of pounds were taken in to benefit the unfortunate children either left or given to the care of the hospital. John Christopher Smith continued conducting the charitable concerts until 1768, after which the blind organist and composer, John Stanley, took over the responsibility until late in the 1770s. He was the last to continue the annual event. Soon after, the tradition was lost and forgotten. The music of *Messiah* fell into obscurity.

Forever and Ever

_____

RAIN POUNDED THE ROOF OF DR. DAVAN WHETTON'S home all night long. He could not remember a single day since the first day of January 1896 when sunlight had found its way to the ground. The inclemency of the weather weighed upon his already heavy heart. The sound of the huge drops on the windows and walls seemed to pound the anxiety he was feeling even deeper into his mind and heart. Although he was physically and mentally drained, he could not sleep. He paced most of the night, besieged by a relentless question that wholly troubled him. The Foundling Hospital was overloaded with children and yet perilously short on funds. As the hospital principal and organist, Dr. Whetton had the arduous task of trying to buoy up the coffers and, more importantly, buoy up the spirits of those who believed the institution would not endure the storm. Even some of the hospital's most influential and generous supporters were debating the institution's viability.

As Holy Week approached, it was expected that music should accompany the celebration of Easter. Dr. Whetton tried in vain to find an appropriate piece for the occasion. He wrote several hymns to invoke a spirit of renewal and worship, but none felt true. He tried to dismiss the gnawing emptiness inside him, but felt a great urgency to pursue the problem further. Certainly he could be justified in ending his quest, as he had spent innumerable hours contemplating the best solution.

Earlier that same day, he had announced the music that would be performed for the service on Good Friday. The news was well received and he had been congratulated for his diligent efforts. The governor was pleased with the decision. The balance of the administrators fell in line to demonstrate their approval once the governor was in full support. In reality, there were few times previous when the common consent was so unanimous. The decision was made.

Dr. Whetton was pleased with the outcome. In spite of his hesitation, the full consensus of approval far overshadowed any misgivings he might have had. But as the night hours wore on, the larger his apprehensions became. What made the situation particularly difficult was that there was no obvious right answer. The music that he had announced would be performed was wonderful and praiseworthy in every way; it simply wasn't right. He knew it, and he knew that God knew it.

Before dawn arrived, he went out. He walked through the damp streets, no clear destination in mind. As it happened, habit eventually carried him to the Foundling Hospital. He entered the chapel, humbly listening and thinking through the dark hours before dawn. The sun was just beginning to glow below the east horizon when he stood to leave. He walked to the front of the chapel, crossed himself, and walked past the pulpit to the door near the front of the chapel. When he opened the door he saw something he had never noticed before: in back of an old stand of antiquated bookshelves behind the pulpit was the outline of a narrow door. He thought at first that it must be an old priests' dressing room. He started to leave but was suddenly compelled to investigate further. He moved aside the shelf in front of the door and spotted a brass knob. He was certain it would be locked, but, to his surprise, the door squeaked open.

It was a small room, full of dust and cobwebs. He did not know when the last time was that someone had entered there. Shelves lined the walls. On those shelves were stacks of music. Dr. Whetton flipped through the pages of music, certain that his prayers were answered; he needed only find the right piece.

He pulled a stack of papers and turned to leave. Out of the corner of his eye he saw something unusual. Above him was a curious box with a distinctive line of wood grain on the side. He put down the papers and lifted the box from the thick cobwebs gathered around it. He pulled it from the shelf and stared at it. He inhaled deeply, then blew the fine dust off the lid into a cloud. On the lid of the box were three letters: G.F.H.

A shaft of sunlight streamed through the small window high overhead to where he stood. Dr. Whetton carefully slid back the lid, light filled the interior of the box. To his wonderment, he read the top sheet.

"*Messiah.*"

Near the bottom was the name of the author.

"George Frederic Handel."

Dr. Whetton recalled from the hospital journals that there was mention of an annual performance of an oratorio of like name nearly one hundred years before, but never had he heard it, nor had he thought of it. As he stared at the cover page, he knew that this was the answer he had sought. He walked from the bright beam in the small antechamber, box in hand, to the chapel. He sat down at the organ. Light filled the stained-glass windows above him. He flipped through several pages of manuscript and pulled out the first choir number he found. He laid the handwritten score on the organ. While his feet pumped, his fingers pressed the keys; music filled the hall. He sang aloud the words. As he did, choirs of voices filled his heart with song.

"'And the glory, the glory of the Lord shall be revealed. And all flesh shall see it together for the mouth of the Lord hath spoken it.'"

Handel's *Messiah* has endured through time to become the most widely performed oratorio ever written. It has become a universal celebration of Christianity through Scripture and song.

"I should be sorry if I only entertained them, I wished to make them better."

Epilogue

IT HAS ALWAYS BEEN THE AUTHOR'S INTENT THAT THIS BOOK
be historical fiction. Certainly there is much in the book that is historically accurate, but creative license has been exercised in many instances.
With that said, the reader may desire some clarification regarding what
parts of the story are factual. Following are some general notes that may
be helpful.

The timeline of the story is compressed significantly. Approximately
twenty-seven years elapsed from the time that Handel arrived in London
(1714), and his writing of *Messiah* (1741). Early on, Handel enjoyed
many successful years of opera and association with royalty.

The competing operas, the Royal Academy of Music, and Handel's
up-and-down string of performances came years after his arrival in

London. His eventual failure, indebtedness, and fall into obscurity were not fully realized for several more years.

The events portrayed during the years prior to writing *Messiah*—the duel with Matheson and Matheson's sword striking his button, the King's flotilla and *Water Music*, competing operas, encounters with divas, pushing Cuzzoni out the window, musical duels, the cat-fight on stage—these are all well-documented events. Time was shortened to facilitate the sequence of events in the subplots of Jonathon, Rachel, and the Packrat.

It should be noted that the crown changed hands from King George I (r.1714-27), to King George II (r.1727-60), in the early stages of Handel's career. Handel served as Kappelmeister to George I in Hanover. The incident on the river and the amnesty given were granted by George I. The opera wars and the remainder of Handel's life was lived out under the reign of King George II. The enmity between George II, and his son, Prince Frederick, is well chronicled. The King hated the Prince and many of the lines spoken by the George II regarding Frederick are recorded quotes. Frederick hired Buononcini to contend with the King's opera and Handel, thus setting up the "factions of fiddlers" spoken of. As Handel's entanglement in the conflict between the King and son was a continuing story element, the two kings were merged into one.

For the most part, the events, circumstances, and biographical information relating to Handel are historically accurate. Some characters were created based on recorded events. The Packrat emerged from the fact that Handel's enemies hired street urchins to tear down playbills; the ruffians emerged from his enemies hiring bullies to wreak havoc among opera patrons. As there is little information available, liberties were taken regarding the transpirings within and without Handel's house during his writing of *Messiah*.

Jonathon, Rachel, Christina, and all those characters directly relating to their specific story lines are fictional. It is true that Handel oft directed proceeds from *Messiah* performances to freeing prisoners from debtor's prison, and his philanthropic relationship with the Foundling Hospital is also well recorded.

It should also be noted that the author was greatly influenced by the information attributed to Handel's manservant, Peter LeBlonde, who was closest to Handel during the writing of *Messiah*. As LeBlonde was given a substantial gift in Handel's will, it is plausible to assume that Handel had a high regard for him. The spirit and feel of this book was greatly influenced by the words and recountings of Peter LeBlonde. He is principally responsible for giving insight as to Handel's heart and mind during the writing of *Messiah* and the last days of his life.

Handel's faithful friend, Mrs. Delaney (Mary Pendarves), did not actually marry Dr. Patrick Delaney until two years after Messiah was written. Dr. Delaney was not musically apathetic as portrayed in the book. Like Mary, Patrick was a supporter of Handel.

Rolli is a factual character. He wrote several librettos for Handel, including his last, *Deidamia*. Rolli was chosen as a principal antagonist because of the slander and gossip filled letters he wrote about Handel. His letters affirm that he was two-faced and sought to undermine Handel in spite of his close association and reliance upon him. The olive wood box and his suicide were invented.

There are certain quotes or statements that the reader may want to know are authentic:

> "My Lord, I should be sorry if I only entertained them, I wished to make them better."
>
> Handel to Lord Kinnoul

> "I shall shew you a collection I gave Handel, called Messiah, which I value highly, and he has made a fine entertainment of it, though not near so good as he might and ought to have done. I have with great difficulty made him correct some of the grossest faults in the composition, but he has retained his Overture obstinately, in which there are some passages far unworthy of Handel, but much more unworthy of the Messiah."
>
> Letter from Jennens to Holdsworth

> "I wish to breathe my last word on Good Friday, in hopes of meeting mine good God and sweet Lord and Savior on the day of His resurrection."
>
> Handel to Peter LeBlonde

"I did think I did see all heaven before me, and the great God Himself sitting upon His throne."

> Handel to Peter LeBlonde
> (in reference to Hallelujah chorus)

Any questions or comments can be e-mailed to jsflorien@aol.com

HALLELUJAH
Order Form

Postal orders: Lorien Entertainment
2850 E. 3300 South, Suite # 101
Salt Lake City, UT 84109

Telephone orders: (801) 461-0267

E-mail orders: jsflorien@aol.com

Please send *HALLELUJAH* to:

Name: _____

Address: _____

City: _____ State: _____

Zip: _____

Telephone: (_____) _____

Book Price: U.S. $28.00   Can. $40.00

Shipping: $3.00 for the first book and $1.00 for each additional book to cover shipping and handling within US, Canada, and Mexico. International orders add $6.00 for the first book and $2.00 for each additional book.

Or order from:
ACW Press
5501 N. 7th. Ave. #502
Phoenix, AZ 85013

(800) 931-BOOK

or contact your local bookstore